James von Leyden grew up in Durham and studied Philosophy and Modern Languages at Oxford University. He worked for thirty years as an advertising copywriter. He first visited Morocco in 1985, leading to a life-long love affair with the country. He is married with two children and divides his time between Lewes, East Sussex and Oualidia, Morocco.

You can follow James on Instagram at
www.instagram.com/jamesvonleyden.

DISCARDED

A Death in the Medina

JAMES VON LEYDEN

CONSTABLE

CONSTABLE

First published in Great Britain in 2019 by Constable
This edition published in 2020 by Constable

Copyright © James von Leyden, 2019

1 3 5 7 9 10 8 6 4 2

The moral right of the author has been asserted.

*All characters and events in this publication, other than
those clearly in the public domain, are fictitious
and any resemblance to real persons,
living or dead, is purely coincidental.*

A CIP catalogue record for this book
is available from the British Library.

ISBN: 978-1-47213-062-4

Typeset in Adobe Garamond by Hewer Text UK Ltd, Edinburgh
Printed and bound in Great Britain by Clays Ltd, Elcograf S.p.A.

Papers used by Constable are from well-managed forests and other responsible sources.

Constable
An imprint of
Little, Brown Book Group
Carmelite House
50 Victoria Embankment
London EC4Y 0DZ
An Hachette UK Company

www.hachette.co.uk
www.littlebrown.co.uk

A Death in the Medina

For my mother

The Medina of Marrakech

Prologue

The man stopped pushing and stood up to catch his breath. Despite the fierce afternoon heat he was wearing a black *jellaba*, the hood over his head, and sweat was dripping from his chin. He glared at the handcart. The wheels were of unequal size and the constant effort of pushing harder on the left side was giving him a blister. He had half a mind to leave the cart where it was but, with a sigh, he grasped the handles and set off again. He collided with a lamppost, dislodging the stack of cardboard in the cart and causing some of the sheets to slide off. Swearing, he walked around, rearranged the cardboard and started up again.

At the traffic lights he stared at the ground as a bus came to a halt. The passengers, pressed against the windows, were too hungry or exhausted to give him a second glance. He crossed the road carefully. It took him three hard shoves to get the wheels onto the kerb on the other side.

The rush hour traffic had dwindled by the time he reached the city walls. It was half an hour before sunset and the white-belted policeman who usually directed traffic had gone home. The man pushed the cart along an alley of high, windowless buildings. He had got used to the odd-sized wheels by now and the cart only scraped the walls of the alley once. Two boys ran out of a house ahead of him, laughing and pulling on each other's T-shirts, and disappeared into another house a few doors up. Passing the open doorway, he heard the clatter of plates and a woman's voice, '*Ara al-hobz a Yasmina oo al-qahwa!* Fetch the bread, Yasmina! And the coffee!' The smell of freshly baked bread reminded him that he hadn't eaten since daybreak.

When he emerged at Bab Taghzout the square was deserted. There were no motor scooters, street traders or donkeys to break the silence. The grocery and household goods stores were closed, a broom laid across the entrance to signal that the owner's absence was only temporary. Quickening his pace, the man pressed on through the archway at the end of the square then turned left through two rows of shuttered workshops and through a final arch with a woodwork and stucco facade. Here, a few yards from the mosque, he halted. He wiped his eyes, then, as an afterthought, ran the sleeve of his *jellaba* over the cart handles. He lifted his palm to examine his blister and cursed.

A sudden crackle made him jump. The call to prayer had started. A moment later the call was taken up by the other mosques in the city.

Chapter 1

Ten hours earlier

The first day is the hardest. Karim tried to swallow but swallowing requires a modicum of saliva and he had none. In a few hours, his lips would crack. By afternoon the griping pains would begin. He had only himself to blame. His mother had shaken him at dawn with a jug of water and said, '*Shrob!* Drink!' Instead he had rolled over and gone back to sleep. By the time he woke again the sun had risen.

A fly buzzed on the windowsill. Karim watched it crawl up the pane, fall off, then crawl up again. The neighbourhood was full of flies. It was nothing to do with the rubbish – there wasn't any rubbish nowadays, not with those shiny new cleaning vehicles that came whirring into the Jemaa with their jets and brushes – but as long as there were juice carts and fried food stalls and barrows piled with sticky dates, there would be flies. And it was only a few hundred yards from the square to the commissariat.

The desk to his right was empty. Abdou was spending Ramadan with his family in the Ourika Valley. The trees by the river would be heavy with figs. Karim imagined funnelling the soft flesh into his mouth, the juices running down his chin. '*Astaghfiru Allah*,' he said quietly. I seek God's forgiveness.

Down in the forecourt he could see the parking attendant covering the windscreen of the captain's car with a piece of cardboard. It had been over forty degrees for twenty-six days now – the hottest, they said, since records began. Karim remembered that when he was a small boy he had seen a man collapse and die in the heat. It turned out that the man was diabetic and didn't have to fast, but he had fasted anyway. Karim had asked his father, 'What's the point of fasting if he dies as a result?' 'Because he will go to heaven,' his father answered. He said the words without conviction.

The fly careered around the room, bumped into the open door of the filing cabinet, zigzagged upwards and settled on a blade of the fan. When Karim had arrived at the commissariat eighteen months ago, fresh out of police college, he'd put in a request for the ceiling fan to be repaired. He'd filled out three forms, one for the captain's secretary, one for the quartermaster and one for the maintenance department. Abdou and Noureddine had laughed, whether because getting anything fixed in the Sûreté was a joke, or because they scorned his need for womanly comforts, Karim still wasn't sure.

Apart from the buzzing of the fly the only sound was the *clack-clack-clack* from Noureddine's keyboard. The old man took Ramadan in his stride. He didn't sigh, or fall asleep, or lose his temper. Was he hardened after years of practice? Or did he guzzle in secret? Karim immediately felt ashamed at the thought. Nour was a good man, a devout man, not like those so-called believers who closed their shutters during daylight and stuffed their mouths. If they did that in the street they would go to jail. *He would see to it personally.*

He opened his drawer and rummaged through an assortment of new-looking pens and watches. He took out one of the watches, adjusted the time, opened the ring binder on his desk and started reading.

1. Assess its weight

Both the head and the band of a Breitling chronograph are made from stainless steel. Because of this Breitling chronographs are usually heavy. In contrast, a fake Breitling may have a head or band that is quite light.

Karim's eyelids drooped. The fly droned ... the keyboard clacked ... his thoughts drifted to Ayesha and Lalla Fatima. They would be chopping vegetables in the kitchen. How did they manage to prepare such delicious food without testing the seasoning? Perhaps, when evening came, everyone was in such a hurry to eat that they didn't notice details like seasoning. When a hungry lion tore into the flesh of a gazelle did it stop to ask for salt?

There was a clatter: the watch had fallen on the floor. Karim opened his eyes. He checked to see if the old man had noticed but he was still *clack-clack-clacking* away.

Tomorrow, God willing, the fast would get easier. At least he wasn't alone. All over the Maghreb, all over the *ummah*, men and women were abstaining from eating, smoking, drinking and engaging in profane activities. Of course, there would be accidents. Last year there had been nine hundred traffic accidents in Marrakech alone. But there would be few crimes. Who has the energy for crime when they have to fast for sixteen hours a day?

He heard laughter from the staircase. Women's voices . . . British – or American? Despite taking English classes for two years Karim found it hard to tell the difference. He slipped the watch on his wrist then got to his feet. *Too hasty!* He clutched the side of his desk to steady himself. There was a knock at the door.

'*Bonjour?*'

Without waiting for a reply, a girl stepped into the room. She was European, brown-haired, about twenty, with large sunglasses and baggy cotton trousers. Her shoulders were sunburned and there was a half-full bottle of water in her hand. Two other girls followed. One was tall – taller than Karim – and wore a cowboy-style hat and tight-fitting T-shirt. The other had long blonde hair tied in a bunch, bracelets on both wrists and a purple sarong around her hips. Karim recognised the type. They came on the cheap flights from Europe, haggled for trinkets in the souks then swept off to Essaouira or the mountains.

'*Parlez-vous anglais?*' The brown-haired girl looked from one policeman to the other.

Noureddine pointed at Karim and carried on typing. Karim was thrown into confusion. Elsewhere in Marrakech Western women with bare thighs and plunging necklines were nothing special, but in the commissariat they were almost unheard of. Like exotic animals escaped from their natural habitat, their features were magnified, heightened. Karim's gaze was drawn to the hips of the tall girl, to her bronzed midriff, the tattoo of a cat chasing a mouse down towards her—

'Do you speak English?' the girl repeated.

Karim blinked. 'A little. Please sit. Let me . . .' He fetched three tubular metal chairs, wincing with pain as one of them banged his shin, and placed them opposite his desk. The brown-haired girl sat down and took a drink.

'I want to report a theft. They stole my bag, my wallet, my phone, my passport, everything.'

'You need to report it to the *police judiciare*, the tourist police on the square Jemaa.'

'There was a queue,' the girl said curtly.

Karim gave the slightest of nods. He unscrewed his fountain pen, wondering if the girls could tell the difference between a real Mont Blanc and a fake.

'What is your name?'

'Melanie Murray.'

Karim put the pen to paper but no ink came out. He shook the pen and tried again. He replaced the pen on his desk and booted up his ancient computer. 'Melanie . . .'

'Murray. M-U-R-R-A-Y.' The girl stood up and stared at the computer screen. 'No, not *Murray Melanie*. Melanie is my first name.'

Karim ignored her. He turned to the other two girls. 'Your names, please.'

'Emma Stephenson.'

'Julie Stassinopoulos,' said the tall girl with the cowboy hat. 'S-T-A-S-S-I-N-O-P-O-U-L-O-S.'

'Passports?'

'Mine was stolen. Like I told you,' Melanie snapped.

The other girls handed over their documents to Karim. The passports felt warm and damp. He wedged one in the back of his keyboard and started tapping. 'Do you have photocopies?'

'Why would we have photocopies of our passports?' Julie asked irritably.

'Look, is this really necessary?' said Melanie. 'You've put the information into your computer. Plus – it was *my* things that were stolen. You don't need *their* details!'

'If you report an incident you must show proof of who you are.'

Melanie leapt to her feet. 'Hello! That's me! It's nothing to do with them. They didn't have their stuff nicked!'

Karim took the passports and stood up. 'Please wait here.' He walked out of the room and down the steps, glad to be away from the troublesome women with their revealing clothes and loud voices.

In the ground-floor office the heat was even more oppressive. The smell of sweat caught in Karim's nostrils. A civilian in a short-sleeved *gandora* robe was talking in a low voice to an officer. Another policeman with pockmarked cheeks was slumped in a nearby chair, asleep.

'*Salaam ou alikum*,' said Karim. No one stirred.

While he waited for the photocopier to warm up he leafed through one of the passports. There were stamps from India, Vietnam, the United States, Australia and Indonesia. Karim didn't know anyone who had been outside the Maghreb apart from his cousin Majid who lived in France. He checked the time on his chronograph. The word *chronograph* appealed to him. He liked the weight it added to his wrist. It felt heavy, reassuring. He made two copies of the documents and turned off the machine. As he left the room he was aware of the other men watching him.

When he got back to the office Nour had left. Perhaps the old man had gone to pray. Or he had felt uncomfortable being alone with three Western girls. Karim handed back the passports, sat down and flexed his fingers. 'Please continue.'

'It happened last night,' Melanie said. 'We were walking across the Jemaa el-whatsitsname –'

'Jemaa el Fna,' Karim said, typing the location and '31 July'.

'It was quite late, about one o'clock.'

Karim deleted '31 July' and typed '1 August'.

'We were a bit drunk.'

Karim frowned. He knew that Western women drank alcohol. *But on their own, after midnight?*

'It was my hen party,' said Emma.

'What is hen party?' he asked, puzzled. 'Hen – like chicken?'

Julie threw back her head and laughed, a rich, hearty laugh that welled up from her belly. Karim had never heard a woman laugh like that before.

Emma explained. 'When a girl gets married – in England – she has a hen party. She invites all her girlfriends and they have a night out. I thought it might be fun to go to Marrakech for the weekend, just the three of us.'

'You come to Marrakech to do your chicken party?'

'It's called a hen party – Jesus Christ!' Melanie jumped up, knocking over her chair. 'Can we get this done? We're in a hurry! We have to go to the airport!'

'Of course.' Karim returned her stare. *What were her problems compared to his?* 'Which riad you stay at?'

'Dar Zuleika. The staff gave us a map but we got lost.'

Karim nodded. When he was a boy he used to guide tourists out of the medina for a dirham or two. Now the local kids asked for twenty. He had even heard a boy demand sixty – more than most Moroccans earned in a day!

'We were on our way home after a night out at a club. A young guy asked if he could help. We said *yes*.'

'This guy – what he look like?'

'All Moroccan men look the same,' muttered Julie.

'He had a blue Italia football shirt,' said Melanie, 'and bad teeth.'

Karim ran his tongue reflexively over his upper teeth. 'How old this guy?'

'Twenty-four? Twenty-five? I don't know! I was tired!'

'And then what happen?'

'He took us along one alley, then another, until we came to a dead end. I said, "This isn't Dar Zuleika." He grabbed my shoulder bag – he was gone in a second.'

'What was in your bag?'

'My phone – a white iPhone – my passport, my boarding pass and all my credit cards.'

'I understand, you want to make insurance claim.' Karim's tongue was stuck to the roof of his mouth. He felt as if his saliva glands had been removed by a malicious *djinn*.

'No!' wailed Melanie. 'Well, yes, I suppose I do – but that's not the point! I want my phone back. It's got all my pictures, the pictures of our last night together! And I've lost my passport!'

Emma checked her watch. 'We should go.'

Melanie gave Karim an angry look. 'I'm going to be stranded in this effing city without money or passport for days! Do you understand?'

Karim made a mental note to look up the word *effing* in his dictionary. He loaded a sheet of paper into his printer. 'You need to buy a *timbre*, a stamp. Twenty dirhams.'

'What then?'

'Go to consul, get new passport.'

'How long will that take?' Melanie cried.

Karim shrugged. He passed the paper across his desk. 'Please sign.'

Marrakech Menara Airport was quiet. The week before, the terminal had hummed with middle-class Marrakchis keen to escape Ramadan. Now the place was quiet apart from a handful of tourists, porters and desk clerks. The doors of the arrivals lounge opened and a smartly dressed woman with dark hair and sunglasses came out into the blinding sunlight.

The taxi drivers sprang into action. *Où allez-vous, madame? Palmeraie, Guéliz, Hivernage?*

A scuffle broke out between two of the drivers. An officious-looking man with a walkie-talkie walked through their midst, took the woman's suitcase and escorted her with an air of authority to the taxi at the head of the queue. He placed the case in the boot of the car, opened the rear passenger door and held out his palm with a smile. The woman ignored him as she took her seat.

The driver grinned in his rear-view mirror. 'First time Marrakech?'

'*J'habite ici. Bab Taghzout. Je connais le tarif – soixante dirhams.* If you ask for more I'll report you to the police.' The driver's smile faded.

Kay McKenzie gazed happily out of the window. Her shopping trip to Cairo had been a success. She had acquired a Byzantine cross, an inlaid mother-of-pearl box, two eighteenth-century candleholders, a Coptic textile and a portfolio of 1920s gelatin photographic prints. Sébastien had been right. The political turmoil had created a once-in-a-lifetime buying opportunity. Even the antique dealer in Zamalek had been in no mood to haggle.

She had her hands full in the week ahead: close the riad for the holidays, start arranging the boutique, meet a client, organise Sébastien's birthday party. But that was how she liked it. She needed projects, as she told her friends, preferably several on the go at once.

Her phone pinged. It was a text from a guest unable to make the party. That was the downside of holding a party in the hottest month of the year: everybody who was anybody had left town.

The familiar sight of the Koutoubia came into view. It was so simple, so stately, compared with the minarets of Cairo. As they drove towards it, the roses along the roadside were a sea of colour. On the horizon the Atlas mountains shimmered in the haze. Yes, she was glad to be back. This was her town.

She noticed a billboard promoting a condominium development. *L'appartement de vos rêves à partir de 100,000 Dhs!* Photoshopped on the poster was a woman with a plunging neckline, a glamorous actress whom Kay recognised from an American TV show. She shook her head in disbelief. The new development was aimed at a mainly Muslim clientele. Which marketing genius had decided that the best way to woo them was with an image of a woman showing off her tits?

Ten minutes later the taxi dropped her at Bab Taghzout. The square was empty in the afternoon heat. The merchants had retreated into the dark interiors of their shops. An onion seller was asleep under his barrow. In a butcher's hatch flies swarmed around an unrecognisable hunk of flesh. The only sign of life came from two boys crouched under the *bzar* trees, poking a dead bird. They looked up when they saw Kay step out of the taxi and half-heartedly asked for *un dirham*.

Kay's spirits sank. The regeneration of the medina was supposed to be improving run-down neighbourhoods like Bab Taghzout. Kay wondered what her guests must think, fresh off the plane, their heads filled with notions of dreamy minarets and Arabian Nights-style palaces, when they clapped eyes on the festering rubbish and crumbling, graffiti-strewn walls. Her gloom deepened when she spotted Driss waiting by the rubbish dumper, dressed in jeans and a T-shirt. What was the point of designing uniforms for the staff if they didn't bother to wear them?

Driss was a recent hiring, lured from a rival riad with the offer of a job as operations manager. Seeing him in casual clothes, striding ahead with her suitcase, Kay was glad that she hadn't made him manager. He was setting such a fast pace that the back of her dress was damp with sweat. Driss glanced over his shoulder, addressing her in French.

'A guest wants to stay on.'

'Who?'

'Mademoiselle Murray.'

'*Pas possible*. We're closing the riad tonight.'

'Her bag was stolen.'

'Not my problem,' Kay panted.

'She cannot move out.'

'*Pourquoi pas?*'

'She has nowhere to go. Her passport was stolen as well.'

Kay glowered. This was an inconvenience she could do without. She followed Driss past a crumbling wall, sidestepped a beggar and stopped in a tiny alleyway outside a salmon-pink frontage, forty feet high, with fretwork-covered windows. Driss rang the bell. After a few seconds, the door swung open to reveal the smiling face of the housekeeper.

'*Bonjour* Samira,' Kay gasped. '*S'il te plaît*, get me something to drink before I die of thirst.'

She walked into the courtyard, sat under an orange tree and kicked off her heels. The fountain was playing and the air was heavy with the smell of lavender. A tortoise was making its way slowly through the bougainvillea litter. A maid came out with a glass of juice and a bowl of snacks. Her spirits restored, Kay rested her feet on a chair and gazed up at the palm tree that soared towards the sky. Of all the features of the riad, Sébastien told her, the hundred-foot palm tree was the one that made it special.

Sébastien had arrived in Marrakech in the 1990s just as Europeans were starting to buy up the city's riads. He noticed their fondness for old-fashioned Moroccan building techniques like polished *tadelakt* plaster, chiselled stucco, filigree grills and wooden latticework. Soon he was employing five teams of craftsmen to cope with the demand. When Kay came to Marrakech a few years later, flush with money from her divorce settlement, Sébastien was the architect that everyone recommended. It was Sébastien who encouraged her to buy the crumbling pile near Sidi bel Abbès, Sébastien who demolished the interior walls, raised the ceilings and installed an illegal plunge pool, even going to the *moqaddam* at the planning department with a bundle of dirhams to get the necessary permission. Shortly after the refurbishment was complete Sébastien's wife announced that she was returning to Paris with the children.

There was a splash from the swimming pool and Melanie's face appeared above the surface. She lifted herself out of the water and sat in the sunshine, knees hunched to her chest, while a circle of water collected around her. She saw Kay looking at her and reached for her towel.

'Oh, hello, you must be Kay. I'm Melanie.'

'Our reluctant stayer-on.'

'Did Driss tell you . . .?'

'Yes. It's really too bad.'

Melanie stood up. 'I've been to the police. The consul was closed today but I'm going to see them tomorrow. Apparently they can issue me with a new travel document, or something, although it might take a day or two.' For a few seconds, the only sound was the drip of water onto the hot *tadelakt*. 'My friends left me some money so I should be OK for a few days.'

'You can stay until the end of the week. On Friday I'm having a party so I'll need you out of the riad. Oh, and the kitchen is closed so you'll have to sort out your own meals.'

'OK.' Melanie gave a little wave and padded off, leaving a trail of water.

Kay reached down and picked up the tortoise. 'Have you missed me?' she cooed.

My Medina
(Extract from Kay's blog)

Ramadan Mubarak! When I arrived in Marrakech Ramadan fell in winter. The days were short and cool. Now the days are sixteen hours long and the temperature is over forty degrees. Fasting is a real effort. As a Westerner you have to make allowances for the fact that the people around you are tired and irritable and prone to accidents. If some hapless individual burns your best saucepan, simply shrug your shoulders and say: 'C'est le Ramadan.' I was in the kitchen just now when our maid Aziza smashed an antique ceramic bowl on the floor. She looked at me, terrified. I just laughed. C'est le Ramadan!

It was mid-afternoon in the Palmeraie. In the shade of palm trees the camel boys lay dozing. In an hour or two they would rouse themselves, saddle their camels and holler at passing tourists to come and take a ride. For now, they were content to spend the long afternoon hours asleep. In the smart hotels and country clubs guests relaxed by the pool while uniformed waiters strode back and forth with iced drinks. Occasionally one of the guests would look up from their lounger and frown. A deep rumbling noise was disturbing the peace.

Half a mile away jackhammers, bulldozers and excavating machines were grinding up four hectares of red earth. To the sound of revving engines and beeping cranes, an army of builders was lining trenches, mixing cement and welding steel.

One of the cranes stood next to a high, domed building covered with scaffolding. Five workmen were at the foot of the scaffolding, grappling with a curved brass panel which they were attempting to attach to the sling of the crane. A tall Frenchman towered over the Moroccans like the crane above the building. The panel weighed half a ton and its curvature made it awkward to handle. The workmen held it upright while Sébastien, his sandy hair plastered to his forehead, shouted instructions to a foreman who relayed them to the workmen in barks of Arabic. Finally, they succeeded in fastening the panel and the foreman waved his arm at the crane operator. Sébastien watched, shielding his eyes with his forearm, as the jib of the crane swung over to the roof, the panel turning and flashing in the strong sunlight.

While he was watching, a boy came up to him and tugged at his sleeve. He pointed at a man in a *jellaba* standing by the gate. Sébastien nodded. When the panel was safely in place he walked down to the gate. The man in the *jellaba* showed him a large cardboard box with holes punched in the side. Sébastien peered through the holes and gave a broad smile.

The square at Bab Taghzout was coming back to life. With shouts and laughter, bare-chested youths splashed water at each other from a standpipe. Street vendors laid out watermelons and prickly pears on barrows. Women in headscarves settled down on the edge of the pavement to sell flatbreads still warm from the oven. One of the women stared as a yellow Renault 4 parked in front of her. It wasn't the colour that attracted the woman's attention: the car had no roof.

When Sébastien told the owner of his car repair shop that he wanted to *couper le toit* of his Renault 4 the owner replied that Sébastien should have his own head cut off for considering such a ridiculous idea. However, when the work was finished and the car had been sprayed bright yellow the owner had to admit that it had a certain beach-buggy charm. Wherever it went motorists hooted and gave thumbs-up signs. Passers-by took selfies when it was parked at the kerb. Isabelle, Sébastien's ex-wife, refused to have anything to do with the car, declaring that Sébastien had ruined a perfectly good *quatrelle* and that, *en plus*, driving it around the dusty streets of Marrakech made her clothes dirty. When they separated, Isabelle took the Shogun back to Paris while Sébastien was left with the *quatrelle* and a pile of debt.

Sébastien reached into the back seat and lifted out the cardboard box. He headed into the bustling medina, peering around the side of the box every few seconds to avoid collisions. When he'd gone halfway he stopped to rest beside a vacant lot. A group of young men was playing football. They were stripped to their waists, yelling and charging around madly. Sébastien was fascinated by these displays of manic energy during Ramadan, the way youths liked to show off their toughness, their resilience to the rigours of fasting. The ball came bouncing towards him, closely followed by one of the boys. Sweat was running down his lean brown torso. Sébastien caught the ball, gazed at the boy for a moment then let the ball roll onto the ground. A breathless '*merci mssyoo*' and the boy was gone.

Sébastien walked on until he reached Dar Zuleika. He placed the box on the ground behind him and knocked. A maid came to the door, her face blotchy and tear-stained. When Sébastien asked her what was wrong she turned away with a mumble. A few seconds later Kay appeared, smiling, and reached up to give Sébastien a kiss.

'Aziza looks like she's been crying.'

Kay gave a dismissive wave. 'Oh, she smashed a bowl – the nice blue and green one from Fez. I told her she had to pay for it out of her wages. Come in out of the heat!' Her attention was caught by a thud as the box toppled on its side. 'What was that?' Kay looked at Sébastien suspiciously. He gave a grin. Turning his back he reached into the box and wheeled around, holding a monkey. It looked as surprised as Kay.

'Sébastien, what on earth—?'

'Cute little guy, isn't he?'

'Where did—?'

'He's for you,' said Sébastien, walking past Kay with the monkey clinging to his shirt. 'Don't you like him?'

Kay grimaced. Why couldn't Sébastien, for once, bring her an ordinary present? What was wrong with flowers – or a gift from the *chocolatier* in Rue de la Liberté? She took a bottle of champagne from the fridge and went up to the roof terrace. Sébastien was lying on a rattan recliner smoking a cigarette. He had attached the monkey to the leg of the recliner with a piece of string.

'Keep him for now,' said Sébastien. 'If you decide you don't want him we'll donate him to a sanctuary.'

'A sanctuary? This is Morocco! They don't have sanctuaries for monkeys – especially not for monkeys bought by cruel Frenchmen in a shameless attempt to win over their girlfriends.'

Sébastien chuckled. 'Other riads have a spa. You have a monkey. Maybe you could train him to serve cocktails.'

'What does he eat?'

'*Filet mignon.*'

Kay stared a moment, then threw a cushion at Sébastien. He held one hand in front of his face, laughing. '*Je sais pas!* Ask Driss, he'll know.' He propped the cushion behind his head.

'Where am I supposed to keep him?'

'In the courtyard . . . in the library . . . *comme tu veux*. I bought him from one of the *mecs* in the Jemaa. Look at him! He's going to be a big hit with your guests.' Sébastien stubbed the cigarette out on the ground. Kay picked up the butt as if it was a dead wasp and dropped it over the parapet.

'Aren't you going to ask about my trip?'

'Ah yes – Cairo. It went well?'

'I bought some lovely old Byzantine crosses. And ten original Lehnert and Landrock prints.'

'Nudes?' Sébastien's eyes twinkled. '*Des femmes déshabillées?*'

'No. They're landscapes, of the Nile delta. Talking of which . . .' Kay gave a sidelong glance. 'The riverboats are empty. What do you say we go on a Nile cruise? I've always wanted to see Abu Simbel and Luxor. The sites will be deserted.

We'll be like nineteenth-century travellers, travelling in splendid isolation! Perhaps when the Serafina is finished—'

Sébastien's face clouded. '*If* the Serafina is finished! Ramadan has fucked everything up. We're low on materials and the men are like zombies. Jamal is supposed to start in September but we haven't even completed the *gros oeuvre*, the main building work. *C'est une catastrophe!*'

Kay said nothing. Six months ago, when Sébastien was asked to take over the Serafina project, he described it as the answer to his prayers. It was *un projet cinq étoiles* that would pay off his debts and get his career back on track. Yet now all he did was complain. Kay refilled his glass.

'Let's talk about something else. Like the party! Have you any last-minute requests? Fire-eaters? Gladiators? *Barbecued monkey?*'

Sébastien got up, walked to the parapet and gazed at the nearby mosque. The call to prayer was in progress. He waited for the prayer to finish then turned around. 'I think we should cancel it.'

Kay was incredulous. 'Cancel the party?'

'People are away, it's Ramadan . . .'

Kay marched over and grabbed Sébastien's arm. 'It's your fiftieth birthday! I've sent out invitations! It might be fun! You know – *fun?*'

'This is not a good time.'

'With you it's never a good time!'

Sébastien freed himself. 'I have to go.'

'*Go?* You've just arrived!'

'I'll call you tomorrow.' With a wave Sébastien disappeared down the stairs.

'But Samira has prepared supper!' Kay sank on the recliner in a daze. She stared at the monkey. The monkey scratched its head and stared back at her.

Melanie walked gingerly through the food stalls in Jemaa el Fna. The closely spaced kitchens and eating areas made her claustrophobic. Every leering man looked like the brute who had robbed her. The cooked sheep's heads were straight out of a horror film. And what were those rubbery things on trays?

She had left the riad two hours ago to find somewhere to eat. After wandering down endless alleyways, taking wrong turns into cul-de-sacs, she chanced upon an Internet café. It was dark and smelled of sweat. She paid three dirhams, sat down at the unfamiliar-looking keyboard and sent an email to her place of work, telling them what had happened. She glanced at the youth at the next desk. He was watching a porn video. She left in a hurry. How different things had been when she was with Emma and Julie – riding around in a horse-drawn *calèche*, gawping at the sights and laughing until the tears ran down their faces!

'Only look good price Number 21 best food in town cheaper than Ryanair come back here excuse me!' A waiter with a cheeky grin was standing in her path, trying to steer her to his stall. '*Couscous d'agneau quarante dirhams le moins cher pourquoi pas chérie?*'

Melanie hesitated. The men couldn't all be muggers and sex fiends. She allowed the waiter to show her to a trestle table occupied by a handful of other tourists. A salad of chopped tomato and onion appeared in front of her, followed by a saucer of sliced aubergine. The aubergine was fried in olive oil and, to her surprise, very tasty. She could hear the beat of tam-tams interspersed with the wail of a wind instrument. It sounded like a street party was taking place around the corner. Toy rockets flew into the sky, flashing red and green, then drifted to the ground.

Perhaps this isn't so bad after all, she decided.

When Karim left the commissariat the sun was sinking and a stork was flying slowly to the ruins of the Badi Palace. Oh, to be free like the bird! Karim would normally have been looking forward to breaking the fast with his family, to enjoying the novelty of water on his tongue, to tasting a date as if for the first time. But he knew that his mother would want to discuss Khadija's wedding. The ceremony was just twelve weeks away and he still hadn't arranged a restaurant or booked the Turkish singer that Khadija was so keen on.

He went through the figures in his head. His mother had given him eleven thousand dirhams, Khadija another four thousand, and he had eight thousand in his post office account. Even if he saved his salary for the next two months, skimped on the catering and hired a cut-price venue he would still be short by ten thousand dirhams. But he was the head of the family. It was his responsibility to take care of things.

He considered asking Khadija's fiancé for a contribution. He didn't like the idea of being in debt to his future brother-in-law, but Zak was a wealthy man with a successful business and an apartment in Daoudiate. Perhaps he would pay for the food. When Karim's sister Naïma got married the guests feasted on ten spit-roasted lambs and danced to the best orchestra in Marrakech. Of course, his father had been alive then and prices had been lower. It seemed like everything had doubled in the last few years apart from his salary, which remained stubbornly at four thousand dirhams a month.

Karim thought of the English girls. Which one was getting married – the bad-tempered one, what was her name, Melanie? Or the girl with the sarong? How much would her father have to pay for her wedding? Would she insist, like Khadija, on four changes of costume?

Around him people were hurrying home with breads, yogurts and fruit for the evening meal. Those who had to work – parking attendants, filling station personnel and the like – sat on the pavement in little groups around pans of *harira*, waiting for the call to prayer. As he passed the round-about he heard a crash. A people carrier had jumped the light and hit the rear of a *grand taxi*. The drivers leapt out and started haranguing each other. Karim should have taken charge, told the drivers to move their vehicles to the side of the road until a uniformed officer arrived, but like the rest of the crowd he was bent on getting home as quickly as he could. He entered the souks: hundreds of bodies, carts, scooters and donkeys pushing in every direction, a fug of rosewater and exhaust fumes.

It was with relief that he turned into the quiet alley of Bourahmoune Lkbir. Ayesha welcomed him at the door, her hands wet from the kitchen. Ayesha had lived with Karim's family for eighteen years. Abandoned on their doorstep as a baby, she had been raised by Karim's parents as one of their own. They always referred to her as their daughter but, while Naïma and Khadija had gone to college and then to office jobs in Guéliz, Ayesha was the one who stayed behind to help with the housework.

She took Karim's jacket and followed him into the courtyard. The courtyard was open to the sky, the floor paved in tiles around a concrete fountain that had long since been disconnected from the water supply. In the corner was a small sofa and a birdcage with a pair of finches. Five rooms led off the courtyard, including a tiny kitchen that Karim's father had equipped with a gas cooker when Karim was born. Few home improvements had been carried out since then apart from an occasional coat of paint and a garland of plastic roses that Khadija had draped around the fountain. Karim peered into the *salon*. The television was on but no one was watching. Karim's mother, Lalla Fatima, came out of the kitchen. She looked careworn, older than her fifty-three years. She gave Karim a kiss on the cheek.

'Abderrezak is joining us.'

Karim's heart skipped a beat. If he found a moment alone with Zak he would broach the subject of money, *inshallah*.

He went up to his bedroom and took a fresh shirt from the pile of laundry that Ayesha had left on his bed. He padded to the shower room, tapped the bulb above the sink until it flickered into life then washed his face. He was wondering whether to have a shave when he heard voices in the courtyard.

He came downstairs to find a pair of Italian leather brogues outside the *salon*. Karim kicked off his sandals and walked in.

The *salon* was a narrow windowless room, the walls tiled half-way up with blue and white faience. At one end was a wooden shelf unit with a forty-two-inch television and a photo of Naïma and her husband on their wedding day. At the other stood a low table with divans on three sides. Abderrezak was sitting on the far divan, absorbed in his mobile. Karim stood for a moment contemplating his future brother-in-law. Zak had left school at sixteen to work for a stone merchant. Eight years later he was running his own business. Karim knew that Zak was a good match for Khadija even if, in his heart of hearts, he had doubts about the marriage. Did all men feel the same way about their sisters' fiancés?

'*Salaam ou alikum.*'

'*Oualikum salaam.*'

Zak shook Karim's hand without raising his eyes. Khadija came in with a plate of sweetmeats and greeted her brother. She was wearing her best caftan and her cheeks were flushed with excitement. Everyone said that Khadija looked like Karim. They had the same green Chleuh eyes, the same gently upturned nose. Karim hoped that Khadija's children would inherit her looks and not those of Abderrezak, with his hawk-like nose and prominent chin.

Lalla Fatima wheeled in a trolley laid with hard-boiled eggs, yoghurts, black olives, flatbread, a silver teapot and a flask of coffee. Ayesha followed with a large bottle of Coca-Cola and a tray with cups and glasses. She muted the volume on the television, checked to see that everything was ready then perched next to the doorway. Karim took a seat between her and Zak.

He glanced at his chronograph: two minutes to go. Zak peeled an egg, arranging the fragments of shell in a little pile.

Khadija placed three dates and a sweet pastry on her plate. Ayesha poured a glass of milk. Lalla Fatima sat with her arms in her lap. One minute to go. Karim closed his eyes and prayed that he would be able to give his sister the wedding that she deserved.

A prayer made at the time of breaking fast is always accepted, according to the Prophet, Peace and Blessings upon Him.

A loudspeaker blared from the mosque. As the first '*Allahu Akbar*' died away – before the second had sounded – everyone pounced on their food. Zak shovelled egg into his mouth, Ayesha munched a date and Khadija helped herself to a *shebbakiya* dripping with honey and sesame. Lalla Fatima, murmuring *bismillah*, poured five cups of coffee. Karim raised a glass of water to his lips and took a long drink.

Oh Allah, I fasted for Thee and I believe in Thee and I break my fast with Thy sustenance.

They ate without speaking, the women following the soap opera on television. When the show ended Lalla Fatima spoke. 'I saw the *negafa*, the wedding organiser. She said we should have two of the *takshitas* made to measure and hire the other two.'

This was news to Karim. A tailored *takshita* wedding dress would cost between six and ten thousand dirhams. 'Couldn't we have one of the dresses made and hire the other three?'

'Two made to measure and two hired, that's the rule!' said Khadija.

'What about Ayesha?' Zak grinned. 'Is she getting a *takshita*?'

'She's having a red *takshita*,' said Khadija. 'With gold braid. Isn't that right, Ayesha?'

Ayesha blushed. '*Inshallah.*'

'A red and gold *takshita*?' Zak gave a wink. 'Who are you out to catch, Ayesha?'

Lalla Fatima spoke. 'She's not out to catch anyone. She just wants to look pretty, isn't that so, Ayesha?'

Ayesha blushed again. She mumbled a few words and retreated from the room with a handful of empty plates.

Zak wiped his mouth with a napkin and turned to Karim. 'I'm going to have a cigarette. Coming?'

The men put on their shoes and climbed the stairs to the roof. They ducked under the washing line and sat down on an old metal bedstead. Like other families in the medina, the Belkacems used their roof as a dumping ground. It was home to a fridge, a chair without a back, two old car tyres, a mattress, a solidified bag of cement, several lengths of plastic pipe, wooden crates and assorted jars and bottles, overlooked by a rickety satellite dish.

Zak took out his cigarettes. Karim had intended to give up for Ramadan but one of Zak's Marlboros would concentrate his mind. He inhaled deeply.

'How's business?'

Zak reached up and gave the satellite dish a prod. 'Everyone's going crazy for Ouarzazate stone. A man came in yesterday and ordered a hundred and fifty square metres.'

'You must be doing well.'

'Yes – except I spend all my time in Ouarzazate.'

'Do you like Ouarzazate?

Zak shrugged. 'Ouarzazate is Ouarzazate.'

'Have you decided if you're going to take time off for a honeymoon?'

'Don't worry, I'll take your sister somewhere nice . . . like Ouarzazate!' Both men laughed. They heard the chink of glasses and the sound of foreign voices from a nearby terrace.

Zak peered across the rooftops. 'Have you thought of that?'

'What?'

'Selling the riad to foreigners. You could get forty *milyoon*. More if you get rid of this rubbish.' He kicked the bedstead.

'Zak, can I ask—'

'Your mother could buy a nice modern apartment and she wouldn't have to worry about money for the rest of her life.'

'I need to talk to you—'

'You might even get fifty *milyoon*! How much do you earn at the Sûreté – four or five thousand a month? You could retire! I heard of one family who sold their place for sixty-eight *milyoon* and it's a dump.'

Karim's palms were sweating. 'Zak, the wedding venue—'

'What about the wedding venue?'

'It's going to cost twelve thousand dirhams. Thirty thousand with the food and musicians. That's more than we can afford. And Khadija wants a Turkish singer!'

Zak considered a moment then jabbed his finger against Karim's chest. 'Exactly!'

'What do you mean?'

'That's exactly why you need to sell the riad!'

Karim sighed. He heard a commotion from the courtyard, then footsteps on the stairs. Khadija came onto the roof, panting.

'Karim, come quickly!'

Karim went to the railing. In the courtyard his mother was

talking to a ten-year-old boy whom Karim recognised as the son of the local muezzin. Karim called down.

'What's wrong?'

'You're needed!'

Karim ran down the stairs and into the courtyard.

'*Ooqat moseeba*.' His mother's face was pale. 'Something terrible has happened.'

'Come!' The boy clutched Karim's hand. '*Ajee!*' He led Karim out of the front door then started running down Derb Bourahmoune Lkbir. Karim quickened his pace, then broke into a run as well. The boy looked over his shoulder to check that Karim was still behind him. At Bab Taghzout he headed right towards Sidi bel Abbès.

A knot of men had gathered in the alleyway by the mosque. Karim recognised the muezzin and a couple of local shopkeepers. A tall, loose-limbed man in shirt and rolled-up trousers was arguing with another man in a *jellaba*. Karim's first thought was that there had been a fight. The group parted to let him through. The tall man pointed to a parked handcart. In a loud voice he said that the cart was his, that it had been stolen and, as God was his witness, he had nothing to do with what was inside. At first all Karim could see in the cart was a stack of sheets of cardboard. He lifted off the top sheet and caught a glimpse of red cloth. He took off another sheet and saw a sleeved arm. One more layer, and there was the body of a girl of about twenty wearing a red dress. She had long black hair and was curled up as if asleep. For a brief, panic-stricken moment Karim thought it was Ayesha. But this girl was plumper, her lips fuller, and she was wearing make-up. He felt her neck for a pulse. On the side of her head above her ear was an ugly swelling. The hair around it was matted with blood. Judging by the discolorations on her arms she had been dead for at least twelve hours. Beside her was a strip of cardboard on which was scrawled, in black marker pen:

My name is Amina Talal and I am a whore.

Chapter 2

The library-cum-boutique of Dar Zuleika was a long, high-ceilinged room crammed with antiques and furniture. One wall was covered with mirrors, textiles, Orientalist paintings and old maps of Morocco. A bookcase stood against another wall, its shelves filled with sculptures from sub-Saharan Africa, tiles from long-demolished synagogues, nineteenth-century Fassi bowls, Berber jewellery and colonial-era bric-a-brac. From the ceiling dangled chandeliers and lanterns in every shape and size. In the middle of the room, on a high-backed chair flanked by piles of rugs and carpets, sat Kay.

'My dear Kay! You look like the Queen of Sheba!'

Lucinda Parker glided through the room and kissed Kay on the cheek. Lucinda was a recent arrival in Marrakech who'd left London at the age of sixty to buy a rundown villa in the Hivernage district. She set about restoring the property, much to Kay's irritation, with a series of good-looking young Moroccan men whom she referred to as 'advisors'.

Lucinda sank into an armchair, took a magazine from the coffee table and fanned herself.

'Talking of the Queen of Sheba, how was Cairo?'

Kay offered her a flute of champagne. 'Hot.'

'As hot as here?'

'Nowhere is as hot as here.'

'Did Sébastien go with you?'

Kay gave a little laugh. 'He was busy.'

'He works too hard, that man! I hope he's going to take time off for his party. How does he feel about being fifty?'

'Who knows?' Kay paused to reflect. Was Sébastien having a mid-life crisis? Were his mood swings symptoms of existential angst (how appropriately French!)? Or were they a warning of something more troubling – the end of their relationship? In November his contract came to an end. What if Mohammed offered him another job, this time in the Gulf? What would become of their relationship then? She changed the subject.

'How are you settling in?'

'Fine,' said Lucinda, fanning her neck. 'Some things are still beyond me.'

'Such as?'

'How much to tip taxi drivers. Whether to have blinds or curtains.'

'Nothing and curtains, that's my advice. Would you like to have a look at some of the things I picked up in Cairo? I've got a shipment arriving in a fortnight but I brought some of the best items with me.' Kay placed a tall brass object on the coffee table.

'Goodness, it's heavy!' said Lucinda. 'What is it?'

'An Ottoman candleholder. Eighteenth century, possibly earlier. The bell shape is typical of Mamluk design.'

Lucinda examined the decoration on the base. 'I suppose it's frightfully expensive.'

'Well, it's true that Ottoman candlesticks in this condition are rare. The antiques dealer in Zamalek was very reluctant to part with them.'

'There's more than one?' Kay produced a second candlestick and Lucinda picked it up with her free hand. 'They would look marvellous in my dining room.'

'My thoughts exactly.'

'And the price . . .?'

'I could let you have them both for . . . let me see . . . five hundred euros.'

'Would you take four hundred and fifty?'

'Of course.'

As Kay wrapped the candlestick she repressed a smile of delight. Three hundred profit! Not bad considering she had only recently started a career as an antiques dealer. That was the marvellous thing about Marrakech: as long as you had the confidence, you could pass yourself off as anything you liked.

Lucinda went over to look at some fabrics. 'These are nice. Are they bedspreads?'

'They're antique Yemeni sarongs. You could use them as bedspreads if you wished.'

Lucinda pointed to an embroidered muslin. 'And that?'

'It's a burial shroud from the Beqaa Valley. It would make a nice tablecloth.'

Lucinda examined the price tag, then took the shroud and placed it on the coffee table next to the wrapped candlesticks. She sat down again and arranged the folds of her dress.

'How do you manage to find so many beautiful things? Places like Cairo must be stripped bare by now!'

'It's not as easy as it used to be,' agreed Kay. 'It's not just

Cairo. Istanbul, Rajasthan . . . wherever I go, I get the feeling that the best items have already gone.'

'What's the solution?'

'I hunt twice as hard as other buyers. If all else fails – if I can't find what I'm looking for – I design it myself. That chair, for example – the one you're sitting on.'

'This?' Lucinda shifted her knees for a better look. 'I'd no idea you designed your own furniture.'

'Oh, I design a lot of things,' said Kay airily. In truth, she had only designed two pieces: a chair and a garden bench. But there was no reason why she couldn't be a furniture designer. All it took was a scribble and a competent craftsman to execute it.

Lucinda considered a moment. 'I wonder whether I should get you to design my dining table.'

'I'd be delighted.'

Lucinda put her hand on Kay's knee. 'Do you know what, my dear? It's ridiculous you just supplying bits and pieces. You should do the whole lot – the decoration, everything! Why don't you come by and take a look?'

'It would be a pleasure.' Kay was so gratified that she almost invited Lucinda for dinner.

It was after midnight when Karim returned from the mortuary with Amina Talal's father. A passer-by would have found it hard to tell which was the bereaved man. Omar Talal shuffled along the alley, glassy-eyed with shock. Karim walked slowly beside him, staring at the ground, lost in a world of his own.

He had been a boy of eight when he last saw – properly saw – Amina Talal. Omar Talal was a different man in those days, an intimidating figure with bushy black eyebrows who owned a small *hanoot*, or grocery store, in Derb Esh-Shems. Karim's father had taken him to the Talals' house because the two men 'had business to discuss'.

Omar answered the door without smiling and the two men went off to talk. Karim found himself alone with Amina, a little girl of seven with unruly hair and large black eyes. After a few minutes, Karim took out the wooden top he always carried with him and spun it on the floor. As he picked it up, he noticed Amina watching him intently. He wound the string around the top and went over to where she was standing. Planting his feet behind her he reached around and positioned the top between her thumb and forefinger. He wrapped the end of the string around her hand then stepped to one side. She looked at him and he nodded. She yanked. The top flew out of her hand and skittered along the corridor. It would have gone on spinning forever had a door not opened and knocked it over.

It was only years later that Karim found out that his father and Omar had been discussing a marriage betrothal between himself and Amina. But they had quarrelled and the arrangement had been called off. In the years since, Karim had passed Amina a few times in the medina. Apart from an occasional *salaam* they hadn't spoken.

Karim could hear sobbing as he helped Omar Talal over the threshold. Amina's mother was in the front room, surrounded by weeping women. Amina's brother Abderrahim, a bearded twenty-five-year-old in a white *galabiyya* robe, led the two men into the *salon*. On the table were plates of half-eaten food. Abderrahim clapped his hands and a woman came in, eyes averted, and cleared the plates away. Abderrahim placed a chair in the middle of the room and helped his father to sit down, then stood with his hands on the back of the chair and looked at Karim expectantly. Karim took out his notebook.

'When did you last see Amina alive?'

Si Omar stared into space. Abderrahim spoke on his behalf. 'On Sunday evening at seven o'clock. She went to her friend Leila Hasnaoui's house to revise for an exam.'

'Where does Leila Hasnaoui live?'

'Guéliz.'

'How did Amina get there?'

'She took the bus.'

'Not a taxi?'

'We don't have money for taxis.'

Karim was surprised. Even Ayesha could afford to take a taxi every now and then. He gazed around the room. There was a simple sideboard on which stood a silver teapot. The only decoration was a small Quranic wall-hanging. This was the room, he realised, where his father had quarrelled with Omar all those years ago.

'Did she go to Leila's house often?'

'Whenever she needed to use the computer.'

Karim looked up again.

'We don't have a computer,' Abderrahim explained.

'Couldn't she use the *seeber* – the Internet café off the square?'

'My father does not approve of *seebers*.'

Karim glanced at Omar, shrunken and haggard in the glare of the ceiling lamp. It was hard to imagine him as a forbidding father. The dark bushy eyebrows were now white tufts, more comical than threatening.

'What was Amina wearing when she went out?'

'A grey *jellaba* and a headscarf. She never goes out without her *jellaba* and headscarf.'

Karim's thoughts flicked back to the figure in the red dress, her hair cascading onto the floor of the handcart. 'Were you worried when she didn't come home?'

'Amina usually stayed the night with Leila then went straight to college the next morning. We were not expecting her until *ftour*, the breaking of the fast.'

At the mention of *ftour* Si Omar stirred in his chair and motioned in the direction of the table where the food had been.

'What was Amina studying?'

Abderrahim took a plastic loose-leaf folder from the sideboard and handed it to Karim. It was titled *Tourisme et hotellerie, Etape 2*. Karim leafed through the pages.

'Did she go to college yesterday morning?'

'No. I called her teacher to check.'

'I need the phone number of Leila Hasnaoui. And a photo of Amina.'

While Abderrahim went to fetch them Karim put a consoling hand on Omar Talal's shoulder. The old man stared straight ahead, rubbing his knuckles. He reminded Karim of a lobotomy patient he had seen in a hospital in Kenitra. Abderrahim returned with a scrap of paper and a passport photo.

'Have you spoken to Leila?'

Abderrahim shook his head. 'Amina has been taken from us. That is enough for now.'

Si Omar rose unsteadily to his feet. He looked at Karim, as if suddenly aware of his presence. 'Who . . . who would . . . who would . . .?' His voice trailed off.

Who would murder a good Muslim girl? Who indeed, Karim wondered. Had Amina been mistaken for someone else? If so, how to explain the clothes? And the sign – that terrible sign? He was glad he had covered it up and left it inside the mosque with the handcart. The family would find out about the sign soon enough. Would Abderrahim conduct himself with such compo-sure when he discovered how his sister's name had been sullied?

'I shall be in touch.' Karim searched for something else to say, an epitaph for his almost-fiancée, a girl whom he'd once instructed in the art of spinning a top. In the end all he said was, 'Can I keep the photo?'

In the corridor more women had arrived. They were pressed in the doorway to the front room, keening and mopping their eyes. Out in the alleyway, Abderrahim clasped Karim's hand to his chest. 'Our honour and your honour depend on this,' he breathed.

Karim made his way back to Bab Taghzout through a stream of families, the children skipping in merriment, delighted at being allowed to stay up late for Ramadan.

It was a hazy morning, the sun palest yellow. At Bab el-Khemis the market was in full swing. Porters were pushing handcarts laden with second-hand goods. Scribes sat at tables writing documents for illiterate customers. A crowd had gathered

around the last table. As Karim approached, the crowd parted
to reveal a scribe with his back to him. Karim drew nearer
until he could see over the man's shoulder. On a piece of paper
were the words *My name is Amina Talal and I am a whore*. The
man turned around, his mouth gaping, black and toothless.
He started to laugh. The rest of the crowd started laughing
with him.

Karim jerked awake. He threw back the sheet from his bed
and sat upright. His pillow was drenched with sweat. It was
still dark. He experienced a second of confusion then the
events of the evening came flooding back.

The daughter of his father's best friend, a girl he was once to
have married, was dead. She had gone to a friend to revise for
an exam and ended up dumped in a handcart, dressed like a
prostitute. Was it possible – was it *conceivable* – that Si Omar's
daughter had been punished because she sold her body to
men? Even if she had lain with men for financial gain no
mortal has the right to kill another. That right belongs to God
alone!

In just over an hour his mother would come to wake him.
He wiped his forehead and opened the window to the alley.
The air was hot, heavy. He could hear foreign voices drifting
through the stillness. Were they the same voices that he and
Zak had heard hours, years, centuries ago? He went back to
his bed even though he knew he wouldn't be able to fall asleep.
He decided that as soon as he arrived at work he would get the
cart swabbed. He would summon a handwriting expert and
he would talk to Leila Hasnaoui.

He caught a faint smell of argan oil. A shadowy figure was
standing in his doorway . . . Ayesha! She was wearing a white

caftan and her hair was loose around her shoulders. She padded over in bare feet and sat on the side of his bed.

'I heard you cry out.'

Karim propped himself on his elbows. 'I had a nightmare.'

'Where did you go to last night?'

'Sidi bel Abbès. A girl was found dead in a handcart.'

Ayesha shuddered. 'Who was she?'

'Amina Talal. I knew her family. A long time ago.'

'*Allah irhemha*, may God have mercy on her. Were there any witnesses?'

'No. Everyone was at *ftour*.'

'Shall I heat up some food?'

Karim shook his head. He drew Ayesha towards him and buried his face in her sweet-smelling hair. They sat holding each other for several minutes then Ayesha kissed Karim on the cheek and tip-toed out of his room.

Karim went to the bathroom and rinsed his mouth thoroughly. He put his feet under the shower, cleaned his hands up to the elbow then dried himself with a towel. He unrolled his prayer mat, raised his hands to his ears and started his prayers.

The air in the new town of Guéliz was cool and fresh. Early morning, before the sun rose above the buildings, was the only time of day when Sébastien found the heat bearable. After ten o'clock, driving an open-topped car through Marrakech was like sticking your head in a fan oven. He parked the *quatrelle* outside a café, strode past the pile of tables and tried the door, only to find it closed. He remembered that it was Ramadan. He went to the tobacco kiosk but it, too, was shut.

'*Merde!*'

Sébastien got back into the car and drove slowly along the street looking for somewhere to park. As luck would have it, there was a space right outside his office. He stopped and reversed only to hear a *crunch*.

'*Putain!*' He had hit a parked car, a black Lexus. He looked around to see if anyone had noticed. On the pavement a Moroccan man in a suit, phone to his ear, was staring at him. Sébastien jumped out to inspect the damage. The licence plate of the Lexus was smashed and the bumper was hanging at an angle. The man in the suit marched up to him. He was in his early thirties, with moustache and clipped hair.

'*Ça va pas la tête?*' he exclaimed. 'Are you crazy?'

Sébastien stood up. '*Ce n'est rien.*'

The Moroccan was almost speechless. 'What do you mean, it's nothing?'

Sébastien ignored him. He took his leather bag from the back seat of the Renault and walked off towards the building. The Moroccan crouched down and ran his fingers over the broken bumper, following Sébastien with his eyes.

Sébastien took the elevator to the top floor and pushed open the heavy glass doors of Al-Husseini Group SARL. He gave a brief nod at the receptionist, walked down the corridor, sat at his desk and put his head in his hands. The accident had unsettled him. It wasn't the shock of the collision. It was the fact that the Moroccan had been driving a Lexus.

For years Sébastien had enjoyed a lifestyle that most Moroccans could only dream of. Even when his business had collapsed he had been able to console himself with the thought that, however bad things were, he hadn't sunk to the level of a Moroccan. As a French citizen, he was the superior race. Now the boot was on the other foot. In recent years the Moroccan economy had boomed while the French economy had tanked. Marrakchis half his age were driving around in shiny Lexuses while he drove a beaten-up *bagnole*. Only last week a Moroccan couple in their twenties had asked him, Sébastien de Freycinet, *diplômé* of the École nationale supérieure des Beaux-Arts in Paris, *maître-architecte* of riads and hotels, if he would submit a proposal for their *kitchen*!

'*Monsieur de Freycinet?*' Latifa, the secretary, was standing by his desk. '*Vous desirez un café?*'

Sébastien nodded. He turned on his computer and waited for it to boot up. On a table by the window was a 3D model of the Serafina Hotel. Back in March, at his interview, Mohammed Al-Husseini had stood Sébastien in front of the model, placed his arm around Sébastien's shoulder and declared in a loud voice that he needed someone of Sébastien's calibre to take over the project because the current architects were *a bunch of shitheads*. Over the next five months, through a combination of incentives and shortcuts, Sébastien had managed to get the construction back on track. In return, a grateful Al-Husseini had promised him a bonus of a hundred thousand euros if the Serafina opened on schedule.

Sébastien scrolled through his emails. There was a message from his son, Laurent, stating his arrival time in Marrakech on 27 August. Laurent was the only one of his two children with whom Sébastien still had contact. His visit would be the first time Sébastien had seen his son in ten years. He was about to send a reply when Latifa showed up with an espresso.

'Don't forget you have a telephone call with Monsieur Al-Husseini at nine-thirty. Also, an inspector from the Wilaya is coming to the office with some documents for you.'

Sébastien gave a weary sigh. He had expected a visit from the planning department. A week ago an official had made a surprise visit to the Serafina construction site and made a fuss about safety procedures. Now the man's superior had decided to follow him, probably sniffing for *baksheesh*. Sébastien would introduce the inspector to his assistant in the next-door office and let the two men hammer out a deal, one Moroccan with another. That was how these things were done.

The phone rang: the official had arrived. Sébastien drank his espresso, picked up a file and strode down the corridor. The receptionist pointed to a man sitting in a leather chair. Sébastien went over to shake his hand.

It was the driver of the black Lexus.

'I – I don't understand.'

'Aziz will take over. Give your notes to him.' Hamid Badnaoui, captain of the Préfecture of the 4ème Arrondissement, gave a wave to indicate that the interview was over. Karim cast around the room, as if searching for some higher authority to appeal to, then turned and walked out. He had been prepared to argue for the investigation staying with the *quatrième*, rather than being passed to headquarters, but not in his worst nightmares had he imagined that Badnaoui would award the case to a fellow officer – a man of the same rank as himself.

He climbed the steps to his office and slumped at his desk. 'He's given the case to Aziz.'

Noureddine rubbed his spectacles with a cloth. 'Who was the victim?'

'Amina Talal, twenty-one. I knew her – a little. She went to a friend's house on Sunday evening and failed to show up for college the next day.'

'You knew her?'

'Her father was a friend of my father's.'

'Perhaps it's better that you're off the investigation.'

Karim was startled. 'What do you mean?'

'Perhaps you're too close to it.'

Close to it? Of course he was close to it! Amina Talal was the daughter of his father's best friend. He had been betrothed to Amina. Her family were relying on him to solve the case. Abderrahim had told him as much!

'Aziz is a good officer,' continued Noureddine.

Was that meant to reassure him? Karim buried his head in his hands. 'God help me.'

'God helps when the sons of Adam help themselves,' Noureddine said gently.

Karim turned his chair to the window and stared out. Across the road the parking attendant was standing in the sunshine chatting to the upholsterer. Every so often one of them would laugh. How could they laugh with the thermometer at boiling point? Karim realised that his forehead and cheeks were damp with sweat and he looked for a cloth to wipe them with, eventually settling on his shirtsleeve.

Noureddine addressed him again. 'How are plans for the wedding?'

The wedding. Karim felt like he'd been punched in the stomach. 'Weddings cost so much these days.'

'Have you considered taking a night job?' suggested Noureddine. 'As a security guard?' Karim rummaged through his drawer while Noureddine carried on talking. 'It would give you the chance to earn some extra money.' Karim picked out a watch, a Tag Heuer, and scribbled some notes. 'All you'd have to do is sit in a hut all night and keep watch.'

'What about sleep?' Karim retorted. 'I wouldn't get any sleep.'

'*Pah.* None of us sleep during Ramadan. Besides, you're more likely to sleep in a quiet hut on the outskirts of town than in the medina where people stay up all night and chatter.'

Karim thought of his noisy bedroom. He gave a noncommittal grunt.

'I heard of a building site on the Route d'Ourika that's looking for a nightwatchman,' said Noureddine.

'How much are they paying?'

'Thirty an hour. They might pay thirty-five if you tell them you're a policeman.'

Karim reached for his calculator. Thirty-five dirhams an hour . . . two hundred and eighty dirhams a night . . . thirty nights . . . eight thousand four hundred dirhams. That was enough to pay for two dresses. What's more, a night job would take him away from Ayesha, from his annoying brother-in-law, from discussions about the wedding. For the first time since the start of Ramadan Karim felt his mood lift. He picked up the watch and walked over to Noureddine. 'Fake or real?'

'What?'

'The watch.' Karim dangled it in front of his colleague. 'Fake or real?'

With a sigh Noureddine took the watch and held it to his ear. He gave it a shake and listened to it again. 'It's fake.'

'Wrong. It's real. Do you know how you can tell?'

Noureddine shrugged his shoulders. Karim fetched a marble ashtray from Abdou's desk. He placed the watch on the desk in front of Noureddine then, looking solemnly at his colleague, he lifted the ashtray in the air and brought it down with a *CRASH*. The Tag Heuer shattered into pieces. Karim burst out laughing.

'By the beard of the Prophet!' Nour exclaimed angrily. 'What do you think you're—'

There was a tap at the door.

'*Bonjour*, hello again.' Melanie Murray stepped into the office. Karim hastily tidied the fragments of watch into the wastepaper basket. '*Le consul Britannique m'a demandé* – no – *il m'a suggesté . . .*'

Karim returned to his desk and set out a chair. 'Please, sit down.'

Melanie sat gratefully. 'The consul advised me to check with you again in case my bag has been handed in.'

Melanie's morning hadn't gone according to plan. She had turned up at the British consulate expecting to find a sympathetic figure who would listen to her tale of woe and get her onto the next flight home. The consul wasn't even British! He took down her details with a seen-it-all-before indifference, informing her that it would take several days to issue new documents and that, in the meantime, she should contact her parents if she needed funds.

'Sorry, there is no news.' Karim had forgotten about the stolen bag. 'The thief – maybe he sell phone and throw away passport. Or he sell passport and throw away phone.'

'I'll have to come back again tomorrow, I suppose.' Melanie got up wearily. 'Do you have a business card or something?'

Karim took out a ruler. He wrote his name, email address and phone number on a piece of paper, placed the ruler on the paper, tore off the strip and handed it to Melanie.

She read aloud. 'Lieutenant Belkacem.'

'It is pronounced *Belkassem*.'

Melanie folded the paper and put it in her bag. 'Well, so long.'

As she left the room she almost collided with the man with pockmarked cheeks – the second-in-command to Aziz. He gave Melanie a leer then strode up to Karim.

'Your notes on Amina Talal,' he said, holding out his hand.

Sébastien followed Hicham Cherkaoui into the meeting room, trying to gauge the man's character from his clothes. The white shirt, pressed black trousers and neatly polished shoes didn't bode well.

'I apologise for *le petit accident*,' Sébastien began. 'If I'd known the car belonged to you, I would have—'

The inspector turned around. 'You would have what, *monsieur*?'

'I, *eh bien*—'

'You would have paid more attention, is that it, *monsieur*?'

'Yes,' said Sébastien uncomfortably.

The inspector took a file from his briefcase. 'Does that mean you're happy to go around smashing up cars as long as they don't belong to public officials?'

The nape of Sébastien's neck was slippery with sweat. 'I have apologised, *monsieur*. It was an accident, as I told you. I saw no damage to your vehicle, but if you disagree I am happy to pay for repairs. Now, what is it you wish to see me about?'

Cherkaoui gave him a sheet of paper headed '*Chantier Serafina – Infractions de Règlements*'. There were two columns, one itemising breaches in site safety, the other failures to acquire the relevant permits. Sébastien sat down at the table to gather his thoughts. He would start with seventy thousand. That was more than a high-ranking government official made in a year. Then again, the inspector wore leather shoes and drove a Lexus; maybe he was used to receiving bigger bribes. He, Sébastien, had better open with eighty thousand. If Cherkaoui still baulked he would offer him a hundred thousand dirhams and have done with it. Sébastien pushed the paper into the middle of the table. 'I'm sure we can reach an agreement.'

Cherkaoui regarded him blankly.

'A settlement.' Sébastien found Cherkaoui's silence unnerving. 'A *contribution*.'

Cherkaoui's reply was cold. 'Things are not done like that anymore.'

'*Allez*, Monsieur Cherkaoui, we are men of the world!'

'You have twenty-eight days to comply.'

'How much money do you want?'

'If the breaches are not rectified the site will be closed down.'

'Ninety thousand,' stormed Sébastien. 'Take it or leave it!'

The inspector fell silent and Sébastien gave a smile. *Every man has his price!*

'If you continue in this *manière, monsieur*,' Cherkaoui said at last, 'I will include attempted bribery in the charges.'

Just then Sébastien's mobile rang and Mohammed Al-Husseini's name flashed on the screen. Sébastien gestured to the inspector that he would have to take the call. '*Attendez, monsieur, s'il vous plaît!*' Holding up the palm of his hand, Sébastien backed out of the room.

Once in the corridor he put the phone to his ear. The voice on the other end was icy. 'Who were you talking to?'

'No one! Everything's fine.'

'You were talking to someone. Is there a problem?'

'*Paf!* Regulations, you know, these Moroccans—'

'Which Moroccans?'

'An inspector of buildings.'

'What does he want?'

Sébastien wiped the back of his neck. 'Nothing – we were talking, that's all. *Il n'y a pas de problème.*'

'I pay you to sort out problems. Call me when you have done so.'

The line went dead. By now, the planning inspector had walked out of the meeting room and was at the end of the corridor. Sébastien ran after him. 'Please excuse, what I said – I didn't mean to suggest that you – that we . . .'

But Cherkaoui had already gone through the doors.

'We need to take all the furniture out of here for the party.'

Kay was standing in the doorway of the dining room. 'Put roses on the mantelpiece – nice, long-stemmed ones, not the cheap ones they sell at the market.'

'*D'accord, madame.*' Samira wondered how she was going to find time to go shopping for roses when she had so much else to organise.

Kay paused to straighten a view of Meknes by Jacques Majorelle. Sébastien had given her the painting in the early days of their relationship, after a holiday to Meknes. Kay remembered the trip fondly. She sat on a rock reading aloud from the guidebook while Sébastien sketched the ruined city of Moulay Ismail. In the evening, they made love on their hotel bed, laughing at the thought of the eighteenth-century sultan and his 867 children. How many of Morocco's present population, they wondered, could claim descent from the prolific sultan?

The front door slammed. Driss came into the courtyard, cheeks flushed, and gabbled to Samira. Kay frowned: she had told the staff never to speak Arabic in her presence. She was about to reprimand Driss when he turned to her.

'*Madame*, something bad has happened . . . a murder.'

Kay went pale. 'Where?'

'By the mosque.'

'Who was it?'

'A Moroccan girl.'

'How do you know?'

'They're all talking about it in the square.'

Kay was aware of only one thought in her head: *at least the victim wasn't a tourist.* Marrakech couldn't afford another tourist atrocity, not after the bombing in the Argana that had killed seventeen foreigners and caused bookings to plummet all over town. Even so, the murder was cause for alarm. Dar Zuleika stood in the shadow of Sidi bel Abbès. The call to prayer was part of daily life at the riad. One of the first things guests did when they arrived was pay a visit to the mosque, with its picturesque courtyard and mausoleum. She asked Driss what else he knew.

'Her body was left in a *charrette*. They say she was . . .' Driss turned to Samira.

Samira translated, blushing. 'A prostitute.'

'*A prostitute?*'

'Yes.'

Just then there was a movement above their heads. Kay looked up to see Melanie peering over the parapet.

'Is everything all right?' asked Melanie.

'Oh, hello.' Kay tried to sound nonchalant. 'Would you like some lemonade?'

'Er . . . OK.' Melanie disappeared from view.

Kay glared at Samira and Driss. She pressed her forefinger to her lips. '*Vous ne dites rien, vous comprenez?*' They nodded meekly.

Melanie came into the courtyard.

'Did you have any luck at the police station?' Kay asked. 'No? Too bad . . . Samira! *Limonade, s'il te plaît!*'

Samira wiped the tears from her eyes and made for the kitchen. Kay took Melanie by the elbow.

'What's wrong with Samira?' said Melanie.

'Oh, she's just a bit emotional. Ramadan can have that effect. Have I told you how the riad got its name? Let me show you a very special room, perhaps *the* most special room in the riad.'

Melanie was disconcerted by Kay's behaviour but she allowed herself to be led up to the first floor where Kay turned the handle of a door inscribed 'Room of the Moroccan Bride'.

'When I bought the riad it needed a lot of work,' Kay began. 'We started renovations immediately. Dust everywhere, hammers clanging all day long. One morning a builder asked me if he could remove some old skirting tiles from a wall – those ones over there.' Kay pointed to a pane of glass at Melanie's feet. 'I came up to watch, thinking that I might be able to reuse the tiles. The walls are over three feet thick. When the builder had taken away several tiles a hole opened up – a kind of hidey-hole.'

Kay flicked a switch and a light came on behind the glass. 'Take a look.'

Melanie got down on her knees. The hole went deep into the wall. Towards the back was a wooden beam on which were some words in Arabic, with an English translation.

'Read what it says,' said Kay.

Melanie took a breath. ' "My name is Zuleika. I was born seventeen summers ago. My sweetheart Ismaïl lives next door. He has jet-black eyes and his smile makes the birds sing. But my father wants me to marry my cousin Abdillah. Tomorrow I must leave this house. I will never see my house or my sweetheart again." '

Melanie looked up at Kay. 'Is this for real?'

Kay nodded. 'It was written about two hundred years ago. The tiles are similar to ones in the mosque of Sidi bel Abbès, which date from the late eighteenth century. Very few women could read or write in those days so Zuleika probably came from a well-to-do family. Moroccan women still use skirting tiles to hide their possessions.

'There's a twist to the story. You've probably noticed that Dar Zuleika has two courtyards. The second courtyard was once part of a separate building. When I'd been running the riad for a couple of years the building came up for sale. I thought: why not join the two riads together and make a single, extra-large riad? On the day that the contract was signed, I went next door with a hammer.

'I ran up the stairs and into the room opposite Zuleika's. I kneeled down and tapped along the wall. After a few taps I heard a hollow *clunk*. I gouged with the claw of the hammer. The plaster came away easily and soon I could see through to the other side.'

Melanie looked into the hole again. Sure enough, there was a square of daylight.

'The bedroom opposite this one was Ismaïl's room. He – or Zuleika – made the hole. If they both lay down as you just did they could gaze into each other eyes, even hold hands. On the day that Zuleika left to get married she filled in the hole and covered it up. The hole and the message remained hidden until we uncovered them two hundred years later.'

When Melanie stood up her eyes were moist. 'That's the most moving thing I've ever heard.'

'Now, how about that lemonade?' Kay said brightly.

News spread fast in the medina. Carried along the alleyways, infiltrating every *hanoot* and *hammam*, it grew, altered shape, feeding on speculation and rumour. Twists were added, details inflated, sub-rumours spawned. What version would his mother and sisters have heard? As Karim stood outside the riad he felt too weak to face their questions.

He turned the lock and let himself in quietly. The riad was silent. There was no sign of Zak, *al-hamdullilah*. Lalla Fatima was in the kitchen shelling peas in a colander. The moment she saw Karim she fell on his neck.

'What is the news about Amina Talal? *Miskina,* the poor girl! Oh, please let it not be true!'

'Come, Meema.' Karim led his mother into the courtyard and sat her on the little sofa. He crouched down and clasped her hands.

She looked at Karim fearfully. 'Was she murdered . . . *raped?*'

'I don't know.'

'You will find out. You will find out who did this horrible thing.'

Karim took a breath. 'I'm not investigating the case.'

Confusion filled Lalla Fatima's face.

'They've appointed another officer. He will find out what happened, *inshallah*.'

Lalla Fatima stared at her son but she knew better than to press him on the matter. She reached for a box of tissues on the table. 'Your father hoped that—'

'I know what father hoped!' Karim said hotly. 'He hoped that I would marry Amina! That was a silly scheme that he and Omar Talal cooked up a long time ago. Amina is dead – it's a tragedy, and we will find out why, God willing, but please do not talk about what father hoped!'

Lalla Fatima sniffed. 'I will go and visit Lalla Hanane after *ftour*.'

'No. You must stay here. The girls, too. It's not safe outside at night, not at the moment.'

'Couldn't you come with us?'

'*La*.' Karim shook his head emphatically. 'I have business to attend to.'

'What business?'

'Don't worry – I'll be back by midnight.'

'Midnight? But we need to talk about the wedding! There's still so much to arrange – the guest list, whether to hold the wedding before or after Eid – if we don't decide on a venue soon all the good ones will be taken.'

'*Thennay*, calm down. We have twelve weeks to decide all those things. We can talk about them over the meal. Where's Ayesha? I'm starving.'

He picked up his bag. As he was making for the stairs he heard his mother say in a quiet voice, 'I want to sell the riad.'

'*What?*'

She twisted the tissue in her hand. 'I want to sell the riad.'

Karim ran back to the sofa. 'What are you talking about? Has Zak been putting ideas into your head? We have plenty of money, more than enough to pay for the wedding!'

Lalla Fatima stared at her son, terrified.

'You don't believe me? Very well, yes – I admit it. We *don't* have enough money. Not yet. That's why I'm going out later – I need to get a second job, a part-time job, but don't worry, we will manage. *I* will manage.'

Lalla Fatima suddenly looked very small. Ayesha came out of a room to see what the disturbance was about.

'Get the food!' Karim told her. But Ayesha stood her ground, defiant.

His mother gazed at Karim with sad eyes. 'I didn't know that we had money problems.'

'We *don't* have money problems!' cried Karim. 'We're just a little short, that's all. Ten or twelve thousand at most. It would be sheer lunacy to sell the house just to pay for Khadija's wedding!'

'That's not the reason I want to sell the house.' A tear fell from his mother's cheek and soaked into her sleeve.

'By the Seven Saints, woman! Why do you want to sell it, then?'

'The medina isn't safe . . . you said so yourself . . . women are being killed . . . we may end up like that poor child . . .'

Karim realised his error. He fell to his knees and took hold of her hand. 'Mother, please forgive me! I'm tired, I misunderstood. I thought that Zak had been giving you notions about selling the riad like our neighbours. We will catch the man who killed Amina Talal, I swear to God. The medina *is* safe, safer than anywhere else in Marrakech. Don't talk about selling. This is our home, *your* home!'

Ayesha sat down, put her arm around Lalla Fatima and glared at Karim. He walked away unhappily.

In Guéliz the post-*ftour* crowd was spilling onto the streets. Girls strolled arm in arm past men flagging down taxis; families gazed into shop windows while their children played tag in the doorways. In the open-air bar of the Hotel Renaissance, cordoned off by a hibiscus hedge in a row of planters, Sébastien was drinking his second beer. When night fell during Ramadan Sébastien usually retreated to the Renaissance or to the Négociants café on the other side of the roundabout.

Sébastien didn't stay out late purely for pleasure. His tiny apartment was situated on nearby Boulevard Zerktouni, a street lined with cafés and restaurants. During Ramadan the cafés stayed open all night. If Sébastien closed his bedroom window to shut out the noise the temperature in the room rose uncomfortably. If he opened the windows the noise of car horns, conversation and laughter banished any possibility of sleep. As a consequence, for one month a year he went to bed, along with the majority of the local population, just before dawn.

Tonight, Sébastien wasn't thinking about his bedtime. He had a greater dilemma on his hands; one that threatened his very livelihood. The changes demanded by the planning inspector would delay the schedule by several weeks. If he refused to carry them out he could end up in jail. If he complied, his boss would fire him. It was lose-lose. Just like his shithole of an apartment.

'*Monsieur?*' A young West African man was standing a few feet from his table. In one hand he held sunglasses, in the other, designer watches. 'Omega, Longines . . . *tu veux?*'

Sébastien usually ignored street vendors but there was something about the man's finely chiselled features that caught his eye.

'*Viens ici,*' he beckoned.

Karim stared out of the window at the night-time cavalcade. The honey and sesame *shebbakiya* lay heavily on his stomach and the constant stopping and starting of the bus made him feel sick. Normally he would have made the trip to the Route d'Ourika on his scooter. But a week ago he had taken a corner too sharply and the bike was now at the repair shop.

He noticed families walking along the pavements with prayer mats over their shoulders. When he returned from his interview he would go to night prayers. He needed to restore his sense of well-being. Khadija had been hysterical during the meal, imagining serial killers around every corner. His mother had spent the whole time dabbing her eyes while Ayesha sat tight-lipped, hardly eating a thing. After such a stressful day, joining in communal prayers would soothe his soul.

The teenage boy with headphones sitting in the seat next to him was listening to a Shakira song. It was one of Ayesha's favourites. She would turn up the volume on the radio, her scarf around her hips, and sing along as she mopped the floor. The image made Karim smile. When they were growing up he and Ayesha were inseparable. Ayesha was the tearaway, always getting into fights with the boys from the alley or challenging them to acts of bravado while Karim watched through his fingers. When they grew bored of playing with the other children they would go up to the roof and eat pistachios, flicking the shells onto the heads of passers-by. One day, when Karim was fifteen and Ayesha twelve, he came home from school to find Ayesha wearing a *hijab* and talking quietly to Lalla Fatima in the alcove of the courtyard. From now on, his father told him, he must leave Ayesha alone. *She was no longer a child.*

The stars were bright in the heavens when Karim stepped off the bus. He turned off the highway until he spotted a dark building set back from the road. A faded sign read: *Sherezade Résidences de haut standing*. Karim walked down a track flanked by tamarisk bushes until he saw a Dacia with its side-lights on, parked by a hut. A man got out of the car. He was wearing a short-sleeved *gandora* gown over his trousers and carried a torch.

'I'm Khalifa.' The man's brusque manner suggested he had better things to do than interview people late on a Ramadan evening. He went to the hut, unlocked the door and shone the torch over a grubby mattress and a kerosene lamp.

Karim heard a crunch of tyres and turned around to see a *petit taxi* come down the track. There was a man in the passenger seat. At first Karim feared it might be another applicant for the job.

'*Shouf*, look,' snapped Khalifa. He shone his torch at the apartment building. It was surrounded by dense undergrowth like a fairy-tale castle in one of Khadija's old story books. The building was four storeys high, the ground floor hidden from view, with window voids on the upper levels and a chain dangling from the roof – a pulley most likely.

'Check the site at midnight and at three in the morning. Keep an eye out for anyone stealing scaffolding, sleeping on the site or fucking.'

Karim thought he had misheard. 'Excuse me?'

'The nightclub Pacha is half a mile away. Young people come here sometimes.' Khalifa lowered the beam of the torch onto a black rectangular area in the undergrowth. 'Be careful where you put your feet. That's a swimming pool.'

'Why did work stop on the building?'

Khalifa brushed the question aside. He handed Karim the key. 'There's a tap behind the hut. Be here at ten.'

'Have I got the job?'

'From ten at night,' the other man repeated, 'until six in the morning. And bring a torch.' Without another word he got into the Dacia and drove off.

At the same moment the door of the taxi opened and the passenger got out. He was of medium height and build but it was too dark to distinguish his features clearly. He gave Karim a cursory nod and walked up to the hut. Karim wanted to ask him questions, but the taxi was already reversing. He ran up to the driver's window.

'Can you take me back to town?'

'*Tla*, get in.' Karim caught a whiff of tobacco and cologne. 'Are you the new night watchman?' The driver was wearing a denim shirt and his oiled hair still bore the marks of a comb. Bollywood music played softly on the car stereo.

Karim nodded. '*Inshallah*.' He pointed towards the hut. 'Who's he?'

'Fouad? He's the security guard – I mean, the *other* security guard. He usually works here during the day.' The driver held out his hand. 'My name's Rachid. Honoured to meet you.'

'Karim. The honour is mine.'

'Do you smoke?' Rachid held out a crumpled packet of Marquise. 'Where do you live, Mister Karim?'

Karim slid a cigarette from the packet. 'Bab Taghzout, in my mother's riad.'

'You're lucky. I live in Targa. My wife and I rent two tiny

rooms for which we pay the outrageous sum of thirteen hundred a month.'

'At least you have a car.'

'This?' Rachid tapped the steering wheel. 'It belongs to my brother-in-law.'

'Why did work stop on the apartment building, the — what's it called — Sherezade?'

Rachid shrugged. 'It's been like that for as long as I can remember, three years at least. Apart from Fouad no one wants to work out here — it's too far from town, I suppose. Now you're around Fouad will probably be back on the day shift. Do you have a day job, Mister Karim?'

'Yes.' Karim hesitated. 'I work in an office.'

'How did you get here? On the Number 25 bus? I could bring you, if you like. I could drop you when I start my shift then come back in the morning and pick you up again. What do you say? It would be better than stewing on a hot bus, that's for sure!'

'How much?'

'Pay what you like!' Rachid gave a dismissive wave of his hand. '*Keema bgheetee!*'

Karim wanted to ask Rachid more questions but he felt queasy. The cigarette had been a bad idea. He threw it out and leaned on the window to get some air.

They drove past the billboard for the new property development, lit with spotlights. '*L'appartement de vos rêves à partir de 100,000 Dhs!*' Rachid peered at the woman in the low-cut dress smiling down at them.

'She's a *gazelle*, eh? What a beauty! Those breasts are practically popping out, ha, ha!' He turned to Karim. 'Are you feeling all right, Mister Karim? You look pale! Push the seat back

– I'll have you home in no time. Just sit back and listen to the music. Do you like Bollywood? It's the best music in the world!'

Karim closed his eyes. His head was swimming, he needed the toilet, and the driver and his music were driving him crazy. *He wasn't going to take this taxi again, not in a thousand years.*

By the time they arrived at Sidi bel Abbès Karim was on the verge of throwing up. He pushed open the passenger door, propped his feet on the kerb and leaned down with his head between his knees.

Rachid put a hand on his shoulder. 'It's hard, Ramadan.'

Karim gripped the seat and made a supreme effort to suppress the roiling in his gut. Sweat poured from his brow. After what seemed like hours he sat up, reached for a tissue and wiped his face. He took a few deep breaths and managed a painful smile.

'Thank you.' He took out his wallet.

Rachid pushed the wallet back at him. 'There's no charge. It's Ramadan: we must look out for each other.' He handed Karim a business card with his phone number. '*Seer fid Allah*, go in God's care.' With a wave of his hand he was gone.

Karim stared at the card. Under a drawing of the Koutoubia were the words *Taxi 1547 Toutes destinations – Randonnées – Aéroport.* Smiling, Karim put the card in his wallet.

He gave a coin to a beggar outside the mosque, slipped off his shoes and entered. He looked for the handcart that he'd left by the door but every inch of space was taken up with worshippers; so many, in fact, that several had spilled into the courtyard. He decided to join them in the open air. There was a break in the prayers and men were talking in low voices or kneeling in silent devotion. A row of men in white robes moved aside to let Karim pass. As he waited for the prayers to resume he stood, his eyes closed, feeling the soft breeze on his cheeks. The murmuring was soporific. His attack of nausea, added to the upheavals of the day, had left him spent. He would have liked nothing better than to curl up and go to sleep, right there on the floor.

Suddenly he pricked up his ears. The two men in front of him were discussing Amina Talal.

'It's a warning to our sisters . . . she deserved her punishment . . . she has brought shame . . .'

Karim couldn't believe what he was hearing. A girl of good family had been murdered and these men had the gall to defile her memory!

'. . . she was a fornicator, a common prostitute . . .'

How could they utter such vulgarities – in a mosque of all places!

'. . . her sex was still hot from the penises of a thousand lovers . . .'

The despair of the last twenty-four hours exploded in Karim's chest. He gave the man in front a violent shove. The man was heavy and he toppled over the kneeling figure in the row in front of him. A space widened as worshippers scrambled to their feet or backed away. There was an ominous silence and all eyes turned towards Karim. He pushed his way through the crowd and stumbled out of the mosque.

Chapter 3

My Medina

We have a new addition to the team. He's very friendly although he has an annoying habit of going into the bedrooms and stealing the pom-poms from the blankets. In case you hadn't guessed, 'he' is a monkey – a Barbary macaque, to be precise. Suggestions for names welcome! The little guy is house-trained and seems mainly to eat dried fruit and nuts although this morning a carpenter told me on good authority that monkeys also eat chocolate bars. The carpenter is here along with an army of stagehands and electricians to get Dar Zuleika ready for a party. It promises to be quite an event: 150 guests, a troupe of entertainers and three tables of Moroccan, Italian and Japanese dishes. Unfortunately, a projection light just fell off the roof because someone forgot to fix a clamp. It came crashing down through the orange trees, making the monkey practically jump out of his skin. C'est le Ramadan!

Special Autumn Offer: Autumn, when the shadows lengthen and snow appears on the Atlas, is the best time of year to visit Marrakech. Our weekend package includes evening meals and

*airport transfer. Book before 30 August and we'll throw in a
free cookery class!*

Karim was so exhausted after returning from night prayers
that he went straight to bed and slept until eight. He emerged
from his bedroom thirsty and ravenous, annoyed that his
mother hadn't woken him for something to drink and eat. He
looked up at the rectangle of blue above his head. It was going
to be another hot day. He banged the tap, shaved in a trickle
of water and went downstairs, tucking his shirt into his
trousers.

The sweat was already running down his back when he
reached the square at Bab Taghzout. From there he headed to
Shrob ou Shouf, catching a whiff of ammonia from the tanner-
ies a mile away. At Mouassine he lingered over the sheaves of
herbs on the pavement, exchanging pleasantries with the seller
just so he could enjoy the aroma of fresh mint. Emerging into
the blinding light of the Jemaa he clung to the strip of shade on
the east side of the square, then headed past the rubber goods
sellers of Zitoun el Kedim. As he approached the commissariat
he saw Bouchaïb, the parking attendant, looking in his direction. Bouchaïb was a dark-skinned southerner from the Souss
who had lost his leg in a tractor accident. He was leaning on his
crutch, wearing a shabby high-visibility vest over his shirt.

'*Sbah al-khir*, good morning Mr Karim!' he said cheerfully.
'They say it's going to reach forty-five today!'

'God help us.'

'Your lips are blistered. You need to drink more.'

Karim nodded. He could taste blood in his mouth.

'Still no *moto*?'

Karim shook his head.

'Perhaps it will be ready tomorrow,' grinned Bouchaïb. 'God willing!'

At the foot of the steps to his office Karim paused to fasten his shirt buttons. He spotted Aziz in his office and called from the doorway.

'Any news about Amina Talal?'

Aziz looked up. A smile spread across his face. 'She turned out to be quite a party girl.'

'What do you mean?'

'She went to Guéliz.'

'Yes – to revise for an English test.'

'An English test? Is that what you heard?' Aziz glanced at the pockmarked officer, who sniggered. 'Let's just say she preferred swinging her hips to moving her lips.' Pockmark Features gave a coarse laugh.

Karim marched up to Aziz's desk. 'Stop talking in riddles! What did you find out?'

Aziz stood up. 'This is my case, not yours, Belkacem. *Seer fehalek!* Clear off!'

Karim climbed the steps. Now he had a pounding headache as well as a raging thirst. Noureddine was standing in front of the filing cabinet.

'Did you get the job?'

Karim fell into his chair. 'I start tonight.'

'You don't seem very happy about it.'

Karim said nothing. He watched a fly examine a grease mark on the windowpane and brooded. Badnaoui gave Aziz the Talal case because he was a fellow Arab. He – Karim – was fobbed off with menial jobs because he was Chleuh, a Berber from the mountains. Berbers always got the jobs nobody wanted. The only other pure-blood Chleuh at the commissariat was the janitor. You could have the best diploma in the world and it counted for nothing if your father had been born a shepherd in Midelt or the Rif. Aziz wouldn't treat him with such disrespect if he was a fellow Arab! He would tell Karim what he'd discovered, perhaps ask his opinion as the first officer on the scene. Karim blurted out: 'Details of an investigation should be shared among fellow officers.'

Noureddine looked up from the filing drawer. 'Eh?'

Karim focused his attention. 'I need to know what happened to Amina Talal.'

'What are you talking about?'

'Aziz won't tell me but I have a right to know. I don't want to interfere in the investigation, I'm not trying to wrest back control, you understand, I'm quite happy for Aziz to be in charge – like you said, he's a good officer – it's just that – Amina Talal – she was a friend of mine.'

Noureddine's face darkened. 'Karim—'

'She was more than a friend,' Karim swallowed. The effort nearly made him choke.

'Karim—'

'I – I was betrothed to her.'

A silence hung in the air. Noureddine shut the drawer of the cabinet and walked out.

Karim pushed his chair back from the desk and closed his eyes, aghast at his own stupidity. What he had done was wrong, unprofessional. He had asked a senior colleague to intervene on his behalf. Not only that, he had divulged personal information about himself – information that would find its way to Aziz and, in turn, Pockmark Features and the other officers. Would they now make jokes behind his back? Snigger about his betrothal to a prostitute?

When Noureddine failed to return another fear took hold of Karim. He had made his betrothal to Amina sound more important than it was. By exaggerating his relationship with the victim he had justified Badnaoui's decision to remove him from the case. He put his head in his hands. *In the name of Allah, Most Gracious, Most Merciful. Thee alone we worship and Thee alone we ask for help. Show us the straight path. The path of those whom thou hast favoured, not the path of those who earn thine anger nor of those who go astray.*

After five minutes Noureddine came back and sat at his desk.

'Aziz questioned Amina's friend.'

'Leila Hasnaoui.'

'Yes. She said that she and Amina didn't study at the apartment that night. They went to a nightclub.'

'A *nightclub*?'

'Yes. They secretly left Leila's parents' apartment at eleven o'clock. They stayed at the club for two hours, dancing. Amina left the club on her own at around quarter to one. Leila came home soon afterwards. She never saw Amina again.'

'Which club did they go to?'

Noureddine folded his arms. 'That's all Aziz told me.'

Karim was scandalised. Amina went to nightclubs! She had flaunted her body. She had lied to her brother and parents. The men in the mosque were right: she deserved her punishment. *Stay quietly in your houses and make not a dazzling display* – wasn't that what the Holy Quran said?

'I didn't mention your betrothal to Amina Talal,' said Noureddine. 'If you take my advice you won't mention it, either.'

Karim jumped up and headed for the door.

'Where are you going?'

Karim walked out without replying.

The email's subject line read 'Cancellation'. The guests didn't give a reason. There was no way of knowing if it was related to what had happened at the mosque. But it added to Kay's fear that the girl's death was a disaster for business.

Kay had arrived in Marrakech with warnings ringing in her ears. *Morocco is fine for a holiday but it's no place to start a business; there are hundreds of riads in Marrakech – why should anyone choose yours?* This last from her ex-husband Jack, who mocked her decision to open a boutique hotel in a crummy neighbourhood where few Westerners ventured.

She proved them all wrong. Dar Zuleika's shabby-chic location and its exquisitely themed bedrooms made it the darling of travel writers. Guests loved the soaring palm, the exotic furnishings, the combination of Moorish tradition and modern luxury. Sidi bel Abbès, with its ancient mausoleum and cemetery, provided a dramatic backdrop. Kay hired a chef and bookings rocketed. Fashion shoots followed. For two years the riad was full every night. Then, almost imperceptibly, demand tailed off. Newer, hipper riads came on the scene, with better locations and a more contemporary look. Orientalism was out, minimalism was in. There were still enough guests to keep the place going and it was still listed in some of the guidebooks, but Dar Zuleika had lost its pre-eminent status. Contemplating the empty spaces in her reservations diary, Kay thought that her clientele was like a herd of skittish gazelles that had vanished over the horizon in search of shinier watering holes.

Her business had suffered another blow in April, when the bomb exploded in the Argana café. Every hotel and travel company in Marrakech had felt the effects of the blast. And now this: a murder on her doorstep – a murder of a prostitute, no less. The death of Amina Talal threatened more than Kay's livelihood. Her entire *raison d'être* was in jeopardy. She had worked hard to cultivate the image of a successful woman leading a glamorous existence in Marrakech. As long as she wafted around the courtyards, arranging ornaments, giving orders to the staff, flirting with her French boyfriend, she could believe in the dream as well. But in the face of death the dream turned sour. When her friends in London heard the news they would look upon Kay with pity, even schadenfreude. There was always the nuclear option: to sell up. She could return to London with a million pounds in her pocket. But what would she do in London? Start a business? As what – a designer? With no experience and no contacts? No, there was nothing for her in London. Her future lay in Marrakech. This was her home now.

She sat in the office, cradling a cup of verveine tea, and let her gaze wander. The narrow room was functional and office-like, a late addition squeezed between the kitchen and the laundry, but she had decorated it with as much care as the grandest of the riad's bedrooms. Above the desk was a row of neatly arranged box files, each carrying the logo she had designed: a 'Z' hennaed on the palm of a hand. On the floor was a deep-pile Beni Ourain carpet, leading to a bougainvillea-framed window that overlooked the courtyard. She had a good eye, everyone told her so. This summer she would find a proper showcase for her talents. The boutique was a start. Lucinda's commission would help.

And on Friday there was the party.

From the dome of the Serafina Sébastien had a panoramic view. To the south lay the Atlas Mountains. Hundreds of years ago water was brought along aquifers from the mountains to the city of Marrakech, a feat of engineering that Sébastien had long admired. He was fascinated by water, by its technical challenges, its possibilities for landscaping. Below he could see the outline of the basin that surrounded the hotel on three sides. In a month's time this would be a lagoon with an archipelago of villas and palm trees. Leading away from the building was a five-hundred-foot long, ten-foot wide channel that Sébastien had created down the middle of the driveway. Called the Line of Water, it ran on a north–south axis and reflected the domed palace in one direction and the Atlas Mountains in the other.

Since taking over from the original architects Sébastien had greatly improved the design. The Serafina was now an ambitious undertaking, a landmark project that employed hundreds of local workmen, that would provide permanent jobs to staff and bring in millions in revenue. Yet all the bureaucrats could see were petty infringements of building regulations!

'*Excusez-moi, mssyoo!*'

A young man with a shirt wrapped around his head was pushing a wheelbarrow towards him, his sandals flapping on the wooden walkway. Since the plank was only forty centimetres wide Sébastien had to lean back to let the youth pass. Sébastien watched him tip out a load of sand. He added cement powder, creating a little well in the centre, whereupon a second man carefully hosed it with water. Sébastien had a raging thirst. In his bag, slung over his shoulder, was a litre bottle of water. But he refused to drink in front of his men, not during Ramadan. Most Europeans wouldn't bother with such niceties but Sébastien knew how the men must be suffering. He liked Moroccan construction workers. He admired their can-do attitude, the way they shunned protective clothing, the way they worked twelve-hour days for modest reward. *Compare that to the overpaid prima donnas on French building sites!*

Hassan, the site foreman, came along the walkway, his face wet with perspiration. '*Nous faire les dalles?*' he said in his broken French. 'Shall we make the slabs?'

Sébastien considered. If they did things the proper way, the way that Hicham Cherkaoui demanded, using concrete separators and a regulation mesh size, they wouldn't be able to start pouring the concrete until tomorrow. If they used Sébastien's methods they would be finished by sundown.

'*Vas-y!* Do it!'

Karim thought about catching the bus. Then he searched for a taxi. Finally, he decided to walk. He had passed the Koutoubia when he suddenly remembered that he didn't have Leila Hasnaoui's address. He retreated into the doorway of a plumbing supplies shop, took out his mobile and scrolled to the number that Abderrahim had given him. A female voice answered.

'*Alloo?*'

'Leila Hasnaoui?'

'Who wants her?'

'I'm a police officer, Karim Belkacem, from the *quatrième arrondissement*—'

'My daughter has already spoken to the police.'

'I – I wanted to ask a few more questions.'

'She's at college.'

'Which college does she go to? When will she be back?'

There was no reply.

'I'm a friend of Amina Talal.'

'I thought you said you were a police officer.'

'I am a police officer *and* a friend.'

There were a few seconds of silence then the phone went dead. Karim pressed redial. The phone rang for half a minute before the woman answered.

'Don't put the phone down, *a lalla*, please,' Karim begged. '*Allah ikhalleek*, may God spare you! I have just one question: Leila and Amina went to a nightclub on Sunday night. Which nightclub was it?'

'My daughter will not be going to any more nightclubs. She disgraced us. *Khellee-na*, leave us alone.' The woman hung up.

Karim sat down in a heap. His tongue was horribly swollen and he felt faint with hunger. The road was still, silent, shimmering, as if the sun had annihilated all sound and movement. On the other side of the road, casting the smallest of shadows, stood a handcart. There were ten thousand handcarts in the city; red, brown, green, rectangular, square, metal-sided, wooden-sided, carts with large wheels, carts with small wheels, carts with handles made from scaffolding tubes, carts with writing on the side, carts with missing panels. All they had in common was the size: the perfect size for a medium-height human body when curled up asleep – or dead. There was a faint murmur of men's voices from behind him, from deep inside the plumbing store. Karim rested his head on his knees and closed his eyes . . . it was peaceful . . . he was drifting . . . he was lying on the baking deck of a boat in the middle of the sea . . . he could taste the dried saltwater on his lips . . . there was nothing but the sun and the sea . . . he imagined rolling off the deck . . . sinking into the calm waters . . . drifting down . . . the keel of the boat far above his head . . . he was on the seabed, being wafted back and forth . . . it was blissfully cool down here in the sunlit shallows, strands of seaweed like shiny tresses, moving back and forth, back and forth . . .

Rum-rummmm. A motorbike went past. Karim opened his eyes with a start. He decided to go to Dar el Bacha to see if his bike was ready. He stood up and brushed the dust and dirt from his trousers. He could imagine Noureddine upbraiding him for being so slovenly: *This is not how an officer of the Sûreté behaves.* Both sides of the street were in full sun and by the time he reached the repair workshop the sweat had formed little rivers down his back and chest. To his dismay the scooter was exactly where he had left it, the fork still buckled and bent out of shape. The mechanic emerged from the interior of the workshop, his face and forearms black with oil. '*Salaam*,' he grinned.

'You haven't fixed my *moto*.'

'Next week, *inshallah*.'

Karim's heart sank. He couldn't bear the thought of trudging around the city for another week. 'Can't you fix it today?'

'*Mashee momken.* Not possible.'

'Why isn't it possible?'

'Ramadan.'

'What's Ramadan got to do with it?'

'We close at two.'

'Tomorrow then.'

'*Mashee momken.*'

'Why not?'

'Ramadan.'

'What's Ramadan got to do with it?'

'No spare parts.'

'Why are there no spare parts?'

'Ramadan.'

Disheartened, Karim retraced his steps to the commissariat. He wondered what excuse he could give Noureddine for his absence. At the filling station just beyond the Koutoubia he had a flash of inspiration. He would go to the shop of his friend Youssef and ask him questions about counterfeits. He could tell Nour that he had gone to do research. Cheered, he turned left down Moulay Rachid, right at the Two Brothers Restaurant, and stopped outside a shop window displaying new and second-hand electronic goods.

It took his eyes a few moments to adjust to the darkness of the interior. The floor and shelves were filled with appliances of every kind: air-conditioning units, routers, satellite receivers, mobile phones, DVD players, laptops, joysticks, surge protectors, headphones, loudspeakers, kitchen blenders. Youssef was standing behind a glass counter, headphones in his ears, dismantling a mobile phone with a miniature screwdriver.

'*Salaam ou alikum!*'

Youssef stepped from behind the counter with a smile, removed the earpieces and embraced Karim. He was six feet tall with heavy subcutaneous stubble.

'*Ou alikum salaam!* How are you, my friend?'

'Good. And you?'

'*Bekhir al-hamdullilah!* I bet it's as hot as the fires of hell outside. Would you like a pair of sunglasses? Here, take them. A present.'

Karim laughed. 'No thanks.'

'How about an air-conditioning unit for Lalla Fatima? The poor lady must be suffering!'

'Lalla Fatima is fine, thanks to God.' Karim looked around. 'I remember when your father ran this place. Everyone wanted a ghetto blaster in those days.'

'I remember. They had slide controls and those funny graphic equalisers!' Youssef smiled. 'What brings you here?'

'I'm doing an investigation into counterfeit goods.'

Youssef narrowed his eyes suspiciously.

'*Thenna!* Relax! If I went after everyone who sold fake goods I'd have to arrest half of Marrakech.' Karim looked around. 'Where does all this merchandise come from?'

'The electronic items come from China. Clothes and bags are made here in the Maghreb. We Moroccans are good at copying – look at all the fake fossils we make for tourists!'

Karim showed off his 'Breitling'. 'What about this?'

Youssef took Karim's wrist. 'That's what I call a *fake* fake. See how the second-hand clicks? Quartz movement. Very cheap to manufacture. Has a tendency to stop suddenly.' He reached under the counter and took out another watch. 'This has a self-winding mechanism, like a real Rolex, so it's what I call a *genuine* fake. They last for years. I sell them for a hundred and fifty dirhams. What did you pay for that thing – fifty, sixty?'

'Wait a minute – you're saying there are two types of fake? Fake fakes – poor-quality fakes – and good-quality fakes, or real fakes?'

Youssef laughed. 'There are dozens of types of fake. It would take an eternity to list them all.'

'I'm in no hurry,' said Karim pulling up a stool. He no longer felt tired and his thirst had gone. He listened with interest as Youssef gave a detailed explanation of the fake designer goods market, listing the subtle decreases in price and quality from *as good as the genuine article* to *falls apart after a week*.

Eventually Karim gave a stretch and yawned. 'According to my fake fake timepiece, it's time for me to go.'

'Stay a while longer! How's the family?'

'Everyone's fine, praise God. Khadija is getting married. She wants four *takshitas* and a Turkish singer. I've had to take a night job to pay the costs.'

'*Llah ikimmel bekhir*, may God end it well. If you need a wedding present –' Youssef pointed at a flat-screen television '– made in Guangdong . . . genuine fake . . .'

Karim laughed. 'I'll let you know.'

Kay stabbed a scallop. 'What do you think?'

It had been Sébastien's idea to meet at Goya. As a rule, Kay disliked visiting Marrakech's latest in-places. *I didn't come to this city*, she blogged, *to eat sushi in a fondouk run by an ex-record producer from Paris*. In reality, she was jealous. Goya and other venues were a reminder of her former fame, those heady days when Dar Zuleika was the name on everyone's lips. The boutique, the antiques, interior design, event planning – they were all attempts to recapture the high. Earlier that morning, as she was sitting in the office, another idea popped into her head: a riad renovation company. Its market: wealthy Europeans seeking a place in the sun. She could run the venture with Sébastien, using their complementary talents. As well as raising her profile, it would be fun, the two of them working together as they had when they restored Dar Zuleika, bouncing ideas off each other, flirting, joking until they were helpless with laughter. It would reignite Sébastien's interest in her more effectively than all the love potions from all the apothecaries in the Jemaa el Fna. She had even thought of a name for the company: The Riad Thing.

'Not bad,' said Sébastien.

'What?'

'The restaurant. *Pas mal.*' He pointed his fork at an open-sided wicker cage hanging from the ceiling. '*Qu'est-ce que c'est?*'

'I believe it's used for *burlesque*,' Kay replied tartly. It was the sort of decadent touch that would appeal to Sébastien. She gave him an appraising look. He was still striking for a man of fifty, with his piercing blue eyes, aquiline nose and *beau-laid* face. He didn't deserve to be that attractive, not considering the hours he worked and the alcohol and God-knew-what-else he put inside himself.

'We should invite Mohammed to the party,' Sébastien said. 'He'll be back in Marrakech on Friday.'

'OK. What time does his flight get in?'

Sébastien took out a battered leather organiser stuffed with receipts. The page for Friday was blank, lacking even an entry for his own birthday party. Sébastien was hopeless with organisation, mused Kay. He forgot appointments, lost documents and regarded tax returns as a personal affront. If they went into business together, she decided, she would handle the paperwork.

'*Aucune idée.*'

'Tell him he needs to be punctual if he's coming to the riad. The programme starts at eight.'

'Programme?'

'I've planned a programme.'

Sébastien scoffed. 'You make it sound like your party.'

'I want it to be a success. Don't you?'

'I told you before – *je m'en fous*. A planning officer is breaking my head, Mohammed is breaking my head – that's all I care about!'

They sat for a time. Kay looked around at the other diners. There were two men with flowing hair. Italian, judging by their voices. Further along, a fashionably dressed woman was sitting on her own cooing at an infant in a buggy and, at a far table, a doting couple. The man was running his fingers across the woman's cheek. When was the last time Sébastien had caressed her? When was the last time he had complimented her? When was the last time he had *fucked* her?

'Have you thought of a name for the monkey?' Sébastien asked.

'Driss has christened him Momo.'

'You can't use the word *christen*. He's a Muslim monkey.' They both laughed.

'Well *Momo* it is. Driss bought some nuts and grains from the *hanoot* . . . Oh God! I forgot to tell you!' Kay grabbed Sébastien's hand. 'A girl was murdered in the medina on Monday night!'

'A girl – murdered?' Sébastien sat up in alarm. 'Where?'

'Her body was found outside Sidi bel Abbès.'

'Who was she?'

'A local girl.'

'Was she strangled?'

'I don't know. Her body was left in a handcart.'

'It could have been *les barbus*,' Sébastien said grimly. 'The bearded ones.'

'Islamists? You think so?'

'You only have to look at the mosques during Friday prayers. They're overflowing. The preachers are fanatics.'

'Should I warn the English girl? She might tell her friends. You know how these things spread! I already had a cancellation.' Kay put her hand over her mouth. 'Oh my God, I've just thought – people might be afraid to come on Friday – to the party!'

Sébastien took her arm. 'Calm down, Kay. You're getting paranoid. The death was probably a domestic matter, a jealous husband—'

'You said Islamists were behind it!'

'I don't know who's behind it. But it's a local matter, for the local community. It won't affect visitors.'

'A murder is a murder!'

'We don't know if it was a murder. Let's see what the police say.'

'The area is tainted, don't you see?'

'Kay, *arrête*! One murder is not going to put off tourists. Think of 9/11. That hasn't stopped tourists visiting New York.'

'New York is a big city!'

'So is Marrakech. There are murders and rapes all the time in places like Paris, Rome, London . . . Tourists still visit those cities. At least the attack took place in August when there are no tourists around.'

'You don't think it will stop foreigners visiting Marrakech – buying second homes here?'

'No.'

'Are you sure?'

'*Sûr et certain.*'

Kay summoned the waiter for the bill. 'Sébastien . . . I've had an idea for a business.'

'What sort of business?'

'It could make a lot of money.'

'What sort of business?' Sébastien repeated.

'A riad restoration company. There are companies offering parts of the service but you and I could do the whole lot from start to finish: finding a property, renovation, paperwork, everything. In French *and* English! I could get the ball rolling and you could come on board when the Serafina opens. It would be perfect!'

A cloud fell across Sébastien's face. 'No one's going to buy a riad when people are getting killed on the doorstep.'

'But you just said—'

'I was talking about tourism. Property is different. *Ça ne va pas marcher.*'

'There are always foreigners looking for riads!'

'Do it on your own, then. I'm too busy.'

'You wouldn't have to do a thing until November.'

'November? I can't think that far ahead!'

'What are you going to do in November?' Kay said in despair. 'Go back to your apartment and wait for the phone to ring?'

Sébastien put his organiser back in his bag. 'I have to get back. We're pouring concrete.'

'Sébastien – after the party – let's go away, just for a night or two. We could go to Essaouira, get a room on the beach—'

'*T'as pas compris?* I'm busy!'

'At the end of the month then.'

'Laurent is coming, have you forgotten?'

'Well, at least let's go out for a picnic in the *quatrelle*. We could talk—'

'Talk?' replied Sébastien, getting to his feet. 'What about?'

'Oh, I am not Arab. I am Berber!'

Karim smiled. He was back at his desk chatting to Melanie. She was waiting in the office when he returned from Youssef's. To his relief, there was also a note from Noureddine saying he'd been called away to headquarters.

'We call ourselves Amazigh or Chleuh, which means Berber. We have different language, different culture to Arab people.'

'Does that mean you're not a Muslim?' Melanie gave a nervous laugh. 'Sorry – I didn't mean to be rude.'

'I go the mosque, I am a Muslim. Chleuh people do the fast like everyone else.'

'It must be hard fasting in this heat,' said Melanie.

'We are used to it.'

Melanie gestured at her water bottle. 'Do you mind?'

'Please.'

Melanie took a long drink. 'I usually cool off by the swimming pool in the afternoon.'

'Your riad has swimming pool? You are lucky.'

'Unfortunately they chucked me out.'

'Your riad made you leave?'

'Just for a few hours, while they get the place ready. They're preparing for a party on Friday. I don't suppose there's any sign of my handbag?'

'No.' Karim realised that he hadn't notified the sergeant in charge of lost and stolen property. 'It's Ramadan . . . things take longer.'

'I like being in Marrakech during Ramadan. I heard the most amazing prayers from the mosque last night.'

'Which mosque? Mouassine?'

'No. I think it's called Sidi bel Abbès.'

'Aha, we are neighbours. I was at Sidi bel Abbès last night. They're called *tarawieh* prayers, the ones you listened to.'

'They were beautiful. I stood outside for an hour. It was like I was in a trance.'

'Wait – you say your riad is near the mosque?'

'Yes. It's just around the corner.'

'You should not go out, not on your own – not after sunset. A girl was found dead outside Sidi bel Abbès on Monday night.'

Melanie reacted with horror. 'Oh my God!'

'Until we know the reason, Sidi bel Abbès is not good area for women. When will you return to the riad?'

'I don't know, I hadn't really thought about it.' Melanie gulped. First she'd been mugged, now there'd been a murder. Marrakech was a scary place!

Karim pressed her. 'When will you go back to your riad?'

'I was going to eat in the square tonight, so probably around eight o'clock.'

'You must go back now!' Karim jumped to his feet. 'Come please! I find taxi!'

Outside, the road was busy with traffic. Karim looked in both directions. It was later than he had realised. 'Bad time!' he shouted. 'Taxis full.'

'I'm fine to walk – honestly,' said Melanie.

A taxi pulled up. 'Sidi bel Abbès,' said Karim, reaching for the door.

'I'm going to Agdal. *Bslemma*, goodbye!' The driver sped off.

Karim turned to Melanie. 'We walk!'

Together they waded into the slow-moving traffic. By the time they reached Jemaa el Fna Karim was starting to feel uncomfortable. Was it his imagination, or were his fellow citizens staring at him? Were they judging him for parading around with an English girl?

Melanie stopped to gaze around. The fruit juice barrows were flooded with colour in the evening sunlight. 'It's so beautiful! I can't believe that anything bad can happen here.'

Karim thought wryly of the bomb attack a few months earlier at the Café Argana. They'd heard the blast in the commissariat and rushed out to scenes of carnage. The building was still draped in plastic sheeting.

'Has it changed a lot – the Jemaa el Fna?'

Karim pointed. 'In that corner used to be – how do you say – a bus station. A bus came every morning with farmers. On the roof they put chickens, vegetables and *bouya – le caméléon.*'

'Chameleons? What for?'

'Magic. The magic men throw them in the fire and *caméléon* explode, pouf! Now they sell the *caméléon* to tourists.' Karim turned to face the other direction. 'I remember, over there, men who walk across broken glass.'

'What happened to them?'

'Gone. Bad for tourism. The fortune-tellers . . . the beggars . . . the men who pull out teeth . . . all gone.'

'I'm leaving on Saturday,' said Melanie, after a pause. 'That's what I came to tell you. I'm getting my documents from the consulate tomorrow.'

'I understand. Please come, it is getting late.'

They reached Dar Zuleika as the sun was sinking behind the roofs. Kay opened the door.

'This is Lieutenant Belkacem,' Melanie said tersely. 'He says there was a murder near here on Monday night. Did you know about it?'

Kay was evasive. 'Driss did mention something . . .'

Melanie turned to Karim. 'Goodbye, lieutenant.'

'*Au revoir*, Mademoiselle Murray. Take care during your last two days in Marrakech.'

When Karim returned to Derb Bourahmoune Lkbir he found Abderrezak sitting in the *salon* with one sleeve rolled up, examining a nicotine patch. Karim was puzzled.

'Are you allowed to use a nicotine patch during Ramadan?'

'The Quran only forbids substances that pass the mouth or pierce the skin.'

'Surely it forbids any substance that passes *through* the skin.'

Zak rolled down his sleeve. 'A nicotine patch is no different to moisturising cream. You wouldn't object to your mother using moisturiser, would you?'

'You can't compare a nicotine patch to moisturiser! If you use a nicotine patch you're putting nicotine into your bloodstream.'

'What is this?' Zak chuckled. 'An interrogation?'

'The point of fasting is to go without,' said Karim, growing heated. 'You might as well as smoke cigarettes all day!'

'So all of a sudden you're an expert on the Quran?'

'*A draree!*' Lalla Fatima came in with a pot of coffee. 'Boys, please, no arguing. Sundown is nearly upon us.'

Ayesha placed a large bowl of vermicelli with chicken and

cinnamon on the table and Khadija followed with plates. Karim made an effort to collect his thoughts. *O Allah, for Thee I fast and with the food Thou givest me I break the fast, and I rely on Thee.*

The call to prayer rang out. *Allahu Akbar!* Karim had looked forward to this moment all day but now that it had arrived he had little appetite. He forced himself to eat some chicken vermicelli and settled back to watch the Wednesday night soap opera with the others. Nothing was said about the matter uppermost in everyone's mind but as soon as the show was over Zak spoke.

'Khadija tells me that it was you who found the dead girl at the mosque, Karim. Left in a handcart like a sack of flour. Is it true that she was a prostitute?'

'There's no truth in those rumours,' said Lalla Fatima. 'Amina Talal was a good girl.'

'Forgive me, *a lalla*, I meant no harm. I'm just repeating what I've heard.'

'Do you think it was a crime of passion?' asked Khadija.

'More likely to be a religious fanatic. Why else would he leave the girl's body outside a mosque? Come now, Karim, what have you discovered? Or is it *hush-hush*, as they say?'

'A colleague is handling the investigation.'

Zak was amazed. '*Bletee*, wait a minute – you're not on the case? But you were the first on the scene! I was here when the boy came to take you! Why aren't you leading the investigation?'

Karim made no reply. Zak stared at him for a few seconds then clicked his tongue. 'Well, all I can say is: the Sûreté works in mysterious ways.'

Khadija asked Karim if they could visit the seamstress.

'I've already told you. You're not to go out unless you're chaperoned.'

'Will you chaperone us?'

'I can't. I have to work.'

'I'll come,' Zak said brightly. 'I have no plans for this evening.'

Karim scowled. 'It's bad luck for the groom to see the wedding dress before the wedding.'

'I won't look – I promise!' laughed Zak. 'You ladies can go inside and talk to the seamstress. I'll stand outside and have a cigarette. You'll come too, won't you, Ayesha?'

'I've got things to do.'

'Do come, Ayesha!' Khadija pleaded. 'I'll help you do the dishes!'

'You can choose that gold braid you wanted,' said Zak.

Ayesha shook her head. 'I have to go to the *hanoot*.'

'We can pick up groceries at a *hanoot* on the way.'

'I want to go to the *hanoot* in Kbour Chou.'

Khadija's face broke into a grin. 'Aha! That's where the cute boy works – the one with the dreadlocks.'

'Is he your sweetheart?' Zak taunted. 'What's his name? Come on, tell us, Ayesha – is he the one you want to marry?'

Karim, who had been growing steadily angrier, erupted. 'You teased her about boyfriends on Monday night. Now you want to marry her off to a grocer! What business is it of yours?'

Ayesha spoke. 'No.'

Everyone was taken by surprise. 'No, what?' asked Khadija.

'Zak asked if I was going to marry the boy in the *hanoot*. The answer is no.'

'How do you know?' needled Zak.

'I have my heart set on someone else.' Ayesha gave a long stare at Karim. Then she turned on her heel and walked out.

Khadija started gathering the plates. Karim, scarlet-faced, went up to his room to pack his bag. What was Ayesha thinking? She had announced to the world that she was going to marry him. It wouldn't happen, *it couldn't happen* – not in a thousand years! He waited until Ayesha was alone then marched into the kitchen and seized her by the elbow.

'What are you playing at?'

'I'm not playing at anything,' Ayesha replied.

'You know I can't marry you. Why go around making insinuations? You might as well tell everyone our secret!'

Karim's mother appeared in the doorway with a pile of dirty plates. 'Why are you scolding Ayesha?'

Karim let go of Ayesha's elbow. 'I'm not scolding her. I don't think she should discuss her love life with a man who isn't part of this family, that's all.'

'Abderrezak is hardly a stranger. And Ayesha was not discussing her love life. She didn't mean anything by it, did you, Ayesha?' Lalla Fatima put the plates in the sink. 'We've had an awful shock in the last two days. Let us be kind to one another. Come, give her a hug.'

On his way back from lunch Sébastien came up with a plan to thwart the planning inspector. Rather than halt the building work he would speed everything up. If the inspector tried to shut the site down Sébastien would accuse him of being motivated by revenge for the car accident. Ramadan would slow the wheels of justice. By the time the authorities got around to issuing a second injunction the structural work would be complete. The hotel would be a reality. Given the importance of tourism to Marrakech it was unlikely that the authorities would enforce retrospective compliance. It would be a brave judge who ordered the demolition of a fifty-million-euro hotel because the stair treads were a centimetre too narrow. It was a high-risk strategy but what choice did he have?

He gave orders to get a night shift underway. He told Hassan to recruit any builder who was available, offering top rates. Construction would take place around the clock with breaks for food at 7.30 p.m., midnight and 3.30 in the morning. By sunset the Serafina workforce had swelled to 250 men.

It was now ten o'clock at night. Hassan and Sébastien were standing under a blaze of arc lights, surrounded by the roar of engines and machinery. The smell of diesel and carbide filled the air.

Hassan was worried about supplies. 'If we work around the clock,' he shouted, his cheeks glistening with sweat. '*Pas de sable, pas de ciment!*'

'Call the depot.'

'They're low on stocks. Ramadan!'

'Try Youssouffia or Casablanca, anywhere that has sand, gravel, cement! What about equipment?'

'The last generators are coming tonight.'

'I want you to get a team of men and build a fence!'

'A what?' Hassan's voice was hoarse.

'A fence!' Sébastien shouted. 'Three metres high! Start by the barrier!'

'All round the site?'

Sébastien nodded. 'Use corrugated sheets! Order more sheets as well!'

If they were going to work around the clock, Sébastien thought grimly, they may as well do so unobserved.

'*Labas!* How are you, my brother?' Rachid was sitting behind the wheel of the taxi, smoking a cigarette. 'Are you feeling better? Yes? *Al-hamdullilah!* Me? I had a good day. That's because I was asleep for most of it!'

They drove along the city walls, past the billboard with the scantily clad woman and onto the Route d'Ourika. While Rachid chatted away Karim dwelled on his outburst at Ayesha. His anger with her was born of frustration. He wished that they could make their devotion to each other public, shout it from the rooftops. But it had to remain locked in their hearts. No one must ever know.

When had their relationship changed, undergone the transformation from closeness to intimacy? In Karim's mind it happened when Ayesha reached adolescence. Instead of separating them, his father's admonition simply made them more secretive. They held trysts on the roof when Ayesha was hanging out the washing or they met after lessons in the market at Bab al-Khemis. They shared their interests, their secrets, their jokes, their fears. When Karim got into trouble with his father, or was bullied at school, he would ask

Ayesha's advice. She in turn would tell Karim about the empty-headed girls in the *douar*, how all they were interested in was make-up and clothes while she wanted to discuss Bluetooth and parkour. They counted the hours until their next meeting. Lying on the roof together, out of earshot, Ayesha would ask why they couldn't get married. 'I'm not your real sister so where's the harm?'

Karim's reply was always the same. 'Marriage with a brother or sister, even one born to other parents, is forbidden by the Quran. It is pointless to talk of such things.'

When Karim was accepted for police academy he hoped that the 250 miles between Kenitra and Marrakech would divide them, cool their feelings for each other. For a year the plan worked. He had a brief relationship with a female cadet at the academy. He distracted himself from thoughts of Ayesha by taking extra classes, ending up as the best marksman in his year. Then, just as Karim was starting his first job in Rabat, his father suffered a fatal heart attack. Overnight, the family was impoverished. Karim was recalled to Marrakech and Ayesha had to leave school to help Lalla Fatima. Ayesha and Karim were once again living under the same roof but this time Karim was the head of the family and even more obliged to observe propriety. On the last occasion they had lain together on the roof, gazing up at the night sky, Karim told Ayesha that they were like the earth and the moon, forever attracted to each other, forever subject to each other's gravitational pull, but destined to remain apart.

He was brought back to the present by the wheels bumping along the track. The black outline of the Sherezade came into view, then the figure of Fouad blinking in the headlamps.

'*Labas?*' asked Karim. 'OK?' Once again, the other man said nothing. Karim and Fouad changed places and the taxi drove off, trailing strains of Bollywood music.

Even here, three miles out of town, the heat was stifling. Men went mad on nights like this, Karim thought. He opened the door to the hut. Despite the relative comfort of a bedstead to sleep on there was no window, a fact he hadn't noticed the night before. The kerosene lamp was lit, making the air even hotter than outside. To his relief, the smell of kerosene masked any odour left behind by Fouad. He perched on the mattress. There were marks and stains, too disgusting to contemplate. Tomorrow he would bring a sheet, *inshallah*. He looked around at the four wooden walls which would form his home for the next few weeks. He ran his finger along a slat of pine, rough and splintery. Cobwebs swayed gently above his head. Opening his bag, he realised with annoyance that he had forgotten the torch. *Idiot.* He picked up the kerosene lamp and went outside to the back of the hut where the standpipe was located. He cleaned his hands, forearms and feet, then returned to the front of the hut and unrolled his prayer mat. Kneeling with his hands on his thighs, he placed his palms on the ground and rocked forward, touching his forehead on the mat.

Glory to Thee, O Allah, and Thine is the praise, and blessed is Thy name, and exalted is Thy majesty, and there is none to be served besides Thee.

When he had finished he made an inspection of the site. The path was hard to follow in the light from the kerosene lamp and his trousers snagged on thorns. After ten minutes he gave up and went back inside.

Leaving the door of the hut open to catch any breath of air, he lay on the mattress in his T-shirt and trousers. Through the door he could see the silhouette of the derelict building. He craved a cigarette. He should have borrowed one from Rachid or, better still, bought a packet of Marquise before coming out. He idled away an hour on his phone. A moth fluttered round the lamp, its shadow dancing on the walls. He noticed two dead moths in the cobwebs above his head. He slapped a mosquito on his forearm, then another.

He pictured the way that Ayesha had looked at him when she announced that her heart was set on someone else. What if she was telling the truth? What if she really had found another man? It was several hours before he slept.

Chapter 4

Karim was sitting at his desk, one trouser leg rolled up, scratching his shin.

'The kerosene lamp stank but I didn't dare put it out in case an intruder thought the place was empty. And because the door was open half the insects in the neighbourhood flew in and feasted on my blood.'

Noureddine smiled. ' What about you? Did you eat?'

'An orange.'

'That's not enough. It's Ramadan and you're away from home. You must remember to eat and drink more.'

'*Wakha*, OK.' Karim picked up a swatter and swatted a fly on the window. He gave a yawn. 'So – what's new?'

'Aziz has arrested Amina Talal's brother.'

'*What?*'

'He's being interrogated in the Breeze Block.'

Karim threw aside the swatter and headed towards the door. Noureddine jumped up to block his exit.

'I know Abderrahim Talal!' protested Karim. 'He's an engineering student! It's madness to think that he murdered his sister!'

Noureddine put one hand on Karim's chest and steered

him back towards his desk. 'It's always the one you don't suspect.'

'But the Talals are a respectable family! What possible reason could Abderrahim have for killing his sister?'

'You said yourself that the brother was prudish. Who's to say he's not an Islamist?'

'By the Seven Saints!' Karim exclaimed. 'Having a beard doesn't mean that he's an Islamist! And even if he *is* an Islamist, that's no proof that he murdered his sister! Ever since 9/11 we've jumped on the nearest idiot with a beard and pinned any unsolved crimes on him!'

'In cases of this type you always start with members of the family.'

'*Cases of this type?*' cried Karim. 'How many cases have you come across where a female is found dead, placed in a hand-cart, and left outside a mosque with a sign on her body proclaiming her name and reputation?'

Before Noureddine could respond Karim strode through the door and down the steps. He ran across the courtyard and into an ugly single-storey building. The officers dubbed the building the Breeze Block because the money had run out (been pocketed, the more cynical ones said) before the exterior could be rendered. The result was a mass of grey cinder blocks which, together, resembled a giant breeze block. Into this unloved building strode Karim, his face set, scanning the windows along the corridor until he spotted Amina's brother. He marched into the room without knock-ing. To his dismay, Captain Badnaoui was standing by the wall.

Karim faltered. 'I – this man – he's innocent.'

No one spoke. Pockmark Features walked over and stood with the tips of his shoes against Karim's so that his nose was inches from Karim's face. 'What do you want?'

Karim pointed at the figure at the table. 'I can vouch for this man. I have already interviewed him!'

'*Seer*, go.' Pockmark Features pushed Karim into the corridor and closed the door.

Karim put his hand on the wall and took several deep breaths. A passing secretary gave him a wide berth.

'In the name of Allah! What have you done now?' Noureddine exclaimed as Karim slunk back to his desk.

Karim said nothing. He logged on to the intranet of the Interior Ministry and clicked on the directory of suspected Islamists. Sure enough, Abderrahim Talal's name was on the list.

Melanie walked along the alleyway. Little children ran after her, giggling, *un dirham, un stylo!* Every time she turned around they fled away, shrieking. She could feel the sun burning through her blouse and wished she brought some factor 30. On the corner a leathery-faced woman was sitting cross-legged behind little heaps of vegetables. Melanie pointed at some tomatoes. The woman weighed out a kilo and pulled a thin plastic bag from the folds of her caftan. Melanie leaned down with a handful of change, the woman took three coins and Melanie went on her way, pleased with this minor triumph.

After wandering some more, she came to a pair of rusting, half-open gates. Behind lay a cemetery, a wilderness of earthy mounds and cracked stones. The only signs of life were two jackdaws cawing around a headstone. At the far end loomed the minaret of Sidi bel Abbès.

'*Engleesh?*'

Melanie turned around. In the doorway of a shop stood a man in a white and brown *gandora* and pillbox cap. '*Kbour Chou.* Cemetery of Sidi bel Abbès, maybe two hundred years old. You like some pottery?'

Melanie was on the point of refusing then noticed the colourful plates laid out on the pavement and decided that eight of them would make an ideal wedding present for Emma. The shopkeeper wrapped them in sheets of newspaper.

'Is this where the girl was murdered?' Melanie asked.

The man looked at her for a moment then used his teeth to tear off a strip of brown tape. 'Very bad, bad for Marrakech.'

'Who was she?'

'Very bad,' he repeated. Melanie waited for him to expand on this observation but he continued wrapping and taping, every now and then sucking his teeth or shaking his head. Eventually he handed her two bundles tied with string. 'Please tell your friends Marrakech not like this. Marrakech people friendly people.'

Melanie paid and the man went back into his shop. Taking her bearings from the minaret she retraced her steps past the *hanoots* and kitchenware stores. She made a few wrong turns before arriving at a long courtyard flanked by workshops. The minaret rose directly ahead of her. In the alleyway, around the entrance to the mosque, was a line of beggars, hunched in wheelchairs or sitting on the ground. Something about the tilt of their heads suggested they were sightless. Melanie put down her shopping and opened her guidebook.

Sidi bel Abbès is one of the seven patron saints of Marrakech. He was born in 1130 in Ceuta and died in Marrakech in 1205. He spent his life caring for the weak and the handicapped. In the early seventeenth century, a mosque and a cemetery were built next to his mausoleum. The '*zaouia*' or shrine is now a charitable foundation for the blind. Non-Muslims are forbidden to enter the mosque.

Melanie heard a low murmuring from the wheelchairs. One of the beggars had sensed her presence. The other beggars started mumbling and holding out their palms. Melanie picked up her bags and walked towards the first beggar. His eyes were filmy. The hood of his *jellaba* was folded back over the crown of his head and his face was the colour of leather. Unsure what to do, Melanie handed him the bag of tomatoes. The man lifted the bag, gave it a sniff then thrust his hand out again. Assuming that he didn't want the tomatoes, Melanie took the bag away but the beggar shrieked loudly and tried to grab it back. She took out a single tomato and placed it in his lap, then went down the line of beggars handing each one a tomato in turn. The murmuring grew louder and more insistent.

Confused and frightened, she stepped away. A porter wearing a baseball cap and threadbare jacket came towards her with a handcart. He pointed at the heavy parcels by her feet. '*Charrette?*'

Melanie nodded. The porter loaded the pottery into his cart and followed her back to Dar Zuleika.

It was noon and sunlight flooded into the room, raising the temperature several degrees. Karim's shirt buttons were undone and he was scratching a mosquito bite on his stomach.

'You know as well as I do that men end up in the dossier simply because they've sprouted a beard or because some neighbour with a grudge whispers in a policeman's ear. It doesn't prove that he killed his sister!'

'Maybe he didn't mean to kill her,' said Noureddine. 'Maybe he hit her and she fell. It could have been an accident.'

'If it was an accident, then why would the brother incriminate himself by leaving a sign? No, Amina Talal's death has been dressed up to look like an honour killing and the police have bought it!'

'Whatever happened, it's not your concern. You've already caused a nuisance by barging into the interrogation. Get on with your work. And for goodness sake, do your shirt up.'

Karim stood up and searched the office. He found a large sheet of cardboard which had been used for photos of a crime scene and propped it against the window to block out the sunlight. Then he sat in front of his computer and read a report about contraband merchandise.

La fabrication, la commercialisation et l'importation d'une marchandise contrefaite sont punies comme un délit de confiscation et d'une amende, outre la destruction des choses contrefaites et la réparation du préjudice.

He spotted a fly on the rim of the wastebasket and swatted it to the floor.

*En cette ère de production délocalisée, il est de plus en plus
coûteux de vérifier l'origine des produits. Du fait même que la
contrefaçon est par définition illégale il est très difficile
d'estimer . . .*

He swatted another fly. He wondered if Abderrahim was still
in the Breeze Block. The telephone on his desk rang, giving
him a jolt. It was Captain Badnaoui, demanding a progress
report.

'Progress?' Karim stammered. His mouth was sticky and his
tongue felt two sizes too large.

'With your investigation. There is only one investigation
that you are involved with. Do you want me to come up to
your office and remind you what it is?'

'No, sir.'

'Tomorrow first thing.'

'Yes, sir, *inshallah*.' Karim put the phone down and stared
helplessly at Noureddine. But the older man didn't have any
words of solace.

'Kill one fly and seven others come to the funeral.'

'What?'

'The flies. Don't swat them. It only attracts others.'

Kay put her phone on the side of the bath and turned the cold
tap. She tied her hair in a knot then sprinkled a few drops of
lavender oil. Stepping over the rim, she lowered herself in the
water and breathed in sharply. A cold bath always sent her
metabolic rate into overdrive. She sank down by degrees until

the water came up to her chin and her toes touched the far end. The bath had been designed by Sébastien to accommodate two people and she always felt like a child when she bathed in it alone.

She wondered if Sébastien was having sex with other women. Open relationships were part of the local expatriate lifestyle, like keeping a horse or going for Sunday lunch at the Beldi club. She knew plenty of women who found him attractive. An affair she could tolerate; Sébastien staying with her out of convenience, or for her money – that was a different matter.

Samira knocked on the door. 'I'm leaving, *madame*.'

'OK, Samira, *merci*.'

'The men have assembled the stage. All they've got to do now is wire up the cables for the loudspeakers. We've cleared the dining room.'

'*C'est bon*.'

Samira paused a moment, then said, 'There has been news about the matter at Sidi bel Abbès. The police have arrested the brother of the dead girl.'

Kay turned around violently, sending water sloshing over the side.

'He was a bearded one,' continued Samira. 'He found out his sister was going to bars and having relations with men.'

'You mean it was an *honour killing*?'

'That's what they're saying, *madame*.'

'Good God.'

'One more thing,' Samira hesitated.

'Yes?'

'Fatiha doesn't want to work on Friday night. She's scared to walk home through the medina. Shall I look for a replacement? Or ask Driss to accompany her?'

'Yes,' said Kay, distracted.

'*A demain, alors.*'

Kay stared at the sponge in her hand. The water suddenly felt icy. She stepped out of the bath, put on a robe and checked the news on her phone. Sure enough, there it was: *Sidi bel Abbès: arrestation du frère.* She walked into her bedroom, trying to make sense of this development. Honour killings were carried out by illiterate fanatics in distant countries. Surely they couldn't happen in Marrakech with its modern apartment blocks and branches of Starbucks! But, if it was an honour killing it ranked low on the scale in terms of threats to her business. An honour killing could be rationalised, compartmentalised, dismissed as something that posed no risk to foreigners. She could already hear the voices of her friends: *see how Islam oppresses women.* The murder would be gossiped about for three weeks then forgotten. She called Sébastien, who was in the *quatrelle* on his way to the office. He had just heard the news on the radio.

'Don't you think it's far-fetched?'

'Men go crazy during Ramadan. And with this heat . . . there have been killings reported in Casablanca and Settat.'

'So . . . if the brother killed her, that means foreigners aren't affected?'

'No.' Sébastien accelerated to beat an amber traffic light.

'The medina is still a desirable place to live?'

'*Évidemment.*'

'People will still buy property?'

'Yes.'

'In that case can we talk about my idea – The Riad Thing?'

'The what?'

'My plan for a riad development company.'

'No.' Sébastien slowed down outside the office. The *gardien* signalled that there was a parking space.

'You just said that the killing won't affect people's confidence!'

'*J'ai plein de choses en tête!* I'm super busy. We've just started night and day operations.'

'We could announce the idea at the party.'

'With Mohammed there? Are you crazy?'

'Why should he mind? I'm not talking about launching the company immediately, but when you've finished the Serafina. Making an announcement in front of Mohammed might stop him taking you for granted, make him realise that you're an architect with big plans, not a has-been clinging to his only source of income.'

Sébastien gritted his teeth. Didn't Kay realise that he was no longer interested in refurbishing riads for rich Europeans? Marrakech was over. In a year he planned to be on the other side of the Mediterranean. Mohammed had already talked to him about his next project, the renovation of a hotel in Beirut. Beirut was a place where a man could make a fresh start.

'Is that how you think of me? As a has-been?'

Kay backtracked. 'No, it's just – this could be an opportunity for both of us.'

'I can't hear you. I'm in the *quatrelle*.' He pressed the accelerator, even though the car was stationary.

Kay raised her voice. 'Are you coming over for dinner tonight?'

'I have to be at the *chantier*.'
'In that case I won't see you until the party tomorrow.'
'No.'
'Make sure you're here by eight!'

Hicham Cherkaoui was angry. He was parked outside the Serafina watching the workmen erect a gate. He knew what the architect was up to. He was using Ramadan to speed up construction. If he, Hicham, tried to serve a second injunction nothing would happen until September. Then the matter would move out of the planning department and into the hands of the judges. Those mercenary bastards would do anything for a few euros.

Zero tolerance – that was the policy of his planning department. He had closed three sites in the last few months alone. There had been dissenting voices, editorials in *La Vie Eco* and *L'Economiste*, warning about deterring investors, but if officials like him didn't enforce basic safeguards Marrakech would be concreted over within twenty years. He wasn't against development, far from it. He wanted the world to look at his city with admiration. But Marrakech was not some flyblown African town where foreigners could behave as they liked. It was a modern metropolis, with proper laws and governance.

By God, it was hot! He refused to put on the air conditioning: air conditioning cost money. He spat a mouthful of phlegm into the dust. Taking his binoculars he watched a lorry driver in conversation with the guard at the gate. Behind them, work was taking place on a channel or pool – a very long one by the look of it. Hicham's father had worked as a pool attendant at the Hotel Mamounia. He held the job for twenty-five years. One day he came home early. He sat in their two-bedroom house on the Route de Safi with his head in his hands. It took hours of questioning by Hicham's mother before the truth came out. He had been arranging towels when a guest, a Frenchman, complained that his sun lounger was broken. He was a big man with an enormous belly and Hicham's father suspected that the lounger had collapsed under his weight. He advised the guest to sit on a chair instead. The Frenchman flew into a rage and hurled the lounger into the swimming pool, then ordered Hicham's father to jump in and pull it out. His father refused, whereupon the other man frog-marched him into the manager's office and demanded that he be sacked. The only job his father could get afterwards was as a road sweeper. He died before Hicham finished school.

Putting the binoculars aside, he took the repair bill from the glove compartment and stared at it for the umpteenth time. He had bought the Lexus with the money he received when the Wilaya ordered compulsory purchase of his family's house to make way for development. He polished the car every day until he could see his face in it.

He would find a way. Yes, he would find a way.

Karim stood in the shower with his eyes closed, taking care not to let any water pass his lips. As he dried himself he peered through the window into the courtyard. Khadija, Ayesha and his mother were going back and forth from the *salon* to the kitchen, talking in agitated voices about the arrest of Abderrahim Talal.

He changed into jeans and a long-sleeved shirt, put a sheet, a torch and a Quran into his bag and went downstairs. The women were waiting for him in the *salon*.

'Do you think he could have done it?' Khadija said at once. 'Could he really have killed his sister?'

'I don't know.' Karim sat down heavily. 'Allah will decide.'

'You must speak to the poor boy,' cried Lalla Fatima.

'If he has an alibi he will be released, God willing.'

'I think he's guilty,' said Khadija.

'How can you even think such a thing?' asked Lalla Fatima.

'Maybe he beat her because she was whoring around.'

'Don't use that word! Amina Talal was not a *wh*—, she was a respectable girl.'

'How do you know, Meema?' asked Khadija. 'How do you know what goes in other families? I feel sorry for Amina, of course I do, but if she was going to nightclubs and sleeping with men then you can't say that she wasn't to blame.'

'Hush, Khadija!' said Lalla Fatima. 'The poor family has suffered a double tragedy! First Amina, now Abderrahim. What agonies must their parents be going through?'

Khadija turned to Karim. 'Father was right to call off your betrothal to Amina.'

Ayesha looked up with astonishment. 'Karim was going to marry Amina Talal?'

'It was just a hare-brained idea of Si Brahim. A passing fancy. He soon changed his mind.'

'Si Brahim was always marrying off his children in his head!' said Lalla Fatima, laughing. 'He married Khadija off to half the young men in the medina.'

'Who did he marry me off to?' asked Ayesha. The others were spared from answering her question by the cry of the muezzin.

Karim poured himself a coffee. It was the fourth day of Ramadan and his appetite had returned, thank God. After a bowl of *harira* soup he ate an omelette and *msemmen*. He usually found the wheat pancakes too heavy for his stomach but the first one went down so easily he spread a second with a dollop of jam. He reached for a toothpick, put his feet up and watched the soap opera, glad that Khadija's fiancé wasn't around to ruin his digestion. When the commercials came on Lalla Fatima turned to her son.

'You must talk to them, Karim.'

'Talk to whom?'

'Whoever is in charge of the investigation. Tell them that Abderrahim is a good man. He goes to the mosque five times a day.'

'That's precisely why they think he killed Amina.'

'No, no. He would never do such a thing!'

'I've told them, Meema. If I tell them again I will lose my job. If Abderrahim can account for his whereabouts on Sunday night and Monday night, and they don't have any evidence linking him to the crime, then all will be well, *inshallah*.'

Lalla Fatima stood up. 'I shall visit Lalla Hanane. The poor woman must be beside herself.'

'No.' Karim was quick to forbid her. 'You're not to go out tonight. Not until we're sure we've got the right man.'

Sitting in Kay's private quarters, Melanie felt like she'd been invited for tea with the headmistress. Except that a headmistress wouldn't have a dining room like this: twenty feet in length, the walls painted a lapis colour so intense it almost hurt the eyes. On the dining table stood a vase of bird-of-paradise flowers.

'I need you to serve cocktails. In return, I'll deduct the cost of your last night's accommodation.'

It didn't take Melanie long to accept. She had been wondering where she would spend her last night in Marrakech. Having observed the preparations for the party, she was curious to see the event itself. It would provide plenty to gossip about when she returned home.

'What should I wear?'

Kay cocked her head. 'You look about my size. Come with me.'

Melanie followed Kay into the bedroom. The curtains were closed and a shaft of sunlight fell across a white deep-pile carpet. Melanie noticed a metal-framed four-poster bed with muslin curtains. Kay opened a cupboard and took out a strapless dress. 'Something like this perhaps?' She held up a frock. 'Or this?'

Melanie baulked. The dresses were for a woman twice her age. 'I would hate to spill anything on them . . . I do have something of my own. It may be a bit racy . . .'

'Racy is good,' said Kay, putting the dresses back on their hangers.

'Do you want to see it?

'No.' Kay led Melanie back through the dining room. On the way she opened a drawer and took out a pair of oversized sunglasses.

'Are these yours, by the way?'

'Yes!' Melanie exclaimed. 'I've been looking for them everywhere. Where were they?'

'Momo must have got hold of them. I found them under the orange tree.'

'I'd have thought that Ray-Bans were more his style,' Melanie quipped.

Kay gave a thin smile.

The girl was pretty, with shoulder-length hair and black jeans. She was standing at the corner of Avenue Mohammed Cinq when she flagged them down.

'Route d'Ourika?'

'*Tlaeee*, get in,' said Rachid. The scent of perfume filled the taxi. 'It's hot again tonight!'

'Are you talking to me?' the girl replied without enthusiasm. 'We have air conditioning where I work.'

'Where's that – Pacha?'

'Bô-Zin.'

'Bô-Zin! I hear that's a nice place!' Rachid turned up the stereo. 'Do you like music?'

The girl examined her fingernails. 'Not that kind.'

'My friend here is off to work as well. He works as a nightwatchman on a building site. He's paid to guard the place but, between you and me, I think he sleeps all night, ha ha!'

The girl remained silent. Karim marvelled at the way that Rachid chatted away without a response. If he had even dared to address the girl he would have clammed up as soon as he sensed she wasn't responding. After ten minutes the taxi pulled up outside Bô-Zin and the girl stepped out. Rachid watched her walk up to the entrance, her hips swaying in her tight jeans.

'We always want what we can't have, eh, Mister Karim?'

Karim rolled his eyes. 'Just drive.'

Shortly afterwards the taxi trundled down the dark track to the building site. Fouad came out of the hut. Karim made an effort to be friendly.

'May God protect and preserve you! *Kulshee bekhir?* All well?'

Fouad mumbled a response. What a strange individual, thought Karim. He was the opposite of Rachid and his non-stop banter. Perhaps spending sixteen hours a day in a hut turned you into a tongue-tied recluse.

When the two men had gone he made an inspection, happy to have remembered his torch. Picking his way along the path he distinguished murky shapes in the undergrowth: an old cement mixer, fence posts, the black outline of the swimming pool. The interior of the building looked dark and forbidding. He couldn't remember if Khalifa had instructed him to look inside. He stopped and listened. The hot night air was broken by a *boom-boom-badda-boom* from Pacha. Somewhere to the south a dog barked.

He pulled a wooden fence post free of the tangle and retraced his steps to the hut. Fouad had left the kerosene lamp burning and the moths were trembling in the cobwebs. The heat in the confined space was almost intolerable and before long Karim was bathed in sweat. He hid the fence post under the bed, in case he needed to use it as a weapon, and ran his torch over the stained mattress. The side was slit by a gash as long as his forearm. Was that a rustle he could hear from within? It was like the night: thick, impenetrable, filled with nameless horrors. He went outside to wash then unrolled his prayer mat on the ground.

God is the greatest, God is the greatest. Glory to Thee, O God, and Thine is the praise, and blessed is Thy name, and exalted is Thy majesty. Thee alone we worship and Thee alone we ask for help.

The first thing he learned at police college was that you could only arrest a suspect if you had evidence.

Show us the straight path. The path of those whom thou hast favoured, not the path of those who earn Thine anger or of those who go astray.

Aziz must have evidence against Abderrahim Talal.

My God, forgive me, forgive me. God listens to those who praise him.

If Aziz didn't have evidence – evidence that would stand up in court – he must have faked it. Karim was too distracted to complete his prayers. He put his head under the tap and held it there for a full minute. Then he went inside, stripped off his clothes and did thirty press-ups. He wiped his body with his towel and covered the mattress with the sheet. The stains showed through the thin cotton. He lay down and closed his eyes. *Boom-badda-boom* went Pacha. *Arf-arf* went the dog.

Whine-whine went the mosquitoes. Even with the towel wrapped around his head he couldn't shut out the noise. *Boom-boom, arf-arf, whine-whine.*

He had a dream that he and Ayesha were lying naked on the roof of the riad. He woke from it with a cry. Then he sat on his sodden sheet and opened the Quran.

Chapter 5

'As I was on my way to work a bird fell out of the sky.'

Bouchaïb was arranging one-dirham coins on the bonnet of a car. 'It fell right in front of me – *plaf!* – no further than where you're standing. I've never seen a bird like it. Blue with brown wings. Maybe it came from the north, or perhaps it came from the south. You would know better than me, Mister Karim. Picture it, the bird might have flown a thousand miles across the desert only to drop dead when it was within sight of water.'

'Like a man dying of thirst on the last day of Ramadan.'

'*Besahh!* Indeed! What brings you here at this ungodly hour?'

'I have to write a report for Captain Badnaoui.' Karim was dropping with exhaustion and his mouth felt as if it had been stuffed with cinders. Any hope that he might sleep better on the Route d'Ourika had been dashed.

Bouchaïb looked up at the sky. The last stars were disappearing in a flood of orange. 'I think we're in for another inferno. How long before we reach fifty degrees?'

The commissariat was deserted. Even the duty officer was asleep. As he was walking past the downstairs office Karim stopped and stared at Aziz's desk. On an impulse, he strode across the room and sat down. The desk had been cleared of everything apart from a wire in-tray and a desk blotter. Karim went through the drawers. What had Aziz done with the cardboard sign? As he was tugging at the top drawer, someone spoke.

'*Sbah al-khir.* Good morning.'

Karim almost had a heart attack. But it was just a cleaning woman in a tabard. She emptied the wastebasket. As she moved off with her trolley Karim got to his feet.

'Stop!'

Pretending that he had thrown away an important document he rummaged through her sack but there was nothing of interest, only a scrunched-up handbill, a few toothpicks and yesterday's newspaper.

Any doubts Kay had harboured about her ability to take on Lucinda's commission vanished the moment she set foot inside the villa. The interior was an ugly mix of faience floors and cheap partition studwork. Hidden under the paint and varnish were some beautiful 1930s features. All she had to do to transform the place was remove the modern additions and put in a nice armchair or two. As they looked around she made appreciative noises.

'I would put in a wall behind the bed with openings here –' she pointed '– and here, to make a walk-in wardrobe. It would allow you to show off this fabulous cornicing.'

'A wall?' Lucinda said doubtfully. 'That's quite a big job. Wouldn't we need Sébastien to do something like that?'

'Not really. I'm thinking of a wall like the one we built in the Room of the Arabian Merchant.'

'Perhaps Sébastien could oversee things?'

'There's really no need,' Kay said testily. 'The builders could manage quite easily if I told them what to do. In any case Sébastien's got his hands full with the Serafina.'

'Have you seen the hotel yet? I read an article in the *Tribune*. It sounds simply astonishing!'

For months Kay had pestered Sébastien to show her round the construction site but he never seemed to have the time. She'd seen the plans, however, and she had no doubt that the hotel would be a success. With Sébastien's ingenuity and Mohammed's deep pockets it would stand out, even in a city of beautiful hotels. Although she was pleased for her boyfriend, happy that he finally had a prestigious project worthy of his talents, she was also envious. The hotel would make Sébastien famous.

'It's going to have the most marvellous gardens,' Lucinda enthused. 'A sort of lagoon arrangement, with water everywhere.'

'So I've heard. Shall we press on? What about the bed? Are you happy with it?'

'No! Tofiq – you know, that chap who's been helping me – he gave the job to a carpenter he knows but he made it too low. Moroccans seem to like their beds an inch off the floor.'

'I could make you a custom-designed bed with a carved plinth and headboard. You could have it any height you want.'

'Excellent!'

Kay made notes. 'What about the French doors?'

'Replace them. They're the devil to open.'

'Personally, I would keep them. A little restoration is all that's required. The handles are pure art deco.'

'I was thinking of a nice pair of sliding doors.'

'It's true that sliding doors would give you a better view of the garden.'

'Who did those lovely sliding doors in your library?'

Kay scowled. 'Sébastien.'

'I've got him the most marvellous present,' said Lucinda. 'You know how he's always carrying bits of paper around?' She picked up a leather shoulder bag. '*Voilà!*'

'Beautiful,' said Kay. She'd seen hundreds like it in the souks. Sébastien would hate it.

'I want it to be a surprise so don't go telling him.'

'I wouldn't dream of it.' Kay gathered up her belongings. 'I should be getting back – I've still got some things to sort out before the party.'

'I can't wait!' As she said goodbye Lucinda whispered, 'Promise me you'll consider involving Sébastien in the refurbishment. Just for the *complicated* things.'

Captain Badnaoui skimmed the two pages of typescript. 'What's the biggest problem – handbags? Trainers? Watches?'

Karim didn't know what to say. His report was little more than a summary of what Youssef had told him and some statistics he'd gleaned from the Internet.

'All three are a problem,' he faltered. 'Production of all three is rife and, er, all three are—'

'I don't see any recommendations here.'

Karim's tongue felt like one of the slabs of rubber tyre that the craftsmen in Rue Riad Zitoun el Kedim made into sandals. 'There's no point trying to stop the sellers. We cannot control things at the other end, at the – the point of production, at least not the goods made in China, which are, er, ninety per cent of the total . . .'

'What about the distributors? Are they Maghrebi or Chinese?'

Karim would have given a thousand dirhams for a glass of water and an excuse to drink it. 'They, er, I'm not sure.'

Badnaoui leaned back in his chair. He contemplated Karim for a few moments. 'What did you get at college – a distinction?'

'A merit, sir.'

'So find me something of merit.'

'Meaning what, sir?'

'Something I can show the ministry. Something they can show the Europeans. This stuff –' he held up the pages '– I could find on the Internet.'

Karim reddened. '*Wakha*, yes sir.'

'And stay away from Amina Talal's brother,' he said, tossing the report back across the desk. 'Forget about Abderrahim Talal. Concentrate on Calvin Klein.'

My Medina

Some visitors never see the real Morocco. The nearest they get to meeting local people is when they tip the staff in their five-star hotel. But away from the air conditioning and expensively irrigated gardens are quiet alleyways where women still get their water from standpipes and cats sun themselves outside mosques. Apart from electricity and mains sewerage, life in the medina has stayed the same for centuries. You may be jostled by a donkey pulling firewood or a water-seller ringing his bell, but you'll experience the real Morocco in all its wonder.

Monkey News: A couple of readers have written to say that we shouldn't be keeping a monkey as a pet. My response is that Momo was rescued from the Jemaa el Fna. Although the Jemaa is a lot of fun to visit, the animals are kept in boxes and made to perform day and night. Momo has a much better life in the courtyards of Dar Zuleika where he has the run of eight orange trees and all the nuts he can eat. So no wagging fingers, please!

On Fridays in Ramadan the officers and staff usually left the commissariat before noon prayers. By late afternoon the building was deserted apart from the duty officer and a solitary stenographer catching up on her work. Karim crossed the yard, blinking in the sunlight, then entered the Breeze Block. His footsteps echoed along the corridor. The doors were wedged open with cardboard stubs and the heat picked up the smell of disinfectant. He pushed open a further set of doors and descended a flight of concrete steps into the windowless basement. The builders hadn't got around to installing ventilation and the air was as stifling as a *hammam*.

There was a single holding cell which Karim initially thought was empty. Then he made out a figure sitting in the corner with his knees hunched to his chest. A pipe on the wall leaked a rust-coloured ooze.

'Abderrahim!' Karim hissed.

Abderrahim raised his head. His hair was wet and there was a bloody bruise on his chin. He saw Karim then lowered his head again.

'*Abderrahim!*' Karim said more loudly. 'I had nothing to do with this. You saw how they treated me when I came into the interrogation room. I've been taken off the case.' He looked to left and right, then pressed his face to the bars. 'Listen to me – if you're in here it means they've got nothing on you, do you hear? No evidence! Tell them where you were on Sunday night – give them an alibi!'

A low laugh came from the corner. For a moment, Karim thought that Abderrahim had lost his reason. Then the other man raised his head.

'How old were you when you started Ramadan?'

'Twelve.' Karim remembered the day clearly.

'I was seven. I have fasted since I was seven years old. I have prayed five times every day like my father before me. I have never touched alcohol or tobacco. One day a week I give lessons at a school for disadvantaged children. Next year, *inshallah*, I will make the *haj* to Mecca. Your colleagues have accused me of being an Islamist. If Islamism means devoting your whole life to Allah then they are right. I am an Islamist.'

'Your parents have already lost a daughter! Don't deprive them of their son as well!'

Abderrahim spat into a bucket on the floor. 'You would have made a good husband for Amina.'

'Where were you between Sunday night and Monday morning? Were you at home the whole night, until your parents awoke? Could they attest to this – could they provide an alibi?'

'An alibi? If I provide an alibi I won't be the only one in this stinking cell.'

Using the wall for balance, Abderrahim rose to his feet and shuffled painfully across the floor. Karim realised that he had been foot-whipped. The punishment left no marks but the pain was almost unendurable. Foot-whipping was still used to get a confession, especially in terrorism cases, but it was despised by officers like Karim and Noureddine, who believed that it had no place in the modern Sûreté.

Abderrahim grasped the bars. His eyes were red and bloodshot. 'The first night of Ramadan is a holy night. Not for my sister, evidently –' he gave a bitter laugh '– but for myself and for those who revere this holiest of months. I attended allnight prayers and I celebrated the meal before dawn with my friends—'

'There you are! You have an alibi!'

'– my friends in Al-Adl wa Al-Ihssane.'

Karim recognised the name. Al-Adl wa Al-Ihssane was a shadowy, semi-legal Islamist organisation whose meetings the authorities had been trying to suppress for years.

'To prove that I didn't kill my sister I would have to give the names of my friends. Your colleagues will then go to my friends' houses and arrest them. Given what I know of your colleagues, they'll probably string them up by the ankles. So you see, I can provide an alibi and incriminate others, or I can stay silent and incriminate myself. Tell me, lieutenant – what would you have me do?'

Abderrahim spat a gobbet of bloody phlegm onto the floor then hobbled back and sat down with his knees to his chest.

No one would call Boulevard Zerktouni attractive. A ragbag of 1960s apartment blocks, unremarkable shops, cafés and eateries, and a filling station, the street had one redeeming feature: the jacaranda trees that produced a bright blue blossom from March to October. That Friday afternoon even the jacaranda blossom failed to lift Sébastien's spirits. A hot dry wind had started to blow, creating eddies of dust on the pavement. The few pedestrians walked with their heads bowed, as if the hot wind had sucked the life out of them. The parking attendant was sitting forlornly on a plastic chair, a scarf tied from his head to his chin like a cartoon character with toothache. Sébastien parked the *quatrelle*, leaned back and sighed. He thought about the party that evening. Would he have to give a speech? Chaperone his boss? He pictured his friends – those who would attend – and felt ... nothing.

He was fifty years old. He was working harder than he had worked in his life. His relationship was on the rocks. His apartment was a joke. And a *connard* of a planning inspector was out to get him.

He read a birthday greeting from his son. From the day that his children had left Marrakech Sébastien had been conscientious in maintaining contact. He remembered their birthdays, sent money when they passed exams. Then, one day, Sophie stopped answering and changed her email address. She gave no explanation but it made Sébastien even keener to keep the lines of communication open with his son. Laurent's visit was the only thing he was looking forward to.

He walked up to his apartment, took off his boots and threw himself on the bed. The pillow felt cool and inviting.

Karim felt the hot wind on his cheeks as he walked along Houmane Al-Fatouaki. The minivan drivers who usually gathered in the public parking lot had gone home, leaving a faint smell of urine. When he reached the Koutoubia he paused and gazed up at the golden orbs on the minaret. According to a story his father told him, the highest of the three orbs had been donated by the wife of Sultan Youssef ben Tachfine as penance for eating during Ramadan. It had taken all her gold jewellery, thrown into the melting pot, to atone for her transgression. Karim couldn't imagine breaking the fast, even in the most testing circumstances. He had that in common with Amina's brother. This weekend, with God's infinite guidance, he would devote himself to prayer, pure thoughts and pure deeds.

In Souk Semmarine the shops had reopened after Friday prayers. As he was passing Arset ben Brahim, Karim spotted a lanky figure in rolled-up trousers – the porter from Sidi bel Abbès! His long arms were draped over the handles of his cart and he was deep in conversation with another porter. Karim quickened his step.

'*Salaam ou alikum.*'

'You're that cop,' drawled the porter.

Karim looked closely at the cart, noting the mismatched wheels and the missing side panel.

'When did the police return your cart?'

The porter unfurled himself from the handles. 'What are you talking about?'

'When did they return your cart to you?'

'*Mafhemch*. I don't understand.'

'I told you on Monday that we would collect your cart to check it for evidence and that you would have it back by the end of the week.'

'Nobody came. I went to the mosque on Tuesday and they gave me the cart back.'

'What time?'

'Before noon prayers.'

'Did anyone interview you – an officer from the Sûreté?'

'No.'

Karim was starting to grow concerned. 'Have you used your cart since then?'

The porter grinned, exposing a row of decayed teeth. 'How do you think I feed my family?'

Karim was appalled. Aziz had neglected the most basic police procedures. Any fingerprints or DNA left in the cart or on the handles would have long since been contaminated.

'What did you do with the sheets of cardboard?'

'The cart was empty when I picked it up.'

'Empty?' Karim's temple started to throb. He tried to think of an explanation. Aziz could have raced to the mosque, swabbed the cart for evidence and taken the cardboard, all before noon prayers. The alternative – and more likely explanation – was that Aziz had done nothing. Karim kept his thoughts to himself.

'You told me on Monday evening that you normally keep your cart here, outside the *hanoot*.'

'Yes.'

'It was stolen during *ftour* on Monday evening – correct?'

'No. It was stolen on Sunday night.' *Another surprise!*

'Why didn't you tell me?'

'You didn't ask.'

Karim began to wish he'd gone home a different way. 'You next saw the cart on Monday evening, with the girl inside it?'

'Yes.'

'Who found the cart?'

'The muezzin, of course,' the man said, as if speaking to a five-year-old. 'He sent his son to fetch you – remember?'

The second porter spoke. He was clad in tracksuit bottoms and a grubby cotton jumper. 'People are saying you've arrested the girl's brother.'

'He's being questioned, that's all.'

'I've seen him at the mosque. He's one of the bearded ones.'

Karim thanked the porters. If he hadn't been a religious man he might have wondered if some malign force was setting obstacles in his path, or at least playing tricks with him. But there were no devils in Ramadan. *The gates of hell are closed and the devils are locked up, said the Prophet, Peace and Blessings Upon Him.* Karim repeated the words all the way home.

'*Salaam!*'

Karim's voice rang out in the empty courtyard. He found Ayesha in the kitchen.

'Where are the others?'

'Zak has taken them to see the apartment.'

'Didn't you want to go with them?'

'Somebody has to cook the meal.'

Karim leaned against the counter and watched Ayesha shell some hard-boiled eggs. He wondered how to dispel the tension.

'What do you think of my watch?' he said eventually. 'I can get you one if you like – a woman's version. Which would you prefer – Tag Heuer or Breitling?'

'As you wish.'

Karim sighed. He would have to wait an hour before he could enjoy the blessing of water and the even greater blessing of paracetamol. Lacking anything else to say, he launched into an account of his day.

'I spoke to Amina's brother. He claims he was at an illegal prayer meeting but refuses to use it as an alibi in case he incriminates his fellow worshippers. Although I don't like the man, I believe him. I also spoke to the owner of the handcart. It wasn't stolen on Monday night but on Sunday night – the night that Amina disappeared.'

Ayesha listened with interest. 'Where is the nightclub located – the one that that Amina and Leila visited?'

'Guéliz.'

'Had they been there before?'

'Yes.'

'How did they get the money for nightclubs?'

'Many nightclubs are free, at least for women. You can stay the whole night and not spend a dirham, as long as you don't drink anything.'

Ayesha started cutting the eggs into slices. 'What time did they leave?'

'That's the interesting thing. Amina left on her own, just before one o'clock. There are no buses at that hour so she must have walked back to the medina. It's possible that she took a taxi, although Abderrahim claims that she didn't have enough money for taxis.'

'What was Amina wearing?'

'A red dress.'

'Make-up?'

'Eye shadow and lipstick.'

Ayesha arranged the slices on a serving plate and sprinkled cumin. 'Amina did not go back to the medina.'

'How can you be so sure?'

'No girl would risk her father's wrath by coming home late from a nightclub.'

Karim was unconvinced. 'So you think that Amina's attacker killed her in Guéliz, then stole the cart from outside a *hanoot* in the medina, wheeled it all the way out to Guéliz, put Amina's body into it then wheeled it back to the medina twelve or fifteen hours later? That doesn't make sense.'

'I'm not saying she was killed in Guéliz. All I'm saying is that she wouldn't go home to the medina – at least, not without getting changed first.'

'If she wasn't returning to the medina she must have been heading to Leila's house. If that was the case, why didn't she go back with Leila?'

Ayesha shrugged. 'Ask Leila.'

The front door opened and a few moments later Lalla Fatima and Khadija came into the kitchen, breathless with excitement.

'The apartment is amazing,' said Khadija, taking off her scarf. 'It even has a dishwasher!'

Lalla Fatima started preparing food. 'We chatted to a couple who live downstairs. They have a little girl of four who's just started school.'

'A *private* school!' gushed Khadija.

Karim left them to their chatter and wandered into the *salon*. To his dismay Zak was reclining on the divan, tapping his phone. He sat down warily.

'Ah, Karim, *salaam*. I'm just calculating my charitable donation. This year I think I'll give half my *zakat* to the poor of Hay Mohammedi. The other half I propose to donate to a home for the elderly. Have you given any thought to your *zakat*?'

Karim was so focused on saving for the wedding that he had forgotten he would need to put some money aside for charity.

'Are you discussing *zakat*?' said Lalla Fatima, carrying in a tray laden with dishes. 'I've donated two hundred dirhams ever since I got married. That's twenty-six years now! I haven't missed a single *zakat* – not even when times were hard.'

'You should increase it to two hundred and fifty dirhams, *a lalla*,' Zak laughed. 'Inflation, you know!'

Lalla Fatima chuckled. She arranged plates, cups and cutlery on the table, placing an ashtray in front of Zak. *An ashtray*. Karim could hardly believe his eyes. Zak was going to be allowed to smoke in the *salon* after the meal. If Karim had had the gall to light a cigarette at the table his father would have boxed his ears.

'I've had a good year,' continued Zak. 'So I'm going to give five thousand dirhams.'

Lalla Fatima nodded approvingly. 'Good actions bring a greater reward during Ramadan.'

'Very true, Meema. I'll tell you what – I shall double it to ten thousand!'

Karim jumped up angrily. 'Charity is supposed to be an act of devotion! It's not an excuse to show off!'

Lalla Fatima and Zak exchanged looks of surprise, then Lalla Fatima gave Zak a wink.

'Take no notice of Karim. He's just hungry.'

Sébastien was asleep when his mobile rang.

'Where are you?' said a voice.

It took Sébastien a moment to realise that it was Mohammed Al-Husseini. He grabbed his watch: eight thirty. He had been asleep for four hours. He jumped out of bed and pulled an ironing board from the cupboard. While the iron was heating up he took his suit from the back of the door and pulled on the trousers, trying to remember if Kay had mentioned a dress code. Snatching a crumpled shirt, he ran the iron over it then threw on his jacket and hurtled downstairs. Out in the street he realised he had forgotten the car keys. He dashed back upstairs and plucked the keys from the bedside table. Opening the drawer he took out a wrap of cocaine, tipped half the contents on the surface, cut two lines, snorted them and dashed out again. Back in the *quatrelle* he pressed the phone to his ear.

Kay was in the courtyard, surrounded by guests. 'Hey, birthday boy! Where are you?'

'On the way to the airport.'

'What?' Kay almost spilled her cocktail down her dress.

'I have to pick up Al-Husseini.'

'But the party has started!'

'*Ne t'inquiète pas.* I won't be long.'

'Sébastien, listen to me. Turn around and come straight to the riad. Do you hear?'

'I'll be there in an hour.'

'Everyone's waiting for you!'

'*A très bientôt.*'

'Don't even—'

Sébastien switched off his mobile and threw it on the passenger seat. He turned off Avenue Mohammed Cinq and drove through Hivernage. The streets were empty. The wind had died down and the stars were beginning to shine. Approaching the roundabout, he saw one sign for the airport, the other for the Tizi n' Test pass. If he took the road up to the mountains he could be in Taroudant by morning. He circled the roundabout once . . . twice . . . then, with a howl of resignation that summed up his *bordel* of a life, he turned off to the airport.

His boss was in the parking lot, talking on his phone. Mohammed Al-Husseini was a short man in a suit, impeccably groomed, with an actor's range of expressions. He walked back and forth, gabbling into his phone, widening his eyes in horror or curling his lip in scorn. Sébastien drummed his fingers on the steering wheel. He felt hot and uncomfortable in his suit, impatient to get to the party not because of any pleasure he might derive, or because he feared Kay's wrath, but so that he could get drunk as fast as possible. Eventually Al-Husseini switched off his phone and came over.

'Where the fuck have you been?'

Mohammed wiped the dust from the passenger seat before settling in. Sébastien put his case in the boot and turned the ignition.

'We can park in Bab Taghzout and walk from there.'

'Bab Taghzout? We're not going to Bab Taghzout.'

'You want to go to the Méridien first?' Sébastien was filled with dismay. Going to his boss's hotel would mean more delay while Mohammed took a shower and preened himself in front of the mirror.

'Of course not.'

Sébastien let out a sigh of relief.

'I want to see the Serafina.'

Sébastien choked. 'But the party—'

'I want to see the new night shift you told me about. Come on, let's go! *Allez!*'

'But . . . I planned to show you the site tomorrow morning!'

'Tomorrow morning – *pah!* Better to turn up unannounced. Then we'll catch those lazy bastards off guard.' Al-Husseini wagged his finger. 'I know what Moroccan workers are like, Sébastien. Don't forget – I was working on the Serafina long before you arrived!'

Melanie was in her bedroom looking at herself in the mirror.

When she, Emma and Julie had checked in to The Room of the Ottoman Sultan they had tittered about the name on the door and the painting above the bed depicting half-naked women dancing in front of a reclining sultan. But now that

Melanie was about to leave she realised she would miss the room and its opulent furnishings. Through the latticework window she could hear the babble of voices and the thrum of music.

She ran her hands over her hips. She was wearing the red velvet catsuit she had worn on the girls' last night together. She had lost weight since then and the suit showed off her body to perfection. Was it too revealing? She toyed with the zipper before deciding that it was her last night in Marrakech – she'd never see these people again – *what the hell*. She applied eyeliner and stepped out.

She nearly collided in the passageway with two women, one in a gold lamé bathing costume and the other in a skin-tight dress – no, it wasn't a dress but a *body painting*! Before she'd had time to recover from the shock she was engulfed in sound and spectacle. Acrobats were performing on a long stage, picked out with tramlines of lights that ran diagonally across the courtyard. Techno blared from loudspeakers. Wherever she looked, people were dancing – on chairs, on the roof – even in the swimming pool!

Samira came towards her carrying a tray of cocktails. Instead of her modest caftan she was wearing a white chiffon dress and a headband entwined with roses.

'Hello, Mademoiselle Melanie. Please – your mask. And your tray.' She handed Melanie a white carnival mask with two black teardrops and placed the tray of cocktails in her hands.

'*Bonne soirée!*'

Karim washed the grime and sweat from his body and said his prayers, included two *duas* for forgiveness. He propped himself up on the mattress which he had covered liberally with citronella and flea powder before spreading with his sheet. Tonight, with God's help, he would find rest and solace. He opened the Quran and started reading.

Those who spend in God's Cause in prosperity and in adversity, who repress anger, and who pardon the people; verily, God loves the good-doers.

He grew drowsy. The citronella and the flickering flame were soporific. Just then, something brushed his leg. He lifted the book. Horror! A rat was crouched at the end of the bed. It was the size of his foot, with yellow eyes and a slick of tail. It looked like it had crawled from the bowels of hell. Keeping it in his sights he groped for the fencepost under the bed. Lifting it sideways he slammed it into the rat. *Missed!* The rat sprang off the bed, shot through the door and vanished into the darkness. Karim jumped out of bed and crouched down to examine the mattress. With trepidation he reached into the gash, probing with his finger, and pulled out a chicken bone. Had the rat made a nest in there?

He ran outside and collected several armfuls of brushwood, dead branches and fence posts. After arranging them in a pyre he located a container of fluid that Fouad used to fill the kerosene lamp and poured the contents over the top. Then, using both hands, he heaved the mattress out of the hut and onto the pyre. He tossed a match and the ensemble exploded into flame. He stood and watched for a few minutes, sweat coursing down his face. The wood was bone dry and flames quickly enveloped the mattress, rupturing the ticking like the hide of an animal and laying bare the entrails. Alarmed that the flames might spread to the hut he used a fence post to prod the mattress away. The hairs on the back of his hand vaporised in the heat. Now the fire was dangerously close to the under-growth. Faced with this new threat Karim ran back and forth with containers of water, pouring them over the undergrowth. He tried to stamp the brushwood flat but he tripped on an empty bottle and put his foot in a pile of shit. The mattress was now billowing plumes of acrid smoke.

By the Seven Saints!

The trip to the Serafina had gone well. Mohammed sat in the front seat of the *quatrelle*, watching the night shift, and declared himself satisfied. They didn't stay for longer than ten minutes. Better still – that *salopard* Cherkaoui had gone home!

They walked from the car park to the riad, the Frenchman looming over the five-foot six Qatari. Sébastien buttoned his jacket, took a deep breath and pressed the bell. The door to Dar Zuleika flew open with an outpouring of music and laughter. Sébastien was enveloped in a hug by his friend Yves, a stocky, shaven-headed Frenchman. Other guests crowded around, ruffling Sébastien's hair and slapping him on the back. '*Salut, vieux connard!* Where have you been, you rascal?' Aware of his boss's presence, Sébastien begged everyone to step aside and the two men made their way through the crowd like rock stars. Kay came up, wearing a gold mask, and threw her arms around Sébastien's neck.

'Happy birthday, darling!'

Sébastien was agreeably surprised. If Kay was angry with him for being late she was hiding it well. She held out her hand.

'Mr Al-Husseini, Kay McKenzie. It's a pleasure to meet you.'

'Thank you, Miss McKenzie.' Mohammed took in a black waiter wearing nothing but a mask and a tutu. 'This is a remarkable – ah, party.'

'Can I offer you a *jus panaché*? Some tea? We have orange blossom, verveine, hibiscus, mint – or perhaps you would prefer something stronger?' Kay linked her arm and led him towards the bar.

Sébastien was transfixed. Well-wishers pressed from all sides. A buxom woman whom he half-recognised kissed him on the cheek.

'Happy birthday, Sébastien! It's me – Lucinda!'

A waitress with feathery white wings took him by the hand onto the stage and settled him in a high-backed chair shaped like a throne. He looked up to see a female acrobat on a tightrope, her white costume and gold sash bright against the night sky.

As Kay chatted to Mohammed Al-Husseini she noticed Sébastien gazing around in wonder. So much for his carping! He was like a child at the circus. The entertainers, the food, the costumes – everything had succeeded brilliantly. As for her own forebodings, not one guest had mentioned events at Sidi bel Abbès.

The tightrope walker reached the other end of the rope, turned around and walked back, this time carrying a flaming hoop. Everyone clapped and whooped. Startled by the applause, Momo jumped down from a first-floor railing and ran along the corridor. A bathroom door opened and a giggling couple tumbled out. Momo scurried past them, leapt onto the railing of the second courtyard and hopped onto the branch of an orange tree that had been garlanded with fairy lights. A female guest in a black lace mask looked up.

'There's that darling monkey again!'

Melanie was standing nearby with her tray of cocktails.

'Watch out,' she giggled. 'He's a menace. He stole my sunglasses!'

The guest cocked her head at Melanie's accent. 'An *English* waitress? Now, that's exotic.'

'My name's Mel. I'm a bit tipsy but don't tell anybody.'

'I'm Léticia. Your secret's safe with me – as long as you give me another of those delicious cocktails.' They heard the sound of applause from the other courtyard. 'Shall we take a peek?'

Melanie hesitated. 'I've still got drinks to serve.'

Léticia took four cocktails and tipped them into the flower-bed before handing the last one to Melanie. 'Not any more you haven't!'

They climbed the stairs and took up position on a corner of the balcony. The space on either side of the dais below them was thronged with guests.

Léticia pointed. 'There's the golden boy.'

Melanie leaned forward. *The famous Sébastien.* There was something about the fair-haired man that seemed familiar – a film star quality – but it could have been the fact that he was the only guest not wearing a mask or fancy dress. Kay was standing next to Sébastien holding a microphone. She appealed for silence.

'When I first arrived in Marrakech everyone told me that the best architect in town was Sébastien de Freycinet. He's a magician, they said, *un sorcier*. He conjures palaces out of rubble. As soon as I met him I fell under his spell. But nobody warned me that the magician had a flaw . . . he's always late!' Everyone laughed. 'His excuse for being late tonight is that he's been showing our distinguished guest, Mohammed Al-Husseini, progress on the new Serafina Palace Hotel which, when it opens, is going to be *the* hotel in Marrakech . . . after Dar Zuleika, of course!' There were claps and hoots. 'Like his creations – like that awful car he drives around in – Sébastien de Freycinet is a one-off. Here's to you, my darling – fifty years old today!' Everyone raised their glasses and applauded.

'But wait!' Kay gave a theatrical wave. 'It seems that our magician is not properly attired. What do you say – shall we put on his robe?'

The crowd roared their enthusiasm. As the courtyard darkened a musician started drumming a slow beat on a tam-tam. A spotlight picked out the tightrope walker above the crowd. She looped the ends of her sash to the tightrope then descended in a series of graceful arcs. When her feet touched the dais she tugged and the sash wafted down into her hands. She folded it over itself then folded it a second time. Taking two corners, she held it up with a flourish: it had transformed into a golden robe. Everyone cheered wildly. Another girl in a white leotard came running down the dais, somersaulted twice and landed directly in front of the throne. The spotlight was now on Sébastien. The girl turned and arched her back until her hands grasped the arms of his throne. She performed a slow back bend followed by a handstand, so that her legs were in the air and her head, upside down, was level with Sebastien's. She kissed him on the lips. All around the crowd watched, too spellbound to cheer. The acrobat tucked in her legs, then silently flipped onto the back of the throne, feet balanced on the rim. She was now standing above Sébastien. While her colleague stood ready with the gold robe, the girl on the back of the chair reached down, raised Sébastien's arms and lifted off his jacket. As she folded it over her arm a slim object fell from the pocket and landed on the floor. It looked like a credit card.

Along with the other guests, Melanie and Léticia craned their necks to see better. Kay, who was standing closest, reached down and picked the card up. It was a Moroccan *carte nationale* bearing a photo of a girl in a headscarf and the name: 'Talal, Amina'. Sébastien jumped up with a look of terror and snatched the card from Kay's hand.

Chapter 6

'You're supposed to prevent accidents, not cause them!'

Rachid couldn't restrain his mirth. The taxi was speeding back to town in the grey light of dawn.

'That mattress should have been destroyed long ago! It was full of rats.'

'Rats don't live in mattresses!' laughed Rachid.

'It was covered in stains! The devil alone knows what they were.'

'Couldn't you just get a new one? Did you have to set it on fire?'

Karim started laughing as well. He felt light-headed with exhaustion. He brushed some soot from his trousers. 'What will you say to Fouad about the mattress?'

'*Thenna*, relax. I'll tell him that the lamp fell over and it was only your quick thinking that saved the hut from going up in flames. You'll be a hero by the time I've finished.'

'What do you and Fouad talk about? He hasn't said a word to me all week.'

'It's true he doesn't say much. Mind you, I talk enough for two men.'

'Where's he from?'

'He's Khalifa's nephew or the son of his cousin or something. He's a bit . . .' Rachid made a circling motion around his temple.

'I thought as much,' Karim muttered. 'No one but a half-wit would do that job.'

'Look on the bright side,' said Rachid, 'it's Saturday. You don't have to do anything today except sleep!'

Back home, Karim hung his jacket on the fountain, tiptoed upstairs and took off his dirty sweater and jeans. He was about to step into the shower when his mobile buzzed. For an awful moment he thought it was Khalifa, calling about the fire at the Sherezade, but he recognised the number as Noureddine's.

'*Sbah al-khir*, good morning,' said Noureddine. 'There have been developments in the Talal case. Abderrahim Talal is no longer being charged with his sister's murder.'

'*Al-hamdullilah!*' Karim was so relieved that he didn't think to ask Noureddine why it was necessary to call him at six-thirty in the morning with the news.

'Aziz has made another arrest.'

'Who?'

'The father.'

'*The father?*' Karim clutched at the shower curtain, almost yanking it from its moorings. 'That's crazy!'

'Not so crazy, it seems.'

'Arresting the brother was bad enough! Arresting the father is beyond belief! Aziz has fallen straight into the trap! It's not an honour crime – doesn't he realise? That's what the perpetrator wants us to think! This is total and utter—'

'Omar Talal has confessed.'

Karim's words died in his mouth.

'You're needed at the commissariat,' said Noureddine. 'Now. The old man says he won't sign anything unless you're present. Oh, and before you ask – Abderrahim Talal has not been released. He's been sent to Kenitra for questioning about his membership of Al-Adl wa Al-Ihssane.'

Karim put his clothes back on and walked slowly downstairs. The finches were chirping in their cage and last night's washing up was still in the sink. It felt like a normal weekend. It was only when he closed the front door behind him that he had the sensation that the sky had fallen in.

Momo scampered downstairs and clambered onto a table in the courtyard. He examined the dirty plates and prodded a half-eaten slice of cake. A minute later Driss came out brandishing a broom.

'*Seer!* Away with you!'

Upstairs, Sébastien was sprawled across Kay's bed in his shirt and trousers, eyes closed. Kay was standing grim-faced at the end of the bed.

'Well?'

'Mmm?'

'What was that card doing in your pocket?'

'Nothing.'

'You know whose card it is, don't you? Amina Talal's! The girl whose body was found at the mosque!'

'There are probably lots of Amina Talals.'

'What were you doing with her? Were you *fucking* her?'

'*Calme-toi.*'

'Answer me – or I'll take the card to the police!'

'*T'es folle . . .*'

'You're right, I am crazy – putting up with you all these years, throwing a party with a hundred and fifty guests and God-knows-how-many entertainers. Have you any idea how many months it took to prepare?'

'I didn't want a party.'

'And all the while you're fucking prostitutes! Killing them as well, for all I know!'

Sébastien sat up and scratched his belly. 'She wasn't a prostitute.'

'Who was she, then?'

'She was looking for a job.'

Kay was thrown off guard. 'What do you mean, *looking for a job*?'

Sébastien gave a yawn. 'Lot of girls come to our company for jobs. Half of Marrakech wants to work at the Serafina. The girl turned up at the offices last week. As our HR person was away the receptionist asked me to interview her.'

Kay was suspicious. 'Why did she give you her *carte nationale*?'

'Instead of acting like the fucking Gestapo, how about making some coffee?'

Sébastien got off the bed and walked unsteadily to the kitchen, followed by Kay. His speech was slurred. 'When a Moroccan applies for a job they have to produce proof of identity. Surely you know that! The girl seemed well quali-fied – she'd just finished a diploma in *hôtellerie* – and I told her to leave her student card so we could check her references. She didn't have the card with her so she left her *carte nationale* instead. She said she would come and collect it but she never showed up. I was going to drop the card off at her college but forgot.' He filled the cafetière with hot water. When Kay didn't respond, he turned around. '*Quoi?* You think I killed her?'

'No. But—'

'I didn't even realise that the girl was the same one who was found dead at Sidi bel Abbès. *La pauvre*, she spoke good French and English – she would easily have got a job as a desk clerk, perhaps even as a trainee manager.'

Kay held up the card, which had been lying on the table.

'What are you going to do with this?'

'*Je m'en fous*, I don't give a fuck.'

Kay knew that at any minute Sébastien would launch into one of his *I'm too busy to think about anything* speeches and storm off to the Palmeraie. She placed the card on the kitchen shelf and watched him pour two cups of coffee.

Most of the faithful were still in bed, keen to prolong sleep and shorten the hours of fasting as far as possible. Karim barely noticed the handful of souls in the souks as he hurried, pale-faced, to the commissariat. He wondered what he'd find when he got there. He'd seen Omar Talal on Monday evening when he identified Amina's body at the mortuary, the way he crumpled to the floor – that was not the reaction of a man who had killed his daughter!

As he crossed the Jemaa, squinting in the early morning

sunshine, he formulated a defence for Omar, one that would convince Aziz. If Omar Talal was the sort of man who would kill his daughter for visiting a nightclub then, as Ayesha had pointed out, it was inconceivable that the daughter would risk her life by returning home from the nightclub dressed in dancing clothes. But how could he help Omar if he'd already confessed?

Bouchaïb was his usual cheery self. 'Another early start? You'll be coming in at night-time next! Did you hear the news?'

'What news?'

'Cases of heatstroke are up. Twelve dead so far!'

Pockmark Features showed Karim into the interrogation room – the same room from which he'd unceremoniously ejected him two days earlier. Aziz was sitting at the table facing a shapeless brown sack. It took Karim a moment to recognise the sack as Omar Talal, dressed in his *jellaba*, his lips moving as he ran his fingers over a string of prayer beads. Karim went straight to him.

'*Salaam ou alikum a sidi*,' he said gently. 'It's Karim *wld* Brahim, Karim son of Brahim.'

Si Omar's cheeks were hollow and his skin had a sickly yellow colour. 'Praise be to Allah, Allah the Merciful . . .'

'I'm the son of Brahim Belkacem.'

'Praise be to Allah, Allah the Merciful . . .'

'Brahim was my father, your friend. *Wesh aqeltee alih?* Do you remember him?'

Omar Talal stared at his beads. 'Allah is all-knowing, all-wise . . . I seek pardon from Allah . . .'

Aziz jumped up. 'This is a waste of time! The rascal has already admitted he did it!'

'He's a *hajj*!' Karim cried. 'He's been to Mecca! Show some respect!'

Aziz leaned aggressively across the table. 'Do you admit killing your daughter?'

'. . . Glory be to Allah . . .'

'Come on, old man. She came back from some repulsive African nightclub stinking of tobacco and alcohol. You did what any respectable father would do – you gave her a thrashing. But you lost your temper, didn't you? You hit her too hard, she fell and broke her head, isn't that what happened?'

'. . . Praise be to Allah the Forgiving . . .'

'Are you guilty? Yes or no? Tell us!'

'The man's not well!' Karim exclaimed. 'He needs a doctor!'

A croak came from Omar Talal. Pockmark Features leaned over him.

'What was that, old man? What did you say? Are you guilty?'

'Mmm.'

'Is that a *yes*?'

Omar held out his palms. 'We are all guilty.'

Pockmark Features rolled his eyes. Aziz pushed a paper and pen across the table. 'Sign.'

'In the name of Allah who sees all . . .'

Pockmark Features grabbed Omar by the shoulder. 'For the love of God, you've admitted you did it, you old fool. Just sign the fucking paper!'

'Blasphemer!' Karim cried, pulling away Pockmark's hand and shielding Omar as if he was a child being attacked by dogs.

There was a silence. Si Omar looked at each of the three men in turn. 'We are all guilty,' he smiled sadly. 'Do you not see? We are all guilty. *Ma shallah!*'

'Sign!' said Aziz, slamming the pen on the table.

Si Omar held up his thumb.

'What do you want, old man?' Aziz softened his tone, as if he'd had a sudden realisation. 'This?' He held up an inkpad.

Omar Talal gave a gesture of assent. Aziz carried the inkpad around the table and placed it before him. Omar put his thumb on the ink.

Karim was aghast. 'Think what you're doing, Si Omar – please! I beseech you!'

Omar pressed his thumb slowly down onto the piece of paper, leaving a black thumb print. In a flash Aziz snatched the paper away. Pockmark Features pulled Si Omar to his feet and dragged him to the door. Aziz followed, glancing over his shoulder at Karim.

'You can go.'

Karim sank in the chair, horrified. Everything had happened so fast. Omar Talal had just confessed to killing his own daughter. The poor fool was so far gone that he would have confessed to anything. He had signed his own death sentence, in front of three police officers. He had signed with his thumb. *His thumb!* Karim jumped up and raced down the corridor, stooping to grab one of Si Omar's yellow slippers.

Out in the forecourt Pockmark Features was bundling Si Omar into the back of a police car. Aziz was giving instructions to the driver.

'Stop!' cried Karim. '*Houwa oomee!* He's illiterate! Omar Talal – he can't read or write!'

Aziz stared at Karim blankly.

'Don't you understand? He couldn't have written the sign!'

'Sign?' replied Aziz. 'What sign?'

He banged his fist on the roof of the car and it sped off.

The *traiteur* was a tall, jovial man. He sat in the foyer of his banqueting room, under the light of a single chandelier, talking to Karim and Lalla Fatima about modern fashions.

'Some couples don't bother with dancing. Some don't even bother with music. It's different from the old days, isn't that right, Lalla? I remember when this room had an orchestra playing until six in the morning!'

Karim was stony-faced. 'Can we get down to the matter of my sister's wedding?'

'Of course.' The *traiteur* took a notebook from the pocket of his *gandora* and started making a list. '*Aiwa*, let's see now . . . one barbecued lamb *mechaoui* . . . rice, salad and dessert for a hundred people . . .'

'And a video,' prompted Lalla Fatima.

'Of course: a video.'

While the *traiteur* chatted away, Karim replayed the dismal scene in the commissariat. He had had a chance to intervene, to mitigate the cataclysm engulfing the Talal family, and he had blown it. Events now had taken on a momentum of their own. Si Omar would not survive for any length of time in Boulmharez prison. Karim had seen conditions in the cells. Even a man with youth and health would struggle. Going back over the interrogation, however, he found one scrap of information, one straw to cling to. Aziz had unwittingly let slip that the club was African. Karim took out his mobile and tapped in his browser. A result came up: 'Club Afrique, Rue Oum er Rabia, Guéliz'.

The *traiteur* was singing the praises of a video cameraman that he knew. 'He makes documentaries for national television! And he charges only two thousand dirhams for weddings!'

'*Bezzaf*, too much,' Karim said sharply, without raising his eyes from his phone. 'We need to look elsewhere, or get him to reduce his price. What about musicians?'

'I can get you four musicians with tambourine, violin, lute and electric keyboard for two thousand dirhams. Another five hundred and you can have a singer.'

Lalla Fatima mentioned the name of the Turkish singer that Khadija had requested. The *traiteur* whistled through his teeth. 'Someone like that would charge over six thousand dirhams.'

'Too much.'

Lalla Fatima implored Karim to relent. 'Khadija has her heart set on that singer!'

'The Turk or the guests. Khadija must choose. If she wants the Turk she has to have fewer guests.'

The *traiteur* broke the silence that followed. 'I assume you want palanquins?'

Lalla Fatima was enthusiastic. 'Of course!'

'Two palanquins with five bearers apiece, in costume, let's see now, two thousand dirhams.'

'Does everything cost two thousand dirhams?' Karim exploded. The idea of his brother-in-law being carried around like a pasha set his teeth on edge. 'We're not paying for palanquins!'

His mother looked shocked. 'You can't have a wedding without palanquins!'

'That's not strictly true, Lalla,' the *traiteur* said, trying to defuse the situation. 'The families from the villages, for example, they don't usually have palanquins.'

'Are you implying that we're poor?' Karim snapped.

'Not at all, sir!' The *traiteur* realised he was fighting a losing battle. 'Let me see if I can come up with a figure that is acceptable to you.' He took out a calculator. 'Food and drink for one hundred and twenty guests—'

'A *hundred* guests.'

'A hundred guests . . . and waiters . . . and the Turkish singer . . . and filming . . . that makes fifty-six thousand six hundred and forty dirhams. Shall we say fifty-five thousand?'

'Forty thousand. That's our last offer,' said Karim.

The *traiteur* looked affronted. 'By Allah, I don't know what to say, *a sidi*! I tell you what: I will give you a five-thousand discount in honour of your dead father – there you have it: fifty thousand.'

'Forty-two thousand or we take our custom elsewhere.'

'I cannot go any lower, *a sidi*. I'd be taking the food out of my children's mouths!'

Karim helped Lalla Fatima to get up.

'Very well,' the *traiteur* sighed. 'Forty-two thousand. Let us shake hands.'

Karim took a roll of banknotes from his pocket. 'Here's ten thousand. I'll give you another twenty thousand at the end of the month.'

Out in the street Lalla Fatima unfurled her parasol. The heat and the glare were overwhelming. Karim suggested to his mother that they take a taxi but Lalla Fatima refused; they needed to save money for the wedding, even with the bargain that Karim had struck.

The flight to Manchester was carrying few passengers. Melanie lay across a whole row of seats, eyes closed, trying not to inhale the sickly aroma of toasted cheese wafting from the seat behind her. The party had passed in a blur. It was still going on in her head, woozy beats and odd flashes, fragments of conversation, laughter. She couldn't wait to tell Emma and Julie about the tightrope walker, and the Japanese food, and the good-looking Italian guy with the skin-tight trousers who pressed his body against hers at the door to her bedroom. Who knows where that would have led if Driss hadn't interrupted them, begging her to come quickly as the taxi was waiting? Stumbling across the debris-strewn courtyard she'd felt a pang of guilt as she passed the flowerbed where Léticia had emptied the cocktails. Fortunately, Kay had been too wrapped up with Sébastien to notice.

Sitting up, her eyes half-open, Melanie swigged from the bottle of Sidi Ali that she'd wedged in the seat pocket. She flopped down again.

She suddenly remembered where she'd seen Sébastien before.

Lalla Fatima moved slowly along the white-hot alleyway, leaning on her son's arm, pausing every few seconds to mop her forehead or catch her breath. Karim was worried that she might faint at any moment. Here and there a tattered palmetto afforded some protection. They sheltered in tunnels and covered passageways, sharing the shade with cats and beggars. When they reached the souks a kindly shopkeeper offered his stool. As she sat down, shaking, Karim implored his mother to drink some water, to break her fast in the name of God the Merciful, but she refused.

They sat for a time and watched the passers-by: a stooped old man in a white *jellaba* returning from midday prayers; a young woman with a baby on her back, buying rice and olives. The shopkeeper offered Lalla Fatima the cardboard from a notepad and she fanned herself while Karim crouched by her side.

'Meema, I've been meaning to ask you something. Why did my father fall out with Omar Talal?'

Lalla Fatima stopped fanning. 'Why do you ask?'

'I'm curious.'

'You know the story.'

'Tell me again.'

Lalla Fatima let out a sigh. 'Your father and Omar had been friends ever since their boyhood in the mountains. They herded their family's goats together. They came to Marrakech together. They found jobs together. But afterwards your father went to night school. He learned to read and write and managed to get a position as an accountant.'

Karim thought of the photograph on Lalla Fatima's bedside table. Taken in a studio, it showed a well-groomed figure in a dark suit standing with one foot raised, his arm on his knee.

'Omar used the money he had saved to go on a pilgrimage. He was very proud of the fact that he was the first man from his village to go to Mecca. When Amina was born he and your father made a vow to betroth the two of you in marriage, as was the custom in Chleuh families, but with the passing of the years the men saw each other less and less. They drifted apart.'

'I remember them arguing when we were at Omar's house.'

Lalla Fatima nodded. 'Omar accused your father of being interested only in money. Your father told Omar that he'd become a narrow-minded zealot. *Safee* – it was over.' She put the cardboard down. 'They never spoke to each other again.'

'Mother,' Karim began gently, 'I was at the commissariat this morning. Si Omar – he was there. With two police officers. In a room. He confessed to killing Amina.'

A look of agony crossed Lalla Fatima's face. '*Ashnou hadshee lee katguliya?* What are you saying? Omar was a strict father but he loved his daughter! He wouldn't kill her, not in a thousand years! What did they do to him? Did they force him to confess? God let it not be so!' Her eyes filled with tears. 'Why can't they leave that poor family alone and find the man who committed this awful crime?'

Karim remained silent, staring at the ground and twiddling the handle of the parasol between his fingers. His mother suddenly got to her feet.

'Take me home. I'm going to see Lalla Hanane.'

Sébastien knocked on the door of the hotel room.

'Ah, Sébastien!' Mohammed Al-Husseini opened the door in his dressing gown, holding a cup of coffee. 'Where's Jamal?'

Typical, thought Sébastien: straight down to business, not a word of thanks for the party.

'He'll be here shortly.'

While Mohammed took a shower Sébastien sat at the coffee table and took stock of what had happened at Dar Zuleika. He'd been as surprised as everyone else when the card fell from his pocket. He'd forgotten it was there. Luckily, the stage was raised and Mohammed – like the other guests – had been either too far away or too low down to see what it was. As for Kay, he was still unsure if he'd succeeded in convincing her. He'd taken every opportunity to lavish praise on the party and to brush off the card as an oversight.

He looked around the hotel room. It was a two-room suite, the type that Mohammed preferred. His boss could have afforded the Mansour, or even the Royal Golf Palmeraie, which was only minutes away from the Serafina. But he opted for the Méridien. It was functional, inexpensive, anonymous: he could slip in and out without anyone keeping tabs or asking questions.

Mohammed reappeared in a long-sleeved white shirt and blue jeans. 'Those men on the night shift. How much are you paying them?'

'A hundred and fifty.'

'They're good workers? Not deadbeats or lowlifes that nobody else wants?'

'They're all experienced. Hassan checked. Most of the other building sites are closed for Ramadan so we could take our pick.'

'Ha!' Mohammed chortled. 'We keep going while everyone else sleeps. I like it!'

There was a knock and Jamal appeared at the door. Jamal Boussoufa was an amiable, broad-shouldered bear of a man who ran a successful Casablanca interior design practice. Sébastien found him a useful ally in the face of a difficult boss.

'*Mehrba, tafaddal, tafaddal, kayf haalek?*' Mohammed gave a broad smile. 'Welcome, come in, how are you?'

'Everything is fine, praise God.' Jamal sat at the coffee table. After a few minutes of small talk he opened his laptop and looked at the others. 'I'm concerned about timings.' The Serafina had been scheduled to open in the New Year but Mohammed had brought the launch forward by two months when he learned that a competitor was planning to open a rival hotel in December.

'To hell with the timings!' Mohammed breezed. 'Let's see what you've got!'

As Jamal went through the latest round of refinements Sébastien nodded in agreement. He liked Jamal's idea of a white stucco ceiling for the atrium and a thirty-foot reception desk in polished travertine. Jamal had also come up with an ingenious scheme to bring the Line of Water into the building, solving a long-running argument over where the Line of Water should end. When Jamal had finished Mohammed gave his verdict.

'There's no chandelier.'

Jamal was caught off-guard. 'Chandelier? We haven't got enough time to have a chandelier made, do you really—?'

'Buy one, for fuck's sake! You've heard of the Internet, haven't you? And where's my marble floor?'

'I thought Ouarzazate stone would make a better—'

'I asked you for marble.'

'Marble is expensive, around twenty-nine euros a metre.'

'Where are you getting the fucking stuff from – Beverly Hills?'

Beads of sweat appeared on Jamal's forehead. 'You definitely want marble?'

'I said I wanted marble eight weeks ago – weren't you listening? And make sure it's decent material. I don't want a load of off-cuts. Oh, and I hate that water in the restaurant. It looks like a fucking swimming pool.'

While Sébastien felt disappointed on behalf of his colleague he also felt relief that, for once, he wasn't on the receiving end of Al-Husseini's temper. He tried to cheer Jamal up as he drove him back to the train station.

'Working for him has shortened my life, I swear to God. He made me late for the party last night – my fiftieth birthday party! We arrived two hours after everyone else because he insisted on being taken to see the site first. I think he did it deliberately.'

Jamal smiled. 'Was he a nuisance at the party?'

'He stood in the corner ogling the women but, *grâce à Dieu*, he didn't make advances. I saw him drink a cocktail when he thought no one was looking. Come to think of it, he's probably suffering from a hangover – that's why he was in such a foul mood. I'm sure he'll come around to your ideas in the end. You might have to find him a chandelier, however!'

They drove down Mohammed Cinq, the hot wind in their faces. 'Why's he still using you as a taxi driver?' asked Jamal when they reached the station. 'Why doesn't he hire a chauffeur?'

'Chauffeurs talk. He trusts me not to tell tales about him.'

'Yes, but – this car – I love it, but it's not exactly a limousine.'

'Limousines cost money,' chuckled Sébastien, 'You know Mohammed – *economy before style.*'

Can a man lose his faith? Can a once-devout Muslim turn away from his religion? As Karim spread his prayer mat in the courtyard he tried to remember when his father had stopped going to the mosque. Was it after the quarrel with Si Omar?

When Karim was a young boy his father made him learn ten verses of the Quran every day. There was a test after dinner and he was forbidden from going to bed until he could recite the verses fluently. On Saturdays he had to recite all fifty verses in front of friends or neighbours who happened to be visiting. Then, when Karim was eight – around the time they made that fateful visit to the Talal house – the lessons stopped. His father shut himself away and started reading the works of Sufi mystics like Ibn Arabi. He looked down on those who made the *haj*, saying they were trying to buy their way into heaven. Towards the end of his life he told Karim that the only path was the path of one's conscience.

Karim glanced at the door of his father's old study. It had been taken over by Lalla Fatima when she could no longer manage the stairs. He checked his watch. She'd been asleep for two hours. She'd returned in a state of total exhaustion from visiting Hanane. Although Karim feared for his mother's health, he was glad that she had gone to the other woman in her hour of need. She had managed to overlook the long-standing feud between the families, shown greater forbearance than her late husband. He, Karim, should also strive to be conciliatory, especially in his dealings with Ayesha. Resentments hardened if neither party was prepared to back down.

Karim put his hands to his chest and prayed to the One God who made the heaven above and the earth beneath and the sea and all that is therein, adding a *dua* of supplication to remove conceit and arrogance from his heart. He was about to wake his mother when the front door slammed and Ayesha came in, dangling a chicken. Karim had so much to tell her that he didn't know where to begin. While he poured out the details of Omar Talal's arrest she stood silently by the fountain, listening.

'Do you know what I think?' she said at last.

'What?' Karim asked eagerly.

'I think you need to slow down.'

'What are you talking about?' said Karim, following her into the kitchen.

'You seem overwrought. These last few days . . . you haven't been yourself.'

Karim sighed. 'I have said things I regret. I have allowed myself to become agitated by recent events and have taken that agitation out on others.'

Ayesha sat at the table, placed a bucket between her feet and started plucking the chicken.

'You should have told me about your betrothal to Amina Talal.'

'It was nothing, I swear to you! I was just a boy; it was like being told that my name had been put down for college when I reached sixteen. It was abstract, it had no meaning. I had forgotten all about it until Monday night.'

Ayesha nodded. She tugged the feathers with a quick downward motion, four or five at a time. 'You're sure there was a sign in the cart when you found Amina's body?'

'One doesn't imagine something like that. It was written on a piece of cardboard the size of a Quranic recitation tablet.'

'Did anyone else see it?'

'None of the men who were present mentioned it.' Karim watched Ayesha turn the chicken over and start plucking the feathers on the other side. She was good with her hands, he reflected. When one of the family had a practical task they went to Ayesha. She had mastered Lalla Fatima's recipes by the age of twelve and could dismantle a mobile phone by fourteen. If she were the one leaving to get married, he thought wryly, the household would fall apart.

'You must go back to Sidi bel Abbès,' she said. 'Find witnesses.'

'There weren't any witnesses.'

'Are you sure?'

'There may have been a beggar or two outside the mosque but they're all blind.'

'Blind people hear things.'

'Not the ones at Sidi bel Abbès! They're touched by the *djinn*. All they hear are the voices in their heads.'

'As you wish.' Ayesha removed the last feathers from the carcass with the blade of a knife then stood up and brushed the feathers from her lap. She placed the bird upside down in the sink and washed her hands. She turned around and wrinkled her nose.

'You stink of smoke.'

Karim realised that he was still wearing his dirty clothes from last night. He told Ayesha about his adventure with the fire and her face broke into a smile. When he managed to make her smile like that Karim felt his heart leap.

'Why don't you take the mattress from the roof?' she asked.

'That old thing? It wouldn't fit in the taxi. It probably wouldn't fit in the hut, either! Why don't we go to Bab el-Khemis? We can wander around the market and look for a mattress together. There's always so much to see on a Saturday!'

'*Momken*, perhaps.' She rolled up her sleeves and started chopping some carrots. 'Was Amina very beautiful?'

Karim showed her the photograph that Abderrahim had given him. It was of a girl in headscarf with high cheekbones, dark eyebrows and an impish smile. Ayesha stared at it for a long while. When she looked up her eyes were moist.

'How could anyone kill such a beautiful girl?'

While the staff were clearing up Kay climbed to the roof to think. The party had been worth the months of planning. She had re-established herself as a doyenne of the Marrakech social scene and two journalists were returning to write profiles. The only sour note had been the card in Sébastien's pocket.

She gazed over the roofs to Sidi bel Abbès. She had stood in the same spot on the day she met Sébastien. She had been thirty-five, newly divorced, *in her prime* as her friends assured her when she was fretting over what to do with her life. She had found the riad online. The property was dilapidated and far from the old square, but she needed a project and everyone said that Marrakech was on the up, so she took the next flight from Gatwick.

Her first impressions were not encouraging. The rooms were dark and warren-like and she had to hold her nose as she peered at the hole in the floor that served as a toilet. Nevertheless, the riad was vast and the price, according to the estate agent, was a steal. When Kay asked how one would go about restoring such a heap the agent put her in touch with Sébastien. He turned up at the riad the same afternoon.

Roaming the building, measuring tape in hand, Sébastien indicated with a sweep of his arm where he would put in a staircase or bathroom. He began chalking outlines on walls until Kay, laughing, pointed out that the riad wasn't hers yet. While they were chatting, Kay's solicitor called from London with the news that Jack was contesting the divorce settlement.

Kay told Sébastien everything – how Jack had squandered their money, slept around, poured scorn on her creative ambitions. Sébastien declared that it was *le destin* that had brought her to Marrakech. He said that he, too, had been guided by fate; that here, amid the intense light and red earth, he had found fulfilment. Kay was enraptured. How refreshing to meet a man who talked about his feelings, who disdained material things! She loved his enthusiasm, the way he touched her arm or gesticulated when he wanted to make a point, oblivious to the Moroccan housewife hovering nearby with a tray of mint tea. He made her feel giddy with possibilities. Restoring a riad was daring, crazy, the opposite of the domesticated life she had led in Belsize Park. As they stood on the roof together, watching the swifts soar and swoop across the evening sky, Kay had had a sense that her life – the life she was meant to lead – was about to begin.

Samira's voice called up from the courtyard. '*Le riad est prêt, madame.*'

'*J'arrive.*'

Kay walked downstairs. It was a coincidence, she decided, that Amina Talal had applied for a job the week before she died. She was not a prostitute, simply a girl who dreamed of the opportunities that Western women like herself took for granted.

At Bab al-Khemis Karim and Ayesha wandered happily among the wardrobes and old bathtubs. Ayesha peered inside a fridge freezer.

'Khadija and Zak should come here to furnish their apartment.'

Karim laughed. 'Zak doesn't need to visit second-hand markets. He's a wealthy man.' He treated Ayesha to a new cover for her mobile phone and they bought a mattress wrapped in polythene that the stallholder assured them was a genuine Simmons – *d'origine*! Karim lugged it to the waiting area for taxis and they sat on a wall, watching shoppers load their purchases.

'I want to go on a journey,' Ayesha murmured dreamily.

'Where to?'

'The Zat Valley.'

Karim was taken by surprise. 'Why do you want to go there?'

'I was born in Zat,' Ayesha smiled. 'Si Brahim told me.'

Karim's mouth fell open. He was unaware of Ayesha's origins. She had been left on their doorstep when the mountain women came down to sell their produce. How could Si Brahim have known if Ayesha's mother came from Zat, rather than Amizmiz or Ouirgane? Ayesha slid her hands under the backs of her thighs and swung her legs.

'You see? You're not the only one who's got secrets!'

'When did he tell you?'

'The year before he died, while you were at college. Zat is a green valley with a rushing river. There aren't roads, not proper ones. Si Brahim said there's a spring in a little place called Tighdouine that produces bubbly water.'

'Like Ouelmes?'

'Sweeter! He said it's the sweetest water in the Maghreb. There are sheep on the hillside with curly horns and a hundred types of butterfly.'

Karim pictured the scene. 'It sounds beautiful.'

Ayesha gave him a sidelong glance. 'You could take me there on your *moto*.'

Karim laughed. 'It's being repaired! And the mechanic can't get any spare parts.'

'When it's fixed, *inshallah*.'

'Even when my scooter's working it only does thirty-five

kilometres an hour! How do you think it's going to get up a mountain?'

Ayesha's expression hardened. She jumped down from the wall. '*Khasnee nimshee.* I have to go. Lalla Fatima will be waiting.'

Karim gave her money to hire a handcart for the mattress then hailed a taxi to Guéliz.

Oum er-Rabia street was in a part of the new town that Karim didn't know. Modern apartment buildings lined one side of the road, hotels and restaurants the other. Walking past the restaurants Karim came to a sign with a silhouette of a girl dancing. Underneath was the name 'Club Afrique'. The night-club was dark and the doors were padlocked. As he pressed his face to a window he heard a man calling.

'The club is closed for Ramadan, *a sidi.*'

A parking attendant was standing in the road. He was in his seventies and wore a blue Atlas Peintures work coat over shirt and trousers.

'*Salaam ou alikum!*' Karim smiled. He cast around at the empty streets. 'This seems like a quiet neighbourhood.'

'It gets busy. You can't get a parking space after nine.'

'Were you working on Sunday night?'

'I work here every night. Have done for twenty-nine years!' The man flipped a coin in the air and caught it in his palm.

Karim walked over and took the photo of Amina Talal from his pocket. 'Did you see this girl on Sunday night?'

'Is she your girlfriend?' The attendant held the photo at arm's length and squinted. 'Yes, she was here.'

'You're sure?'

'I know all the girls – the pretty ones anyway! She was wearing a red dress. She came with her friend – she's pretty, as well. They've been before.'

'Did you see the girl with the red dress leave the club?'

The attendant nodded.

'With her friend?'

The attendant pondered the question. 'No. She left with a *berranee*. A foreigner.'

'A foreigner?' Karim could feel his body tense. 'What sort of foreigner?'

'*Ma arfch*. I don't know . . . he was wearing a suit, that's all I remember. There was a crowd outside the club, everyone was waiting for drivers or looking for taxis. I made good tips that night!'

'Did they take a taxi?'

The old man scratched his chin. 'I don't know. I was going back and forth all night, fetching taxis, helping drivers get their cars out – I didn't stop for a minute. Has she run off then, your girlfriend?'

Karim hesitated. 'In a manner of speaking.'

'She looked drunk.'

'*Drunk?*'

'She was swaying like a palm tree. Mind you, most of the girls who come here like to drink alcohol.'

Karim considered this information. Then he reached into his pocket and handed the attendant a ten-dirham coin.

The old man held the coin to his forehead. 'God keep you and protect you! God reward you a thousand times!'

Rachid strapped the mattress to the roof of the taxi. It was an hour after sunset and the lights were on in the shops, *coiffeurs* and food stalls of Bab Taghzout.

'How much did you pay? Four hundred? Not bad. Dolidol mattresses are the best – that's what they say on TV. Mind you, you can't trust anything they say on TV, it's all lies and nonsense.'

'It was two nights' pay,' Karim grumbled.

'*Maalesh*, it's better than that filthy old one.' Rachid leaned out of the window and reached up to push the mattress into position. 'I would buy a new jacket if I had the money but my wife says she needs all our money to buy food.'

'Our money's not our own anymore,' Karim agreed.

'The only things I buy are cigarettes and CDs,' Rachid said, as he pulled out of the square. 'Listen to this – Shreya Ghoshal. What a voice, eh?'

Karim picked up the cover of the CD. The singer sounded to him like a wailing cat. It wasn't proper, melodic singing like Fairouz, but he kept his opinion to himself. 'Are the CDs knock-offs?'

Rachid nodded. 'Three dirhams in the souk.'

Karim removed the insert. It was a poor-quality photocopy, the colours blurred like the wrappers of the DVDs that Khadija bought. The market for counterfeit goods went well beyond bags and watches, he reflected.

'Bollywood music seems very popular in the Maghreb.'

'I know every singer,' Rachid enthused, 'the women, anyway. My favourites are Shreya Ghoshal and Sunidhi Chauhan – voices like angels. Well, you have to have company if you're working nights, *iyek*?'

As they drove past the walls the shops and *harira* stalls gave way to packed cafés and restaurants. The whole of Marrakech seemed to be out celebrating.

'Do you always work nights?' Karim asked.

Rachid put a pistachio nut in his mouth and cracked the shell with his teeth. 'I alternate. At the moment I'm on nights.'

'You must know all the nightclubs.'

'Naturally! I'm a taxi driver, aren't I?'

'Have you heard of a place called Club Afrique?'

'Club Afrique?' Rachid slowed down. 'Yes – it's behind the Hotel de Marrakech. Why?'

Karim shrugged his shoulders. 'I'm curious.'

Rachid laughed. 'You haven't got the money, my brother. The women there . . .' He rubbed his thumb and forefinger together.

'What – they're prostitutes?'

'That's what I've heard.' Rachid cracked another pistachio. 'Go to Pacha or the Three Fives. I know the doormen, they'll let you in free.'

'Do you know the doormen at Club Afrique?'

'I don't bother with the place, to tell you the truth. Too small. And it closes early, so everyone leaves at the same time. The roads are more congested than Marjane on a Friday night. The big, out-of-town clubs have their own parking and they stay open until five so there's a steady stream of people. Some nights that's all I do

– go back and forth to Pacha or Three Fives, sixty dirhams one way. Four trips and I've made enough for the night.'

'What time does Club Afrique close?'

Rachid lit a cigarette. 'Two o'clock.'

Karim was so absorbed in the conversation that he had forgotten about the fire. He was startled, therefore, to see Fouad standing outside the Sherezade, poking the half-burnt mattress. Smoke was rising from the embers and there was a stench of burning rubber.

Rachid found the scene highly amusing but Karim jumped out and went straight to Fouad. 'Everything good?'

'*Mashee mezyan*, not good.'

For the split-second that Fouad looked up Karim registered that had he sharp, darting eyes; not the eyes of a half-wit, but rather of someone pathologically shy, unused to social situations.

'It was old and dirty,' Karim said gently. 'I've bought a new one – a better one.'

'Did you hear that? He's got you a new mattress!' Rachid said in a loud voice, untying the mattress from the roof rack. 'Here, take it inside. *Andek!* Careful! Don't drag it on the ground!'

While Fouad was struggling with his burden, Karim picked up his stick and tried to scatter the blackened remnants of rubber and ticking.

'I've got a better idea,' said Rachid, opening the boot of the taxi. He pulled out a jerry can of petrol and poured it over the heap. Flames shot in the air. Within minutes the old mattress was a pile of ashes.

As the taxi drove off, Rachid leaned out of the window. 'Sleep well, my brother!'

Chapter 7

Si Brahim had been fond of maxims. *Never sleep on an empty stomach. Eat breakfast like a king, lunch like a prince and dinner like a beggar. Treat Ramadan like a journey; use the prayers as staging posts during the day and the meals as beacons during the night.*

Karim had eaten the food that Ayesha had prepared. He had drunk a litre of water and said his prayers, yet sleep still eluded him. He sat on the step and stared into the hot night. How many nightwatchmen had sat on the step before him, chewing their nails, smoking their cigarettes, pining for their loves? Visible in the light from the lantern were rags, empty bottles, a discarded takeaway carton. No wonder there were rats. He half-hoped another would appear so that he could exact revenge. All that remained of the fire was an area of blackened ground and a lingering smell of burnt rubber. Wearily, he picked up his torch and made his rounds.

His father once told him that the king needed honest subjects; that, after the Years of Lead, the kingdom was going through a golden age – a period of openness and prosperity when hard work and a clear conscience were all that a man needed to succeed. Yet here he was, tramping around a rat-infested wasteland in the middle of the night, while evidence about Amina Talal's murder was ignored and his colleagues laughed behind his back. He'd have been better off herding goats in the mountains!

Whoa! He was on the edge of a black void. One step further and he would have fallen into the pool. He shone the torch. Tiles were coming away from the side. At the deep end dangled a rusting ladder covered with bird droppings. He kicked a stone and watched it skitter along the bottom, coming to rest among dried eucalyptus leaves.

Returning to the standpipe, Karim washed his hands and feet. He found an unscorched area of ground and unrolled his mat towards the east. He held out his hands palm upward, then folded them against his chest.

Surely my prayer and my sacrifice and my life and my death are for God, Lord of the Worlds, who has no equal.

After half an hour he went inside and settled on the new mattress. Covered with the sheet, it felt little different to the old one, spongy and lifeless. He closed his eyes, Nothing. So much for a Simmons *d'origine*! He slapped a mosquito and lay on his back, gazing up at the cobwebs. He turned on his side. Sweat collected at the base of his back. Somewhere a cock crowed. He recited the 109th surah in his head. He said it again, eleven times, to keep Shaitan away and bring on sleep. Through the open door the abandoned building rose in the moonlight. Rachid would be driving the last customers home from Pacha. His mother and sisters would be eating *suhour*, their last meal of the night.

As the minutes passed he could make out greens and mauves in the half-light, then the drum of the cement mixer and the branches of the cypress trees. Dawn came and went, the pink clouds dissolving in a sea of blue. With a heavy sigh, he extinguished the lamp. Then he sat on the step with his head in his hands until taxi 1547 arrived and Fouad stepped out. This time Karim was the one who stumbled past without speaking.

'Good morning, my friend,' said Rachid cheerily. '*Wesh naastee mezyan?*'

'No, I didn't sleep well,' Karim replied, his shoes crunching on pistachio shells. 'In fact, I didn't sleep at all.'

'Even with your new mattress? God preserve you! Perhaps you should have bought a Dolidol. I told you they were the best.'

'That hut is cursed. Nobody could sleep there.'

Rachid laughed. 'Fouad manages to sleep.'

'Is that what he does all day – sleep?'

'I have no idea. He could spend the whole day with his cock in his hand for all I know.'

Karim stared out of the window. His head was splitting and Rachid's banter and the *la-leely-la* of his infernal Bollywood music were making it worse. As they approached the roundabout at the end of Avenue Guemassa something made him sit up.

'Look!'

They were driving past the billboard. The cleavage of the semi-clad woman was covered with black paint. 'The poster – it's been . . . censored!'

'Yes. I saw it earlier,' sighed Rachid. 'Someone got hold of a ladder and a pot of paint. They must have been quick. It was already done when I drove past at four.'

'Who do you think did it?'

'Fanatics. The bearded ones. Who else?'

Karim remembered the conversation he'd overheard at the mosque. 'People are getting more intolerant.'

'You're right, my brother. It's like living under the Taliban!'

In Bab Taghzout the sap seemed to simmer in the *bzar* trees. People with errands moved quickly, anxious to get under cover as soon as possible. Anyone foolish enough to venture outside without a hat or headscarf risked sunstroke. Sébastien walked close to the buildings, hugging the precious line of shade. By the time he arrived at Dar Zuleika his head was pounding.

Samira opened the door with a look of surprise. '*Bonjour, monsieur. Madame n'est pas là.*'

'*Aucun souci.* I've come to pick up some of my things.'

The stage had gone from the courtyard. Carpets were draped over the chairs, drying in the sun. He felt sorry for the staff having to work on the hottest day of the year. Momo eyed him from the shade of the orange tree as he trotted up to Kay's apartment. His birthday presents were in the kitchen where he'd left them. He put the bottles of champagne in a bag. He would chill a bottle in his fridge – the one appliance in his apartment that worked properly – and open it when he returned from the *chantier*. That would be his birthday present to himself, his little reward. He glanced at the shelf where Kay had placed the ID card. His heart stopped. *The card had gone.* He ran his fingers along the surface. He climbed onto a stool, nearly toppling over in his hurry, and went through the cookery books, holding them by the spines and fanning the pages. He searched the drawers and window sills then went into the bedroom. Had Kay hidden the card in the office? *Or handed it to the police?*

He drank a glass of water and tried to think straight. It wasn't a big deal. He wasn't guilty of anything – not really. After replacing the cookery books he gave one last look around the kitchen then opened the door. Samira was coming up the stairs with a carpet. He was about to ask her if she'd seen the card then thought better of it.

'*J'ai récupéré mes affaires.*'

Samira gave a nod.

'Thank you for helping at the party,' he said in Arabic.

'You're welcome. *La chukran allah yjeeb.*'

As Sébastien walked across the courtyard he turned to see Samira staring down at him from the parapet.

While Sébastien was making his way back to Bab Taghzout, Karim was heading in the other direction to Sidi bel Abbès. He could feel the hot cobblestones burning the soles of his feet through his shoes. Everything was dazzling. The piles of rubbish left in the alley had dried to desiccated heaps. He was almost fainting when he finally arrived at the stuccoed arch-way in front of Sidi bel Abbès. Noon prayers were about to start and the beggars had taken up position outside the mosque.

Alms for the love of Allah, sidi, God bless your parents, sidi, please you sidi, God bless you, sidi . . . al'Allah! Al'Allah!

A skinny youth wearing tatty red trousers was sitting a few yards from the entrance with his legs splayed in front of him. Karim went over.

'May Allah make your life easy! May He grant you prosperity and length of days. Do you know anything about the dead girl who was found here on Monday evening?'

The young man turned his unseeing eyes towards Karim. 'Alms for the love of Allah!'

Karim repeated the question. When the youth failed to reply the next beggar, an unshaven old man in a filthy *jellaba*, raised his head. 'Praise God, I heard the cart.'

Karim stared at the man. His legs had been amputated above the knee and he sat in a wheelchair operated by two handles.

'What did you hear?'

'I heard the cart arrive, may Allah preserve your parents and your children.'

The youth in red jeans spoke. His speech came in slurs.

'. . . came . . . cart . . . wheels . . . der-*dah*, der-*dah*—'

'Silence, Bashir!' said the old man. 'You didn't hear a thing. You just want this good man to open his wallet for you. Be quiet!'

'Der-*dah*, der-*dah*!'

The old man leaned over and cuffed him on the head but the youth grabbed the old man's hand and bit it, causing him to howl in pain. Karim grew alarmed.

'Stop! I will pay both of you but only if you stop fighting! Did you hear anything else?'

The old man growled at the youth, then, nursing his injured hand, he said: 'I heard his voice.'

'You did?' Karim felt a stab of excitement. 'Was it a foreign voice?' He stood up to allow two worshippers in white *jellabas* to walk past, then squatted down again. 'Was it a *foreign* voice?'

The youth rocked to and fro, mumbling, 'Der-*dah*, der-*dah*.'

'Imbecile!' the old man hissed.

'Was it a French voice?' Karim said, more urgently. 'Or English?'

'English? He was not English.' The old man thrust out his palm. Karim felt in his pocket and pressed a five-dirham coin into the man's hand. The man balanced the coin as if assessing its weight.

'What did you hear?' Karim asked.

'What I heard should be heard by no man, only by Allah, the All-Hearing, the All-Knowing.'

With a sigh, Karim placed another coin in the man's hand. He leaned in close, close enough to smell the man's rotten breath. The man shouted in his ear.

'May God curse the donkey that gave you birth!'

Karim drew back in disgust and started to walk away. The old man called after him.

'That's what he said! *Allah inaal l-hmaar lee weldek.* May God curse the donkey that gave you birth!'

Four miles outside Marrakech, French families were splashing in the pool of the Beldi Country Club. The club came into its own in the summer months when its pools and shady gardens provided a welcome respite from the heat.

'Ah, there you are!' said Lucinda, sashaying up to Kay's lunch table.

Kay gave Lucinda a peck on the cheek. 'Did you come here by taxi?'

'Yes, I've made the fellow wait outside. The last thing I want to do in this heat is stand by the road trying to hail a cab.'

'Spoken like a resident.'

'Congratulations on a splendid party, by the way,' Lucinda said after she'd given her order to the waiter. 'The tightrope walker was a master stroke.'

'Thank you.'

'I talked to Mr Husseini. Such a sweet man!'

'Yes, I don't know why Sébastien complains about him.'

'*Dear* Sébastien! Did he enjoy himself?'

Kay laughed. 'I believe so.'

'I imagine you have lots of catching up to do, now that the party's out of the way.'

'Oh, a few things – closing the riad for the holidays, washing the carpets, preparing an inventory for the boutique. I'd like to launch it in September, when Dar Zuleika reopens. Shall we discuss plans for your villa before the food arrives?' Kay took out her notebook.

'Must we? It's so lovely just to sit and enjoy the shade.'

'Let's just get a few details out of the way. The painter is tied up for Ramadan but the carpenter is available and he's the one that matters. He's going to build a walk-in wardrobe with two hanging areas. I've made sketches. Here – take a look.'

Lucinda took off her sunglasses. 'Do you know what, my dear? I've made a decision. I think we should put the decoration on hold for the time being, with Ramadan and you being so busy and everything.'

'What do you mean?' Kay cried in astonishment. 'I've got everything planned, I've made space in my diary!'

Lucinda popped an olive in her mouth. '*You* have other things to attend to, *I* have other things to attend to, the painter has obviously got other things to attend to. Let's pause for breath and see where we are in the New Year. Apart from anything, Sébastien will be free by then and can give us a hand.'

'But what about the furnishings – the table and carpets? You can't live in a campsite until January!'

'Oh, Tofiq can sort that out. It's basic stuff.' Lucinda gave Kay's hand a squeeze. 'Beneath your talents.'

Kay's face was crimson. She got to her feet. 'If you don't need me then, as you said, I have other things to attend to.'

'But my dear – the food! It's just arriving!'

Kay found the two taxi drivers chatting in the shade of a wall. They jumped up with surprise. While her driver held the car door open Kay addressed Lucinda's driver.

'You can go. You're no longer needed.'

Kay sat, her face clenched, all the way back to town, hardly listening to what the driver was saying about the latest twist in the Talal affair.

'First the brother, now the father. They'll be arresting the mother next!'

When Karim arrived back at the riad every bone in his body ached and he was faint from lack of food and sleep.

There is joy in self-denial. There is joy in abstinence.

When had he last felt joy? As a child perhaps, running through the alleys with Ayesha. He couldn't remember feeling joy as an adult. Being an adult was nothing but care and responsibility.

Lalla Fatima was in the kitchen arranging pastries on a plate. 'What news of Si Omar?' she asked fearfully.

'I don't know, Meema,' said Karim, leaning against the doorframe. 'I've been out for a walk.'

'Are they treating him well, at least?'

'I don't know.'

'What made him sign that confession?'

'Why do you think I know the answer to everything?' Karim threw himself down in the chair by the table. 'Forgive me, Meema, I didn't sleep last night. *Ana mhlouk*, I'm shattered.'

Lalla Fatima cupped her son's cheeks. 'You poor boy! That job is not good for you.'

She reached up to the wall cupboard and handed him a packet of pills. Karim looked at them dubiously.

'What are these?'

'They'll help you sleep. I took them when your father died.' Karim tried to protest but Lalla Fatima closed his hand over the packet. 'Take them with you. Just in case.'

She went back to the counter, tore off a sheet of clingfilm and covered the pastries. 'I'm going to Lalla Hanane.'

'Again?' asked Karim. The two families hadn't spoken in years, yet his mother was going to visit Lalla Hanane for the third time in a week!

'She needs me, Karim.'

'What she needs is a lawyer.'

Lalla Fatima looked at him with hope in her eyes. 'Can we give her money for a lawyer?'

'No, Meema. We need every dirham to pay for the wedding. Even if we had a pot of money it wouldn't do Hanane any good, not if Omar insists that he's responsible for Amina's death.'

His mother sat beside him at the table. 'Has Abderrahim been released? Can he help his father?'

'Not yet,' Karim replied in a softer tone. 'Soon, *inshallah*.' He thought it best not to reveal that Abderrahim had been transferred to Kenitra. 'Has Hanane said anything to you – anything that might shed light on Si Omar's confession?'

'Only that he was very strict with Amina. Once he found lipstick in her bedroom and beat her black and blue. He checked her bag whenever she went out. Perhaps he thinks he was too harsh, that his inflexibility caused her to rebel by going to nightclubs.'

Karim knew that this information would count against Omar, confirm everyone's suspicion that he took his daughter's life in an honour killing.

'If you want to help Omar, ask Hanane the name of the college that Amina and Leila attended.'

His mother nodded. '*Wakha*.'

Karim watched her get ready. 'Do you have to go and see Hanane now? The sun is pitiless!'

'It's not far. I'll soak my *hijab* in water. *Always keep a cool head*, that's what your father said.'

'I don't think that's what he meant.'

'God will protect me.'

'At least let me come with you.'

'No.' Lalla Fatima wet her scarf and put it over her hair. 'You need to sleep.'

'Shall I ask Ayesha to accompany you?'

'Leave her be. She's been in an odd mood these last few days.'

When she was safely out of the riad Karim turned and went upstairs. Seeing the door to the roof open he climbed the last few steps and crouched, half-hidden, on the last step. Ayesha was hanging out the washing. He observed the sunlight in her hair, the easy movement as she leaned over, the curve of her hips. He tried to imagine that he was a stranger, spying on a girl with a pretty face and a shapely body. Ayesha picked up the basket and came to the door, almost tripping over him.

'Oh!'

Karim reached up to stop her falling, catching her by the midriff and holding her suspended like a Russian ballerina. The laundry basket clattered down the steps. He could feel Ayesha's muscles tense, then relax. He sensed the weight of her body, the softness of her stomach. He smelled argan oil and sun-warmed skin.

Warnings rang in his ears. *Unclean women are for unclean men, and unclean men are for unclean women! Who is more astray than one who follows his own lusts without guidance from Allah?*

'You gave me a shock!' said Ayesha finally, regaining her balance. She smoothed her hair then sat on the step beside him, her cheeks flushed.

'I didn't mean—' Karim began.

The moment had passed. 'Tell me what happened at the mosque.'

'The mosque?'

'Did you find any witnesses?'

Karim repeated the curse the beggar had heard.

'That's not a curse just anybody would utter,' said Ayesha. 'You should tell your colleague – the one in charge.'

'Aziz?' Karim's frustration came rushing back. 'What would that achieve? I told him about the sign and he did nothing. He hates me, they all hate me. Why do you think I was taken off the case?'

'Because you knew Amina?'

'That's just a pretext, don't you see? I'm young, educated, Chleuh. That makes me different to them. They treat me like an outsider.'

'Are you sure you're not imagining it?'

'You keep asking if I'm imagining things! The Sûreté is a clique: the officers look after each other, they share out the interesting assignments while I get the crumbs from the table – dull, menial jobs that nobody else wants!'

Ayesha gathered the laundry basket. 'Now you know how I feel.'

'What do you mean?'

'You went to police academy, Naïma went to college, Khadija works in an office. I do the washing.'

Karim was taken aback. 'It's not like that!'

'Yes, it is. You treat me like a servant that you can do what you want with.' With those words she marched downstairs.

Dar Zuleika was quiet when Kay returned. The gentlest of breezes stirred the leaves of the orange tree in which Momo sat, half-asleep. A long, empty August beckoned. She would be alone in the riad except for periodic visits by Driss to water the garden and check on Momo. She would have to wait until Samira returned from holiday to start work on the boutique. And her first commission – the refurbishment that would make her name as a designer – had been kicked into the long grass.

Throwing her bag on the kitchen table she noticed a cookery book on the floor, underneath the sideboard. As she replaced it on the shelf she saw that the *carte nationale* was no longer there. She distinctly remembered placing it on the shelf yesterday. She went down on her knees and searched the floor, then took out her phone.

'Samira?' Kay could hear Samira's children playing in the background. 'Did the maids clean my apartment today?'

'No, *madame*, we were busy with the carpets. Do you want them to clean it?'

'Was anyone else in the riad?'

'No one apart from Monsieur Sébastien.'

Kay's heart skipped a beat. 'Monsieur Sébastien?'

'Yes. He came to collect his birthday presents.'

Kay felt a cold dread creep over her.

Chapter 8

On Monday morning at eight o'clock the receptionist of Al-Husseini Group opened the doors of the office. On Mondays she liked to arrive early to lay out the magazines and place fresh flowers in the vase. She had just sat down to sort the mail when she rose to her feet again.

'*Salaam ou alikum, ya sayyid Al-Husseini, kayf haalek?* Greetings, Mr Al-Husseini, how are you?'

She had not been warned about the boss's visit and was relieved that she had bought long-stemmed roses for the vase. She led the great man along the corridor and ushered him into the meeting room.

'The others should be here shortly.'

Mohammed Al-Husseini felt bloated. At midnight his hotel had served chicken *m'kalli* with lots of oil and onions. Moroccans always overdid things! Tonight he would take some fresh fruit and retire early.

When the meeting was over he intended to spend the rest of the day at the site. The Frenchman fussed like an old woman but he had done the right thing in starting night-time operations. The Serafina would be ready to open on 9 November, the day after the Feast of the Sacrifice and a full five weeks before the Mandarin Oriental. The project would have taken just eighteen months from breaking ground to opening doors – a timescale even his father hadn't matched, and he had run his own construction company!

When Anwar Al-Husseini became a minister he gave Mohammed a cheque for ten million rials and told him to get the hell out of Doha. Mohammed plumped for Marrakech. Marrakech had more tourist potential than Dubai, where he had attended school, and better tax breaks than London, where he had studied for his MBA. But the best thing about Marrakech was that it was three thousand miles away from his father.

There was a knock at the door and two of his employees entered. Mouna was the marketing manager of AHG, a harassed-looking young woman in a business suit. She had received a text message while still in her pyjamas informing her of the meeting. She was followed by a pudgy-faced IT guy with some cables in his hand. Mouna arranged a laptop on the table while the IT guy fumbled under the table for a power source. Mohammed smiled. He liked to see his employees scramble to attention.

'We're going to fast track completion of the dome so we can feature it in publicity,' Mouna began.

'You're telling me things I already know. Show me some ads.'

Mouna brought up a layout on her screen, a computer-generated image with text and headline. 'As you can see, we've made the headline larger. We've booked full pages in the UAE, Qatari and Moroccan papers, at an average of twenty per cent off the rate card. Would you like me to email you the media schedule?'

Al-Husseini grunted. He glowered at the pudgy-faced man who was still on his hands and knees. A good kick, that's what he needed!

'We've filled the office positions. We're interviewing for front of house tomorrow. We've had some very good applicants.'

An image appeared on the projection screen at the far end of the meeting room and the IT guy emerged from under the table.

'Right,' Mouna said with relief. 'Let's run through—'

There was a knock at the door and the receptionist came in, looking worried. 'Excuse me, *ya sayyid Al-Husseini*. There is a problem.'

'What sort of problem?' Mohammed barked. 'Can't you see we're busy?'

'There's been an accident on the building site. A man – he's fallen—'

'Why are you bothering me with this?'

The receptionist struggled to get the words out. 'Sorry, it's just that – he's dead.'

Nobody could remember it this hot. Not Lalla Fatima. Not the *hajj* down the street. Not the woman on the nightly weather forecast. Throughout Morocco there was a spike in deaths among the very young and the very elderly. The Ministry of Agriculture issued wildfire alerts. Radio talk shows offered tips on fasting in the heat.

Karim had spent another sleepless night at the Sherezade.

He felt so fragile that the slightest knock would shatter him into a thousand pieces. According to the scales in the bathroom he had lost three kilos. Trudging miserably to the commissariat he stopped at a cobbler to get another hole punched in his belt. While he waited he tried to make sense of the weekend's developments. First, Omar Talal's so-called confession was nothing of the sort. Second . . . what was the second thing? A *djinn* leered in his face. It could have been the overheated air, or a man on a bicycle.

'Good morning, chief!' Bouchaïb hailed him when he arrived, panting for breath. 'Did you hear about the fire on the Route de Fès? Caused by the sun reflecting off a mirror. Killed ten people.'

Karim didn't answer. It was the start of a new week but all he wanted was to crawl into a hole.

Noureddine was behind his desk, immaculate as ever, stapling papers.

'*Sbah al-khir*, good morning. I hear the Talal girl's father has made a confession. So you can concentrate on your counterfeit investigation. Badnaoui tells me he's given you a direction to pursue.'

Karim fixed Noureddine with a stare. He'd been wrong when he complained to Ayesha that all the other officers hated him. Nour didn't hate him. Not only had he mentored Karim during his first year at the commissariat, he had invited him to eat with his family. He was more like a kindly uncle than a superior officer. He deserved Karim's gratitude and obedience. Karim's words came out in a rush.

'Amina Talal was last seen alive with a foreigner but her body was dumped at Sidi bel Abbès by a man who swore in

Arabic dialect. Her father can't read or write so he couldn't have written the sign that was found with her body, which means that two people were involved in Amina Talal's death, neither of whom was her father. Aziz has arrested the wrong man.'

Noureddine grasped the sides of his desk. For a minute Karim thought he was going to hurl it at him. 'Karim, what you're doing . . . poking your nose into the Talal case . . . it's not normal, it's not . . . *healthy*.'

Karim was defiant. 'I didn't ask to be present at Omar Talal's interrogation. You told me to be there.'

'I didn't tell you to come into the office and make wild allegations!'

'The interrogation was a farce. Aziz browbeat a sick old man and ignored a crucial piece of evidence. He didn't even bother to check the handcart.'

'Do you have proof?'

'Aziz had no proof that Abderrahim Talal killed Amina and he has no proof that Omar Talal did, either. He's not fit to call himself a policeman!'

Karim gulped. Now he'd gone too far. Casting aspersions at a respected fellow officer was a sure-fire way to get yourself posted to a police station in the middle of nowhere where the most serious crime was stealing sheep.

Nour rose to his feet. 'Come.'

'Where to?' asked Karim with surprise.

'The police in the Palmeraie have requested assistance. If you can't attend to your own work you can at least help with mine.'

'What's the case?'

'A death.' Noureddine put on his sunglasses. 'On a building site.'

Karim was reminded of photos he'd seen of the Dome of the Rock in Jerusalem. Even with scaffolding around it, the cupola of the hotel shone like gold. He and Noureddine introduced themselves to the architect and the foreman and the four men walked to the side of the building where they found a rumpled tarpaulin next to a parked ambulance.

'He was the security guard,' said Hassan.

Karim crouched down and lifted the tarpaulin. Underneath was the twisted body of a man in his mid-forties. One leg was splayed out at an impossible angle. His nose was crushed, caved into what remained of his moustache. A wound gaped open from his left eyelid to his right temple, like a grotesque pair of lips.

'When did it happen?' asked Noureddine, addressing the others in French.

'*A sept heures du matin*. He fell from the scaffolding.'

Karim gazed up at the gangway above his head. Every few seconds a shadowy shape passed along it and the wood buckled slightly.

'*Il faisait quoi?* What was he doing up there?'

'Finishing his rounds.'

Karim felt a fleeting affinity with the dead man, a fellow guard working the nightshift.

Sébastien spoke. 'I arrived at six-thirty and went up to the roof. I saw him walk past us – he said *bonjour*. Next thing I knew there was a shout from below and the guard was no longer on the roof.'

'How did he seem when you saw him, *monsieur*?'

'Tired, a little grumpy. It was the end of his shift.'

'Did anyone see him fall?'

'An electrician – he was laying a cable in that trench over there. He's in a state of shock.'

While Hassan went to find the witness Noureddine caught Karim's eye and directed his attention to the walkway. Karim nodded. He made his way around to the entrance. The interior was dark, immense – at least two hundred feet across and a hundred feet high – the gloom cut through with shafts of sunlight. Plasterers were applying fibreglass mesh to the walls. Karim climbed the wide curving staircase, past a plasterer's platform. Just then his phone vibrated. It was a four-word text from his mother: 'Polytechnique du Sud, Guéliz.'

Buoyed by this new information, he crossed the floor and emerged through an arched window void into a forest of scaffolding. The roof dazzled where the sunlight hit it. Reaching the walkway, he noted that all of the boards appeared to be intact. The railing looked sound but there was a three-foot gap between the rail and the walkway through which the security guard could have slipped. Karim rested his hands on the rail then took them away sharply: the metal was too hot to touch. But what a view! He could see across the palm trees all the way to the bus station at Bab Doukkala. Below him, the construction site was an expanse of churned earth, humming with earth-moving machinery. There were enough figures to populate a small town. He could see a yellow vehicle that looked like a Renault convertible parked alongside Noureddine's

Peugeot. There was a third car parked in front of the site entrance, a black vehicle with a man standing beside it. Looking straight down through the walkway he could see the tops of the heads of Noureddine and the foreman, talking to the witness. Where was the Frenchman?

'*Ca y est?*' Sébastien was standing behind him. 'Finished?'

Karim almost fainted from shock. 'No, I'm not finished,' he said when he had recovered his composure. '*Et vous, monsieur?* Have you done your checks? What do you think happened to the watchman?'

'He came up here to finish his rounds, he was tired, he lost his footing.'

'He fell? That's all?'

Sébastien shrugged. '*C'est le Ramadan.*'

'Have you had many accidents on this *chantier?*'

'A cut or two, nothing serious.'

'Did anyone approach the guard or talk to him while he was up here?'

'No,' Sébastien replied impatiently. 'Accidents happen. *C'est dommage, mais c'est le Ramadan.*'

Karim took a dislike to the Frenchman, who seemed to regard the death of an employee as nothing more than a tiresome inconvenience. With his phone Karim took photographs of the gangway, the rail and – because he was still in the way – Sébastien.

'*Qu'est-ce que tu fais?* What are you doing?'

Karim ignored him. When he was back in the car he asked Noureddine what the electrician had said.

'In a great many words, that he saw a blur hit the ground.'

As they were following the ambulance, the corpse inside, a

man flagged them down at the gate – the man Karim had spotted from the roof. His hair and clothes were flecked with dust.

'Are you police? My name is Hicham Cherkaoui. I'm with the Wilaya, the council. I'm investigating breaches in safety regulations. I heard that a man died this morning. Did you see any evidence of poor safety – lack of gangways or scaffolding ladders, for example? If the man died because of negligence you have the power to shut the site down.'

Karim exchanged looks with Noureddine. 'We shall have to await the autopsy.'

'Autopsy?' Hicham jeered. 'What do you think the autopsy will show you? That the man had a knife in his back?'

'*Momken*. It's possible,' Karim shrugged.

'He wasn't killed! He fell because this place is unsafe! I've been watching it for days. Everywhere you look there's an accident waiting to happen. Hey! Where are you going?'

'Ramadan brings out the crazy in people,' observed Noureddine as they drove onto the road.

Sébastien had seen the policemen talking to Hicham Cherkaoui. He stormed into the site office, a prefabricated cabin with a single window, slamming the door so hard the building shook. Just then his mobile rang. Kay's name flashed up on the screen.

'Were you fucking her?'

It took Sébastien a while to understand what Kay was referring to.

'You came to get the girl's card,' she spat. 'The only possible reason is that you have something to hide.'

'I didn't take the card!' Sébastien said with mounting frustration. 'I told you – the girl was looking for a job! I didn't know she was the same girl as the one who was murdered until you told me!'

'The fact remains that you came back here to get the card.'

'I came to fetch my presents!'

'In the middle of the day?' Kay's voice was full of scorn. 'When you knew that I would be out?'

'I had to drop Mohammed at his hotel and I called on my way back to the site.'

'You took the card.'

'I came for the champagne! The card was gone when I looked on the shelf.'

'So – you admit that you looked for the card? You said you came for your presents.'

'I did come for my presents.'

'If you're going to play games then there's no point in having this conversation!' Kay rang off.

Sébastien was outraged. How dare she accuse him! Any doubts he had harboured about ending his relationship with Kay melted away. It was over.

There was a knock and the errand boy came in with a silver tray. He was a fifteen-year-old who did odd jobs and helped in the mess tent. He put a glass of mint tea on the desk with two rectangles of sugar then stood silently in the corner. Sébastien sat down and lit a cigarette with a trembling hand. For a minute he thought of calling back and telling Kay to fuck herself. Then he remembered that he had a death to deal with, as well as Hicham Cherkaoui skulking at the gates. He couldn't afford to fight a battle on another front. Instead he called Jamal and told him about the death of the security guard.

Jamal was appalled. 'Was he drunk?'

'I don't think so. He was probably just half-asleep.'

'Do you think there'll be an inquest?'

'*Dieu nous en garde!* Heaven forbid! I've already got the town hall breathing down my neck.'

'What did Mohammed say?'

'He blames me, *évidemment*. He said that the guard shouldn't have been on the roof. But the reason he was there was because Mohammed is worried about the men stealing the copper or smoking kif on the job.'

'Did the police talk to Mohammed?'

Sébastien laughed. 'He hid inside, like a naughty schoolboy.'

They spent a few minutes discussing work. Jamal had tracked down a supplier who could deliver marble in the first week of September. Sébastien removed the cap of a black marker with his teeth and wrote *Marbre* on the wall calendar behind him against 5 September.

'*Écoute*, Jamal – I want to take three days' holiday on 27 August. Can you cover for me? We should have finished the *gros oeuvre* by then.'

'*Aucun souci*. I'll chaperone his majesty.'

Sébastien drew a line under the last three days of August and wrote above it *S congé*. Then he finished his tea and told the boy he could go.

The mortuary room was pleasantly cool, with a white tiled floor that smelled of antiseptic. Noureddine was deep in conversation with a pathologist. Excusing himself to go to the bathroom Karim walked off down the corridor and pushed open a set of rubberised doors. The temperature dropped several degrees and he caught a whiff of sulphur. Pipes ran along the ceiling above four stainless steel examination tables, separated by a run-off channel.

'Yes?' said a voice.

Karim turned around to face a mortuary technician. He was wearing a plastic apron over white scrubs.

'Karim Belkacem, Sûreté.'

The technician looked at Karim's ID. 'Belkacem. *Wesh nta Shilh?* Are you a Chleuh? Are you related to Si Brahim Belkacem?'

'He was my father.'

The man held out his hand. 'My name is Mounir Ouheddou. We are from the same family – my father is your father's cousin!'

'*Mutsharrifin!* It's a pleasure to meet you, Mounir.'

Karim's first impression was of a cheerful man in his early thirties, with tightly curled black hair and deep-set eyes. He asked Karim what he was doing at the mortuary.

'We're investigating the death of a security guard,' Karim replied, glancing at the doors, fearful that Nour might walk in at any moment. 'Tell me, Mounir – I brought in a female last Monday night by the name of Amina Talal. Has her autopsy been completed yet?'

'Amina Talal?' Mounir checked a computer screen. 'Talal . . . Talal . . . no, not yet.'

'A week has passed!'

'We're on reduced hours because of Ramadan. And then with the heatwave – well, you can imagine the casualties.'

Karim lowered his voice. 'Mounir, there was an important item with the body, a cardboard sign. The paramedics may have brought it in separately.'

Mounir scrolled down the computer screen. 'It hasn't been logged on the system. Do you want me to see if it's with the cadaver?'

Karim nodded. He was sweating despite the freezing cold. *He could lose his job for this.*

Mounir put on a pair of latex gloves and went over to a wall of cold chambers. He pulled out a drawer containing a body bag and pulled the zip halfway down. Karim gazed at the grey-white features of Amina Talal. He averted his eyes out of respect while Mounir felt around the corpse.

'There's nothing here.'

Karim's heart sank. Mounir zipped up the bag and was about to peel off his gloves when he noticed something clinging to them.

'Where was the body found?'

'Outside the mosque of Sidi bel Abbès. Why?'

Mounir held up his forefinger and Karim noticed tiny grains on the latex.

'Sand?'

'Yes.'

'Like you might find on a beach?'

Just then the doors swung open and Noureddine marched into the cold room. He spotted Karim talking to Mounir. 'This is Mounir Ouheddou,' Karim stammered. 'He's a relation of mine, we're just catching up . . .'

Mounir and Noureddine bowed stiffly to each other.

'Come.' Noureddine said to Karim. '*Yellah.*'

The two detectives left, only for Karim to dash back a few seconds later.

'Can I keep the gloves?' he asked Mounir breathlessly.

'I hope you weren't sticking your nose into the Talal case back there,' Noureddine said as he parked the Peugeot outside the commissariat.

'Not at all!' said Karim, trying to hide the panic in his voice. 'We had a lot to talk about, Mounir and I.'

Noureddine stared at Karim for a long moment. 'He who digs a hole for his brother will fall into it himself.'

'I don't know what you mean!'

'Stay away from the Talal affair. It's Aziz's case. I'm not going to warn you again, *fhemtee*? Open a case number for the dead security guard and write up your notes. Inform the man's widow, if he has one.'

As the two men walked into the commissariat a man's voice rang out. '*Belkacem!*' The duty officer was looking through his window hatch, holding up a scuffed handbag. Karim looked blank.

'The bag that the English girl reported stolen, perhaps?' said Noureddine.

De : Belkacem Karim [mailto:kBelkacem46@wanadoo.ma]
Envoyé : lundi 8 aôut 14:00
À : <Melanie Murray>
Objet : Hand bag

Dear Mademoiselle Murray,

I hope you are returned safely to your home. Today your hand bag was found in Derb Jdid, medina. The bag is here at the commissariat. There is:

1, one leather bag 'Top Shop'

2, one lipstick 'Rimmel'

3, one 'Lillet' lady's item

4, one Easyjet boarding pass (half), with luggage sticker

5, one Manchester Public Library card

There was no money, credit cards, passport, and no iPhone.
I am, sorry.
With the most distinguished salutations,
K. Belkacem
Lieutenant

The heat hit Kay like a sledgehammer. She had only gone a few hundred feet before she had to stop and take a drink. When she reached the sloping enclosure on the north side of the mosque she stopped again and watched some of the local children playing hopscotch. She had visited the religious foundation of Sidi bel Abbès only once, shortly after her arrival in Marrakech, when she went to complain about the noise from the loudspeaker. The following day the volume was turned even higher. Mosques were not welcoming places for women, least of all Western women.

She paused at the entrance to a second courtyard, larger

and more elaborate than the first. On the left was a green-roofed mausoleum containing the bones of the saint; on the right stood a sort of covered arcade, in which blind men and women sat in wheelchairs. Kay was used to being stared at and it was pleasant to stand in the courtyard without feeling a Moroccan's gaze upon her. The pleasant feeling didn't last long. A young man sidled up to her.

'*Vous cherchez quelque-chose, madame?*'

Thinking him to be a tourist guide Kay turned her back. '*Non, merci.*'

'*Je suis le gardien de Sidi bel Abbès.* Would you like some information?' He pointed to the squat building in front of Kay. 'That's the abattoir.'

Kay wrinkled her nose in distaste.

'If someone donates a lamb to the *zaouïa* we kill it in the abattoir and distribute the meat to our – how you say – community. We run a foundation for blind persons, the only one in Marrakech. We depend on donations,' he added pointedly.

'Where was the girl's body found – the one in the handcart?'

It was the *gardien*'s turn to express repugnance. 'Outside in the alley.'

Kay left him standing in the courtyard and walked into the alleyway. Almost immediately the ragged line of beggars started murmuring benedictions. *You are infinitely kind in the name of God the most gracious the most merciful may God preserve you in well-being.* Kay looked down the alley. It was cobbled, about ten feet wide, with high walls that curved away on one side. Half of the buildings had been renovated with terracotta render and varnished wooden doors. The rest were ramshackle affairs, clumps of plaster falling off the walls. A tailor's shop looked on to the alley.

'God reward you a thousand times!' shouted a voice. It came from a beggar in red trousers, his face swivelled in Kay's direction.

'*Je n'ai pas d'argent.*'

A man in a wheelchair called out, '*Pas de problème, madame, la prochaine fois, inshallah!*'

The boy in red trousers started to speak but the other man thumped him and he lapsed into silence.

The deceased, Abdel-Latif Blaoui, CIN. A454188, was in a prone position approx. 2.5 metres from the scaffolding.

Karim stopped typing. The case of the dead security guard was interesting but the effects of his exhaustion, combined with the heat in the room, were making his eyelids close. He dug his nails into his palms and looked around for an object or activity to keep him awake. How was it that he failed to sleep in the hut by night but, come the daylight hours, he dropped off at every opportunity? The sheet of cardboard over the window had warped with the heat. Four dead flies lay under it next to a yellowing photograph of a crime scene that had fallen from the cardboard. Karim remembered the case: a woman in Casablanca who, with her lover, had carried out the murder of her husband by hiring an assassin to shoot him. The three of them were now serving life sentences. On the other side of the room Nour was wrapped up in an interminable conversation with someone from headquarters. Karim looked at the items from Melanie Murray's handbag, still arrayed on his desk. He picked up the lipstick and twisted the tube out of its container. The lipstick might lubricate his blistered lips. *Better not.* Wearing lipstick was probably forbidden during Ramadan and, besides, if Noureddine caught sight of his colleague wearing bright red lipstick he would think he'd finally gone over the edge. He laughed, quickly putting his hand over his mouth to stifle his laughter. Laughing for no reason was just as likely to alarm Noureddine. That thought made him laugh as well. Karim reached down to the empty handbag by his chair, placed it on his lap and put his nose inside. It smelled musty with a hint of perfume. Using both hands he turned the bag upside down to check there was nothing left inside. A scrap of paper fluttered down to the floor, among the dead flies. It was a cloakroom ticket. Karim turned it over and saw a girl dancing . . . *a silhouette of a girl dancing*. In a flash, he was at his keyboard.

Dear Mademoiselle Murray,
Is it that you visited Club Afrique when you were here in Marrakech? I found a garderobe ticket in your handbag. The dead girl Amina Talal who I told you about went to Club Afrique on 31 July. I remember that you said you were at a club on the night that your handbag was stolen. Is it that you were at this club on 31 July? Please, let me know. I am attaching a photograph of Amina Talal for identification.

With distinguished salutations,
K. Belkacem
Lieutenant

Half an hour later came the reply:

Dear Lieutenant Belkacem
Yes! We were at Club Afrique that night. It was our last
night. We arrived at the club about 10.30 p.m. and left
about 1 a.m. How horrible to think that we were there the
same time as that poor girl! I sent your email to Emma and
Julie but none of us recognise her. It was dark, there were a
lot of people and we were rather drunk, to be honest.
Yours, Melanie Murray
P.S. Thank you for the news about the handbag. It's only a
cheap one – you can throw it away.

By the Seven Saints! It was painful to piss. Karim came out
of the cubicle and stared at the cracked mirror over the
sink, trying to picture that fateful night in the African
club . . . a band playing, Amina in her red dress, the three
English girls celebrating their hen weekend, everyone
laughing and dancing. Something had happened to make
Amina leave. To find out, he would need to talk to Leila.
While he was washing his hands a figure loomed in the
mirror: Pockmark Features. Pockmark leaned over the sink
and blew his nose with his thumb and forefinger, flinging
the mucus in the sink. He washed his hands, grinning at

Karim, then dried himself on a grubby towel. He gave Karim a final smirk and walked out, the door slamming behind him. Karim reached for the towel, baulked, and wiped his hands on his trousers instead. When he got back to the office there was an email waiting for him.

Dear Lieutenant Belkacem,
It occurred to me that there was another person at Club Afrique on Sunday night.
His name is Sébastien de Freycinet, a French architect. He's the boyfriend of the woman who runs Dar Zuleika. You could ask him about the dead girl, perhaps?
Yours,
MM

At ten to five, under a gunmetal sky, Karim trotted up the steps to the Polytechnique du Sud. Despite the crushing heat, he had a spring in his step. There was now a candidate for the mystery foreigner seen leaving the nightclub with Amina. The Frenchman who had been so rude to him on the building site had another death to answer for! The Talal affair was about to come apart like one of those wooden puzzle boxes they sold in the souks!

Students were drifting out in twos and threes. Karim spotted a sleepy-looking concierge in the lobby. In answer to Karim's question he pointed at two girls coming out of a classroom. Karim ran up to them.

'Leila Hasnaoui?' The girl was petite, with almond eyes, and wore a long-sleeved smock over blue jeans. 'My name is Lieutenant Belkacem, from the Sûreté. Can I ask you some questions?'

Leila's companion peeled off. Leila quickened her stride.

'It won't take long,' said Karim, hurrying alongside.

'My brother is waiting.'

'You went to Club Afrique with your friend Amina Talal on the evening of 31 July.'

A pained expression crossed Leila's face and, for a moment, Karim thought she was going to burst into tears.

'Did you leave the nightclub together?'

They were now outside the building. Students were chatting in small groups or wandering towards the bus stop. A young man in a grey sweat-top walked up to Leila, grabbed her by the elbow and tried to lead her away.

'Hey!' Karim cried, putting a hand on the man's shoulder. 'This is police business!'

The young man pushed Karim aside. 'Police business – *tfou*! She has answered enough questions. Leave her alone.'

Karim grabbed the man's arm and twisted it behind his back, causing him to cry out with pain.

'No, *you* leave her alone, unless you want to spend the night chained to the bars of a cell, *fhemteenee*? Do you understand?' He released his grip and the man shrank back, scowling.

Leila looked from Karim to her brother.

'Tell me what happened,' Karim said firmly.

'It was very busy in – in the club,' Leila faltered. 'There were lots of people . . . I went to the lavatory. When I came out I couldn't see Amina . . . I went out into the street, but she wasn't there either.'

'Why did you think she might be outside?'

'The Frenchman said that she'd left.'

'Frenchman?' Karim's heart started racing. Out of the corner of his eye he saw Leila's brother climb onto a *moto*.

'We met a Frenchman in the club . . . he sat and chatted with us . . . when I came out of the lavatory he said that Amina hadn't been feeling well and had gone home.'

'Back to the medina?'

Leila strode towards the *moto*. Her brother was gunning the engine. 'I don't know.' She clutched her bag in both hands and sat on the pillion behind him.

Karim caught her up. 'The Frenchman – was he tall? Around fifty years old?'

Leila's brother kicked the stand and the *moto* roared off. Karim ran after them, shouting, 'Did the Frenchman leave with Amina?'

The scooter disappeared around a corner.

Chapter 9

The heat covered the land like a blanket. Karim tore the filter from a cigarette, lit it from the lamp, inhaled deeply and gazed into the darkness.

And among His signs are the night and the day, and the sun and the moon. Prostrate not to the sun nor to the moon, but prostrate to God who created them.

Creatures of the night fluttered and buzzed around him. He had no appetite for the food he'd brought.

Starting a day of fasting without food in your belly is like setting off on a tightrope without a safety net.

The elation he'd felt earlier had been replaced by a familiar despair. His brain had ceased to function, his reasoning replaced by random quotations and half-remembered phrases.

Four takshitas and a Turkish singer. God curse the donkey who gave you birth.

Where did the Frenchman go with Amina? It wasn't a puzzle but a tangled heap of *seffa*, hundreds of strands of vermicelli tangled and interwoven. With each passing hour the clamour in his head grew louder.

Kill one fly and seven others come to the funeral. C'est le Ramadan.

He took out the sleeping pills Lalla Fatima had given him, turning the box in his hand. But he couldn't bring himself to take one. It might fill his head with disturbing dreams. He should eat. He should drink. *He should pray!* Karim washed the sweat from his eyes, brushed his teeth then laid his mat on the ground.

O God, suffice Thou me with what is lawful, to keep me away from what is prohibited, and with Thy grace make me free from want of what is besides Thee . . .

Once again, he found it hard to concentrate on his prayers. The air was like a furnace, all moisture sucked from it. *The flames of hell await the sinner and unbeliever.* A dog barked, setting off the other dogs in the neighbourhood. He thought of Ayesha and how he had supported her at the top of the stairs; the touch of her skin, her shallow, expectant breaths. All pretence at prayer had now gone. Returning to the standpipe he took a swig of water then went into the hut, sat on the bed and mechanically crammed a hard-boiled egg into his mouth. He choked and spluttered, fell to his knees, struggling to dislodge the crumbs of egg in his windpipe. When he had recovered he wiped the yolk from the floorboards and dabbed his eyes. He drank some milk and picked up his Quran, opening at the bookmark.

Haram for you are: your mothers and your daughters and your sisters, your maternal aunts and your paternal aunts, your brothers' daughters and your sisters' daughters, your foster mothers who have suckled you, your foster sisters by suckling . . . An hour passed.

Karim jolted awake. The noise sounded like a twig snapping. Putting his Quran aside he crept to the door with the torch, the switch in the *off* position. He stood on the threshold and peered into the gloom. He could hear a faint murmuring. He tiptoed down the step. After a few feet, smooth clay give way to springy undergrowth. Palmetto spikes snagged at his thighs. He had a sense that others were listening, holding their breath. He switched on the torch.

'*Aieeeee!*' A girl was lying on the ground looking up at him, screaming. A young man sprang to his feet and yanked up his jeans. The girl got up and groped for her shoes, shielding her eyes against the dazzle of the torch.

While Karim stood and watched, the couple stumbled towards the road, every so often casting a baleful glance behind them.

Lalla Fatima and Ayesha sat at the kitchen table in their night clothes eating yoghurt. It was just before dawn and their eyes were puffy with sleep. As they put down their spoons the call to prayer sounded. Ayesha spoke.

'Who were my parents?'

Lalla Fatima was shocked. 'In God's name, Ayesha, it's half-past three in the morning! Why do you ask such a question?'

'Because I want to know. Tell me. Please.'

Lalla Fatima sat down heavily. 'I've already told you.'

'Tell me again.'

'It was so long ago! *Yanni*, it was the time of the cholera epidemic . . . a lot of people died that winter. Khadija was only a few months old. We had to buy bottled water because the water from the tap wasn't safe to drink. But you know all this!'

Any hope that she would be spared from further explanation was dispelled by the sight of Ayesha, tight-lipped, regarding her intently. Lalla Fatima gave a sigh and carried on.

'It was Thursday, after *asr* prayers . . . we heard a knock at the door. Si Brahim told me to answer. When I looked out there was no one in the alley. Then I saw you on the ground, wrapped in a blanket, a tiny bundle by my feet. You couldn't have been more than five weeks old.'

'You don't know who left me?'

'*La.*' Lalla Fatima shook her head. 'I hurried to the end of the alley but I didn't see any strangers. Women from the mountains sometimes came to Bab el-Khemis for the Thursday market. We think one of them left you as *kafala*, a foundling for us to look after.'

'Why did she choose our house?'

'Perhaps our door looked like that of a well-to-do family. Perhaps the woman – your mother – knew that we were Chleuh. All I know is that we accepted you as a blessing from God. We looked after you and cherished you. Si Brahim loved you like his own daughter.'

'Si Brahim told me I was born in Zat.'

Lalla Fatima's mouth gaped. 'He told you that? I don't know why Si Brahim told you that. His relatives lived in the neighbouring valley – perhaps he heard that the epidemic was bad in Zat.'

'They have a spring in Zat. And a river. Surely they would have escaped the worst of the cholera?'

'*Ma arfch.* I don't know.'

Ayesha toyed with the lid on the yoghurt carton. 'I want to look for them – my parents.'

'That's madness! Your parents could be anywhere – they

could be dead! Even if they're alive, seeing you after all these years would only cause them distress. Let it be!'

'I can still be a daughter to them.'

'You're a daughter to *us*, Ayesha!'

They heard footsteps and Khadija padded into the kitchen, scratching her hair. 'What time is it? Have I missed *suhour*?'

After another night without sleep Karim's emotions were shredded. He felt exuberant one minute, terrified the next. The idea of Abderrezak and his donations to charity – Zak and his *zakat* – gave him fits of laughter. Then the mystery of the sand, its obscure origins, plunged him into despair. He started to see faces in the knots in the wood of the hut; an old crone, a grinning child. He said his prayers. *God is the Greatest, Glory be to my Lord, the most High. My God, forgive me.* Then he recited the Surah al-Baqara, all 286 verses, from memory. The first streaks appeared in the eastern sky. When the taxi arrived, and Fouad gave his usual wary nod, Karim reacted violently.

'*Sbah al-khir!* Good morning! Good morning! Good morning! What's the matter – can't you even say *good morning*?'

Fouad backed away, as if circling a rabid dog.

Rachid was tidying the back seat of the taxi. 'Can you believe my brother-in-law?' he said when Karim got in. 'He told me to clean the taxi. Said it stinks!'

Karim gave him a vacant stare. 'I found a couple having sex.'

'*Besahh?*' Rachid was agog. 'Really?'

Karim related the details in a monotone.

'Was the girl naked?'

'What? No.'

'You must have given them the fright of their lives,' Rachid cackled.

'That's why Khalifa hired me,' Karim said mournfully. 'To stop people having sex.'

'Don't look so long-faced! Now and again you catch couples having sex – so what? It's better than sitting behind a steering wheel all night!'

Karim eyed the cigarettes on the dashboard greedily. *Keep me away from what is prohibited and with Thy grace make me free from want of what is besides Thee.*

They drove along the deserted Route d'Ourika. In the Almazar shopping centre a single light shone in the lobby.

'Do you know anywhere sandy?' Karim asked suddenly.

'The Sahara desert?'

'Nearer.'

'Essaouira?'

'Nearer than that.'

'Why do you want to know?'

'I'm investigating a case.'

'You're a private investigator?'

'I'm a policeman.'

Rachid hit the brakes. '*Ya salaam!* I thought you worked in an office!'

'I do – sort of. I'm a plain clothes detective in the Sûreté, *quatrième arrondissement*. I took the night job to pay for my sister's wedding. Why do you look so alarmed?'

'Because I'm on the fiddle, of course! I don't turn on my meter. If my brother-in-law finds out he'll kill me.'

'We don't care about stuff like that. I'm more likely to ask where you get your CDs from. I'm investigating counterfeit goods.'

'Counterfeit goods? What's sand got to do with counterfeit goods?'

'Stop the car,' said Karim, looking out of the window. 'Give me a piece of paper.'

Rachid, thoroughly confused by now, tore a receipt from a pad. 'Like this?'

They were just outside the city walls. The grey light gave the outskirts of the city a washed-out appearance. Squatting down by some thorn bushes Karim started prodding the ground with the rim of his torch. Rachid stepped out of the taxi and went behind an oleander bush to relieve himself.

'I should have guessed you were a policeman,' he called to Karim.

'Why's that?'

'You're intelligent – not like some nightwatchmen I know! Besides, you ask a lot of questions. You should make me your assistant! You wouldn't believe what people say in the back of a taxi.' He zipped up his fly and wandered over. Karim was putting a pinch of sandy earth into the folded wrap of paper.

'What are you doing?'

'Comparing.'

'Marrakech is a desert town, my brother, there's sand everywhere you look. If you want we could drive to the Agafay hills. Plenty of sand. Or the *barrage*, they've got an entire beach. We could go now, we'd be back in a couple of hours . . . oh, I forgot – I have to clean the car for my son-of-a-bitch brother-in-law.'

'*Blesh*, forget it. Take me to the commissariat in Arset al-Maach.'

For the rest of the way Rachid listed all of the reasons why he hated his brother-in-law. Karim wasn't listening. He was too busy thinking about sand.

Il baise des prostituées – He fucks prostitutes
Il baisait des prostituées – He was fucking prostitutes
Il a baisé des prostituées – He has fucked prostitutes

Kay rolled the words on her tongue, seeing how they sounded. It was now clear to her that her boyfriend was mixed up with the girl. But was it infidelity, or something worse? Years ago, after she and Sébastien started their relationship, he told her that he was not the stay-at-home type. He had been married once and needed his freedom. He never made it clear what he meant by freedom, and Kay never asked. She knew that he had a taste for Marrakech's low life, for visiting nightclubs with Yves, his drinking buddy. But prostitutes?

Il a agressé une prostituée – He has attacked a prostitute
Il a assassiné une prostituée – He has killed a prostitute

Kay couldn't help laughing. What would her old sixth-form French teacher say if he could hear her conjugations?

She went back over the day she returned from Cairo. Sébastien was on the roof terrace with her when the evening call to prayer rang out at seven-thirty. Lucinda arrived at eight-thirty, by which time Sébastien had left. According to reports, the corpse was left during the hour of *ftour* – in other words, between seven-thirty and eight-thirty. So if Sébastien killed the girl he would have had to arrange for a second person to dispose of the body.

Was it possible that Sébastien, *her* Sébastien, her gentle, diffident, hopelessly disorganised Sébastien, who loved to paint and travel, who delighted in giving her rare and exotic gifts, was a whoremonger and a killer, so meticulous in his depravity that he engaged an accomplice to cover his tracks? An accomplice, moreover, who had the effrontery to leave the body in a handcart outside a mosque? No! It was an honour killing. The father was motivated by religious zeal to kill his sinful daughter. The police had arrested him, hadn't they? As far as Sébastien was concerned, the daughter had gone to AHG to enquire about a job, handed over her identity card, Sébastien had forgotten it was still in his pocket, it had fallen out at the party, then he had returned to Dar Zuleika to avoid the staff finding it (imagine!) or having to answer awkward questions from the police. But that still left one, uncomfortable truth: Sébastien had lied to her about taking the card from the shelf.

She was sitting in the smaller of the two courtyards, drinking a cup of verveine tea. It was only six-thirty in the morning but the heat had made it impossible to sleep. For once, there was no sun on the palm tree and the sky was a greasy colour. She could see a column of ants running across the ground, up the leg of a table and onto the table top where she had left a peach stone the night before. She picked it up to throw in the bin. There was a piece of litter under the orange tree where

Momo sat. At first Kay thought it was a sweet wrapper; that Momo had eaten one of those disgusting Turkish chocolate bars the workmen had given him. Curious, Kay went over to have a closer look. It wasn't a sweet wrapper at all . . . it was an ID card . . . *it was Amina Talal's ID card.*

Oh, the joy! Kay picked it up and looked at Momo with tears in her eyes. What an idiot she had been!

Cherchez le singe!

Bouchaïb was covering a car with tarpaulin when Karim stumbled out of the taxi.

'*Sbah al-khir!* Early again, Mr Karim? Perhaps you should sleep here!'

Karim regarded him dully.

Bouchaïb pointed to the sky. 'Something strange is going on up there, *wahakallah*, I swear to God.'

Karim looked up. The sky was grey-yellow, the colour of brimstone.

Bouchaïb tapped his stump. 'I can feel it in my leg. Remember when we had that rainy spell in March? The *météo* didn't predict it but my leg—'

Karim stalked off without waiting for Bouchaïb to finish. Upstairs he sat down at his desk, unlocked his drawer and took out the latex gloves Mounir had given him. After unfolding them carefully he used a penknife to scrape the sand onto the surface of his desk and looked at them through a magnifying glass. Did the grains resemble the sand that blew about the city, that found its way into pavements and handcarts? If not, it meant that Amina had gone elsewhere between the time she left the club and the time her body was found. Trembling with excitement, Karim emptied out a second pile of sand from the little envelope he had made at the roadside. He separated the grains in each pile with the blade of his knife then peered at them through the magnifying glass. There was no doubt: the sand was different. The grains he had gathered that morning were smooth and rounded whereas the grains from the gloves were coarse, angular in shape. The next test was whether the sand from the gloves tasted of salt, like seaside sand. He dabbed a finger . . . *stop*! Karim realised that he would be breaking his fast if he placed salt on his tongue. He would do a taste test later.

He folded a second tiny envelope, labelled the two envelopes 'Corpse' and 'Roadside' and tucked the envelopes into his pocket. He went over to the map of Morocco on the wall and pinpointed Essaouira. Essaouira lay on the coast, 110 miles from Marrakech. Did the Frenchman take Amina to Essaouira on the night of 31 July? If he killed Amina Talal in Essaouira, why go to the trouble of bringing her body all the way back to the medina? It was absurd. *Absurd!*

'What's absurd?'

Karim wheeled around to see Noureddine in the doorway. The older man ran his eyes over Karim's appearance. 'You look terrible.'

'I, er, I've come straight from the Sherezade.' To fill the awkward silence he added, 'I found a couple having sex on the building site.'

'Consensual sex?'

'I, er, yes. It wasn't rape, if that's what you mean. I think they came from the nightclub across the road.'

Noureddine kept his gaze on Karim, weighing his words. Then he went to his desk, took off his jacket and draped it over the back of his chair. He started writing notes. Karim craned his neck to see what Noureddine was writing. Noureddine turned to face him.

'What are you doing?'

Karim pretended to examine the map. 'I'm looking at the – er, map. You know, finding possible entry points for black market goods . . .' *A lie! A despicable lie! In Ramadan the ears, eyes and tongue should abstain from lies.*

'Have you made progress with your investigation?'

'Yes, praise God. I'm making a list of – er, ports and frontier posts with weak security.' *Another lie!*

'And what is your conclusion?'

Karim pointed to a town on the Algerian border. 'Oujda has weak security.'

'It's not likely to be Oujda, is it? Not unless the goods are coming on the back of a donkey.'

Karim went back to his desk. He sat down and opened the ring binder. Several sheets of papers fell onto the floor, followed by his calculator. *Behave normally,* Karim told himself. *But how does a normal man behave? A normal man does not lust after his sister and allow a foreigner to kill his fiancée.* He tried to put the batteries back in the calculator but they sprang out and rolled across the floor.

'Maybe the night job wasn't such a good idea,' said Noureddine, more softly. 'You seem . . . not yourself. Have you written up the case report on the dead security guard?'

'Yes.' Another lie. *Truthfulness is righteousness and righteousness leads to Paradise!*

'Find out from the mortuary if they've done the autopsy.' Karim sprang to his feet and headed for the door.

'Where are you going?'

'To the mortuary.'

'You don't have to go there in person! Pick up the phone, man!'

Karim returned to his desk. He bit his nails for a few minutes then got to his feet again.

'It's better if I go in person. My cousin said they've got a backlog of cases. If they haven't done the autopsy I'll give him a kick up the backside!'

He hurried out of the room. At the foot of the stairs he halted, stricken with panic. Had he left the gloves on his desk in plain view?

'Forgotten something?' Aziz called out from his desk in the ground floor office. Pockmark Features was standing beside him. Karim turned to face them.

Why did they hate him so much, these lowbrows? They saw him as an interloper yet he had been born and bred in Marrakech while Aziz came from Tangier and Pockmark Features hailed from some Godforsaken town in the east. Was it because he was a Berber, a Chleuh from the mountains? There had been racism in the early days when Berbers were supposed to aspire to no more than shop keeping, carpet selling at best, but now they had their own TV channel and the language was being taught in schools. Besides, half the population of Marrakech had Chleuh in their blood. Scratch a Marrakchi – uncover a Chleuh!

'Can't remember what you've come down for?'

Karim looked at Aziz's desk. *What had he done with the sign?*

It was probably lying on a rubbish heap covered with eggshells.
'He deserved better, Omar Talal!'

'What's that? Omar Talal? Last I heard, he was refusing to eat. They say he'll be dead by Saturday.'

The sky was overcast. A dusty wind had started to blow, hotter and more enervating than the wind of last week. The desert – the unseen hinterland of the city – was stirring, marshalling its forces. At the Serafina building site the workmen drooped as if a pestilence had swept over them. In the souks the shopkeepers sat slumped on their stools, surrounded by their pottery and exquisitely worked lampshades, waiting for tourists who never came.

On the way to the mortuary Karim saw a dead dog lying next to a rubbish bin. When he finally arrived he was dropping from fatigue. He headed straight for the autopsy room, pushed open the doors and leaned against the wall, eyes closed, luxuriating in the cool air. He heard laughter.

'We should ask you for payment!'

Mounir and a colleague, dressed in scrubs, were grinning at him from across the room. Mounir came over with a smile.

'For the air conditioning, I mean! It's a joke! *Kee dayr*, how are you? *Bekhir?* All well, I hope? The family is well?'

Karim was stony-faced. 'I've come for the autopsy results on the security guard.'

'You could have phoned, you know,' Mounir said, still smiling. He checked the computer. 'Nothing unusual, as far as I recall . . . multiple fractures at the base and front of the skull, cerebral contusions, subdural haematoma, a sternal fracture, various internal injuries. No alcohol, no kif, nothing unusual in his bloodstream, no signs of a struggle. He probably just missed his footing.'

'Or was pushed!'

'Pushed? It's possible. Although that probably wouldn't show up in the autopsy.' Mounir looked Karim in the face. 'Are you feeling all right?'

'Yes.'

'The heat is terrible, *iyek*? They say the wells are starting to run dry.'

'What about the girl?'

'Girl? You mean the Talal girl? The autopsy still hasn't been done.'

'Is someone deliberately delaying things?'

'Excuse me?'

'How is it that you have time to examine the corpse of a man who has been dead no more than twenty-four hours but not that of a girl brought here seven days ago?'

Mounir stiffened. He glanced at his colleague who was watching from the far side of the room.

'Do the autopsy,' Karim commanded.

'What?' Mounir was unsure if this was a joke.

'Do it,' said Karim, pointing at an instrument trolley. '*Now*.' There was an uneasy silence. 'Do you want me to do it myself?'

Mounir's reply, when it came, was cold. 'I shall have to ask you to leave.'

'Leave? You want me to leave? Amina Talal's father is dying in jail while her French killer, whose DNA is all over her body – and probably inside it as well – walks free just because no one in this laboratory can be bothered to do their job!'

By now the other technician had joined them. He looked Karim up and down.

'What's your business here?'

'More important than yours – since you don't seem to do anything!' He tossed a coin on the floor before striding out. 'That's for your air conditioning,'

Karim had a nagging feeling that he'd behaved badly at the mortuary. He'd forgotten to give Mounir the two sand samples, that much he knew. He sat for an hour in the gardens of the Koutoubia, biting his fingernails. When he finally showed up at the office it was so late that Noureddine sent him home.

Lalla Fatima was dismayed by his deterioration. 'Noureddine is worried about you.'

'He told you that? What did he say?'

'He thinks you're not getting enough food and rest.'

'It's his fault if I'm not getting enough rest! He told me to take the night job!'

'Karim, listen to me. If you still want to go – and I understand if you do – you've got plenty of time before you have to leave. Why don't you have a shower and lie down?'

'I'm fine. Give me coffee and a few dates and I'll be fine.'

Karim rubbed his temples, causing stars to appear before his eyes. *Was he going blind like those poor wretches at Sidi bel Abbès?* He heard laughter, then a man's voice: Abderrezak.

He found Zak in the *salon* with Khadija and Ayesha. A

portable air-conditioning unit was humming on the table. Ayesha was leaning into it, eyes closed, her hair blowing about her ears, a smile playing about her lips. *Why wasn't she wearing her headscarf?*

Zak looked up as Karim walked in. 'It's an Electrolux,' he said, as if that was all the explanation that was needed.

'God be praised,' said Khadija.

Karim stared at Zak, his face like thunder. *You buy toys to impress your fiancée while I work all night to pay for your miserable wedding!*

'Isn't it wonderful, Karim?' said Ayesha.

'Wonderful.'

Lalla Fatima followed Karim into the room. Zak grinned at her. 'You can wheel it into your bedroom at night, Meema.'

Lalla Fatima laughed. 'I'd be afraid that it might blow up!'

Karim wished that he were alone with Ayesha, just the two of them. They could go up to the roof and talk, the way they used to when they were children. He wanted to vent his exhaustion and frustration, to sob in her arms while she soothed him, reassured him that he wasn't going mad.

'I said, did you remember to pick up bread?'

Karim blinked. 'Bread?'

Khadija was looking at him. 'I sent you a text this morning to buy bread on the way home.'

'Why do we need bread?'

'Because we haven't got any!' Khadija rolled her eyes.

His sister was making fun of him – her own brother – in front of another man!

'We didn't have time to make bread today,' Lalla Fatima

said quickly. 'I was at Lalla Hanane's all afternoon and Ayesha has been busy with *ftour*.'

'And Khadija – why can't Khadija make bread?'

'What's the point of making bread when we can buy it for a dirham?'

Karim quivered with rage. *You think we're so grand that we no longer have to make our own bread! Remind me – was it three takshitas you wanted, or four?*

'Four what?' asked Khadija. 'What did you say?'

Karim stomped into the kitchen, opened the cupboard and pulled out a bowl and a bag of flour. He took them into the *salon* and threw them on his sister's lap.

'You want bread? Then make it yourself!'

When the sun shall be folded up; and when the stars shall fall; and when the mountains shall be made to pass away; and when the camels ten months gone with young shall be neglected; and when the seas shall boil; and when the souls shall be joined again to their bodies; and when the girl who hath been buried alive shall be asked for what crime she was put to death; and when the books shall be laid open; and when the heavens shall be removed; and when hell shall burn fiercely; and when paradise shall be brought near: every soul shall know what it hath wrought.

Karim looked up from his Quran. Thoughts crowded his brain like anxious relatives at the front desk. Where was the sand from? How much money had he earned? Who did Ayesha want to marry? Why was he such an idiot? He gave a sob. If the devils were locked up during Ramadan then why was he being tormented so? *Badda-boom, badda-boom* went Pacha.

He needed a radio to sleep. *Yes, a radio was the answer. He would buy one from Youssef.* The thought of seeing his friend again made him almost weep with happiness.

He picked up the sleeping pills and swallowed one to add to the pill he'd taken at midnight. He tore the filter from his last cigarette and smoked on his side to drive away the mosquitoes. Bitter flakes of tobacco fell on his tongue. Surely the pills should be working by now? He rolled on his other side and closed his eyes.

The girl he'd met at police college was called Fatima Zohra. She had almond eyes and wore her hair in a chignon. They went out a few times, walked around town, ate ice cream in a café. He stopped the relationship after a month. What was the point? He had no intention of marrying her. Just before he graduated, a fellow cadet invited him to a brothel. *They have girls with big breasts, girls with blonde hair, even one from Senegal with skin that shines like ebony.* Karim refused. It didn't seem right, somehow.

The cigarette was burning his fingers and he sat up to stub it out on the floor. He felt in the pocket of his shirt and took out the little sachet marked 'Corpse'. He unwrapped it carefully in the light from the kerosene lamp. He moistened his index finger, dabbed it on the grains and put it to his tongue. It felt strange – intimate – licking sand from Amina Talal's body. *The sand tasted strongly of salt.*

He put the sachet away, went to the door and looked outside. The cypress trees stood like sentinels around the abandoned building. The moon was hidden by a thick layer of cloud and the wind was picking up.

It was still dark when he arrived home.

'You're early,' Lalla Fatima said. Judging by the TV remote control in her hand and the blanket on the divan, she'd been waiting up for him.

'I called Rachid and told him to come and fetch me,' Karim said morosely. 'I couldn't stand it there any longer.'

Lalla Fatima led him into the *salon*.

'Put your head in my lap, come.'

Karim lay on the divan and Lalla Fatima stroked his head, caressing his hair like she used to when he was a boy. Karim felt a delicious tiredness creep over him.

'You've been working too hard,' she said gently.

'*Baalee mshroul*, my head is distracted, Mother. It won't give me peace.'

'If you perform your prayers you will sleep.'

'I perform my prayers. I read my Quran. But God is angry with me.'

'*Shhh*. Don't say such things. God is Merciful.'

'Those pills you gave me – they don't work.'

'They *do* work. You're so anxious that your brain won't let go.'

A few minutes passed. 'I spoke harshly to Khadija last night.'

Lalla Fatima's voice was distant. 'You weren't yourself, you were exhausted. The heat has been insufferable. It's not surprising you've been out of sorts.'

The loudspeaker at the mosque crackled into life.

'Hark, the *fajr* prayer,' she whispered. 'Go and pray in the courtyard. You still have three hours before you set off for the commissariat. After you pray you can catch up on your sleep . . .'

'*Ashhadou anna Mohammadan rasoul Allah . . .*'

Karim felt himself drifting off. '*Hayya ala salaa . . . aaaah haaaya . . . errfff . . .*'

The singing of the muezzin sounded odd, choked somehow, but Karim didn't care. He could feel sleep descending on him like a bird brushing him with his wings.

Lalla Fatima murmured. 'Who is calling the prayer? Si Mohammed? It sounds like he has something in his throat.'

'*Uuurrgh . . . offf . . . fzzzt . . .*'

The singing stopped suddenly. Karim sat upright, fully awake.

'Something's wrong!' He jumped to his feet. Before his mother could stop him he was through the door.

Outside in the empty alleyway he broke into a run. He felt a sense of *déjà vu*. The street lamps . . . the rubbish in little heaps in the square . . . the minaret of Sidi bel Abbès coming into view . . . *Si Mohammed was the muezzin on the night Amina's body was found. He must have witnessed something – something for which he was now paying with his life.* Karim's shoulder clipped an archway: a blinding flash of pain. He ran through the second arch, rubbing his shoulder . . . through the colonnade of shuttered workshops . . . through the third arch with the stucco . . . no beggars around, not at this hour . . . through the doorway and into the mosque. Si Mohammed was lying on a carpet, head against the wall of the *mihrab*, legs folded under his body. The *gardien* was crouched alongside, trying to revive him.

Karim pushed the *gardien* aside. He pressed his fingers against the muezzin's neck to feel for a pulse. Si Mohammed was a good man, a devout man, he had the prayer mark on his forehead to prove it. Allah wouldn't strike His servants down while they summoned the faithful!

'Si Mohammed – who did this to you?' Karim turned to the *gardien*. 'Get a cup of water – now!'

The *gardien* reacted with disbelief. 'If we give him water he'll be breaking his fast! He would never allow such a transgression!'

The muezzin's chest was rising and falling under his *jellaba*, feebly at first, then more regularly.

'I think he's all right,' the *gardien* said. 'Look, he's coming round! Don't you think you should take your hand off his neck?'

My Medina

The ajaj is coming. The ajaj is a hot wind that blows from the Sahara. It is not to be confused with the sirocco or chergui. They are puffs of air in comparison. The ajaj is a rolling wall of sand and dust. The last time it struck Marrakech sixteen people died. Already the wind is gusting and the thermometer has started to rise.

The locals say that the ajaj comes in threes. If it hasn't blown itself out in three days it will last for another three days. It's lucky,

therefore, that the ajaj is a rare event that only occurs in August.
By the time we open in September the weather will be mild and
pleasant again, just in time to welcome our first visitors!

Kay heard a knock at the front door. Her heart fluttered:
Sébastien! She had left a message on his voicemail last night
and *voilà* – here he was! His arrival would give her a chance to
apologise, to make up, to have a laugh about that infernal
monkey! But it wasn't Sébastien. It was the detective who had
escorted Melanie Murray back to the riad. When he spoke, it
was with a thick voice.

'*Bonjour, madame.* Karim Belkacem, Sûreté. *Je voudrais*
vous poser des questions.'

Karim stepped inside without waiting to be asked. He
noted the black and white photographs on the walls, of men
with donkeys and women in *haïks*. What did Europeans see in
these old photographs of poor Moroccans?

'What sort of questions?'

The English woman was taller than Karim remembered,
rude and haughty like her boyfriend. 'I would like question,
madame . . . la mosquée – Amina Talal – Sidi bel Abbès.
Sébastien de Freycinet – he is your boyfriend, yes?'

'Are you feeling all right?' Kay asked, with more annoyance
than concern.

'Your boyfriend may have known Amina Talal. She who
was found dead at the mosque.'

'Is that all you came to tell me? He's already admitted that
he knew her.'

'*C'est vrai?*'

'He interviewed her for a job! They're hiring staff for the new hotel and she applied for a job.'

'Where was Monsieur de Freycinet on evening of 31 July?'

'Why do you want to know?'

'A witness saw him – Monsieur de Freycinet.'

'*Vous êtes mal renseigné, monsieur.* You're wrong. Look, I haven't got time for this.'

'Sébastien de Freycinet was at the same nightclub as Amina Talal, the night she was killed.'

Kay reeled as if she'd been struck across the face. Dear God. She struggled for breath. For several seconds, no one spoke.

'I – I have to close the shutters. The *ajaj* is coming. You must leave,' Kay spluttered. 'Now.'

'Do you know where was he, Sébastien de Freycinet?'

'Go. *Allez!*' Kay pushed Karim towards the door.

Karim gritted his teeth. The woman was typical of her kind. She thought all Moroccans were simpletons. The alleyway outside was a swirl of dust. Karim tried to speak but the heavy wooden door had already slammed shut behind him.

Inside, Kay sank to the floor.

The rest of the day passed in a dream. Karim felt like a primitive organism responding only to sensations. He went to the office and pushed pieces of paper around while Noureddine said things that he didn't understand. The *gardien* from Sidi bel Abbès called to say that Si Mohammed had made a full recovery, praise God. It was low blood sugar, nothing more. On returning home, Karim lashed out at his mother when she told him he was in no fit state to go to the Route d'Ourika. *If I don't earn more money, Khadija doesn't get a wedding.* He ate in silence and left without another word.

Despite the bad weather warnings, the pedestrianised street leading to Jemaa el Fna was full of people. They paraded up and down, eating bags of sticky nuts and buying the latest cheap gimmicks. Karim felt an elbow in his ribs.

Hey, watch where you're going, you moron!

An angel appeared before him. No, it wasn't an angel but a youth selling angel wings. Karim reached out in wonder. The wings were so delicate, so pretty . . .

Aateenee al-floos, pay me if you want to touch them – idiot!

At the Two Brothers Restaurant Karim pivoted down a side street. A few minutes later he stumbled into Youssef's shop, rubbing his temples.

Youssef came over. He said the usual greetings. 'Are you all right?'

'I think I'm having a heart attack.'

Youssef stared at Karim for a second then burst into laughter.

'I'm serious,' Karim said hoarsely. 'What are the symptoms of a heart attack?'

'A pain in your chest—'

'I've got that!' cried Karim.

'An ache in your arm—'

'I've got that as well!'

'And a tendency to talk nonsense!'

Karim wailed. 'I don't know if it's night or day, my brother!

I don't know anything anymore!' He recounted, in rambling sentences, all that had happened over the last few days.

Youssef scratched the stubble on his chin. 'You look done in, my friend. *Nta mhlouk*. Go home. You need to rest.'

Karim shook his head vigorously. 'What I need is a radio.' He picked up a box and studied it.

'That's a toaster,' said Youssef, gently prising the box from his hands. 'Why do you want a radio?'

'I'm alone on the building site and the night is full of horrors.'

'You shouldn't go to work tonight. The *ajaj* will be here soon.'

When Karim didn't respond Youssef called to an assistant to bring over a radio. He turned it on and off then handed it to his friend.

'Genuine fake. Free of charge. How's your investigation going – the one into counterfeit goods? You haven't mentioned it.'

'That's because I've done nothing – *nothing*! What time is it?'

'You have a watch, haven't you?'

Karim got to his feet and headed for the door.

'Hey! Don't forget your radio, my friend!'

Chapter 10

When Karim and Rachid arrived at the Sherezade, a Dacia was parked by the hut. Karim immediately assumed that Khalifa had come to fire him, or at least issue a warning about his behaviour. As he approached the driver's window he noticed Fouad sitting in the passenger seat. Khalifa handed Karim some money.

'Your pay,' he said tersely. Karim took it without checking. As the Dacia drove off he saw Fouad staring back at him through the rear window.

He returned to Rachid and impassively held out his hand. 'Take what I owe you.'

Rachid plucked out a couple of banknotes. He looked past Karim, towards the dark building. The pulley was jangling and the cypress trees were swaying in the wind. 'I can see why this place gives you the creeps.'

When he had gone Karim went into the hut, sat on the bed and tuned the radio to a station of Quranic prayer. He sat for half an hour holding the radio in one hand and the lantern in the other, staring at the wall. The repetitive chanting and the mourning of the wind brought a strange kind of peace to his soul. He recited the eighteenth surah of the Quran to the moths that fluttered around him. A scene from his childhood: getting into a fight with Ayesha, tussling on the floor, smelling the argan oil that Lalla Fatima brushed into Ayesha's hair. He started to drift off. Quickly – so as not to lose this precious sensation of drowsiness – he lay down on the mattress and closed his eyes. It was no use. Within five minutes he was upright, sleep as elusive as ever.

He reached down and picked a hundred-dirham note from the floor where it had fallen. He dangled the banknote in the flame of the lamp. He watched until it had burned all the way down to his fingertips, then let go. The ghost of the king spiralled up into the cobwebs before floating slowly back to earth. He thrust the palm of his hand into the flame. Five seconds . . . ten seconds . . . fifteen seconds. With a yelp he snatched it away. He ran to the back of the hut, threw aside a grey *jellaba* that Fouad had left on the standpipe and rammed his hand into the gush of water. He washed himself all over. He wiped his face with the *jellaba*, returned to the front of the hut, unrolled his prayer mat and raised his hands to his ears.

Allah is the greatest. I bear witness that there is none worthy of worship but Allah. And I bear witness that Muhammad is His servant and His messenger . . . Oh Alive and Everlasting One, grant me rest tonight and let my eyes sleep.

After half an hour he went inside and sat down. He had just destroyed a hundred dirhams. His mother could feed four people for a week on a hundred dirhams. His father said that if he saved ten dirhams a day he would end up a rich man. Burning a hundred-dirham note was against all decency. It might even be against the law. *Oh God.* He looked at the hands of his watch, turning inexorably. Rachid would arrive in two hours. *He needed sleep, by Allah the Merciful and Compassionate, he needed sleep!* He bit his fist, hard, until the blood ran.

Seized by an urgent need to pee he grabbed the torch and went outside. He stood at the edge of the undergrowth, his face turned into the hot wind and unzipped his trousers. He gazed up at the building. *How many suns would burn and winds would blow before the building crumbled like the kasbahs of the South? Concrete or mud, everything turned to dust under the gaze of the Almighty, the Merciful.*

All he produced was a few miserable drops, piss-holes in the sandy earth. Somewhere in his brain a synapse fired. He fell to his knees and shone the torch. He scooped up a handful of sand, rubbed the grains between his thumb and forefinger. The grains were coarse, small but angular.

Sand, like you might find on a beach . . . or a building site!

'The *ajaj* will arrive by mid-morning, they announced it on the radio.' Rachid was staring up at the sky through his windscreen. 'It's already reached Taliouine and that's just a hundred and fifty miles away. I picked up a woman outside Marjane who kept flapping like a chicken and squawking: *the storm is coming, the storm is coming.* I put on some Bollywood music to shut her up. I won't be working tonight, that's for sure. Do you want to work tonight? It'll be hard finding a taxi. The sand clogs the air filters, you see. I know one guy who had to replace his fuel line and couldn't work for two days. *Ya salaam!* Look what they've done now!'

Karim looked through the window. On the advertising hoarding someone had gouged out the eyes of the woman and ripped off areas of the poster. *A portent – that's what it was. Like the dead dog and Bouchaïb's bird that fell from the sky. Evil had taken place. Retribution would follow. The Frenchman had lured Amina to the building site at the Palmeraie, he had raped and killed her then told the security guard to dump her body. A few days later he pushed the guard off the roof. No witnesses, no evidence. Just a few grains of sand.*

'You're quiet, my friend. Don't tell me that you didn't sleep – not again, surely! Did you find that sand you were looking for? By Allah, it's windy! That lorry should pull in before it gets blown over. I'll get you home quick and then I'm going home myself, to sleep. It's going to be the mother of all storms . . .'

Karim's grogginess had gone and his head was clear. He would go to the Palmeraie and take a sample of sand from the building site. The Frenchman would be in jail before nightfall.

'There's a change of plan,' he announced.

In the hotels and clubs of the Palmeraie uniformed staff were covering swimming pools and tying down parasols and chairs. The fairways of the golf course were deserted.

Sébastien stared at the dark bank of cloud. They had five minutes – ten at most – to evacuate the site. Hassan had already sent the dayshift home and the site was empty except for the last two workers, a driver and the errand boy who were waiting for him in the truck. *Grâce à Dieu*, Mohammed had gone back to Qatar. Hassan ran up, his head buried in the hood of his *jellaba*.

'The machinery is under cover!'

'What about the saplings?'

'In the tent.'

Sébastien threw him a set of keys. 'Cover the *quatrelle*. Then get in with us!'

As Sébastien climbed onto the truck he saw a taxi stop at the gate and a figure emerge. It was the young policeman. *Fils de pute!* What a time to visit!

Karim locked eyes with Sébastien. A plastic bucket, carried by a gust, bounced along the ground and ricocheted off the bonnet of the taxi. Karim ran over to a mountain of sand and gravel. He funnelled a handful of sand into an empty water bottle. Seeing the truck start to move off he rushed up and banged on the passenger door. Sébastien angrily rolled down the window.

'*Qu'est-ce que vous faites ici?*'

Karim wrenched open the door and, before Sébastien could react, pulled him out onto the ground.

'Was it there?' Karim pointed at the site office. 'Or *there*? Where did you rape her?'

Sébastien slowly rose to his feet, his gaze fixed on Karim. The truck driver and errand boy were watching, fascinated, their anxieties about the storm momentarily forgotten as the Moroccan faced off with the Frenchman. Grains of sand pattered on the roof of the vehicle.

'Answer!' Karim snarled. 'Did you rape and kill Amina Talal?'

'You're insane.'

Sébastien forced his way past Karim and climbed back onto the truck. Fifty feet away a gantry fell over with a loud crash and a splintering of metal.

The *ajaj* had arrived.

The name Majorelle opened a lot of doors, thought Kay, as she looked out of the shop window. Bernard Simonsen, owner of the most exclusive antiques gallery in Guéliz, had only agreed to see her on the day of the storm because she told him she had a painting by Jacques Majorelle to sell.

'Will you excuse me for a minute?'

Simonsen withdrew to the back of the gallery. He was a stout man with a mane of white hair. If anyone could afford to buy the view of Meknes, Kay reflected, it was him. Prices for Majorelle had rocketed since Sébastien gave her the painting. With the proceeds she could open a gallery in the new town, far from the squalor and cares of Sidi bel Abbès. She would put Samira in charge of the riad and devote her time to antiques and design. As for Sébastien, he could go to hell. She glanced through the window again to check that her taxi driver was waiting. The visibility was worsening by the minute. Fortunately he was still there, his headlamps on.

Simonsen switched on the lights and came back with a jeweller's loupe. '*Alors . . .*' He squinted at the label on the back of the painting then flipped it over and looked closely at the brush strokes. Kay watched with bated breath. It wasn't every day that Bernard Simonsen set eyes on a genuine Majorelle!

He put the painting down. 'I'm sorry, *madame*. It's not by Majorelle.'

Kay went pale.

'There's no record of Majorelle ever visiting Meknes. I just checked on the computer. In addition, the brushstrokes are wrong. See here – these daubs of ochre – they were not done with sable. Majorelle only used sable.'

'But it was bought from the Nassim gallery in Rue Yougoslavie!'

Bernard Simonsen spread his arms with a shrug. 'They closed some time ago.'

'Are you sure it's a fake?' cried Kay.

'It *is* a very good one,' he conceded.

'But I – is it – is it worth anything?'

'A hundred euros, perhaps. A hundred and fifty at the outside – purely as a curio, *vous comprenez*.' The dealer replaced the canvas in its brown paper packaging and handed it back to Kay. 'It's growing dark, *madame*. You should return home quickly.'

Momo was agitated. He didn't like being confined to the utility room. Somewhere upstairs a shutter banged, making him screech and bare his teeth. He leapt onto the washing machine, knocked over a box of washing powder, ran along the ironing board and climbed onto a shelf, dislodging a row of jars.

On the other side of Bab Taghzout the finches were hopping

madly in their cage. Lalla Fatima sat in the *salon*, a blanket over her knees, looking anxiously towards the opening above the courtyard. Khadija and Ayesha were on the roof trying to cover the opening with a twenty-by-thirty-foot sheet of tarpaulin. The storm was fiercer than they imagined. Even with their headscarves wrapped around their faces the airborne sand stung their faces.

'Leave it! It's too difficult! Come and help me tie this end!' Ayesha called to Khadija, her words swept away by the wind. 'Leave – help – end!'

Khadija released the tarpaulin and pulled herself along the parapet towards Ayesha. A wooden crate fell past her and smashed into the courtyard. She had lost both of her slippers and the hood of her caftan was flapping madly about her head. She shut her eyes. *We're done for.*

Ayesha, feet planted astride, was trying to guess the force and direction of the wind. Khadija came up and grabbed the corner of the tarpaulin then, together with Ayesha, put all her weight on it, as if forcing it to submit. The girls managed to secure the corner ring to its anchoring point but the tarpaulin instantly billowed like a sail, wrenching the hook from the wall and nearly blowing away. Ayesha flung herself down on the tarpaulin and screamed at Khadija. Khadija was just three feet away but she may as well have been on the other side of Tamansourt.

'–shing – line!'

Khadija nodded miserably. She sank to all fours, sheltered momentarily from the force of the storm, and climbed the last three steps to the roof. At this higher level the airborne sand was vicious, a thousand hornets stinging her arms and legs.

She crouched behind the parapet. The roof was a scene of devastation; posts torn from their sockets, bottles and cylinders rolling around crazily, anything lighter than a kilo already hurled over the edge. She had experienced the *ajaj* before but nothing like this. It seemed like the Sahara had somehow been lifted up, forced through a gap in the mountains, then ejected in a rush of such force that everything in its path was obliterated, trees uprooted and the roofs stripped from houses, exposing the quivering souls within. With a silent prayer Khadija stood up, immediately struck in the face by the sand. She gripped the pole of the washing line and worked at the knot with numb fingers. The knot was double and treble tied and she knew she could never hope to unravel it. She started gnawing through the rubber. At last, her face burned by the wind, she fell back on all fours and crawled back, the line trailing behind her. The return journey produced a new obstacle: broken glass. Despite taking care where she planted her hands and knees, by the time she reached Ayesha she was bleeding all over. Ayesha grabbed the line, ran it through the ring of the tarpaulin and lashed it around a concrete pillar while Khadija fastened the second ring to its hook. Ayesha fought her way along the parapet and fastened the third ring. She searched the side of the parapet for the last hook but to her consternation it was missing.

'Be quick, Ayesha, for pity's sake!' cried Khadija.

Ayesha saw Khadija's distress, her blood-soaked hands, and motioned to the stairwell. The door was swinging back and forth violently, threatening to splinter. Pushing a gas cylinder in front Khadija crawled over the sill and into the safety of the stairwell. She hunkered down and watched Ayesha from the same step from which her brother had spied on Ayesha four days earlier. Ayesha fed the line through the final ring of the tarpaulin and scanned the roof for somewhere to attach it. The parapet was too far away. That left the tower of loosely cemented breeze blocks under the satellite dish. The dish was wobbling precariously; if the tower gave way the breeze blocks and satellite dish would fall onto the tarpaulin, bringing everything crashing down into the courtyard.

'Oh, Karim!' Ayesha wailed. 'Where are you?'

Her voice was lost in the wind.

In Jemaa el Fna the facades of the buildings were bleached out, indistinct. The square was empty, as if the *calèches* and snake charmers and henna ladies had been wiped from the face of the earth. Karim stood rooted to the spot. He should head north, find shelter behind the high walls of the medina. But instead he headed west, one hand gripping the lapels of his jacket, the other clutching his tightly screwed bottle of sand.

A solitary car came down Mohammed Cinq with its headlamps on. On the pavement, a rubbish bin toppled over, spewing refuse. The restaurant at the crossroads was closed, the sign spinning. The lamp posts were shaking in their moorings.

Karim stumbled a few more yards then stopped, his hair thick with sand. He looked down, observing the grains as they collected in the creases of his jacket. *What djinn had sent this storm? Which ghoul had ridden from the south bringing annihilation?* He raised his eyes to heaven. *Would he be judged, he who had lusted after his sister and betrayed his betrothed? Disaster will smother the earth. Nothing will remain except Allah.*

Everything went black.

By the time Kay came out of the shop her taxi was nowhere to be seen. She tried to hail another but the few taxis that went past were full, or refused to stop. A phone call to Driss went straight to voicemail. She took refuge in an empty tourist restaurant where she nursed a can of iced tea until late afternoon. If she hadn't been carrying that stupid painting she could have gone home on foot! She picked up her phone.

'Lucinda? It's me. I'm in Guéliz . . . yes, I know, what a day! I've just been to have a painting valued . . . a Majorelle . . . Worth coming out for? Absolutely! Can I shelter at yours until the storm dies down . . . oh, thank you!'

Kay wrapped her pashmina around her head and stepped onto the street. The street lamps were already lit although it was only mid-afternoon. The wind was ferocious, the whipped-up sand biting every inch of exposed flesh. Her right hand – the one holding the picture – was soon chapped and raw. She got as far as the traffic lights by the *Poste* and decided it was madness to try to make it across the square to Hivernage. She withdrew to a doorway and attempted to call Lucinda but the network was down. She fumbled in her bag and found Sébastien's spare key. His apartment was only three blocks away. What if he was there? Unlikely. He couldn't drive the *quatrelle* in a sandstorm. He would shelter inside his beloved Serafina.

The ten-minute walk to Boulevard Zerktouni took Kay an hour, her unwieldy burden threatening to fly out of her hand at any moment. Finally, on the corner outside the Négociants it broke free, flying into the road like a piece of cardboard and disappearing under the wheels of a bus. Good riddance, thought Kay, shoving her hands into her pockets.

Without the painting progress was quicker. She opened the door to the building, pressed the light switch in the hallway and leaned back with relief. It was at least six months since she'd been to Sébastien's apartment. She unwound the pashmina from her head and climbed the stairs, her hands and legs tingling. On the second floor she turned the latch to the door. To her surprise the light in the hallway was on. Sébastien's boots lay on the floor and there was a half-drunk cup of coffee on the living room table. From the bedroom Kay heard a high-pitched voice . . . Arabic . . . then a grunt . . . a creak of the bed . . .

Kay advanced to the bedroom and flung open the door. Sébastien was kneeling on the mattress, naked from the waist down. He was fucking someone from behind. It was a boy. He looked about fifteen years old.

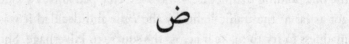

ض

Chapter 11

The following morning dawned clear and bright. Mohammed Al-Husseini stood at his hotel window, stirring his espresso, gazing down at the clean-up operation taking place in the gardens. The storm had caused a lot of damage. His Emirates flight had waited on the tarmac for four hours before finally being told to return to its stand. He'd taken a taxi back to the Méridien and spent all afternoon on the telephone to Doha, rescheduling appointments. He put a photo on social media with the caption *Marooned in Marrakech* and went to bed.

Today was Friday. There were compensations to being marooned in Marrakech on a Friday. He might go to the casino, play a little blackjack. Was it sinful to gamble? Mohammed didn't think so. It was no different to investing in the stock market, an activity pursued by countless Muslims. Mohammed didn't consider himself a bad Muslim. He gave fifty thousand *riyals* a year to charity, said his daily prayers when he remembered and mostly observed Ramadan. Admittedly he drank the occasional coffee, but only in the privacy of his hotel room and only when his blood sugar was dangerously low. Did not the Quran allow breaking of the fast for travellers and the sick? As for his night-time activities, they were not *haram*, except in the eyes of purists like his father. Of course, one still had to be discreet. That was why he let the Frenchman take care of his social arrangements.

He had tried to call Sébastien when the plane was sitting on the tarmac but the network was down. *Adverse weather conditions*, they said. They should see a proper sandstorm. Things only came to a halt in Doha when the windows were breaking!

The storm had blown itself out overnight, *al-hamdulillah*. The builders would be back on site by evening. Any delay would be minimal. Down below, the swimming pool was back in operation. There was a woman in a black swimsuit lying on a sun lounger. She was about twenty-five and had long slim legs. Yes, there were compensations to being stranded in Marrakech on a Friday.

Kay lay on the crumpled bedspread in the Room of the Persian Caliph, staring at the ceiling. After fleeing Sébastien's apartment she had managed to get as far as the railway station where she sheltered for several hours until she found a taxi to take her to Bab Taghzout. Back home, she found a packet of cigarettes and smoked five in succession. Sébastien's lack of interest in sex, his nights off . . . how could she have been so stupid? *Wilful blindness*, wasn't that what they called it? She looked back, almost with nostalgia, to twenty-four hours earlier, when all she had suspected Sébastien of were rape and manslaughter.

Il baise des garçons.

She broke her fingernails beating her fists on the walls and wept hot tears of betrayal. Then she prowled the apartment destroying every item associated with Sébastien. Only Momo was spared.

It was now early afternoon. She hadn't eaten for twenty-four hours. She couldn't get out of her mind the image of the *gandora* hoisted up around the boy's waist, the way the fabric swayed back and forth . . .

My Medina

The gandora is a short-sleeved, ankle-length cotton tunic worn by Moroccan males. It's usually worn over shorts or undergarments and has two vents in the side for accessing inner pockets. Like its female equivalent, the caftan, the gandora is an item of clothing so simple and stylish that – apart from a little detailing here, an embroidered hem there – it has remained unchanged for centuries. A gandora is more elegant than jogging pants and more practical than a dressing gown. As well as being ideal for relaxing around the house it's comfortable to sleep in. Why not buy one for the man in your life? We have a superb selection in a range of colours and embroideries.

Karim woke with a start. He was lying in a room with a high ceiling and white floor tiles. On the back of his hand was a cannula and an adhesive dressing. Opposite the bed was an exercise bicycle and a wardrobe, on top of which was a stack of magazines. Hospitals did not have magazines stacked on wardrobes. Therefore, he concluded, he could not be in hospital. He swung his feet down and walked slowly over to the window. His head was fuzzy but his limbs seemed to work, praise God. Judging by the view of the street below, he was on the fourth or fifth floor, somewhere in the new town. To his left he could see the minaret of the Koutoubia. Directly across from him, in an apartment block crowned with satellite dishes, a woman was doing her ironing. The sky was cloudless. From the position of the sun it was early afternoon. What had happened to the *ajaj*?

He pushed the door open and ventured into the corridor. There was a delicious smell of frying onions. Through the doorway of a kitchen he saw a middle-aged woman laying out a sheet of pastry. She looked up.

'Si Karim! How are you? *Kulshee mezyan?*'

The kitchen was twice as big as his mother's, with a fridge-freezer and a dishwasher. On the sideboard pieces of chicken were steeping in a bowl of water.

'Where am I?'

'Sit down,' said the woman, wiping her hands on her apron. She had a round face and protruding eyes that gave her a startled look.

'I'm Mounir's mother – Mounir Ouheddou. You collapsed outside the mortuary yesterday afternoon – do you remember?'

All that Karim could remember were the palm trees thrashing and the lamp posts shaking in their moorings.

'You've been sick. Mounir was very worried about you. But the colour has returned to your cheeks, God be praised! I hope you will break the fast with us this evening – I'm making *briouates.*' She pointed her knife at two mixing bowls. 'Half with cheese, half with almonds. They're Mounir's favourite! He brought you here in his car. If he'd taken you in the hospital you'd still be waiting to see a doctor. Don't worry – he's spoken to your mother. How is your mother, by the way? Everything well, her health well?'

'The storm – what happened?'

'It has passed. Our neighbours still have no electricity, poor things, but the storm is over, *al-hamdulillah*. Come, I'll show you where the shower is.'

The water felt good on Karim's face. He stood for a long time under it, the powerful jet quite unlike the cold trickle he was used to in Derb Bourahmoune Lkbir. His clothes, freshly laundered, lay on a chair. He dressed slowly and looked in the mirror. His stubble was almost beard-length and he had lost weight, but his eyes had lost their haunted look. He relieved himself and was surprised how full his bladder was. Hearing voices in the corridor he came out of the bathroom, his hair still wet.

Mounir embraced him joyously. 'How are you, my friend? Better? *Al-hamdulillah!* I'm happy to see you!'

'I'm sorry . . . I don't know what . . . how . . .'

'There, there . . .' Mounir soothed. 'Come now, let us sit in the *salon*.'

As he sat down Karim's eyes welled with tears. '*Smeh liya*, forgive me . . .'

Mounir smiled. 'You are forgiven. You must forgive me, too.' He pointed to the cannula in Karim's hand. 'I hooked you up to a drip. There are so many cases of renal failure during Ramadan. I sometimes think we Muslims are too inflexible about our fasting.'

'*Renal failure?*' Karim was shocked.

'You were not well, my friend. Not well at all.'

'The sand – did you . . .?'

'Yes. I had to prise the bottle out of your fist,' Mounir chuckled. 'I guessed that was why you were coming to see me. I looked through the microscope. Your forensic colleagues will need to do further analysis but, on first examination, the sand looks similar to the sand we found on that poor girl.'

Karim felt a flood of relief. 'When will you do the autopsy?'

'Soon, very soon, God willing. *Safee!* Enough questions! Let me take the cannula out of your hand. Have you passed water?' Karim nodded. 'Good. You should rest some more. I have to go back to work but I shall be home at five. We can talk then. You will eat with us, I hope?'

'*La chukran*, no thank you. I have a night job—'

Mounir put his hand on Karim's shoulder. 'Listen to me. You had heatstroke. You could have died. Call whomever you have to call, but you're not going to work, not today, nor tomorrow. I already called the commissariat to tell them.'

'Who did you speak to?'

'A fellow called Aziz.'

Karim groaned. *Why couldn't the duty officer have taken the message?*

'Telephone Lalla Fatima. Tell her I'll bring you home after *ftour*. My mother is a very good cook,' Mounir beamed. 'Why do you think I'm still living at home at the age of thirty-two?'

The front door slammed. This time there was no mistaking who had arrived. Kay steeled herself and went downstairs. Sébastien was crouching by the plunge pool.

'No sand in the pool. And the bougainvillea is still attached to the wall. You're lucky. We lost six palm trees.'

'How dare you walk into my home!'

Sébastien stood up. 'You walk into my home. I should have the right to walk into yours.'

Kay tossed a key on the table. 'You can have your key back if that's what you came for. No doubt you will be needing it for your . . . *friend*.'

'Who? Oh, him.'

'It's so obvious now,' Kay said coldly. 'Why Isabelle left you.'

'We divorced, *c'est tout*.'

'All those nights when you pretended to be out with Mohammed . . .'

'I *was* out with Mohammed.'

'How old was the boy – fifteen? *Fourteen?*'

'*Tsk!*' Sébastien made a gesture of indifference. 'This is Marrakech. Everyone is up to some mischief, some *bêtise*.'

'You call it mischief? Fucking fifteen-year-old boys? And don't give me that *repressed Englishwoman* shit! You're a paedophile!'

'Three days ago you accused me of having sex with prostitutes.'

'That was three days ago. I now know you like boys.'

'I like boys,' Sébastien shrugged. 'I also like girls.'

'You could have given me AIDS!'

'I used a condom.'

'Is that supposed to reassure me? Look at me when I'm talking to you, damn it! How long have we been together? Ten years? For ten years you played me like a fool. I was your cover, your smokescreen, just like Isabelle before me.' Kay strode up to Sébastien, white-lipped with fury. 'Charlatan!'

Sébastien's eyes blazed with anger. '*Je suis un charlatan?* What about you? The story of Zuleika and her pretty little niche? Lies! You paid Samira's sister to write that inscription! You even lie about giving five per cent of your revenue to a children's orphanage! You pretend to be a designer when the only thing you've ever made is a chair that I conceived for you. If I'm a *charlatan* you are *la grande charlatane de Marrakech, toi*!'

'I loved you.'

'Not true! You couldn't bear to be a woman *d'un certain âge* without a boyfriend. That party, when you put me on a throne, to show me off to your guests – they were laughing at you but you were too stupid to realise.'

Kay sat down at the table. Momo was watching from the other side of the courtyard like a scared child seeing a row between his parents.

'I wonder what Laurent would say if he knew his father was fucking fifteen-year-old boys.'

'Laurent?' Sébastien shifted uneasily.

'Secretive activities at African night clubs . . . getting mixed up with murder victims . . . and now this. It's not exactly role-model stuff.' Kay took a piece of carrot from the table. She gave a whistle and Momo scampered across to take it from her hand.

'Are you blackmailing me? I have no money, you know that.'

'I don't want money.'

'What then?'

'Put me in charge of the interiors.'

Sébastien stared in disbelief.

'For the hotel,' Kay continued. 'Persuade Mohammed to fire Jamal and hire me.'

'*T'es complètement folle!* Jamal is one of the best interior designers in Morocco. Why would Mohammed replace him with you?'

'I didn't say it was going to be easy. To remove Jamal, that is. I can handle the decoration.'

'Just because you received some *tout petit* review in *Elle Decoration* you think you can design the interiors for a fifty-million-euro hotel? That's a good joke!'

Kay scrolled through the contacts on her phone. She mimed puzzlement. 'What's the French for *paedophile*?'

'Laurent doesn't care about that sort of thing! He's a student, *il s'en fiche!*' Despite his defiant words, Sébastien's voice was shaky.

Kay tapped the phone on her chin. 'Perhaps I should wait until he's here. He's coming on the twenty-seventh, correct?'

'How much do you want?'

'I told you what I want. This conversation is over. *Degage.* Go now or I'll call the police.' She fed Momo another piece of carrot. 'Leave the key in the hall on your way out.'

Street cleaners in bright yellow uniforms were sweeping up the debris on Avenue Mohammed Cinq as Mounir and Karim drove past. In the plaza opposite couples sat on marble benches gazing at the fountains. The temperature had dropped to a relatively mild thirty-six degrees and some of the men were even wearing jackets.

'My father enjoyed meeting you,' said Mounir. 'Most of his friends from the mountains have passed away, like your late father – God's blessings upon him.'

'The pleasure was mine. I forgot to ask your father if he knew Omar Talal. He's the father of the girl who died – the one whose body is in the mortuary.'

'God preserve the poor man! What an ordeal for a father!'

'It's worse than that. He's been charged with her murder.'

'Her murder?' Mounir was incredulous. 'But that's – is there any evidence?'

'No. At least not yet.'

'Now I understand why you were so keen to see the autopsy results. The Talal case is next on the list. It's scheduled for Monday morning, *inshallah*. I take it you're not the investigating officer?'

'Aziz Al-Fassi is in charge. You spoke to him this morning.'

'You don't like each other?'

'No.' The traffic had slowed to a crawl. There was a fair in El Harti park and cars were double- and triple-parked while families threaded their way towards the entrance. Mounir applied the handbrake and turned to Karim.

'What made you become a policeman?'

Karim smiled. 'I was conscientious at school. I was well-behaved and did everything asked of me. My father told me that marked me out as a tax inspector, a lawyer or a policeman.'

Mounir laughed. Karim continued. 'My father said that nine out of ten cops, tax inspectors and lawyers were rogues or thieves. A few, however, were honest and hardworking and I could be one of them. When I passed the exam for police college he didn't congratulate me – he was a man of few words – but I could tell he was pleased.' Karim suddenly sat up. 'Take the next left.'

Mounir turned out of the queue of vehicles. 'Where are we going?'

They turned into Oum er-Rabia Street. When they were halfway down Karim told Mounir to stop. 'I spoke to a parking attendant a few days ago. He was the last person to see Amina Talal alive.' Karim scanned the street but there was no sign of the old man. Mounir suggested they ask at the *hanoot*, which was little more than a hole in the wall. The owner was arranging flatbreads on the counter.

'*Salaam ou alikum!*' said Karim. 'Do you know where I can find the parking attendant – the one who works in this road?'

'Old Hamza?' The shopkeeper replied without lifting his eyes. 'He's gone.'

'What do you mean *gone*?'

'Been replaced.' The man pointed to a parking meter.

Mounir threw Karim a glance. 'They're installing those things all over Guéliz. We've got one outside our building, a dirham for an hour. Overstay and they clamp your car.'

The shopkeeper said he knew nothing further and waved the two men away so he could attend to another customer. As they walked back to the car Mounir shook his head sadly.

'They'll be getting rid of the shoeshine men next.'

Sébastien didn't regret having sex with the boy. It had made an agreeable start to the evening. It was sheer bad luck, a chance in a million, that Kay walked in on them. He had always been ultra-careful in his recreational activities. He never kerb crawled, never went to the cruising spots in the Cyber Park, never visited the online chatrooms. He had learned his lesson ten years ago when he picked up a boy behind McDonald's. The next night, the boy's father turned up at the de Freycinets' house and shouted at the top of his voice that the *fransawi* who lived there was fucking his son. Sébastien had managed to fob the man off with five hundred dirhams but the episode had cost him his marriage, his home and his children. Now he was in danger of losing his son all over again.

As he sat at the Négociants hunched over a café *nuss-nuss*, he wondered whether to call Kay's bluff. His ex-wife had probably already told the children about his predilection for young men, in which case Kay wouldn't be telling Laurent anything new. His son would still come to Marrakech and Sébastien would have plenty of time to rebuild their relationship.

What made Kay think she could take on Jamal's job anyway? Even if – by some miracle – Mohammed agreed to hire her, the project was well beyond her capabilities. Jamal had designed some of Morocco's smartest hotels and restaurants. He had spent months planning for the Serafina, putting in place a team of highly skilled electricians, cabinet makers, painters and artisans, most of whom would be unaccustomed to taking orders from a woman. If Kay made a mess of things then Sébastien could say goodbye to his bonus as well as any chance of a future career in Lebanon. *Bordel de merde!*

He imagined some pretexts he could give for replacing Jamal: *Mr Al-Husseini, I found out that Jamal is working for one of your rivals; Mr Al-Husseini, Jamal has been embezzling money; Mr Al-Husseini, I regret to inform you that Jamal is a heroin addict.*

Sébastien laughed out loud. The whole thing was insane.

Bouchaïb was drinking mint tea on the pavement with the cigarette seller. He scrambled to his feet when he saw Karim approach.

'Good evening, sir! *Mselkhir!* A nice evening, praise God! What a storm, eh?'

Karim looked up at the night sky. The eye of the bull was crossing the path of the moon. 'Yes, it's lovely to see the stars again.'

He introduced Mounir and the two men exchanged pleasantries. '*Metsharrfeen*, a pleasure to meet you, sir,' said Bouchaïb, emptying and refilling the two glasses. 'Will you share tea with us?'

While Mounir sipped his tea Karim asked, 'Bouchaïb, do you know a parking attendant called Hamza? He's aged about seventy and used to work behind the Hotel de Marrakech.'

'Old Hamza? Yes, everyone knows him. Mad as a snake. He has two wives and lives in the Mellah. He's been an *assas* for longer than me and I've worked since the time of King

Mohammed ben Youssef, God rest his soul!' Bouchaïb made a remark to the cigarette seller who nodded his head vigorously.

Karim told Bouchaïb what the shopkeeper had said about the parking meter.

Bouchaïb sighed. 'It's a scandal, sir. Those idiots at the Wilaya have cotton wool between their ears. When did you last see a parking meter shoo away a thief? Or change a hundred-dirham note?'

'Could you take us to Hamza's house?'

'Now?'

Mounir tried to dissuade Karim. 'It's already nine o'clock. We told your mother we'd have you home by nine.'

'It's good of you to be concerned about me, Mounir. But the Mellah is only five minutes away. Aren't you curious to know who killed Amina Talal?'

'Yes, but—'

Bouchaïb looked from Mounir to Karim, then, sensing that Karim was winning the argument, cried, '*Yellah!* Let's go!'

Sébastien was sitting at the casino bar waiting for Mohammed to arrive. Further along the bar, amidst shouts and raucous laughter, a group of young Moroccan men in suits sat drinking. Sébastien would normally have enjoyed watching them but he was too racked with worry, too desperate to find a solution to an impossible conundrum. He didn't care about his lovers, his friends, his ex-wife or his now ex-girlfriend, but he cared very much about his son. He had no doubt that Kay would deliver on her threat to tell Laurent. He had observed the clinical way she had bankrupted her ex-husband during their divorce.

He pictured two scenarios that might follow Kay's denunciation. *Scenario One*: Laurent knows that his father used to have a penchant for *les garçons*. He then learns that, far from reforming his ways and leading a respectable life in a heterosexual relationship, Sébastien is mired in depravity and has cast aside his broken-hearted girlfriend. Chances of Laurent coming to Marrakech: slim. *Scenario Two*: Laurent, hitherto ignorant about his father's tastes, suddenly finds out that he's a raging paedophile. Chances of him coming to Marrakech: zero. With a sigh, Sébastien got down from his seat and went to the washroom. He ignored the smiling attendant, closed the cubicle door and sniffed a slug of cocaine.

He splashed his face with cold water, dried and looked in the mirror. *Let Kay tell the boy! Who did she think she was, trying to step into the shoes of one of Morocco's leading interior designers? She wasn't fit to decorate the hotel toilets!*

When he returned to the bar he found that his stool had been taken by one of the Moroccans, a man with a grating voice who appeared to have had too much whisky – during Ramadan of all months! Sébastien pushed roughly past. '*Connard*,' Sébastien growled. 'Prick.'

'*Nique ta mère!*' the man shot back. 'Go fuck your mother!'

Sébastien jabbed him hard. The Moroccan grabbed Sébastien by the collar and the two men fell to the floor. Sébastien felt a sharp pain in his chest as the Moroccan landed a punch. He was aware of hands reaching down and separating them, then hauling him to his feet. He shook himself free, brushed down his jacket, withdrew to the back of the bar and sat in the corner, glowering with rage.

Suddenly he had the answer.

Bouchaïb strode lopsidedly ahead. The owners of the souvenir shops near the Bahia Palace, taking down their carpets for the night, stared at the one-legged man with a crutch escorting two well-dressed Marrakchis into the Mellah. The alley led into a dark street smelling of drains, with powerlines spewing from every pillar. Bouchaïb tripped on a broken paving stone and cursed.

'Ever since the Jews left, this place has gone to the dogs!'

He stopped and banged on a door with the handle of his crutch. Karim looked up at the building. Paint was flaking from the windows and weeds sprouted from cracks. It was impossible to tell how many families lived there. Bouchaïb gave the door another rap.

'*Shkoun?* Who's there?'

A woman eyed them through the door grille. Bouchaïb gabbled a few words and the door swung open to reveal a grey-faced woman in a caftan. The three men followed her down a corridor. Shaven-headed children peered from the doorway to the kitchen. The men were ushered into a modest *salon* and a few seconds later Hamza entered. His face broke into a smile when he saw Bouchaïb. The two men embraced and Bouchaïb introduced Karim and Mounir.

'I remember you,' Hamza said to Karim. 'You talked to me outside the nightclub.'

'I'm sorry you lost your job.'

Hamza held out his palms in acceptance. 'God will provide. Did you find your girlfriend?'

'No.' Karim's throat was tight. 'You told me last week that she left Club Afrique with a foreigner.'

'Yes.'

Karim took out his cell phone and showed him the photograph he had taken of Sébastien on the roof of the Serafina. 'Was this the man?'

Hamza studied the face carefully. 'No.'

Karim's heart sank. 'Are you sure?'

'That's not the man.'

Bouchaïb seemed even more disappointed than Karim. 'Come on, Hamza, you're losing your memory. No wonder the authorities got rid of you!'

'He's not the man, I tell you!'

'But you said that she left the nightclub with a foreigner!'

'She did leave with a foreigner. A short man in a suit.'

'A short man?'

'He was no taller than me.'

'How do you know he was foreign?'

'I heard him talking to the girl.'

'In French or in English?'

'Neither,' said Hamza. 'He spoke Middle Eastern Arabic. He sounded like he came from the Gulf.'

Mohammed Al-Husseini's first prostitute had been Moroccan. She gave him oral sex in his BMW in the Dubai marina when he was eighteen. Since coming to Marrakech Mohammed had tried Poles, Latvians, Filipinos and Ghanaians. But he preferred Moroccan girls. They had soft skin from all the exfoliations they did at the *hammam*. And they knew how to please a man.

He walked into the hall of the casino wearing a suit and open-necked shirt. He stopped at the top of the steps and cast his eye around. The two Moroccan girls he could see – a waitress and a cashier – were short and dumpy. When Sébastien greeted him Mohammed pointed with his chin at the blackjack table.

'Her.'

'The croupier?' Sébastien buttoned his jacket and made his way over. The girl was striking, tall, her dark hair cut in a bob. She inclined her head as he sat down at the table.

'*Bonsoir, monsieur.*'

There was one other player, a pasty-looking tourist with thinning hair.

Sébastien lit a cigarette and looked the girl in the eye. 'Russian?'

'Ukrainian.'

Sébastien played a few rounds, making low-stake bets, until the tourist got up and left. He placed a pair of chips on the table. '*Comment tu t'appelles?*'

'Nikita.'

Sébastien switched to English. 'How long have you been in Marrakech, Nikita?'

'Three months.'

'There are easier ways of making money,' he said with a smile.

'Than gambling?'

'Than being a croupier.'

Sébastien took a fourth card on '16' and went bust. Nikita put the deck of cards into the shuffling machine. Quietly but firmly she said, 'I charge three hundred euros.'

Sébastien flicked his eyes towards Al-Husseini. 'He will pay what you ask.'

'Who is he?'

'A businessman from the Gulf.'

'Four hundred euros.'

Sébastien went to Mohammed and murmured in his ear. He received a nod and returned to the blackjack table.

The ousting of Jamal Boussoufa would have to wait.

Khadija flung her arms around Karim's neck.

'Oh Karim, we were so worried about you!'

Karim was touched by his sister's display of affection.

'I'm feeling much better, thank God.'

Lalla Fatima put her hands on his cheeks.

'My poor boy, let me look at you! How you must have suffered, and all because of that wretched night job.'

She welcomed Mounir. '*Ahlan wa sahlan!* It is a pleasure to meet you, how are you? *Labas*, everything well? And your parents – well, I hope? I never had the pleasure of meeting your father but Si Brahim mentioned his name, for sure!'

Ayesha hung back with Karim while Lalla Fatima led Mounir into the *salon*.

'*Yak nta labas?* Are you all right – truly?'

He squeezed her hand. 'Yes.'

'*Al-hamdulillah.*'

'I have so much to tell you.'

'Me too.'

The table was laid with plates of *shebbakiya*, the sesame and honey biscuits that Karim loved. Abderrezak and Mounir were going through the usual pleasantries. Zak embraced Karim, *his brother*, with genuine feeling. While Khadija poured coffee Lalla Fatima recounted how they escaped the worst of the *ajaj*.

'The girls were on the roof. They managed to cover the courtyard but Khadija cut her hands, poor thing.'

'Let me see,' said Karim, taking Khadija's palms. The cuts were already healing.

'It's nothing,' Khadija laughed. 'You should have seen our faces. They were red! We used a ton of Meema's face cream.'

Lalla Fatima raised an admonishing finger. 'Don't forget to replace it.'

'Well, the tarpaulin seems to have held,' said Karim, leaning back to look up at the roof. The tarpaulin was sagging with sand.

'It was so hard to attach!' said Ayesha. 'One of the anchoring points was missing and the other snapped off. Will you help me take it down after we've eaten? I can show you what needs doing.'

'Of course.'

Mounir spoke. 'It was the worst sandstorm I can remember. They said on the news this morning that the wind reached fifty miles an hour.'

'Ayesha nearly got blown away!' Khadija grinned.

'So did you!' Ayesha said, indignant. She remembered how terrified Khadija had looked, crawling across the roof.

'Nonsense, Ayesha, you're as light as a feather. A gust would carry you off. Look at me, shovelling down *shebbakiya*. I've put on a kilo since the start of Ramadan.'

Despite their banter, Karim could imagine how the girls must have struggled. He was grateful that Zak didn't ask questions about his absence during the storm.

'Eat some *shebbakiya*, Mounir.' Lalla Fatima held out the plate. 'Ayesha made them.'

Mounir put one in his mouth. 'They're as good as my mother's! Thank you, Lalla Ayesha!'

Ayesha bowed her head. '*Bessahouraha*, good appetite!'

'I nearly got hit by a motorbike during the storm,' said Zak. 'Blinded by the sand, the rider said.'

'Was he wearing a helmet?' asked Karim.

'Of course not,' grinned Zak. 'Nobody in Marrakech wears a helmet.'

'They should do,' said Mounir. 'So should you, Karim. They're issuing on-the-spot fines – three hundred dirhams.'

'Not for policemen, surely,' joked Zak.

'Twice as much for policemen!' Mounir said with a chuckle. 'Marrakchis are crazy. They'll do anything to avoid paying for a helmet. When I was driving to the supermarket the other day I saw a motorcyclist wearing a strange-looking helmet. It was shaped like an oval, with green stripes. I overtook him to get a better look. Do you know what it was?'

Everyone shook their heads.

'A watermelon!'

The room erupted with laughter.

'The law says you have to wear a helmet. It doesn't say what the helmet has to be made of!'

Everyone laughed again.

Karim leaned back against the divan. Apart from a dull ache behind his eyes, he felt like his old self. *God had been merciful.* He watched Ayesha in her satin caftan, her face glowing as she followed the conversation. He noticed Mounir stealing glances at her. The time had come, he realised, to tell Lalla Fatima their secret. With Khadija leaving to get married, he and Ayesha would be thrown together and he feared the consequences. Perhaps his mother would allow him to move out, apply for a transfer to Rabat or Casablanca. Undistracted by his presence, Ayesha could start looking for a husband. The time had come for them to lead separate lives.

Chapter 12

Under strict orders from Mounir, Karim spent Saturday rest-
ing. He called Khalifa to tell him he was sick, caught up on his
sleep, went to the hammam and attended prayers at the
mosque. By Sunday, however, he was trying to piece together
the final hours of Amina Talal's life from Leila's account of
what happened, from the presence of sand on Amina's body
and, above all, from Hamza's recollection that he saw Amina
outside the nightclub with a man who spoke Middle Eastern
Arabic. When Khadija and Lalla Fatima went out to see the
dressmaker on Sunday morning he told Ayesha his thoughts.
She was mopping the courtyard.

'The French architect works for a Qatari businessman called
Mohammed Al-Husseini.'

Ayesha prodded Karim with the mop. 'Move your feet.'

'Mohammed Al-Husseini may have been in the club that
night.'

Ayesha pulled out the sofa and cleaned the tiles underneath.
She squeezed the mop into the bucket.

'The oath the beggar heard – tell me again.'

'*Allah inaal lhmaar lee weldek.* May God curse the donkey
that gave you birth.'

'Local dialect.'

'Yes. If the Qatari killed Amina then a Marrakchi disposed of the body.'

Ayesha moved the sofa back into position and mopped under the birdcage. 'You need to find out if the Qatari was in Marrakech on the 31 July.'

'I could phone the airport and ask them to check the immigration records.'

'Why not ask your taxi driver? A taxi may have picked him up from the nightclub.'

Karim laughed. 'A Gulf businessman wouldn't need to hire a taxi. He'd have his own driver. Those men are millionaires!'

Ayesha gave her usual shrug. 'As you like.'

Karim realised he had forgotten the most important detail. 'There was sand on Amina's body.'

'From the countryside?'

'No.'

'From a building site?'

Karim was struck by the way Ayesha arrived at the same conclusion that had taken him days to figure out. Not for the first time, he thought she would make a better detective than him. 'It matches sand from the building site in the Palmeraie where the Qatari and the Frenchman are building a hotel. Unfortunately, I can't prove it's identical. I can't talk to forensics without arousing suspicion.'

Ayesha poured the dirty water down the drain. She refilled the bucket and started mopping the stairs. 'You'll have to wait for Mounir's autopsy.'

Karim gave her a sideways look. 'Do you like Mounir?'

Ayesha shrugged. 'He seems nice.'

'I was thinking of inviting him to join us for *Eid es-Sghir*.'

'As you like.'

Ayesha climbed two steps and hoisted the bucket after her. Karim started to follow but Ayesha pointed at his shoes. Karim slipped them off and tiptoed past in his bare feet, perching on a dry step above her.

'Ayesha – we need to tell Lalla Fatima.'

Ayesha prodded his feet with the mop. 'You're in the way again.'

'Did you hear what I said? We need to tell her.'

'Tell her what?'

'You know what I'm talking about.'

'You said you didn't want anyone to know our secret.'

'I want Lalla Fatima to know.'

'Why? We haven't done anything wrong.'

'Ayesha, our feelings for each other are not those of a brother for a sister.'

Ayesha rested her hands on the mop and looked him in the eyes. 'Marry me, then.'

'You know I can't marry you. Marrying you would be like marrying Khadija!'

'So why upset your mother by telling her?'

'*Our* mother,' corrected Karim.

'Why tell her? What would that achieve? The poor woman is in a terrible state. She's devastated about Amina, she's upset about you, about the wedding—'

'Do you think I don't know that?' said Karim, getting heated. 'Do you think I'm not worried about her? The fact remains that Khadija will be married soon and the situation in the household will change. We cannot live under the same roof, you and I. One of us has to move out and it should be me. Meema will want to know why and I will have to tell her.'

'You don't have to tell her about our feelings. Just say you need a place of your own.'

'She would never believe me.'

'Tell her you have to live nearer to the commissariat.'

'Ayesha, I want it out in the open. I want her to forgive me.'

'Forgiveness is for Allah to bestow.'

'I've prayed a thousand times for His mercy!' Tears welled in Karim's eyes. 'But I need Lalla Fatima's forgiveness. And if she forgives me – us . . . then maybe . . . one day, by the grace of God . . .'

He didn't finish the sentence.

'Did things go well on Friday night?' Sébastien was sitting in his boss's suite at the Méridien while Mohammed stood at the window with a coffee.

'Yes.'

'The Ukrainian girl was pleasing?'

'Yes!' Al-Husseini snorted. 'What do you want – a commission?'

'Latifa tells me she has booked you a seat on Tuesday's flight.'

Mohammed grunted.

'We're getting fresh supplies of sand and gravel on Monday afternoon. I'll take you for an inspection before your flight leaves.' Another grunt.

'Can I talk to you about Jamal?'

'What about Jamal?' Mohammed said irritably.

'We might have to replace him.'

Mohammed wheeled around. 'Are you crazy?'

'He said something – *ahem* – worrying.'

'Why should I care what Jamal said?'

'I think he's no longer suitable for the job.'

Mohammed strode over to where Sébastien was sitting. 'Six months ago you begged me to hire Jamal. Now you want me to get rid of him because, what – he doesn't like your dome? Or your precious Line of fucking Water? Listen, fuckwit. We're twelve weeks from opening day. I'm not firing Jamal. I'd rather get rid of you. Is that clear?'

'He saw the Nespresso machine –'

The blood drained from Mohammed's face.

'– a week ago, when he was here.'

Mohammed put his cup down shakily on the saucer. 'And?'

'He said that he had long suspected you were drinking coffee in the daytime.'

Mohammed was livid. 'What – is Jamal playing detective now, the cocksucker?'

'You understand it is not *mon affaire*, but he said . . .'

'What did he say?'

Sébastien paused. 'He said that you were the worst kind of Muslim – one who pretends to observe Ramadan but who breaks the fast when nobody's looking.'

'Son of a bitch!'

'He said it was a big joke that you, the son of a Minister of Islamic Affairs, were breaking Ramadan. I told him he was wrong, that I had only seen you drink at night. But when I took him to the airport he said he had smelled coffee on your breath.'

Al-Husseini curled his hand into a fist. He started to say something, then fell silent.

'I thought you should know.'

Al-Husseini walked back to the window. 'What contract is Jamal on?'

'Jamal is not on a contract.' Sébastien smiled to himself. How many times had he and Jamal commiserated over their boss's refusal to give them a written contract!

'Do you know anyone who could replace him?'

Sébastien braced himself. 'Kay McKenzie.'

Al-Husseini erupted. '*Your girlfriend?*'

'Kay McKenzie is no longer my girlfriend. We separated a short while ago and are no longer on speaking terms. But she is an extremely capable interior designer, as you saw when you attended the party at her riad. She is familiar with the Serafina project and understands what we're trying to do.'

Mohammed said nothing and Sébastien began to think that his stratagem had failed. After a long silence Mohammed spoke. 'Is she available?'

'I know she has just had a commission cancelled. I haven't asked her about the hotel but I believe she could start immediately.'

'Tell Latifa to call her. Now get out of my sight.'

Sébastien was only too happy to oblige.

Night had fallen. Bab Taghzout square was bustling with activity. Karim could smell the aroma of meat grilled over charcoal as he waited with the hawkers of second-hand clothes and household goods. After a few minutes he heard the sound of Bollywood music as taxi 1547 came around the corner.

'How are you, my friend?' smiled Rachid, clearing pistachio shells from his lap. 'You were out of sorts when I last saw you, before the *ajaj* paid us a visit. What a nightmare, eh! A proper hurricane!'

'Yes, I had a fever. I had to take a few days off.' Karim noticed something was different. 'You've got an air freshener.'

Rachid glanced at the pine tree dangling from the rear-view mirror. 'My brother-in-law made me buy it. He wants the taxi to smell like the forests of Ifrane. If I wasn't married to his sister I'd tell him to take a running jump!'

'Rachid – you remember the African club?'

'The place with the prostitutes?'

'Yes. Do taxis wait outside the club?'

Rachid cracked a shell with his teeth and spat out the pieces. 'Where there are nightclubs there are taxis. But, as I told you, the parking round there is a joke.'

Karim gathered his thoughts. 'Rachid ... did you hear about the girl who was found dead at Sidi bel Abbès?'

'Of course! All of Marrakech is talking about the case. Wait – I thought you were investigating counterfeits?'

'That's correct. A colleague is handling the Talal investigation.'

'I heard him on the radio – he said the police have arrested the girl's father. May he burn in hell!'

'The father is only a suspect. He hasn't been before the judge. We don't know yet if he's guilty. At the moment, we – I mean, *my colleague* – is looking into events on the night that Amina Talal disappeared.' Karim told Rachid about the sighting of a Middle Eastern businessman.

Rachid cackled with delight. 'Ha, ha! It's turning into a real detective mystery! A Middle Eastern businessman, you say? It sounds highly likely, if you ask me. Marrakech is full of Arabs from the Gulf. They only come here for one thing. No, two things – to play roulette and fuck whores.' He cleared some more shells off his lap. '*Aiwa*, you want me to find out if a taxi picked up Amina and this Middle Eastern client of hers?'

Karim winced at the mention of *client*. 'Yes.'

'I'll ask my brother-in-law. He was working the night of 31 July. He also knows more of the other drivers than I do. Don't get your hopes up, though. You know what taxi drivers are like in this town, they're all on some scam or other. When someone asks them questions they forget everything except their name and cab number!'

'Don't mention the police enquiry,' Karim said hastily. 'Just say that a businessman left his phone in a taxi outside Club Afrique.'

'*Wakha*. But as I said: Marrakchi taxi drivers are suspicious sons of bitches.'

Rachid turned onto the Sherezade track and trundled past the tamarisk bushes. As they pulled up outside the hut Karim noticed that the light wasn't on under the door.

'Where's Fouad?'

'Oh yes, I forgot to tell you – Khalifa fired him.'

Karim was incredulous. 'Why?'

'Fouad didn't want to work during the sandstorm.'

'*I* didn't work during the storm!'

'You're a cop. Fouad's a nobody.'

'I thought he was Khalifa's nephew?'

'I got it wrong. He's just someone Khalifa knew. I think Khalifa was looking for an excuse to fire him, to be honest.'

'Why do you say that?'

Rachid chuckled. 'Security guards don't last long at this site. Fouad was here for twelve months, that's the longest I've known any man last.'

'Has he found another job?'

'*Ma arfch*, I don't know. The last time I saw him was on Thursday.'

After Rachid had left, Karim stared out over the Sherezade site. Pacha was silent and the facade of the building was bright under the full moon. A donkey brayed somewhere beyond the cypress trees.

He opened the door of the hut with a scraping sound. There was a thin rectangle where sand had entered under the door. Karim sat down on the mattress, lit the lamp and looked around. It felt strange coming back to the hut after three nights away, even stranger now that he was the sole occupant. Although Karim hadn't cared much for Fouad he was sorry that he'd lost his job. Perhaps when he – Karim – handed in his notice Khalifa would reinstate Fouad.

The radio was where he'd left it beside the bed. He opened his bag and took out Lalla Fatima's sleeping pills. He was still unconvinced of their effectiveness but he dared not risk another sleepless night. One pill or two? He checked the back of the packet. The instructions specified *un comprime*. Shouldn't the word *comprimé* have an accent? Were the pills even genuine? Karim was struck by a thought: what if there was a market for fake pharmaceuticals, similar to that for fake designer goods? He would look into it tomorrow, he decided.

His meeting with Badnaoui was overdue. With luck, counterfeit drugs might give him a new, and more rewarding, avenue of enquiry.

He went to the standpipe, washed and said his prayers. Afterwards he felt sleepy. Maybe the pills did work after all. He drifted off to the soft Quranic chanting on the radio.

Chapter 13

My Medina

I'm no fan of property developers. Hardly a week goes by without some lovely old Marrakech building being bulldozed to make way for a block of apartments. But once in a while I come across a good developer — one that builds well-designed buildings in an environmentally sustainable way. One such developer is the Qatar-based AHG (Al-Husseini Group). They're building a beautiful Moghul-inspired hotel in the Palmeraie. And they've just invited me to design the interiors!

Rest assured, dear reader, that I would not have accepted the job if I did not feel the project was true to the principles that I have tried to embody at Dar Zuleika. Nor will it affect arrangements at the riad, where life will continue as calmly and serenely as before.

Meteorological note: I observed an interesting phenomenon yesterday as I was sweeping sand from the roof. The recent storm left a haze of particles in the atmosphere, turning the evening sky blood-red.

Bouchaïb was leaning on his crutch. 'I think we've had the last of the hot weather.' He seemed almost disappointed.

Karim thanked him for his help on Friday night.

'It was a pleasure, Mr Karim. Old Hamza's a wily rogue but he's a good man. The hundred dirhams you gave him will help feed his family.'

When Karim walked into the office Noureddine remarked on how well he looked.

'I've slept better lately,' Karim replied. 'I've stopped smoking and increased my fluid intake as you suggested.' He didn't mention that he had almost died from kidney failure.

Sitting in front of his computer he typed counterfeit medicines into his search engine. Shortly before eleven o'clock he went downstairs and knocked on the door of Captain Badnaoui's office.

'Belkacem. Take a seat. Did you find me a Chinaman?'

'No, sir. That is to say – not yet.'

Badnaoui frowned.

'You asked me last time what the real problem is and I can now tell you that it's not watches, nor sunglasses, nor leather goods.'

'What is it then?'

'Drugs.'

'We have a narcotics squad for that.'

'I'm referring to medical drugs. A third of all drugs sold in the Maghreb are fake.'

'Who cares if a few old men can't get it up because they've taken fake Viagra?'

'I'm not talking about Viagra. I'm talking about drugs for cancer and heart disease, manufactured in China, entering the country by the container-load.'

'So? People get their medicines on the cheap. What's the problem?' Despite his tone, Karim could tell that Badnaoui was interested.

'These medicines are not the same as the real versions. Many have little or no active ingredient. Mothers are giving their babies fake antibiotics. People with serious illnesses are dying because the medicines they rely on contain nothing but glucose, or rat poison. Life-saving drugs are killing people.'

'Where are the drugs manufactured?'

'India and China, as far as we can tell. Mainly China.'

'Do we know who's involved?'

'No. But they're not petty criminals. Some of the medical factories are owned by narcotics cartels.'

Badnaoui put his fingertips together. 'OK, so it's a problem for us in the Maghreb. But this investigation is being funded by the Europeans. What can we offer them?'

'The most popular drugs for counterfeiters are made by international pharmaceutical companies like Bayer and Hoffmann-La Roche that have their headquarters in—'

Badnaoui waved his hand impatiently. 'Yes, I know – Europe. Does Europe have a problem with counterfeit drugs entering their countries?'

'No. Not yet, anyway. But if we can save them millions of euros a day in lost revenue in North Africa, and possibly else-where, I'm sure they'll be happier than if we arrest a few street vendors selling cheap sunglasses. And we'll be saving many of our own citizens' lives in the process.'

Badnaoui considered for a moment. He leafed through the Rolodex on his desk and scribbled some numbers. 'You'll need to liaise with the gendarmerie – this man will tell you the right person. The other number is for OMPIC, the government office dealing with intellectual property. You should also talk to the Ordre National des Pharmaciens.'

Karim saluted. 'Yes, sir.'

'Bring me your recommendations in forty-eight hours.'

Karim saluted again and walked to the door.

'Belkacem?'

Karim turned around. 'Yes, sir?'

'Good work.'

Sébastien watched from the entrance while Kay spoke to Mohammed on the far side of the atrium. Events were moving at dizzying speed. Mohammed had phoned Kay on Sunday morning. By Sunday evening Jamal had been dismissed and Kay appointed in his place. Judging by the laughter echoing across the floor Kay had lost no time inveigling her way into Mohammed Al-Husseini's favour.

When Jamal found out he'd been fired he left Sébastien a furious voicemail. Then another at midnight, full of hurt and recrimination. Sébastien braced himself then dialled Jamal's number. Before Jamal could speak Sébastien launched into a tirade against Mohammed.

'He's acting like a Middle Eastern dictator! He's fired half the engineers and surveyors. He's threatening to tear down the building and start again. As soon as I've finished the *gros oeuvre* he'll fire me as well!'

Jamal harrumphed. 'Do you expect me to believe that?'

'I had no part in your dismissal! When Mohammed offered

me the job in March I told him that I wouldn't do it unless he hired you – *tu ne t'en souviens pas?* Why should I get rid of you now, just when you're about to start work?'

Jamal's reply was laced with scorn. 'And your girlfriend? How does she fit into all this?'

'Believe me, Kay is the last person in the world I want handling the interiors. Mohammed took a shine to her at my birthday party. He's got it into his head that because she did a good job of designing the riad she can do the same for the Serafina. You know much I care about this project. I spend sixteen hours a day on this fucking *chantier*! Would I jeopardise the Serafina by hiring my own girlfriend – someone who has no experience whatsoever?'

Sébastien rang off, unsure whether Jamal believed him. He had deliberately omitted to mention his break-up with Kay, fearing that Jamal might suspect the truth – that Kay was blackmailing him. When Sébastien looked around the atrium, Kay and Mohammed had disappeared. He had an uncomfortable feeling that the balance of power had shifted.

For the rest of the morning Karim immersed himself in counterfeit pharmaceuticals. He called the contact Badnaoui had given him, an official by the name of Elias Alami, and discussed collaboration. He made appointments to see half a dozen pharmacists and compiled a list of websites offering prescription medications. Even Nour was impressed.

'This could be an important case, Karim. Keep going. I'll assign Abdou to help you when he returns from holiday.'

However, at noon, when Noureddine stepped out to pray, Karim put his notes aside and phoned the airport. He asked them to check their records for a Qatari citizen named Mohammed Al-Husseini. Twenty minutes later the answer came back: Mohammed Al-Husseini had arrived in Marrakech on 30 July and left three days later. He had returned to Marrakech on 5 August and would have left on 11 August only to re-immigrate because his flight had been grounded by the storm. In other words – he was still in Marrakech. Karim was so excited by this news that he failed to notice that Noureddine had returned, holding some papers.

'Who are you calling?'

Karim replaced the handset. 'Er – the airport.'

'Why? Are you flying off somewhere?'

Karim was lost for words. He mumbled something about airports and diplomatic bags. Noureddine sat down to study his papers. Karim took the cardboard from the window and stared out at the street. After five minutes he spun around.

'Do you agree that it is wrong to arrest a man for a crime he did not commit?'

Noureddine eyed him suspiciously.

'Amina Talal—'

'By the beard of the Prophet! You insist—'

Karim held up his hand. 'Please, Noureddine, *a sidi*! You've been a friend to me and a mentor, and I'm grateful – truly I am. May God bestow his blessings on you. But I beg of you – listen to me one last time! Amina Talal was killed fourteen days ago. As you know, I was the officer on the scene. Amina Talal was betrothed to me – for a time at least. Her father, who is now in prison accused of her murder, was a good friend of my father. All this gives me a right to speak. Today the autopsy will be carried out, *inshallah*. It has already been delayed for a suspicious length of time but we'll leave that aside. The autopsy will show the presence of sand on Amina Talal's clothes. I know where the sand comes from.'

Noureddine opened his mouth but Karim again held up his hand. 'The last witness to see Amina Talal alive was a parking attendant named Hamza Tantaoui. He says that Amina Talal left Club Afrique at around one o'clock in the morning with a businessman of short height who spoke Middle Eastern Arabic. I have reason to believe that this man was Mohammed Al-Husseini. He is a thirty-year-old Qatari property developer and financier. He's developing the hotel in the Palmeraie that you and I visited after the death of the security guard. I found sand on the building site that matches the sand on the victim's clothing. There's a clear link between Al-Husseini and the dead girl.'

When Karim had finished Noureddine took off his glasses, rubbed his eyes and replaced them.

'Well?' Karim demanded.

'You think we're incompetent, don't you?'

Karim was taken by surprise.

'You think that Aziz hasn't been doing his job,' continued Noureddine. 'That he's been sitting on his backside because of Ramadan.'

Karim could feel the blood pounding in his temple. 'I am requesting permission to interview Mohammed Al-Husseini. I'm happy to do so with Aziz, if necessary.'

'I will not give you permission to interview Mohammed

Al-Husseini, nor anyone else for that matter. Think yourself lucky that our conversation won't go beyond these walls.'

'There's no evidence that Omar Talal killed his daughter!'

'There's no evidence that Mohammed Al-Husseini killed her, either. Even if he left the nightclub with Amina Talal we cannot detain him.'

'Why? Because he's a businessman?' Karim retorted. 'Because his money is so important to Marrakech that we have to turn a blind eye to his activities – even if they include raping and murdering a Moroccan girl?'

'You really believe that Mohammed Al-Husseini raped Amina Talal?'

Karim chose his words with care. 'I believe that Mohammed Al-Husseini went to the nightclub, picked up Amina Talal and took her to the Serafina, where there were no witnesses apart from a security guard. I believe that he raped her, killed her, then got the security guard to dump her body.'

'So a millionaire would go to a rubble-strewn building site to have relations with a girl rather than do so in the comfort of his hotel room?'

'His father is a Qatari minister of state. He can't afford to take risks.'

'You said just now that Omar Talal was a good friend of your father. I, too, was a friend of your father. When you took the job in Marrakech I asked Badnaoui if you could serve in my office. You are a talented young man with a bright future. It is a source of sadness to me that your betrothed was killed and that your father's friend is now in prison. However, you are insubordinate, you are arrogant and, above all – you are wrong.'

Noureddine held up the paper on his desk. 'I have received the autopsy report on Amina Talal.'

Karim felt as if his legs had turned to jelly. Why hadn't Mounir called him?

'The chief pathologist claims that he was told to put the case at the top of today's list – you wouldn't happen to know anything about that, I suppose?'

Karim shifted uncomfortably.

'Shall I tell you what the report says?' Nour read aloud. 'There were no traces of semen.'

'The killer had a whole day to tamper with the evidence!'

Noureddine peered over his glasses. 'Do you think Amina Talal was promiscuous?'

Karim reddened. 'I – I think she liked to go dancing. She may have had sexual relations with men, but I don't see how that is relevant.'

'You think she had sex on the night of 31 July?'

'I think she was raped on the night of 31 July.'

'Amina Talal was not raped on the night of 31 July.'

'She had consensual sex?'

'No, she didn't have sex at all. Not on that night, nor on any other night.'

'How can you possibly know?'

'Amina Talal was a virgin.' Noureddine held out the report. 'Here, see for yourself.'

Hicham Cherkaoui watched the lorry, the third in an hour. Like the others it was carrying a cargo of sand – a cargo that, by the look of it, was in excess of its permitted axle load. After a few minutes the lorry was followed by scooters as men started arriving for the night shift. Hicham had counted 143 men last night, another 165 that morning: over 300 men labouring to build a hotel for rich tourists. Meanwhile, the city's schools were crumbling and the poor of Marrakech had nowhere to live!

Hicham's mobile rang. It was his wife, enquiring whether he would be coming home to eat.

'I don't know.'

He had received an angry call earlier from the director of investment for the Marrakech-Tensift region, asking what Hicham thought he was doing, spying on a new hotel in the Palmeraie. *My job*, Hicham replied, before terminating the call abruptly. So what if he got into trouble? He observed a teenage boy leaving the gates. He looked too young to be working on a building site. Hicham picked up his camera and took a photograph. Something told him he wouldn't be home for *ftour*.

It was a tense mealtime, very different from the night before.

'A virgin?' Khadija said, as soon as Lalla Fatima had left the room. 'It doesn't make sense. If the man didn't rape her why did he abduct her?'

'Maybe he tried to rape her but she fought him off,' replied Ayesha. 'Some women would rather die than surrender their virtue.'

'We don't even know if she was the victim of an attack,' Karim sighed. After Noureddine's bombshell that afternoon he realised that he didn't know anything anymore.

'Come on, Karim!' said Ayesha. 'Someone must have put her in the handcart!'

It was Khadija's turn to speak. 'At least she preserved her honour. All those people who badmouthed her will have to button their lips.'

'You were among the badmouthers!' Ayesha hissed.

'I only wondered what she was doing at a nightclub!'

They fell silent as Lalla Fatima came into the *salon*, sheets folded over her arm. 'I'm going to Lalla Hanane's. She's in no state to make arrangements for the burial.'

'I can help,' offered Ayesha. 'I'll wash the body if you like.'

'Khadija, you come too,' said Lalla Fatima. 'We'll take care of the dishes when we get back.'

Karim chaperoned the women as far as the Talal house, then returned to the square to wait for Rachid. While he was sitting on the wall, munching a deep-fried doughnut, Mounir called.

'The results aren't what you expected, are they?'

'No.'

'There was no foreign DNA on her body, no signs of a struggle. Nothing that points to a perpetrator. Did you read what we said about the trauma to her skull?'

'No. I skimmed everything apart from the paragraph about her being . . . intact.'

'The wound on her temple is not consistent with being hit over the head. It's more likely to have been caused by a fall.'

'A fall? She fell to her death? Why is everybody falling to their death all of a sudden?'

'Ah, that's your domain, my brother! All I can say is that she fell. It could have something to do with the fact that she had alcohol in her bloodstream.'

'Alcohol?' Karim remembered what Hamza had said about Amina swaying outside the club.

'Yes, she had a blood-alcohol concentration of .10 per cent, enough to incapacitate her. Are you going to re-open the case?'

Karim gave a sigh. 'According to my superior officer nothing has changed. There's no new evidence that might point to a different assailant. They're going ahead with the prosecution of her father – may God have mercy on him!'

A few minutes later, Rachid pulled up. He had more bad news. 'I talked to my brother-in-law but he refuses to get involved. As I told you, the taxi drivers in this town are suspicious sons of bitches. They don't like being asked questions.'

'What about you?'

'Me?'

'Can you make enquiries?'

'I'm happy to try. But the drivers I know follow the same routine as me. They wait outside the big clubs like Pacha or the Three Fives, where the parking is easy and there are lots of customers. That African club is too small for most drivers to bother with.'

Something had been nagging at Karim since he last saw Rachid. 'Can I ask you a question?'

'*Maaloum*, of course.'

'How did you know that your brother-in-law was working the night shift on 31 July?'

'He always works nights. He only does the day shift during Ramadan because he likes to put his feet up at his mother's house and stuff his face with *shebbakiya*.'

'Do you trust him?'

'My brother-in-law? He's not involved in the girl's death, if that's what you mean.'

'How do you know?'

'My brother-in-law's a numbskull but he's no killer.'

'Is he married?'

Rachid laughed.

'Why do you laugh?' asked Karim.

'He was married but his wife cheated on him while he was working nights. He says he wouldn't have married her if he'd known what she was like.' Rachid chortled. 'That reminds me of a joke. What's the secret that no man knows about his wife until they're married?'

Karim blushed.

'Er – whether she's a virgin?'

'No – whether she can cook!' When Rachid had stopped laughing he asked, 'Is your sister a good cook – the one that's getting married?'

Karim pondered the question. 'I can't remember the last time Khadija cooked a meal.'

'Tell her she needs to be a good cook if she wants to keep her husband. My wife's a good cook. She made *briouates* this evening with ginger and cinnamon ... mmm!' Rachid smacked his lips. 'Our little girl helped to fold them.'

'You have a daughter? *Tbarekallah!* How old is she?'

'Five – not so little anymore!'

'May God preserve her. Is she at school yet?'

'She starts primary school in September ... then *poof!* Before you know it, she'll be a teenager.' Rachid's face clouded. 'Marrakech is no place for a girl to grow up.'

'Why do you say that?'

'It's so –' he searched for the right word, '– shiny. Everywhere you look – money, money, money. Alcohol and nightclubs around every corner. See over there – the Hotel Mansour? Guess how much they charge for a room? A *milyoon*! For one night. It used to be a public swimming pool! When I grew up Marrakech was a decent city, where everyone earned the same.'

'But you've done well, haven't you? All those tourists with deep pockets?'

Rachid gave a snort. '*The grands taxis*, the people carriers – that's what the foreigners want, with air conditioning and black-out windows. Marrakech has changed, my brother, and not for the better.'

There was truth in Rachid's remarks, Karim reflected. Places like Club Afrique had not existed when he was a boy. Men like Mohammed Al-Husseini had not come in search of sex. Girls had not gone to nightclubs and ended up dead in a handcart.

After Rachid had dropped him off at the Sherezade he sat on the step for a while, gazing at the stars. He took out his phone and sent Ayesha a text message, wishing her well for the long night of washing and anointing Amina Talal's body.

Chapter 14

It was the twenty-seventh day of Ramadan. The heatwave had subsided. At the hospital and mortuary activity had returned to normal. Foreign residents were drifting back from their vacations. Tonight was Lailat al-Qadr, the Night of Destiny, the night on which the first verses of the Quran were revealed to the Messenger of Allah, Peace and Blessings be Upon Him. The night of Lailat al-Qadr was said to be more propitious than a thousand months of worship.

Karim dressed quickly. Lalla Fatima was standing at the doorway to her bedroom, leaning on her stick.

Karim kissed her on the cheek. 'I will go to see Omar Talal today after work.' Omar had been languishing in prison for three weeks and Karim had promised his mother that he would check on him.

'*Inshallah*. Tell him that God watches over him.' When Karim was putting on his jacket Lalla Fatima called across the courtyard, 'Make sure you get back in good time for *ftour*.'

'Have we got visitors?'

'No, Khadija is eating at Abderrezak's parents' house. I thought that Ayesha, yourself and I could have a little celebration together, just the three of us.'

As he set off down the alley Karim wondered if tonight was the night to tell his mother about himself and Ayesha. He considered the reasons in favour. Lalla Fatima had got over the shock of Amina's death; he was nearing the end of his night shifts; the wedding was looming. *Now was the time, now – on the holiest night of the year, when prayers were most likely to be answered!* The prospect of the secret being in the open made him tremble. What impact would the confession have? As Ayesha kept reminding him, Lalla Fatima was frail. What if, instead of forgiving them and knowing what to do, she had a heart attack? Should he remain silent – or was that the act of a coward? *Oh God, truly Thou are the greatest forgiver and Thou likest the act of forgiving. Hence, please forgive us.*

To postpone making a decision Karim decided to go to Dar el Bacha. It was still before nine o'clock. If his *moto* was fixed he would be able to see Omar Talal after work and get home in time to consult with Ayesha. In fact, he decided, he would take the *moto* even if it wasn't ready. He would wheel the wretched thing all the way to the commissariat if necessary, ask Bouchaïb for the name of a different mechanic – one who was prepared to roll up his sleeves instead of standing around blaming Ramadan for his laziness! As he walked into the *mecanique* he almost fell over his *moto*, shining like new.

The mechanic greeted him like a long-lost friend. 'It's been ready for days! Why didn't you come and pick it up earlier?'

Karim was too relieved to argue. He paid, climbed on the scooter and roared off. Praise God! It felt good to feel the wind in his hair, to zip through the shafts of sunlight under the palm trees.

'Behold!' exclaimed Bouchaïb as he arrived at the commissariat. 'The wizard on his flying carpet!'

Karim laughed. 'How are you, my brother? I wish you and your family peace and prosperity for Lailat al-Qadr. What have you got there?' he asked, pointing at a box by Bouchaïb's foot.

'Pomegranates from Ourika.'

'Ourika? Is Abdou back from his holiday, then?'

'He arrived not half an hour ago!'

Karim hurried into the building. Abdou was three years younger than Karim, a good-natured deputy whom everyone liked. He was the only man in the commissariat to whom Karim could give orders without receiving a scowl in return. As Karim approached the steps he heard the sound of laughter. Abdou was in the downstairs office joking with Aziz and some other officers. Abdou spotted Karim and came over, beaming. He kissed Karim on both cheeks.

'How are you, my brother? Everything OK? Health good, the family well? Praise God! I was telling the others how my cousin and I climbed Mount Toubkal. We froze our asses twelve thousand feet up while you were wilting in the heat! Here, I brought you some pomegranates.'

'It's a pleasure to see you again. Let's go to the office.'

Abdou followed Karim up the steps with the fruit box. 'I expect everything's been quiet while I've been away?'

Karim threw him a sidelong glance. 'Not exactly.'

Sébastien walked across the plant room. Here, humming quietly and smelling faintly of chlorine, were housed the machinery, filtration system and reservoirs for the Serafina. Each pool had its own water supply, every valve, pump and conduit clearly labelled. The room was located underground, behind the main building, out of sight of the guests who would enjoy the results of its elaborate workings. Sébastien had designed the plant room himself and he had held a little celebration two days ago when they finally turned on the taps.

He was in a good mood that morning. Laurent was arriving at five o'clock and Sébastien was planning their first evening together: a leisurely drive back from the airport admiring the changes that had taken place in the city, followed by champagne at the apartment, then cocktails in the rooftop bar of the Renaissance and dinner at the Comptoir. On second thoughts, the Comptoir might seem a little *démodé* to a Paris art student. Kosybar was too noisy . . . Bô-Zin too expensive . . . that left Club Afrique. Yes, everyone liked Club Afrique. It had just re-opened and there was sure to be a good band playing. Sébastien put on his sunglasses, stooping to avoid the low door frame, and climbed the ladder to the surface.

Two uniformed policemen were standing in the sunshine. 'Sébastien de Freycinet?'

Sébastien's first thought was that their presence was something to do with the dead security guard. 'Yes?'

'We have reason to believe that you have broken the law,' said the first officer.

'*Vous êtes en état d'arrestation*,' added his colleague.

'Under arrest? What for?' Alarm bells went off in Sébastien's head. 'I had nothing to do with the death of the security guard!

Or the disappearance of that girl! Or is it to do with that other matter? Has my girlfriend been spreading lies about me? No? What are you arresting me for, then?'

'Sand,' came a voice.

Sébastien wheeled around to see Hicham Cherkaoui walking towards him. Sébastien laughed incredulously. '*Sand?*'

'Show me the paperwork for your sand, *monsieur*.'

'*Paperwork?*' Sébastien laughed again.

'For your sand. The sand you use for construction.'

'Are you out of your mind?' asked Sébastien, recovering his confidence. 'This is a five-star hotel we're building. Do you think I have time to check the paperwork for every load of sand?'

'The last time we met, *monsieur*, you adopted the same high-handed attitude. On that occasion it was a matter of compliance with building regulations. Now we have evidence that you have broken the law by buying contraband sand. The buying of contraband sand is an offence.'

'Who cares about sand?' Sébastien spluttered.

'Unauthorised removal of sand for construction is leading to the destruction of our country's beaches. You may not care about such things, *monsieur*, but the government has made it a punishable offence. I have counted a total of ninety-two lorryloads of illegal sand, rendering you liable to a fine of two hundred thousand dirhams or two months in prison.'

Sébastien looked up at the sky. He suddenly felt very tired.

'*Amenez-le*,' said Cherkaoui. One of the policemen took Sébastien by the arm.

'Wait,' cried Sébastien. 'My boss – he'll pay the fine!'

'You can call him from custody.'

'*Custody?*'

'You will be detained until the fine is paid.'

Sébastien was seized with panic. 'I have to go the airport! My son is arriving from Paris!'

'You can call your son from custody as well.'

'Cardiovascular medicines . . . cancer drugs . . . diabetic treatments . . . arthritics . . . tranquillisers . . . antibiotics. They're the most profitable drugs. And Viagra, of course.' Karim was looking at his computer screen while Abdou took notes. 'A doctor told me of a cancer drug that usually costs twenty-two thousand dirhams. This site has a fake version for fifteen hundred.'

Abdou whistled. 'Do the fake versions work?'

'A few. Most are little more than placebos. The worst are cut with harmful substances. Part of our task is to educate people about the risks. We need to show them how to spot fakes.'

'Isn't that a job for the health ministry?'

Karim laughed. 'By the time they get around to doing anything there won't be a genuine medicine left in the Maghreb.'

'So where do we start?'

'The pharmacies.'

'Are they part of the scam?'

'Let's visit a few of them, see what they have to say.'

'Pharmacies in Marrakech?'

'Yes. And ones further afield – Chichaoua, Safi, Ouarzazate. We'll take samples for analysis. We need to draw up a list of all drugs which are being counterfeited and where they're coming from. Next we'll start on the ports. What have you found out so far?'

Abdou looked through his notes. 'Casablanca, Al Hoceima, Tanger-Med, Kenitra and Mohammedia have good security. Tan-Tan, El Jadida and Dakhla are too small for containers. Jorf Lasfar only handles phosphates. That leaves Agadir, Laayoune and Nador.'

'Track Chinese container shipments to those ports.'

'What sort of shipments?'

'Any kind. Green tea, clothes, toys . . . anything they can smuggle drugs in.'

Abdou was bemused. 'You make it sound like heroin.'

'It's worse than heroin. More dangerous, in a way. The profits are *kbar bezaaf*, they're enormous. Let's say a criminal network makes forty thousand dollars' profit on a kilo of heroin. They can make ten times that amount on pirated pharmaceuticals. And compared to heroin manufacture, the cost of making these drugs is very low.'

'Presumably the risks are lower as well? There's little chance of getting caught?'

'*Hakkak*. Correct. As far as I can tell, there's no agency or government in Africa who has the determination or the ability to stamp out the trade. Certainly not here in the Maghreb. Just a few staff at OMPIC investigating intellectual property theft.'

'Not yet!' grinned Abdou.

'What do you mean?'

'Our investigation could change all that!'

Karim was aware of Noureddine listening in on their

discussion and, although he, Karim, was thrilled to have Abdou working with him, he tried to curb the younger man's enthusiasm. 'All we have is the authority to find out what we can. We're not likely to stop the illegal medicine trade by ourselves.'

'Well, it's a start!'

Karim pointed at Abdou's notebook. 'Contact the ports we mentioned. The port authorities will have records of all inbound container traffic and the bills of lading.'

'What if the bills of lading have been falsified?'

Karim gave a sigh of agreement. 'You're right. We can't trust anything. Or anyone. Least of all the port officials. Do what you can. Find out where the containers go after leaving the ports, put tabs on the lorries if necessary. We'll see if a pattern emerges.'

Abdou's eyes were shining. 'This is exciting!'

'It will also be dangerous. You'd better carry your gun from now on.'

While Sébastien was being arrested, Kay was in the atrium taking photos of the workmen laying tiles on the floor. Every *carrelage* workshop in Marrakech had been working flat out to meet her deadline.

'Is everything going smoothly, Miss McKenzie?'

Kay turned to see Mohammed coming down the staircase. In jacket and tie, with his stilted English, he resembled the master of a stately home.

'Yes. How do you like the tiles?'

'I like them very much,' said Mohammed, leaning on the banister. He had exquisitely manicured hands, Kay noticed, very different from Sébastien's rough paws and chipped fingernails.

'It's a traditional Moorish pattern. Two-thirds the price of marble.'

'Ah, saving money – that's the part I like best!'

'I've tracked down a chandelier. It's early twentieth century, a magnificent piece from Murano.'

Mohammed gave a mischievous wink. 'Jamal thought that chandeliers were un-Islamic.'

'Oh, I disagree! The Blue Mosque in Istanbul has the most incredible chandeliers. Nobody would call the Blue Mosque un-Islamic, in fact, it's considered one of the most beautiful Islamic buildings in the world.'

'How expensive is this Murano chandelier?'

'Don't worry. The dealer, Bernard Simonsen, is a friend of mine. You'll be getting a museum-quality piece at a very competitive price – just like the other items you've bought.' It had been a masterstroke, reflected Kay, to use her spare furniture, carpets and *objets d'art* to decorate the Serafina. Naturally, she'd made it seem like Mohammed's idea.

'I hope we're not turning the hotel into a museum.'

Kay rested her fingers lightly on Mohammed's elbow. 'At the very highest level, Mr Al-Husseini, hotels *are* museums.'

Mohammed chuckled. 'We should put that in our publicity.'

'Good idea! We could put something online to whet people's appetite before the hotel opens.'

'Like a blog?'

'Exactly! A blog. Could Mouna write a blog, do you think?'

'Mouna is too busy. What about you? I expect you're too busy as well.'

'Me?' Kay feigned surprise. 'I suppose I could have a go. I could include photos.'

'As long as you include some photos of yourself,' Mohammed leered.

Kay smiled. Mohammed Al-Husseini was a typical Arab businessman. One minute he treated her as an equal; the next he came across as a rampant chauvinist. She, on the other hand, could play him like a fiddle.

'Are you going back to town?' she said sweetly, aware that Mohammed had hired a car and driver.

'Do you need a lift?'

'That would be wonderful. We could discuss the restaurant on the way.'

As they walked out of the building Hassan came running up with the news of Sébastien's arrest.

Laurent was pleasantly surprised by the air-conditioned baggage hall with its marble floor and elaborate ceiling. When he'd left Marrakech ten years ago the luggage trolleys were broken and the toilets stank of piss. He waved to the girl that he'd sat next to on the plane and helped her lift her heavy suitcase from the carousel. They walked together through the sliding doors. The arrivals hall was even more of a showpiece, a vast atrium with arabesque windows and a ceiling that looked like a geodesic dome. He scanned the men with signboards. Was that his dad over there, in the jacket and jeans? No: the man looked seventy at least!

Laurent stopped for a moment. His mother had tried to make him cancel the trip, haranguing him all the way to Orly. *His father never sent any money; his father was a deadbeat.* OK, so the old man hadn't been much of a father but that was no reason to cut him out of their lives!

Maybe he'd sent a driver – yes, that was it! Laurent doubled back to the exit but the men with signboards were already melting away. He sat on a bench and called his father's cell phone. It went to voicemail. His heart sank. If his dad was tied up with work, surely he could have sent his girlfriend – the English woman, what was her name, Kay? Why couldn't she have come instead? But no; there were no middle-aged Englishwomen wandering around scanning the passengers. The girl from the plane was walking away from the terminal with a Moroccan in dark glasses. All Laurent's excitement at visiting Marrakech evaporated. He wished he never had come.

It took Karim only a few minutes to drive to Boulmharez prison. From the outside, Boulmharez looked like a typical government building: a nondescript doorway with a red and green flag hanging limp in the afternoon heat. Only the barbed wire on top of the walls gave away the building's true purpose.

Karim parked his scooter outside the entrance and bought a packet of cigarettes as a gift for Omar. Did Omar smoke? It seemed unlikely. But even if he didn't smoke he could always trade the cigarettes for something useful.

Karim showed his ID and a guard ushered him through the main gate. With each successive gate the conditions grew grimmer. The last gate led onto the wing. The corridor was lit with wire-protected overhead lamps and the floor was still wet from a recent sluicing.

Just when Karim thought they had walked the length of the prison the guard stopped and unlocked a door. Karim could make out twenty or thirty men in the gloom. The smell from the latrine was overpowering. Using his baton, the guard prodded the men aside until he came to a huddled shape in the corner.

'*Jibooh*,' he ordered. 'Bring him out.'

Two of the inmates helped Omar Talal to his feet, pulled him across the floor and sat him on a stool in the passageway. Although Karim was braced for the worst he was shocked at the *hajj*'s condition. His eyes were sunk deep in his head and his limbs were stick-thin, the skin coming off in flakes. He made the beggars of Sidi bel Abbès look like paragons of fitness.

'God look after you, Si Omar! How is your health? Are you eating? Your hearing will take place soon, *inshallah*. Abderrahim is in Kenitra waiting for an appeal. May God preserve him! Did you know that tonight is Lailat al-Qadr. Yes, Lailat al-Qadr!' Karim crouched down. 'Do you want to smoke a cigarette at sundown? Here, take them.' He placed the cigarette packet in Si Omar's lap but they slid onto the floor.

Omar's voice was barely a whisper. 'Karim . . . *wld* Brahim . . .'

'Yes! I am Brahim's son! You herded goats together, do you remember, in Amassine, many summers ago. I saw Ahmed Ouheddou recently, from Aït Ourir. Ahmed Ouheddou! His son works at the mortuary. I had *ftour* with the family. They have a lovely apartment in Guéliz, *tbarekllah*.'

For a long time Si Omar said nothing. Karim was starting to get cramp in his leg. The guard tapped his baton impatiently. Then Omar lifted a bony hand.

'*Bintee* . . . my daughter.'

'Your daughter? What about your daughter?' Karim leaned in close to catch the old man's words.

'My daughter . . . I want . . . to see . . . daughter . . .'

'Amina is buried, may God have mercy on her.'

'I want to see my daughter . . .'

'You will see Amina in the afterlife, if God wills it.'

'I want to see my daughter,' Si Omar repeated, this time clutching Karim's collar.

Karim gently unclasped Omar's fingers. '*Seer fid Allah*, go in God's care.'

He nodded to the guard who unlocked the cell door and jabbed the two nearest inmates. They got up and dragged Omar back into the depths.

The guard led Karim back along the corridor. There was nothing to be done for the old man. His mind had gone and the best lawyer in the world wouldn't be able to save him. Karim was wondering how to break the news to Lalla Fatima when he heard a shout. He looked around to see a white face pressed against the bars of a cell. Taking a step closer, he recognised the Frenchman.

'You!' he cried.

'*Tout à fait!*' replied Sébastien. He was still in the clothes he had been wearing when he was arrested. He told Karim what had happened.

'That sonofabitch *merdeux* planning officer is doing this to get back at me, just because I wouldn't comply with his stupid safety regulations! I paid for the repairs for his car! I even added two thousand dirhams for the inconvenience! Are those cigarettes?' he said, noticing the packet in Karim's hand. '*En donnez-moi!*'

Karim handed a cigarette to Sébastien. The guard produced a lighter and Sébastien drew on the cigarette greedily. 'You've got to get me out of this shithole.'

Karim peered into the darkness. Sébastien seemed to be alone in the cell, which looked like one of the holding cells at the commissariat. 'I'm sure you'll get out in good time, *monsieur*.'

'You don't understand! My son is arriving in Marrakech. He's probably at the airport now!'

An idea started to form in Karim's mind. 'I can't get you out. That's a matter for the judge. But I may be able to help you.'

'How?' Sébastien asked eagerly.

'I can fetch your son.'

'Yes, yes!' Sébastien fumbled in his pocket for a key. 'Take him to my apartment in Boulevard Zerktouni.'

Karim looked him squarely in the eye. 'What happened on the night of 31 July?'

'*Quoi?* Are you fucking with me? You need to go to the airport *now!*'

Karim started to walk away.

'Wait!' Sébastien cried unhappily.

Karim turned and went back to the cell. 'Did Mohammed Al-Husseini kill Amina Talal?'

'No. For fuck's sake, no!'

'What happened?'

Sébastien gave a deep sigh. '*Alors . . .* We went to a club in Guéliz, an African club. Mohammed had just flown in from Qatar and was desperate for a girl. The place was packed. It was the night before Ramadan, a Congolese band was playing . . . apart from the usual *putains* there were two girls on the dance floor, one in a red dress. My boss pointed to her as soon as we entered.'

'Why?'

'He wanted me to chat her up for him. When the girls sat down I went over and offered them a cigarette. I said I'd never seen them in the club before and asked if they'd come to hear the band. The girl in the red dress—'

'Amina Talal.'

'Yes, Amina Talal, she laughed – she had a pretty laugh – she said they had come to dance. They were celebrating because she had completed her exam in *hôtellerie*. We chatted for a few minutes. The other girl became bored and got up to go to the toilet. I told Amina: "Why not come over to our table and talk to Mr Al-Husseini? He's building a hotel in the Palmeraie and might be able to give you a job." It was dark and hard to see anything at the back of the club. I sat Amina down with Mohammed and told her that I'd make sure that her friend could find us. Then I went to the bar to order drinks. The place was full by now, *complètement bondé*. I saw the other girl pushing her way towards me. I wanted to get rid of her so I told her that Amina had received a phone call and gone home. The other girl left immediately.

'I went back to the table. Mohammed was flirting with Amina, saying that it was hard to find staff who had the right combination of efficiency and charm – all that crap. Amina drank her fruit juice. After a while she started looking around for her friend. I told her that I'd seen her friend while I was at the bar and that she'd gone home because she wasn't feeling well. Amina jumped to her feet and almost fell over—'

'Why?'

'She'd been drinking alcohol.'

Karim raised an eyebrow.

'She said she had to get back to Ibn Atya Street where her friend lived. Mohammed told her that we'd take her. He led her to the door—'

'She didn't resist?'

'She'd been drinking, like I said.' Sébastien caught the suspicion in Karim's eyes. '*Eh bien* . . . I put vodka in her drink. A triple measure.'

The muscles tightened in Karim's neck but he said nothing.

'She was *déchirée*, completely out of it. Swaying from side to side. Her handbag fell on the floor and everything came out: her *carte nationale*, make-up, everything. I stayed behind to pick everything up.'

'And Al-Husseini?'

'Outside on the pavement.'

'With Amina?'

Sébastien shook his head. 'When I came out, she'd gone.'

'What do you mean *gone*?'

'She'd run off. Mohammed was stamping his feet and screaming at me to find her. I dashed to the end of the street but there was no sign of her. In the end, I drove Mohammed to el Beqal street so he could pick up a whore.'

Karim let this information sink in then took the key from Sébastien. 'What does your son look like?'

'Tall – my height – eighteen, light brown hair. Wait!' cried Sébastien, 'The cigarettes!'

Karim's voice echoed down the corridor.

'Prison is a good place to give up, *monsieur*!'

Karim rode his *moto* through the airport parking lot. There was a queue of taxis waiting to move to the front. Two drivers had got out of their vehicles and were arguing. As he drove towards them Karim realised to his horror that one of the men was Rachid. He seemed close to blows with the other driver.

'*A kelb!* Dog!'

'Cheat!' said his opponent.

'*Allah yaatek moseeba!* God damn you!'

'Curb your temper. And curb your tongue as well!'

'Son of a whore!'

Karim parked his scooter and ran over. The other taxi drivers were trying to calm Rachid. '*Baraka, baraka!*' Rachid broke free and hit the other driver on the chin. A tussle ensued. Karim helped the other taxi drivers to pull Rachid away. The other man called out.

'You're lucky I don't call the police!'

'Police?' Rachid jeered. 'This man's a policeman! He's my friend! What do you say to that, big guy?'

Karim, by now acutely embarrassed, escorted Rachid back to his taxi. Rachid's eyes were red with anger.

'He accused me of jumping the queue!'

'*Maalesh*. Let it go.'

'I've been in this queue for four bastard hours!'

'Aren't you supposed to be off-duty?'

'What? Oh, my brother-in-law's sick. He asked me to cover for him.' Rachid spotted the helmet in Karim's hand. 'You've got your *moto* back.'

'Yes.'

Rachid got into the taxi. 'That means you won't be needing me to take you to work in the evening.'

'No.' Karim leaned on the window. 'I'll miss our conversations.' With a smile he added, 'And your awful music.'

'I bought another CD to play you, Asha Bhosle – voice like a songbird.' Rachid put the CD in the stereo and Bollywood song filled the car. The line of taxis started moving ahead of him.

Rachid turned the ignition. 'Did you ever find out what happened to the Talal girl?'

Karim gave a sigh. 'No. She didn't leave with the businessman after all. She ran off.'

'Where did she go to?'

'God knows.'

'You haven't found any witnesses?'

'No.'

'No one saw her staggering around?'

'No.' Karim stepped away to let Rachid drive further up the line, then froze. A dawning sensation. He ran after Rachid.

'Why did you say *staggering around*?'

Karim was breathing fast and his heart was pounding. Only a handful of people knew that Amina had alcohol in her bloodstream. *Where else would Amina go to escape from the clutches of the vile Al-Husseini than the safety of a taxi?* He forced himself to remain calm, not to jump to conclusions. Rachid advanced a few feet and braked. He stared at Karim.

'She was drunk, wasn't she?'

Karim searched Rachid's face: did it betray a flicker of alarm?

'I didn't tell you that she was drunk.'

'Well, I heard it from someone.'

Karim's mind went back to that fateful evening outside the mosque. When he looked in the handcart he hadn't smelled alcohol. Could one of the witnesses have started a rumour? He said his next words slowly.

'I think she got a taxi.'

'Back to the medina?'

'No.' Karim made a quick check of the barrier to the car park. It was a hundred yards away – a fifteen-second sprint. 'Back to her friend's apartment.'

'Where does this friend of hers live?' said Rachid, yawning. *He was ice-cool!*

'Guéliz.'

'Where in Guéliz?' The taxi line was moving again. Rachid started the engine and advanced another ten feet.

Karim caught him up and put his hand on the window. 'A street named Ibn Atya.' He glanced again at the barrier. Was it strong enough to withstand being rammed by a taxi?

Rachid scratched his cheek. 'I don't think she took a taxi.'

He opened his glove compartment, took out a street map and unfolded it over the passenger seat. He pointed. 'Here is Oum er-Rabia.'

Karim wasn't paying attention. He had his mobile in his hands, his fingers already tapping out a number for backup.

'. . . and here is Ibn Atya.'

Karim glanced at the map and did a double take. Ibn Atya Street ran into Oum er-Rabia Street. The nightclub was only a stone's throw from Leila's apartment.

'There wouldn't have been any point taking a taxi,' Rachid said, folding the map away. 'She could have walked there in under two minutes.'

Karim blinked. 'I – er –'

The queue started moving again and a horn sounded behind them. 'You'd better go and meet whoever it is you're meeting,' Rachid said. 'Take care, my brother!'

Karim stood rooted to the spot. Then he made his way slowly towards the terminal. He was in such a daze, walking through one door of the terminal building, that he didn't notice Kay and Laurent walk out through the other.

When she listened to Hassan's breathless account of Sébastien's arrest, Kay wasn't unduly concerned. Her first reaction was that Sébastien could stay in prison for the rest of his life for all she cared. But there would be nobody to meet Laurent. As well as thinking it unfair that the son should pay for the sins of the father, Kay was intrigued to meet Laurent. She called briefly at Dar Zuleika to check that everything was in hand for the re-opening, then took Mohammed's car and driver to the airport.

'How long will he be in prison?' asked Laurent, blinking as they walked across the sun-filled forecourt to the parking lot.

'Not long. It's only a silly matter to do with sand.'

'Sand? That seems crazy!'

Kay halted and threw out her arms with a laugh. 'Welcome to Marrakech!'

'Are you taking me to see him?'

'No. Moroccan prisons are not pleasant places. Your father will be out as soon as the matter has been cleared up. In the meantime, I'm sure he would want you to enjoy Marrakech. *Dis-moi* – have you stayed in a riad before?'

Karim didn't waste time looking for the teenager. He drove straight home, overtaking the honking traffic in Unq Jmel and parked his scooter in the alleyway. He felt shattered after the day's events and craved rest. But tonight was the Night of Destiny, the night when all sins would be forgiven. Ayesha was in the salon unloading the food trolley.

'Tonight,' he whispered. 'We should tell Meema tonight.'

Ayesha stared at him for several seconds then shrugged her shoulders. 'As you like.'

Karim passed into the kitchen and embraced his mother. 'My scooter is fixed.'

'*Al-hamdullilah.*' His mother pointed towards the cooker. 'Can you change the cylinder?'

Karim pulled the cooker away from the wall and unscrewed

the gas cylinder. 'I visited *Hajj* Omar.' His words made Lalla Fatima look up. 'His health is not good. But he recognised me, praise God, and he remembered Si Brahim.' Karim walked out and came back a minute later with a full cylinder. 'He said something odd.'

'What was that?'

Karim pushed the cooker back against the wall. 'He asked to see his daughter.'

'His *daughter*?'

'I told him that Amina was dead and buried, but he kept repeating "I want to see my daughter." Poor fellow, his wits have gone.'

Lalla Fatima stared blankly. 'God have mercy!'

Karim went upstairs, took a quick shower and changed. Ayesha appeared at the foot of the stairs. 'Are you sure about this?'

'Yes.'

Lalla Fatima was in the *salon*, tray in hand, placing a plate of gazelles' horn pastries on the table. Karim and Ayesha walked in together. Ayesha switched off the television. Lalla Fatima turned around in surprise.

Placing a hand on his mother's shoulder, Karim said, 'Meema, sit down. We need to talk.'

'What about? What do you want to talk about?'

Karim was sweating so much that his shirt was soaked. He took the tray from his mother and waited until she was sitting on the divan. 'There's something we need to discuss.'

Lalla Fatima looked anxiously from Karim to Ayesha.

'It's been a secret for too long,' Karim began.

'A secret?' Lalla Fatima's face was pale.

'Secrets fester, they eat away at our hearts.'

'Allah protect us!'

'Even though it's a source of shame, it's more shameful to keep it hidden.' Karim turned to Ayesha who gave a nod, allowing him to continue. 'Twenty years ago—'

His mother cut across him. '*Andek al-haq*. You're right. This family has a secret.' Ayesha and Karim looked at each other in alarm. 'And it brings shame to all of us.'

Ayesha gave a sob. Karim started to speak but Lalla Fatima silenced him.

'The terrible things that have happened this month, in Ramadan of all months, have made me realise that the time for secrets is past. You, Ayesha – you have a right to know the truth more than anyone.'

'The truth?' Ayesha was bewildered. 'What truth?'

Lalla Fatima stared at the floor. 'Brahim Belkacem and Omar Talal left the mountains at the age of fourteen . . .'

Karim jumped up. 'We know that, Meema, but what has it got to do—'

'Sit down, Karim. *Kheleenee nhedr*, allow me to speak. As I was saying, Brahim and Omar came to Marrakech. Your father got an education and made something of his life – at least that's how he saw it. Omar took to religion. At twenty-one, they both got married. Omar was already betrothed to a girl from the mountains, Lalla Hanane. They had two children—'

'Abderrahim and Amina,' Karim said impatiently.

'Yes, Abderrahim and Amina, *Allah irhemha*, may God have mercy on her. A year later Omar fell off a ladder and broke his hip. For six months he was unable to work. Hanane was in Zat, pregnant with their third child. There was scarcely enough money to feed the other two. Cholera was rife at the time and everyone was finding life hard. Brahim offered to lend Omar money for an operation but he refused. When the child was born – a little girl – everyone thought she would die. But she survived.'

Karim could hardly breathe. He felt his heart was going to burst through his chest.

'Omar and Hanane had no means of looking after this poor little girl.' Lalla Fatima's eyes filled with tears. 'So your father and I agreed to adopt her.'

Ayesha let out a cry and fled from the room. Karim was scarcely able to comprehend his mother's words. 'You mean *Ayesha*? Ayesha is the child of Omar Talal? Why didn't you tell us? Why didn't you tell *her*?'

'I wanted to,' sobbed Lalla Fatima, 'but your father forbade it. He said it was better that she didn't know, that it would only cause problems and bring shame to her parents. We announced to the world that Ayesha had been abandoned on our doorstep. She was *kafala*, given to us for our protection. The four of us – Brahim, myself, Omar, Hanane – we made an oath of silence.'

Karim opened his mouth, but no words came.

Lalla Fatima got up unsteadily, put her hand against the doorframe and looked into the courtyard. Ayesha was lying face down on the sofa in the corner, weeping. Lalla Fatima limped over and sat down beside her. 'I'm sorry, Ayesha, forgive me,' she said, her voice cracking with emotion. 'I have always loved you – loved you like my own child.'

In Karim's brain tectonic plates shifted and collided.

Opaque words and unexplained actions began to fit together. The conflict between the two men . . . his mother's visits to Lalla Hanane . . . Omar's strictness as a father . . . *Oh, doubly benighted Omar Talal! Punished for giving away one daughter by the loss of a second!*

Lalla Fatima wiped the tears from her eyes. 'Come, let us get ready for *ftour*.'

'Wait – I don't understand,' cried Karim, running into the courtyard. 'Why didn't Omar ask for Ayesha to be returned when he had recovered from his injury and was earning money again?'

'He did.' Lalla Fatima said, her lip quivering. 'A year after we took Ayesha in, Si Omar came to us and said that it had been a dreadful mistake. He asked for Ayesha back, as he was entitled to do. But your father refused. He said that Ayesha was now part of our family. I was partly to blame. I had grown to love Ayesha and pleaded with your father to let me keep her. He told Omar that it would damage the child to uproot her again. Omar became angry. In an effort to heal the rift, Si Brahim proposed a marriage—'

'Between myself and Amina—'

'Yes. But instead of bringing the families together it had the opposite effect. You were there when the two men quarrelled a few years later. Omar accused your father of stealing his daughter. Your father said that he refused to return Ayesha to a family of *illiterate zealots*. The two men never spoke again.'

The call to prayer sounded. Lalla Fatima cast around for her walking stick and hobbled to the kitchen. Karim took her place on the sofa. He put his arm around Ayesha.

'Are you all right?'

Ayesha raised her head. Her voice was steady. 'Take me to see him. Take me to see my father.'

Ayesha rode pillion, her long hair flowing under the helmet. The celebration dinner that Lalla Fatima had planned was a miserable affair. Karim brooded throughout, burning with anger towards his father and Omar Talal. Ayesha said nothing and ate little. Neither she nor Karim broached the subject of their feelings for each other.

Night had fallen and the boulevard was filled with cars and pedestrians. Karim took a right turn along Znqa Oum er-Rabia. He slowed down and pointed to the dark exterior of Club Afrique. 'That's the nightclub.' He carried on moving slowly up the street, looking to left and right.

'No sand,' said Ayesha.

Karim shook his head. They passed a four-storey modern apartment block with broad balconies. 'Leila's apartment.'

Five minutes later they arrived outside Boulmharez prison. A lamp was shining above the entrance. The guard opened, his mouth full of food.

'*Esh-sheebanee,*' Karim said. 'The old man.' He held out twenty dirhams. It took several minutes and another twenty dirhams before the guard let them in. Once over the threshold Karim gave him an envelope in which he'd placed Sébastien's key and a message about the failed rendezvous. 'For the foreigner.' He placed two more twenties in the guard's hand.

Karim and Ayesha walked past two surprised-looking officers sitting at a table with their hands in a bowl of couscous.

The guard pressed a buzzer and an inner door slid open. To Karim's surprise, instead of heading to the wing he made for a flight of stairs.

'Where are we going?'

'Sick bay.'

From deep in the building came a high-pitched scream, followed by gruff shouts. Karim looked over his shoulder at Ayesha. She pulled her *hijab* more tightly around her.

The guard stopped at the entrance to a long room with a row of metal-framed beds, only one of which was occupied. It wasn't Omar. A young bare-chested man lay strapped to the frame, writhing and moaning.

At the far end of the room stood an ancient defibrillator and a gurney. Omar Talal was lying on the gurney, curled up in the foetal position. He was wearing a blue hospital gown. *At least it's clean and ironed,* thought Karim. He tapped the old man on the shoulder, gently at first, then more firmly.

'Si Omar, I have brought your daughter. *Hajj* Omar!'

Ayesha crouched down and stroked the man's hand. A minute passed, then two. Finally, Omar opened one eye. It was rheumy, the pupil almost opaque. '*Shkoun?*'

'Ayesha.'

'Ayesh . . . Ayesh . . .'

Propping up Omar's head with one hand Ayesha poured a trickle of water between his lips. 'Ayesha,' the old man said at last.

Ayesha's voice was a whisper. 'Papa.'

A tear ran down Omar's cheek and disappeared into his white beard. He opened his other eye and for a few seconds Ayesha and Omar gazed at each other. The room was silent apart from the occasional moan from the young man in the bed. Omar closed his eyes, squeezing them tight, his wrinkled cheeks lifting with the effort. He shook his head from side to side. The shaking became more violent, as if he were trying to rid himself of an ill-fitting hat. After a while the shaking subsided and he lay still.

Place Jemaa el Fna was crowded for Lailat al-Qadr. Circles of bystanders, two or three deep, were clustered around the storytellers and sideshow artists. No one noticed the young Moroccan in an Italia football shirt and Nike trainers threading his way through the crowd. He walked past the tea sellers, skirted the Two Brothers Restaurant, went down Derb Si Buluqat and stopped at Youssef's shop window.

Inside, Youssef had just finished with a customer and was saying farewell. The man in the Italia shirt placed a white iPhone on the glass counter.

'*Bshal?* How much?'

Youssef regarded the seller and his broken, stained teeth. He checked the phone. It had a large memory – a rarity in Morocco.

'*Khamsmia.* Five hundred.'

'Six hundred.'

'Five-fifty.'

The man nodded. Taking a wad of cash from his pocket Youssef counted out the notes. The seller picked up the money, nodded again and walked out.

Youssef scrolled through the contents of the phone. There were photos and video clips of two European girls – no, *three* girls. He smiled grimly. The phone had been stolen, just as he'd thought. He watched the second-to-last video. One of the girls was dressed in a tight-fitting catsuit and dancing with uninhibited ease. No wonder the man had held on to the footage! The last video showed the girls outside the nightclub, laughing drunkenly and making thumbs-up signs. In the background Youssef could see a girl in a red dress zigzagging across the road. Curious, he played the clip again, this time zooming in on the girl. She looked Moroccan. He watched her lurch towards a taxi and get into the back seat.

A customer came into the shop. Youssef clicked *hard reset* and drummed his fingers on the counter while the phone cleared its memory. Then he leaned into the shop window and displayed the phone next to all the others.

Chapter 15

Ten weeks had passed since the end of Ramadan. The first snows had appeared on the mountains. In Marrakech, shops and offices were closed for Eid el-Kbir, the feast of the sacrifice. The price of sheep had risen steadily for weeks. Preoccupied with the counterfeit drug investigation, Karim had left it until the last minute to buy a sheep. When he finally went with Bouchaïb to an outlying village the best they could find was a scrawny specimen for two thousand dirhams. Even Bouchaïb couldn't get the farmer to reduce the price. Lalla Fatima tutted when she saw the sheep being led into the courtyard but she tethered it to the fountain and fattened it as best she could.

Today was the morning of the sacrifice. The women stood ready in the courtyard with mops and aprons. In front of them lay a saw, an array of knives and three buckets. Karim was positioned in the middle, wearing *gandora* and sandals, clutching a long-handled knife. His father – perhaps in recognition of his farming origins – had always insisted on carrying out the slaughter himself. Despite the easy availability of door-to-door butchers, Karim felt duty-bound to follow his father's example. He ran his thumb along the knife. *The sheep is offering his life*, his father used to say. *The least we can offer him is a keen blade.*

'Lay the animal down.'

Ayesha flipped the sheep onto its side and gripped its forelegs. Karim could see the outline of the animal's ribs. *If he'd sent Ayesha to the souk four weeks ago she would have found a better sheep for half the price.* The sheep was kicking, panic in its eyes. Khadija reached down to restrain its hind legs. *He should have straddled it while it was upright, cut it from behind the way his father did.* Ayesha pressed the animal's jaw to the ground and looked at Karim urgently. *Now or never!* Karim put the knife to the sheep's throat and whispered a blessing. Dark blood spurted, a guttural sound. *By the Seven Saints! The animal was still alive.* Karim slashed again, this time finding the windpipe. There was a gurgle, the legs jerked twice then stopped moving. With a matter-of-fact air Lalla Fatima started brushing the blood into the drain.

Karim paused to recover his breath. The smell of blood filled his nostrils. He put down the knife and Ayesha handed him a meat cleaver. He leaned over and hacked at the sheep's feet. It took him several attempts before the bone and sinews gave way. One by one he dropped the feet into a bucket. Then he set about severing the animal's head. He hacked doggedly, aware of the women watching him. It was a contest, a battle between himself and this *thing*, this obstinate mass of flesh and bone that resisted his attempts at dismemberment. Once ... twice ... three times ... a splintering sound ... *al-hamdulillah*, the head came away. He placed it in the bucket and stood up, covered in blood and wisps of wool.

Ayesha put a knife in his hand with the efficiency of a nurse exchanging instruments with a surgeon. Karim knelt astride the carcass and cut across the shoulders. He inserted his thumbs and fingertips and had almost finished tugging the fleece away when his mobile phone rang.

Karim wiped his hands on his *gandora* and reached into his pocket. Abdou was on the line, bursting with excitement. A Guangzhou-registered ship had docked in Agadir with a suspicious cargo. The man from OMPIC was already on his way down from Casablanca. Karim relayed the news to Noureddine who told him to collect a police car from the commissariat.

'I'll phone the *préfecture* in Agadir and ask for back-up.'

'OK.'

'You'll need at least twelve men in addition to Abdou.'

'I'm not taking Abdou.' Karim braced himself for what was coming next.

'You're not taking Abdou? But – you need a second-in-command!'

'I want to take Aziz.'

Nour couldn't believe his ears. 'Aziz Al-Fassi?'

'Yes.'

'What – you and Aziz are best friends all of a sudden? Very well, it's your decision,' Noureddine sighed. 'God help you if you get it wrong.'

'God helps when the sons of Adam help themselves.'

'As you wish. I'll tell Aziz to meet you at the commissariat in an hour.'

Karim put the phone away and turned to his mother and sisters. 'I have to go to Agadir.'

'Who's going to do the cooking?' asked Khadija, surprised.

'Phone Abderrezak. Ask him to cook for us for a change!'

'His family have two sheep to slaughter. He wouldn't have time to help us as well!'

'We could do the cooking,' suggested Ayesha.

Karim considered. Barbecuing the lamb on the roof, in view of the neighbours, was usually the job of the men of the house.

'If we fetch the brazier from Abderrezak's apartment we could cook the meat in the courtyard,' said Khadija. 'No one need see us.'

Unable to come up with a better alternative, Karim relented. He picked up the knife to finish the fleecing but Ayesha placed her hand on his. 'Go and get ready. I'll take over.'

Karim nodded. He showered, changed into a hoodie and jeans and took his gun from the drawer. He kissed Lalla Fatima on both cheeks and pushed his *moto* into the alley, slamming the door behind him.

The carcass of the dead animal was now suspended from a hook. Ayesha was busy sawing it down the middle while Khadija held it steady.

'Have you decided on tattoos?' asked Ayesha.

'A bird, a lizard and an eye for luck.'

'What about a swallow?'

'If there's space, yes, I'll ask the henna lady for a swallow.'

Ayesha cracked open the pelvis. 'Jewellery?'

'Naïma said I could borrow hers.'

Ayesha remained silent. She picked up a knife and ran the blade around the sheep's abdominal cavity.

Khadija wagged her finger. 'You're still trying to get me to buy those gold threads!'

'I just think that gold would go well with the *takshitas*.'

Ayesha tugged at the animal's intestines and they slid into the bucket. 'Meema liked them.'

'What did I like?' asked Lalla Fatima, coming into the courtyard with an armful of skewers.

'The lengths of gold that we saw in that shop in Mouassine.'

'I liked them well enough. Who's doing the cooking?'

'By Allah!' cried Khadija. 'We must fetch the brazier.'

From the Serafina Hotel blog
Days to opening: 1

Picture your arrival. As you drive up the 300-yard avenue of water, the dome rising before you like some vision of heaven, you feel your cares melt away. Check-in takes under a minute: just long enough to appreciate the soaring ceiling and the all-enveloping hush.

Follow the white-robed attendant along the causeway, catching reflections of the Atlas Mountains in the water, and push open the wooden doors to your villa. The first thing you notice is the feeling of space. Light floods in from floor-to-ceiling windows. Settle down on the sofa, pour yourself a complimentary glass of champagne and gaze at the rare and beautiful antiques from around the world.

As you walk back along the causeway, now lit by lanterns, consider which of the hotel's three restaurants you will dine at: French-Moroccan, Thai or Indian. With five staff to every guest, service is discreet and unobtrusive.

After dinner take a dip in your private pool. There is almost no light pollution in the Palmeraie and the Milky Way is bright above your head. Linger, and you may see a shooting star. When you're ready for bed put on your towelling robe, slip into the cool 400-thread count Egyptian cotton sheets and drift off to the gentle sound of the fountain.

Breakfast is served in your courtyard. As you enjoy the fresh fruit, free-range eggs, home-made bread, yoghurt and jams, consider your options for the day. Will you visit the hammam with its graceful arches modelled on the Alhambra? Take a quad bike tour through far-flung Berber villages? Or simply lounge by the pool while you await the arrival of lunch?

At the Serafina, the day unwinds as slowly – or as swiftly – as you.

Sébastien squatted over the hole.

Until he arrived in Boulmharez prison Sébastien had thought of himself as a man who could endure hardship. He had crossed the Empty Quarter, survived in the mountains on a packet of dates, even fasted for a week in Ramadan. But he was ill prepared for life in a Moroccan jail. For the first few days the only patch of floor he could find to sleep on was next to the latrine. Around him lay a mass of grunting, snoring, farting bodies. How he longed for his hot, overpriced apartment on Boulevard Zerktouni! He shared the three-metre wide cell with fifteen other inmates. At first they had been hostile. One man demanded to know if he was *un pédéraste*. Sébastien had gone to sleep fearing that he might never wake up. Gradually, using his knowledge of builders' Arabic, he managed to establish a rapport. When Nabil, a hulking *Bidawi* serving life imprisonment for staving in a man's face, asked Sébastien to help with his appeal papers he graduated to a wooden bed near the door. His arms and ankles were pocked with mosquito bites but at least the air was fresher and he could read by the light from the corridor.

No one had visited him apart from his friend Yves and a lawyer who told him that it was *une parodie de justice* that he had been incarcerated but, without payment of the fine by the Al-Husseini Group, Sébastien had no choice but to serve the sentence. Yves came once a week with cigarettes and a change of clothes. They sat together on a bench in the sun, smoking. Yves joked that he had always suspected that Sébastien would end up in prison on account of boys or drugs. But for sand? He laughed so hard that the tears ran down his cheeks. From Yves, Sébastien learned that Laurent was staying in Kay's riad. As for Kay, she had not been to see him once. Nor had Mohammed, nor anyone else from the company.

For the first week Sébastien was sure that his boss would come to his rescue. He was hardly at fault for using black-market sand. Every construction site in Marrakech did the same. Moreover, he was Mohammed's right-hand man, as well as his procurer-in-chief. All Mohammed had to do to get him released was pay the fine – indeed, given Mohammed's status as a Gulf investor, one snap of his fingers and the governor himself would turn up with the key.

After a month had passed the cold truth dawned: he had been abandoned, hung out to dry while Kay and Mohammed swanned around the Serafina, cooing over chandeliers. This was his reward for months of hard work, slaving for sixteen hours a day to meet an inhuman deadline! At least his son had stayed behind in Marrakech. The thought of seeing Laurent was the only thing that kept Sébastien going.

He wiped himself with a torn-off piece of newspaper. The newspaper cost him a packet of cigarettes a week; he couldn't bring himself to perform the task, as his fellow inmates did, with water and hand. As he reached for a second piece of paper his eyes widened. On the page was a photograph of the Serafina hotel – completed! With shaking hands, unable to decipher the Arabic text, he pulled up his trousers and waddled over to the nearest prisoner, a youth with round, calf-like eyes. Sébastien held out the scrap of newspaper.

'*Trjem*, translate.'

When the boy said nothing Sébastien asked Nabil. The big man squinted at the words. 'It's about a hotel in the Palmeraie.'

'Tell me what it says!'

'*Bletee*, hold on.' Nabil tilted the paper to catch the light from the corridor. 'The hotel is opening ahead of schedule . . . the ceremony will be attended by a minister from the Qatari government – fucking Qataris, they get everywhere! And the director of something or other.'

'When?' cried Sébastien. 'When is it opening?'

Nabil showed him the piece of paper to indicate that the rest of the article was missing. Sébastien rushed back to the latrine, picked up the other scraps of paper and handed them to Nabil. Swearing, the other man went through them one by one until he had located the missing section.

'November the seventh.'

'What day is it today?'

'How the hell should I know?'

Sébastien ran to the bars of the cell. '*Ashmin nhar lyouma? Aujourd'hui, c'est quel jour?*' He kept shouting until the guard sauntered down the corridor.

'*Malek a al-fransawi?* What's up with you, French?'

'What's the date today?'

'Why do you want to know?'

'Tell me! I beg of you, may God spare you, *Ilah ikhalleek!*'

The guard glanced at the screen on his phone. 'Sixth of November, French.'

'I have to get out!' screamed Sébastien. 'Today!'

'Everyone wants to get out, French. What makes you special?'

'I have to get out today!' Sébastien repeated. 'Today – you hear?'

The guard laughed and walked off down the corridor.

'I'll give you a thousand dirhams if you let me use your phone!'

The guard stopped, then turned back.

'Monsieur de Freycinet?' Samira knocked on the bedroom door. 'Monsieur de Freycinet!'

The door of the Room of the Uzbek Vizier opened to reveal Laurent de Freycinet in a dark uniform with an arabesque 'S' embroidered on the breast pocket. His face was tanned and his floppy haircut had been replaced by a close-clipped top and sides. Samira adjusted the name badge on his lapel then led the way downstairs. An English couple eating breakfast in the courtyard looked up and smiled.

'Good luck, Laurent!'

'It's only the rehearsal!' he grinned. 'We open tomorrow!'

In the kitchen Aziza handed him a wrapped sandwich. '*Tu vas chercher un taxi?*' Laurent gave a nod.

Outside in the alley, blood and water were seeping under doorways and he had to step carefully to avoid getting his shoes wet. In Bab Taghzout square men were roasting sheep's heads on makeshift barbecues. A tall youth with sheepskins strapped to his arms and legs was staggering around to hoots of merriment. Kay had warned him about the savagery of Eid el-Kbir but Laurent found the scenes exciting, visceral. What a change from staid and sanitised Paris, where everyone went around with long faces!

There was only one taxi at the rank, *a grand taxi*. Laurent reached it just as Khadija and Ayesha turned up in their caftans and headscarves. He graciously offered the taxi to them.

'*Merci, monsieur*,' smiled Khadija, opening the car door.

When Karim arrived at the commissariat Aziz was leaning against an unmarked Hyundai, smoking a cigarette.

'*Salaam ou alikum.*'

'*Ou alikum salaam.*'

'You drive,' said Karim.

'No, you drive.'

Karim's hackles rose. 'You may be the same rank as me but I'm in charge of this operation. Drive!'

'*Mashee momken.* Impossible.'

'Why?'

'I don't have a driving licence.'

Seething, Karim got in and turned the ignition. This was already going badly. His anger turned to incredulity when Aziz reached into his carrier bag and unwrapped a flatbread filled with cooked offal. A delicious aroma filled the car. Aziz proceeded to eat the kebab slowly, savouring every mouthful. He took another kebab from his bag and offered it to Karim.

'*Zid*, go on – take it.'

Karim hesitated then took a bite. The kebab was seasoned with cumin and salt, the way he liked it.

'I had just started cooking when Noureddine called,' explained Aziz.

They headed out of town on the N8 trunk road. It was warm and sunny and they drove with the windows down. After Loudaya they turned onto the motorway. For the first few miles they saw only one other vehicle. Karim briefed Aziz on the mission.

'The ship has called at Douala, Lagos, Abidjan, Conakry and Dakar. We think there may be illegal medicines on board.'

'Are we going to impound the vessel?'

'I don't know yet.'

'What's security like at the docks?'

'One guard and one inspector, possibly bribed, both on holiday leave.'

'Do you think the docking was timed for the holiday?'

'The best time to commit a crime is when no one is around,' Karim continued, an edge to his voice, 'as you know.'

For a while nothing was said. Aziz broke the silence.

'You're referring to the Talal case. *Lee fat, mat.* What's done is done. The father is dead. End of story.'

'The father was innocent.'

'He was a religious fanatic. He beat his daughter.'

'That doesn't mean he killed her.'

'What's done is done,' Aziz said again.

'He couldn't have written the sign,' said Karim with barely contained anger. 'As I told you at the time.'

'We never found a sign. As I told *you* at the time.'

Karim gave a laugh, then spat out of the window for good measure.

Aziz held him in his gaze. 'Was this why you asked for me to come? So you could moan about the fact that Badnaoui assigned the Talal case to me and not to you? Or did you hope to grill me for information? Stop the car. Let me out. Go on – stop the car! I'll find my own way back to Marrakech. Otherwise keep your mouth shut and get on with the job.'

Karim reddened. He should have brought Abdou. They would have chatted and joked all the way to Agadir. They would have planned the operation carefully and executed it efficiently. Instead he had saddled himself with a man who despised him, and who now mistrusted him as well.

Given that it was the quietest day of the year there was very little traffic on the streets of Marrakech. It took Ayesha and Khadija only a few minutes to get to the apartment. They would have liked a little more time to gossip, to discuss the wedding which was just a week away, but they paid the driver and gaily pushed open the door of the building. They smiled at the *assas*, the caretaker, a grey-haired man sitting on a bench and crossed the polished floor.

'It's marble,' whispered Khadija. 'Zak had it done.'

'Why are you whispering?'

'I don't know.' Khadija giggled.

They pressed the elevator for the third floor. The doors closed and the elevator ascended with a whirring sound. The girls stared apprehensively at the ceiling then caught each other's eye and broke into laughter. Khadija looked at herself in the mirror.

'Do you think I've put on weight?'

'You look fine,' said Ayesha, who was admiring the leather padding on the walls.

When they reached the third floor Khadija was so preoccupied with her reflection that she didn't notice the doors closing. Ayesha stepped out, panicked, then jumped back in again. Khadija jabbed the buttons to open the doors but the elevator descended. The girls looked at each other, then laughed. When it reached the ground floor the doors opened. The *assas* was still sitting on his hands on the bench. They nodded at him and he nodded back. When the doors shut the girls burst out in laughter again. The elevator rose to the third floor. This time they both stepped out smartly and walked arm in arm down the corridor.

'When I'm living here,' Khadija said proudly, 'the elevator will be useful when you bring Meema to visit.'

Ayesha felt a pang at the thought of the family being divided. With Karim threatening to leave as well, her future looked lonely.

Khadija stopped outside the apartment and rummaged for the key in her handbag. A neighbouring door opened and a plump middle-aged man came out in jogging shorts and trainers. He stared at the girls. '*Mbrouk al-awashir*, happy Eid.'

'*Mbrouk al-awashir*,' the girls chorused. When the man had disappeared down the stairs they started giggling again.

Khadija put the key in the lock. It didn't turn. She removed the key and tried turning it anti-clockwise, to no avail.

Ayesha took the key, spat on it and tried it, with the same result. 'Are you sure this is the right key?'

'Yes.'

'I'll ask the *assas*.'

The caretaker did his best to be helpful. 'Mr Zak was here yesterday and he didn't mention any problems.'

'What time was he here?'

The caretaker pondered. 'Noon. They left about two.'

'*They?*'

'He was here with a *fransawia*. A French woman.'

Ayesha absorbed this information then walked slowly back up the stairs. She took Khadija's hand.

'I think we should go.'

The MV *Tien Shan* was just over 3,500 TEU, small for a container vessel but a leviathan in the tiny harbour of Agadir. Karim could see an on-board crane and two stacks of containers, two or three hundred in all. Three forty-foot containers marked *China Shipping* were stacked on the quayside. There was no movement on the ship, on the quay or around the warehouses. The entire port was still apart from the trawlers bobbing gently in the moonlight. Karim put down his binoculars and checked his watch. It was midnight. He was cold and his legs were stiff.

He might as well get used to the discomfort. If MEDIHA – the name he had given to the investigation into counterfeit medicines – was rolled out nationwide he would be spending many unsocial hours at docks and ports. A few feet away from him, Elias, the official from Casablanca, was crouched behind the wall talking in a low voice to Aziz.

They couldn't be sure there were any contraband drugs on the quayside or, indeed, on board the vessel. Karim's intention was to watch and wait. If anything illegal was planned it would take place under cover of darkness.

Karim trained his binoculars on the warehouse. A low, squat building set back from the quayside, it housed six policemen in commando uniform. Six men were not enough for a stake-out of this size. Karim half-hoped the night would pass without the need to use them.

His mobile vibrated. Lalla Fatima's name flashed on the screen. She never called at such a late hour! He spoke in a whisper. 'Meema, I can't talk now.'

'Oh, Karim! God preserve us!'

'Calm down, Mother. What's wrong?'

'Poor Khadija! What did she do to deserve such a thing? Oh! God help us!'

'What are you talking about? What's going on?' Unable to get any sense out of his mother Karim asked for Ayesha. There was the sound of fumbling then Ayesha's voice.

'The wedding's off.'

Karim's heart almost stopped. 'What?'

'Zak changed the locks on the apartment. We phoned his mother. After a lot of stalling she admitted that Zak is having a relationship with a French woman.'

'You mean—'

'Yes! Abderrezak has jilted Khadija!'

Karim shut his phone and stared blindly at the wall. Zak had betrayed his sister. Zak – a man whom he had known since his school days, who had accepted his family's hospitality, who had shown them the apartment in which he and Khadija would bring up their children – had been having an affair. The wedding – all the preparation and expense – was now chaff in the wind. What is the right thing to do in such a situation? Demand that honour be satisfied? Seek punishment? *Kill the bastard?* After a few minutes indignation gave way to relief. Khadija may have got off lightly, been spared a greater misfortune. Karim had always suspected Zak was a social climber, interested only in money and status. There would have been trouble down the line, maybe not for a year or two, but eventually.

'A van is coming!'

Karim grabbed his binoculars. An unmarked white van was driving slowly along the quayside without its headlamps. It stopped between the containers and the *Tien Shan*. For several minutes nothing happened. Then the van doors opened and ten or twelve African men jumped out.

'Now?' asked Elias.

'Not yet!'

The Africans ignored the containers on the quay. Moving rapidly, they laid a plank to the deck of the *Tien Shan* and ran across. A tall African with a torch darted in and out of the rows of containers on board the vessel, checking the top of the doors where the identification numbers were displayed. Stopping at one container, he turned the levers and yanked open the door. He went in with a companion and came out carrying a large cardboard box. Together with the other Africans, they formed a human chain and started passing boxes across the gangplank. Within five minutes the van was fully loaded. A second van, its lights off, was already creeping along the quay, coming to a halt behind the first.

'Go!' said Karim.

Aziz barked into his walkie-talkie. Down below, the warehouse door flew open and the commandos fanned out, scattering the Africans before them.

'Tell them to leave the Africans!' Karim shouted. 'Get the drivers!'

Within seconds he was on the quayside. The Africans screamed as commandos pinned them to the ground. '*Je connais rien! Je suis réfugié!*'

'Forget the *Afariqa*! Arrest the drivers!'

Aziz and a commando went to the first van and dragged a terrified-looking Moroccan from the driver's seat. Karim ran over to one of the dropped boxes and slit it open. Inside were blister-packs of Avastin, one of the heart drugs that he and Abdou had on their list of counterfeits. He turned his attention to the *Tien Shan*. There was still no sign of activity on board. Beckoning to a commando he crossed the gangplank and stole towards the open container. He examined the serial number on the right-hand door.

'Aziz!' he yelled. 'Read out the numbers on those containers!'

Aziz shone his torch on the back of the *China Shipping* containers. 'Four-five-two-one-nine, followed by a six. Seven-eight-three-five-eight, then a nine.'

'Got it!'

Elias ran up to Aziz. 'What's he talking about?'

'Every container has a twin. They have the same registration numbers, the same bills of lading. One gets checked; the other doesn't.'

A commando was already at work with a bolt cutter. Aziz ducked inside, reappearing a few seconds later with clothing wrapped in cellophane.

'Sweatshirts!' he called to Karim. 'Calvin Klein!'

Karim smiled, remembering Captain Badnaoui's reference to Calvin Klein two months ago. Just then, he heard a rumble, so low and deep that it felt like it was coming from the bottom of the ocean. Almost imperceptibly the ship started moving away from the quay. There was a splash as the gangplank fell into the water, followed a second later by the crack of hawsers snapping. He took out his gun. There was still no movement on the bridge: whoever was controlling the vessel was doing so from below deck. But the steering was odd. Instead of heading towards the harbour mouth the *Tien Shan* was drifting sideways towards the breakwater.

On the quayside the commandos were running along the water's edge, following the ship as it headed towards the concrete boulders. Karim braced himself. There was the sound of steel grinding against concrete . . . a loud splintering . . . then the ship shuddered to a halt. The commandos jumped on board. A few minutes later they emerged from below deck with five Chinese crewmen, jabbering in broken English.

Karim followed the commandos off the vessel. Aziz and Elias ran up, breathless.

'We thought you were heading for China!' said Elias.

Karim laughed, although his heart was racing and sweat was dripping into his eyes. 'No risk of that,' he panted. 'An eighty-thousand-tonne container ship . . . not a good getaway vehicle!'

Chapter 16

My Medina

We are in the second day of Eid el-Kbir. The sheep have been slaughtered and cooked, the barbecues put away, the shops and restaurants reopened. Now is the time when people distribute meat to the needy and give gifts to their children. I just met the hajj from two doors away, dressed in his white jellaba, bringing his granddaughter back from the toyshop.

Here at Dar Zuleika we're saying farewell to Momo. He's an adorable little fellow but we've decided that it's cruel to keep him cooped up without other macaques for company. The local Worldwide Fund for Nature has agreed to take him to the mountains and release him into the wild. We'll miss him!

STOP PRESS: Mohammed Al-Husseini has invited me to collaborate on his next project, a refurbishment of the Grand Hotel in Beirut. While I'm away Dar Zuleika will be in Samira's capable hands. The Zuleika literary salon opens on 19 November with readings by local authors. We're also hosting an Introduction to Moroccan Cooking with Samir Al-Mokhfi, head chef of the Serafina Hotel. Book now!

'A thousand thank yous, *barakallahufik*, God bless you, my child.' Lalla Hanane's eyes were moist. In front of her was a plate of cutlets.

'I grilled them myself,' Ayesha said proudly. 'On the roof, using the old bedstead. Let me heat one up and make tea. I've brought fresh mint and *sheeba*, a few leaves of wormwood.'

Ayesha found the kitchen in the same state as she'd left it two days ago. In the fridge the milk was unopened, the tagine untouched. She warmed a lamb cutlet in the frying pan and sat on a stool waiting for the kettle to boil. The kitchen was tiny, just two appliances and a sink.

'You haven't been eating, Mother,' she said when she returned to the room.

'Now and then I have a piece of bread.'

'Bread is not enough. *Mohimm thalla f-rasek*, you must take care of yourself.'

Hanane nibbled a piece of lamb while Ayesha swept the salon and plumped up the pillows. She turned to her mother. 'May I see Amina's bedroom?' Lalla Hanane gave a distracted nod.

It was the first time Ayesha had been upstairs. The railing of the walkway had been mended with brown sticky tape. Ayesha smiled. Whoever had tried to fix it was as cack-handed as Karim. A pair of men's flip-flops stood outside the first door: Abderrahim's room, she guessed. He was still in Kenitra prison, *may God protect and preserve him*. The second room was a large *salon* with divans along three walls. Judging by the brown *jellaba* hanging from a hook and the medicine bottle on the table, it was where Omar had slept. There was a plunk as Ayesha walked past. She turned around and walked back.

Another plunk. The tiles on the walkway were loose. For Amina to get to her room she would have had to cross these tiles. They were like sentries, alerting Omar to his daughter's comings and goings.

Amina's room was dark, with one tiny window looking onto the courtyard. Ayesha turned on the light. The room was long and narrow. On the right-hand side was a single bed with a faded green counterpane. At the foot of the bed stood a wooden wardrobe. Against the far wall was a little table on which lay some textbooks, a pencil case and a few pens and pencils. Ayesha opened the wardrobe and gazed at the caftans and gowns on hangers. Below them was a jumble of tracksuit bottoms, T-shirts and underwear and, underneath, two pairs of shoes and a pair of yellow slippers.

She went to Amina's bed and lay down with her head propped against the wall. She gazed at the simple room with its cold stone floor and her eyes filled with tears. If life had unfolded differently she would have shared this room with her sister, lying in bed at night gossiping, complaining about their father, arguing about whose turn it was to switch off the light. Her eye went to the skirting tiles under the table. Something looked odd. One of them was upside down.

Hanane's voice rose from the room downstairs. 'Are you coming, Ayesha? The tea is getting cold.'

'One minute!' Ayesha knelt under the table and tugged at the tile. It came off easily. Behind was a hole the size of her fist. Using the light from her phone Ayesha squinted inside. The hole opened out like a little cave. She reached in and pulled out, one by one, a sequined blouse, a purple skirt, a pair of soft leather boots, a few rolls of lipstick, some mascara and a pair of black enamel earrings. She held the blouse up to her chest.

'Ayesha!'

'I'm coming!'

She felt around in the hole to see if there was anything else. Her fingers closed around a business card. It had a green motif of the Koutoubia and the legend '*Taxi 1547 – Toutes destinations – Randonnées – Aéroport*'.

It was late on Sunday afternoon when Karim steered the Hyundai back onto the motorway. He and Aziz were exhausted. They had spent the day in the Agadir préfecture. As he suspected, arresting the African men had caused nothing but headaches. They all turned out to be illegal migrants and the Agadir police had to fill in reams of paperwork before arranging buses to drive them south. As for the crew, once the Chinese embassy in Rabat heard of their arrest it demanded they were handed over. When Karim and Aziz left the préfecture a diplomatic storm was brewing.

Karim turned his mind to the wedding. It would be difficult and expensive to cancel arrangements so late in the day. Perhaps they could recoup the cost of the food and the dress hire. He was wondering if Ayesha had remembered to ring the *traiteur* when Aziz spoke.

'You were talking about the Talal incident yesterday.'

Karim sat up, suddenly alert.

'Badnaoui was terrified about it appearing on the national news. He said it would be a disaster for Marrakech. Maybe he was under pressure from headquarters. At any rate he told us to make a quick arrest.'

Karim tensed but said nothing.

'The autopsy showed that the girl had been drinking alcohol. We believe that she left the nightclub, drunk, and returned to the medina. The old man was waiting up for her. There was an argument and she fell. It was manslaughter. That may seem harsh, but *al-hyatt saïba*, life is harsh.'

'Before you ask, we searched the house. We found no blood on the floor, nothing in her bedroom – no address book, no letters, no clues of any kind. The last three calls on her mobile were to her brother or to Leila Hasnaoui. As for the clothes in her wardrobe, they were the sort of clothes your sister might wear, not the slut clothes she had on when she died.'

'Just because a woman wears a red dress and make-up it doesn't make her a slut,' exclaimed Karim. He turned into a filling station, got out of the car and shouted at the surprised attendant, 'A hundred dirhams of Super. Ask him for the money!'

The filling station had the look of a new building. Karim washed his hands and face in the washroom then went out to the back and said his prayers, using a piece of cardboard as a mat.

I glorify Thee, God, and give Thee praise, and testify that there is no god other than Thee; and of Thee I ask pardon, and to Thee I confess: I have done evil and injured my soul; O pardon me, since there is none that can pardon sins but Thee.

He felt calmer when he had finished. Aziz was standing by a patch of cactus bushes, smoking a cigarette. Karim whistled and made a drinking gesture with his hand, then went into the cafeteria and paid for two coffees. The two men sat by the window.

'There are still things about the Talal case that trouble me,' said Aziz. 'Such as why Amina returned home dressed in her, ah, fancy clothes.'

'She didn't go home. She would never have gone back home knowing that her father might catch her, especially in her fancy clothes. She was on her way back to Leila's apartment.'

'Not so.'

'How can you be sure?'

'We talked to the driver.'

'Driver?' Karim had a rush of panic.

'The girls had a driver.'

'A driver – like a regular driver? But I've seen Leila's apartment. It's just a stone's throw from the nightclub. Why would they bother with a driver?'

'They used a driver. Leila told us.'

'Impossible!'

'We interviewed him.'

Karim's head was spinning. 'I don't understand! They got changed at Leila's then walked to the club—'

'They didn't get changed at Leila's. Leila's mother was even stricter than old man Talal.'

'What – they changed at the nightclub?'

'No.'

'I don't—' A cold realisation struck Karim. 'By the Seven Saints! They didn't use the taxi to get to the club . . . they used it as a changing room!' He was so agitated that he knocked over his coffee. 'The taxi picks up two girls in caftans and headscarves, drives around for a few minutes then drops them a little further down the street, looking like . . . sluts!'

'Correct. They left their change of clothes with the driver.'

'Who was the driver?'

'I don't remember his name. But his number was 1547.'

'1547?'

'Yes. *Ash andek?* You look like you've seen a ghost.'

'Was his name Rachid?'

'Rachid?' Aziz considered a moment. 'I don't think so. Why?'

'There are two men who drive that taxi. I know one of them. He lives in Targa.'

'He can't be the same man. The one we interviewed – the one listed in the records as the driver – lives in Douar Soultane. Based on his testimony, and that of Leila Hasnaoui, we ruled him out.'

A hundred thoughts were going through Karim's head. 'What did he say?'

'He told us that the girls arranged to meet him outside the club at one o'clock. He got there about twelve-forty-five. Leila Hasnaoui came running out and asked if he'd seen Amina. The driver – whatever his name – said no, he'd just arrived. Leila got into the cab. He drove round for a few minutes while she changed her clothes then he took her home. Leila corroborated his story. She told us that Amina wasn't at her parents' apartment. She tried her number a few times, got no answer and assumed she had returned to the medina with another driver. Either way, the driver is innocent. Only a few minutes elapsed between Leila last seeing Amina and getting into the taxi. The driver wouldn't have had time to abduct Amina and get back to the nightclub in time to pick up Leila.'

'No! Don't you see? You're basing this on the assumption that Amina left the nightclub before Leila!'

'She did leave before Leila. Leila looked for her in the club, but Amina had already left.'

'Not so.' Karim shook his head. 'She hadn't left.'

'How do you know?'

'I spoke to the man who kept her behind.' Karim told Aziz what he'd learnt from Sébastien. 'The club was dark and crowded. Leila couldn't make out in a quick sweep of the room that Amina was still inside the club, sitting at a table at the back.'

'So you think taxi 1547 took Leila home then went back to wait for Amina?'

'Yes.'

'She could have taken another taxi.'

'Why would she take another taxi? She had been plied with alcohol and was trying to get away from a predator! She knew the driver of 1547 and she had her change of clothes in his car.'

'You think the driver killed her?'

'I don't know,' Karim answered.

They drove for the next half hour in silence, each man wrapped in his thoughts.

'Redouane Jabri,' Aziz said suddenly. 'That was his name.'

Driss wasn't happy about taking Momo back to the Jemaa. He'd seen the way the entertainers treated their monkeys, keeping them cooped up in wooden boxes and making them work day and night. But *madame* said that she'd had it up to here. All because Momo had knocked over a vase. Driss asked around in the neighbourhood but he couldn't find anyone willing to take in a pet monkey, so *madame* told him to get rid of Momo any way he saw fit.

As he made his way along the derb with Momo on his shoulder Driss wished that *madame* were getting rid of Samira instead. When he first took the job at Dar Zuleika he thought he was going to be on the same level as Samira, possibly higher. He had worked hard, helping in the office, going to night school to improve his English, but Kay still treated him as a glorified handyman. Maybe it was time to look for another position. His wages wouldn't go far with another mouth to feed.

As he approached the house where the Talal widow lived he took a detour down Arset ben Brahim. It took him another eight minutes but he didn't want to risk being infected by the Talals' misfortune. Not with a baby on the way.

He stopped at the *hanoot* to chat to the owner. Momo jumped off his shoulder and scampered along the wall. Driss made noises with his tongue – *tack, tack, tack*. He beckoned, *ajee*! Momo just sat there, his head cocked to one side. Driss wasn't concerned. Momo always came back. They were a team, he and Momo: the two males of Dar Zuleika, browbeaten by the insufferable females. Driss asked the owner of the *hanoot* to give him a few nuts but when he looked up again Momo had vanished.

Sébastien's lawyer had strong misgivings about applying for an early release. Paying a fine before the release date would undermine Sébastien's defence and preclude any possibility of redress. But Sébastien was adamant so the lawyer went to the magistrate and managed to get Sébastien released three days early, on 7 November, in exchange for a twenty-thousand dirham fine. Yves had to go to an ATM to withdraw the cash. He was waiting in his car when Sébastien emerged, unshaven and straggle-haired, clad in his grubby clothes, blinking in the late afternoon sunshine.

Yves pushed open the passenger door. '*T'as une gueule de déterré*, you look like something a dog dug up.'

Sébastien gave a one-word reply. 'Drive.' He was focused, with every fibre of his being, on getting to the Serafina. He didn't have time for small talk, or to revel in the novelty of seeing trees and cars and people walking in the streets.

'Do you want me to take you to the hotel?' asked Yves as he parked outside Sébastien's apartment.

'*Non! A demain!*'

Sébastien raced up the stairs. He put his key in the lock, pushed open the door, kicked away the envelopes and ran to the shower. *Au nom du ciel!* The water company had cut off the supply. He checked his watch: six-thirty. The ceremony was due to start in an hour. He would wash when he got to the Serafina. He opened a box on the coffee table and took out a wrap of cocaine. He snorted two lines, grabbed his car keys, a clean shirt and a pair of trousers and dashed back downstairs. Out in the street, he stopped in his tracks. Someone had emptied a load of peelings and eggshells into the back seat of the Renault. *Salopard!* With his forearm Sébastien swept the rubbish off the seat. He turned the ignition and drove off, tyres screeching, onto Boulevard Abdelkrim Al Khattabi. He felt as if everyone in the street was staring at him. Perhaps he shouldn't have had that second line of cocaine.

When he reached the Hotel Tichka a gendarme was waving vehicles to the side of the road. Sébastien slowed and called out. '*Qu'est-ce qu'il y a?*'

The gendarme rotated his palm, indicating that something important was going on. Sébastien pulled over, cursing. He got out of the car, bought two cigarettes from a cigarette boy and smoked them both.

After what seemed like an eternity a motorcycle whizzed past, lights flashing, followed by a limousine. The gendarme waved the waiting vehicles back onto the road. Sébastien checked his watch. *Putain!* Half an hour to go. He pressed the accelerator to the floor.

In the limousine Mohammed Al-Husseini was smiling. His father was sitting in the back seat, next to the Moroccan minister of something-or-other. The minister had met them at the airport. He was trying to make small talk with his father – good luck to him! The old bastard was staring ahead, hands folded in the lap of his *dish-dash*.

Mohammed was looking forward to the evening. The hotel was ready, every room booked until Christmas. Many of AHG's investors had flown in to attend the opening. Al-Jazeera was even sending a camera crew. He couldn't wait to see his father's face when they drove along the Line of Water and saw the dome of the Serafina.

354   *James von Leyden*

Fortune had smiled on him when he took on the McKenzie woman. She was an excellent designer, she didn't complain and she saved him money. Her presence by his side had helped him secure the Beirut project.

Had he been harsh in leaving Sébastien to his fate? If the Frenchman's only crime had been to buy a few truckloads of black-market sand he would have paid the fine long ago. He was a forgiving man, after all. But in his mind was the suspicion that Sébastien had lied about Jamal. The story about the coffee machine didn't ring true, somehow; it seemed out of character for the mild-mannered Jamal. Mohammed feared only one thing more than being judged by a fellow Muslim and that was being double-crossed by a Westerner.

Sébastien was due to be released from prison in three days. Mouna had brought forward the hotel opening to avert any risk of a public relations disaster. In three days Mohammed would be on the other side of the Mediterranean. The Serafina would have opened and the first reviews would be in. Even so, Sébastien's imminent release was troubling. Not because Sébastien might sue Mohammed – his legal team would bury the claim the same way they had buried the lawsuit from the Swiss architects – but because Sébastien had evidence of Mohammed's boozing and whoring. What if photos ended up on his father's desk? That would never do.

As the car turned onto the Circuit de la Palmeraie Mohammed decided to have a discreet word with the government minister. Perhaps he could get Sébastien's sentence extended.

'Khadija is sleeping, *al-hamdulillah*.' Lalla Fatima's voice on the phone was hushed. 'The poor thing, she hopes that Zak will call and tell her it's all been a misunderstanding.'

Karim had one hand on the steering wheel and the other on his mobile. He was only half-listening to the conversation. He was waiting for a chance to call Rachid, to confront him about the goings-on at the Sherezade, to find out if he was covering for his brother-in-law. The closer they got to Marrakech the more he burned with fury. No wonder Khalifa had told him to look out for couples fucking. The Sherezade was a rape den. That half-wit Fouad was the lookout!

'We've been on the phone all morning to the guests,' his mother was saying. 'Naïma wants to come anyway. She's booked the time off work and she knows someone who might buy the *takshitas*. Wait – Ayesha wants to speak.'

Ayesha came on the line. She waited until Lalla Fatima was out of earshot. 'Karim! The night when Amina died – I think a taxi took her to the nightclub! All this time we thought that she walked to the club when in fact she went by taxi! Karim! Are you listening?'

'*Kifash arftee?*' he breathed, trying to disguise his panic. 'How do you know?'

'I found Amina's clothes, the ones she wore to go dancing. And a taxi card. He's the driver, the girls' driver!'

'We know about the driver.'

Ayesha could hardly believe her ears. 'You know about him? You must arrest him!'

'*Inshallah.*'

'What do you mean – *inshallah*? You must arrest him now – today!'

Karim glanced at Aziz, worried that he might be listening. 'I'll be home soon. We can talk about Zak then.'

'Zak?' Ayesha cried with exasperation. 'I'm not talking about Zak. I'm talking about the man who killed Amina Talal!'

'There's no evidence that he did.'

'At least bring him in for questioning!'

'We already have.'

'You have? What did he say?'

By now Aziz was staring at him suspiciously. Karim tried to bring the phone conversation to an end. 'We're on the road back from Agadir. I'll be home soon.'

There was a jeer in Ayesha's voice. 'You go all the way to Agadir for a few smugglers but you do nothing to arrest the man responsible for the death of Amina Talal!'

'Don't speak to me like that! I'll be back by nine-thirty. Don't do anything until then. Do you understand? *Fhemtee?*'

He put the phone down and rolled his eyes at Aziz. 'Women!'

Sébastien parked the *quatrelle* by a line of floodlit palm trees. The area of wasteland where Hicham Cherkaoui had conducted his surveillance was now a smart forecourt. Sébastien walked up to the gates, two monumental doors of cedar guarded by an attendant in a black *jabora* and trousers. The attendant ran his eyes over Sébastien's dishevelled appearance.

'*Vous désirez?*'

'*Moi?*' Sébastien retorted. '*Je suis l'architecte, moi!*'

Keeping his gaze on Sébastien the guard radioed for instructions. Just then, a smart 4x4 drew up to the gate and honked. The guard opened the gate to let the car through, then, with an irritated gesture, waved Sébastien through as well. As the gate shut behind him Sébastien looked up and gasped. The Serafina rose before him, luminous against the night sky, the Line of Water running towards it like a river of molten gold. Sébastien plunged his hand in the water channel, as if not daring to believe it was real. And the hotel! The marble architrave, the clerestory windows, the soaring golden dome . . . the nearer he got, the more his excitement grew. But he felt trepidation too, and fury. He was the unwelcome guest, the wicked fairy who had not been invited to the party.

He joined the crowd of smartly dressed guests milling by the steps. A Moroccan in a white tuxedo stared at him with distaste. Sébastien returned his stare, his head reeling with insults. *Casse-toi!* I have been to hell and back on account of this hotel! *Fiche-moi la paix, morceau de merde!* But he said nothing and slunk past the liveried doorman with the other guests.

In the atrium a fez-hatted orchestra was playing lounge music while waiters served cocktails. Kay was off to one side, dressed in a leopard-skin caftan, being interviewed by a reporter and cameraman. A few feet away stood Mohammed Al-Husseini, pointing out a feature on the ceiling to an older man in Middle Eastern robes – Al-Husseini *père*, Sébastien guessed. He was about to march up to them when he caught sight of a straggle-haired vagrant staring back at him from a mirror.

He snatched a cocktail from a passing waiter and darted into the washroom. He downed the drink and snorted the last of the cocaine. Then he took off his shirt and soaped his torso, armpits and face. The warm water and soft towel felt like the most delicious luxury. He cast around, realising that he had left his change of clothes by the Line of the Water. He was standing bare-chested, wondering what to do, when an attendant entered. He raised one eyebrow on seeing Sébastien but said simply, '*Monsieur, la fête commence.*'

Ayesha sat in Khadija's bedroom turning the taxi card in her hand. Returning to Derb Bourahmoune Lkbir after spending the afternoon with Lalla Hanane was like visiting a former life, one that she viewed through a prism of injustice. All the woes of women were caused by men. Khadija had been betrayed by a man, Amina had been destroyed by a man, her own life had been ruined by men. Her first father had given her away then her second father had refused to give her back. As for Karim, he could have married her years ago if he had set his mind to it. She was tired of his weakness and indecision.

Khadija stirred under her covers then went back to sleep, sedated by one of Lalla Fatima's pills. Ayesha was counting the minutes until Karim's return. How could he allow that wicked taxi driver to be at large? The only thing that Amina had done, her sole act of rebellion against a repressive, intolerant father, was to sneak out and go dancing. For this she had paid with her life! Ayesha looked at the sleeping figure of Khadija.

Although she was sorry for Khadija her desire to avenge Amina was fiercer.

She heard the front door slam and ran to the railing. Her face fell: it was Lalla Fatima, leaning on her walking stick, clutching a bag of dried leaves.

'Is she still sleeping?' Lalla Fatima whispered. 'I've got *luiza*, verveine, to make a soothing pot of tea.'

Instead of returning to Khadija's bedroom Ayesha went up to the roof. The air was heavy with the smoke from the city's barbecues. Yesterday evening, while Lalla Fatima was busy consoling Khadija, Ayesha had wrapped the lamb's carcass in muslin and carried it up to the roof where she remained for most of the night chopping, skewering and grilling, only coming down to fetch more charcoal. In the morning, following Karim's instructions, she prepared a plate of cutlets and took it to the *zaouïa* of Sidi bel Abbès. She took another plate to Lalla Hanane.

The tiles underneath the blackened bedstead were splattered with grease. Ayesha gathered up the cooking utensils and tossed a morsel of meat down into the alley for the cats.

Through the vast windows of the Serafina's Moorish restaurant diners could enjoy an uninterrupted view of the Line of Water on one side and the lagoon on the other. The restaurant had a fountain in the centre, one of the few features left over from Jamal's plans for the building. For the opening ceremony a podium had been erected beside the fountain. On the far side of the restaurant, opposite the entrance to the lobby, stood the bar, and behind the bar, watching the guests take their seats, stood Laurent de Freycinet.

He was ecstatic. To think – here he was in Marrakech, serving cocktails at the coolest hotel in town! He had already spotted several celebrities. He couldn't wait to tell his friends back home, as well as his father when he finally saw him. He placed six drinks on a tray and slid it across the counter to a waitress. The chatter in the room subsided as Mouna approached the microphone.

'*S-saada was s-sayyidat, merhaban bikum! Mesdames et messieurs, soyez bienvenus!* Welcome, ladies and gentlemen! A special welcome to His Excellency, Anwar Al-Husseini, Minister of Qatar.' She waited for the applause to finish. 'The Serafina Palace Hotel and Spa has been a long time in the making. It involved over fifteen hundred builders, plasterers, *tadelaktiers, zelligiers, ferronniers*, cabinet makers and painters. Look around you: you will see marble from Carrara, lapis from Afghanistan, lacquerwork from Kashmir. The hotel is a fusion of Islamic and Mediterranean influences, a marriage of east and west. I would like to introduce the man behind the vision – Mohammed Al-Husseini!'

To claps and cheers Al-Husseini bounded onto the podium. 'Thank you! Thank you for coming and joining us here in the Palmeraie of Marrakech for the opening of this incredible building. Please stay behind after dinner, there will be fireworks in the garden and dancing in the ballroom.' The announcement was met with whoops of delight.

'When I was a boy one of my favourite stories was Sinbad the Sailor. Sinbad set off on several long and difficult journeys during which he overcame many obstacles and saw many wonders. I vowed to set off on my own journey one day. I never dreamed that it would bring me to the Country of the Setting Sun, the Land of the Farthest West, Maghreb al-Aqsa, to build a palace fit for a king. As Mouna has said, the Serafina has drawn inspiration from across the Islamic world. But the main inspiration has been my father – a role model not just to me but to millions of Muslims in the Gulf and beyond. So, to my father, who has come here during the holy festival of Eid el-Kbir – or Eid al-Adha, as we call it in Qatar – a thousand thanks!' The audience applauded politely.

'I also want to thank the foreign minister of Morocco, Othmane Kabbani, the director of investment, Mohammed Toufail, and the wali of Marrakech, Sidi Ahmed El-Benghazi. I would like to say thank you to the two hundred and fifty staff of the hotel, many of whom are waiting upon us tonight. And finally, to Kay McKenzie, whose unflagging enthusiasm and expertise—'

'What about me? Don't I get a mention?'

Heads turned as Sébastien barged through the tables. There was a flurry of whispers: was this clown part of the show? Sébastien stepped onto the rim of the fountain and tiptoed along it like a drunken acrobat. Mouna looked frantically for the security personnel but they were all in the foyer or outside on the driveway. Sébastien snatched the microphone from Mohammed and surveyed the sea of tables, feeling the alcohol and cocaine surge through him.

'*Bonsoir!*' he roared. He caught sight of Kay at the nearest table. The bitch had stolen his son, and his glory. The prisoners in his cell had more honour than her! As for Al-Husseini, in his ridiculous dinner jacket, he was a lying, double-crossing son-of-a-bitch. He, Sébastien, had sweated twenty-four hours a day, gone to prison and sat in his own shit for the Serafina. This was his monument, his apotheosis. *This was his moment!*

Kay watched the unfolding spectacle with horror. She should have visited Sébastien in prison, she realised that now. Her desire for revenge had blinded her to the fact that Sébastien might seek vengeance of his own. She saw the television crew zooming in on the podium, keen to capture this unscripted drama . . . she saw Al-Husseini staring at Sébastien and back at her, aghast . . .

At first, Laurent thought that the man on the podium was a tramp. When he realised who it was he wished the ground would swallow him up. His mother had been right all along. With his wild eyes and disgusting clothes his father looked like a lunatic. What awful thing was he about to do?

Sébastien looked around the room, relishing the verbal shitstorm he was about to unleash. Then his eyes fell upon his son and time stopped. Everything receded. He took in Laurent's elegant uniform . . . the smart haircut . . . the agonised pleading in his son's eyes.

'I am . . . I am . . .' – *the architect of this hotel, unjustly imprisoned and left to rot by that bastard who breaks Ramadan and fucks prostitutes –*

'I am . . . sorry.'

There was a ripple of nervous laughter. Sébastien stepped down from the podium and made his way to the exit. A buzz of conversation filled the restaurant.

It was eight-thirty when the two officers arrived back at the commissariat. Aziz spoke first. 'We'll bring Redouane Jabri in for questioning on Wednesday, when the holiday is over.'

'A hundred things could happen between now and Wednesday!' cried Karim. The Talal investigation had been bungled from start to finish. How could he go home and admit to Ayesha that he was as much to blame as anyone?

Aziz faced him. 'Listen to me. You did a good job in Agadir. It was a difficult operation and you handled it well. I was happy to be your second-in-command. But the Talal affair was my case, and it still is my case. Go home. We'll bring the driver in for questioning on Wednesday.'

'*Wakha*,' Karim sighed. 'OK.'

'Give me your word that you will do nothing until then.'

Karim shifted in his seat, then nodded.

The two men shook hands and Aziz walked off in the direction of the medina. Karim fastened his helmet and climbed on his *moto*. As soon as he was past the Koutoubia he doubled back onto Avenue Guemassa and drove out of town to Douar Soultane.

Beyond the airport, past Mhamid, the apartment blocks thinned and the houses grew scruffier. There was no sign to indicate Douar Soultane. The prosperity that Marrakech had enjoyed in recent years hadn't reached this part of town. Half the neighbourhood had been cleared for development; the rest was a raggle-taggle of breeze-block houses, unsurfaced roads and mud dwellings with sheets of polythene for windows. Rachid had always talked about his brother-in-law as if he was well-to-do but this place was a dump.

Karim stopped and looked to left and right. He turned off the highway and drove along a rutted track bordered by prickly pear bushes until he came to a pharmacy, its green and white sign blinking. Like the other shops in the area it was closed. There were no taxis about, no *hanoots* where he could ask directions. Karim was wondering what to do when he heard an ear-splitting roar above his head. An aircraft was coming in to land. It was so low that he could see the hydraulic brakes on the undercarriage. He waited until it had disappeared behind the apartment blocks then knocked on the first door he came to. An unshaven man in a Nike top and sweat pants answered. Karim picked up the smell of cooking as he showed the man his badge.

'*Salaam ou alikum*, I'm looking for a taxi driver who lives in this neighbourhood.' The man looked Karim up and down. 'His name is Redouane Jabri,' Karim added.

The man scratched his balls. 'There used to be a guy next door but he moved to Tamansourt.'

'Any others?'

'There's a taxi driver who lives in the alley over there. A small house with a green door.'

Karim wheeled his scooter around the corner, taking care to avoid the potholes. He saw a *petit taxi* and his heart leaped, but the number on the side was 18211. He knocked twice at the door. After a few seconds it opened a fraction. Karim glimpsed a female face.

'Do you know of any taxi drivers by the name of Redouane Jabri?'

'*Naam?* What?'

Karim repeated his question. The woman called over her shoulder and a man came to the door.

He was in his fifties, with a moustache and a shock of white hair.

'What's the problem?'

'I'm looking for a taxi driver.'

'I'm not working tonight.'

'I don't need a ride,' Karim said impatiently. 'I'm trying to find a taxi driver called Redouane Jabri. He lives in Douar Soultane.'

'There's a Redouane at the end of the street who drives a taxi.'

'*Besahh?*' Karim's heart was in his throat. 'The man I'm looking for works shifts.'

The moustachioed man stepped out and peered down the empty street. 'No, I don't think he works shifts with another driver. The taxi's parked outside when he's not working.'

Karim's shoulders slumped. There could be a dozen taxi drivers in Douar Soultane called Redouane. It was a common name, after all. The moustachioed man was still looking down the street. 'A bit of a loner. Wakes my grandchildren up with that horrible Indian music he plays, *la, leely-la, la*, like cats having it off.'

Karim almost fell over with shock. He thanked the man and walked along the street, a deep, inchoate fury filling his chest. Rachid had played him like a fool. There was no brother-in-law, no wife, no five-year-old daughter. The lying bastard didn't live in Targa but in a slummy neighbourhood from where he preyed on women.

The last building was a single storey with one window and a wooden door. Karim didn't bother to knock. He stepped back and kicked the door open, then took the gun from his holster.

He entered a large room that smelled of cigarettes and unwashed clothes. He groped his way past a table, towards a single bed backed by a metal clothes rail. There was a tiny kitchen at the far end of the room and what looked like the door of a lavatory. On the table stood a computer with a screensaver that cast a feeble glow, a printer, a full ashtray and a dirty plate covered with pistachio shells. He opened the fridge and sniffed an open can of tuna. It all looked innocuous, like the bedsit of a rather dull bachelor. He had a flicker of doubt. What if Rachid was no more than a pathological liar? Amina Talal had not been raped. Her death may not have been intentional. If so, of what crime – other than deception – was Rachid guilty?

Karim pushed open the door of the lavatory with his forefinger. The door only opened a few inches before it hit the edge of the European-style toilet. The space was minuscule, more like a cupboard. Karim activated the torch on his mobile phone. To get inside the lavatory he had to squeeze through a narrow gap then sit down on the toilet and close the door. What he saw next took his breath away. The door was covered with photographs of women. All were lying on their backs, legs bare, clothes in disarray, terror on their faces. Some had their eyes closed. Others had smudged mascara and the glint of tears.

Karim's hands were shaking. He put his gun on the floor and looked again. To his relief, Amina Talal was not among them. Most appeared to be in their late teens or early twenties and, from their clothes and make-up, looked like they'd been on their way to a night out before being raped. This lurid gallery served as Rachid's trophy cabinet and his insurance policy. The women would never dare go to the police knowing that Rachid had evidence of his deeds. Had they done so, they would have suffered a lifetime of shame and disgrace.

A plane roared overhead, long and low. As the roar of the engines died away it was succeeded by another sound – the familiar *la-leely-la* of Bollywood music. The hairs stood up on Karim's neck. In panic he dropped his phone and groped around in the darkness, his cheek pressed against the toilet bowl. Outside, a car door slammed and the music stopped. Karim's fingers closed around the phone. He grabbed his gun, yanked open the lavatory door and squeezed through the gap, buttons popping off his shirt. He braced himself against the wall by the table and listened. As soon as Rachid came through the door he would strike. He would have him in Boulmharez by midnight or wipe him from the face of the earth, *as God was his witness*!

For a few anxious seconds he thought that Rachid had seen the broken door and backed off. Then there was a ringtone . . . Rachid's voice . . . the *click* of the car door locks opening . . . the start of the engine . . . *ya salaam!* Rachid was leaving! Karim dashed out into the street just as the rear lights of the taxi disappeared around the corner. He ran to his scooter, keyed the ignition and took off in pursuit, but by the time he reached the main track the taxi was already turning onto the highway. He could never hope to catch it.

Ayesha felt conspicuous standing in the square although she was wearing a *jellaba* and headscarf and holding a plain plastic bag. She watched the road by the Centre Sanitaire. A white car came along, then a minibus, then nothing for a few minutes. All of a sudden a *petit taxi* appeared and her pulse quickened. As it drew alongside she saw the red 1547 painted on the side. She opened the rear door and got in.

Rachid grinned in the rear-view mirror. 'Did you get my number from a friend? You were right to call me. Most taxi drivers refuse to work on public holidays, even though they can charge double. Not that I will charge you double, you understand, *a lalla!*'

Ayesha stared at the back of Rachid's head. He was wearing a white shirt and had neatly trimmed hair. She could smell cologne. For a second, she wondered if she had the wrong driver.

'Club Afrique.'

The grin vanished from Rachid's face. He stared at Ayesha as if he hadn't heard correctly.

Ayesha returned his stare. 'Club Afrique. You know where that is, don't you?'

Rachid cleared his throat but said nothing.

Ayesha removed her headscarf, letting her long black hair cascade over her shoulders. She opened her bag, took out make-up and a mirror and started to apply lipstick. She unzipped her *jellaba* and slipped it off her shoulders, shifting her buttocks and pulling the robe away. Underneath she was wearing Amina's sequinned blouse, purple skirt and soft leather boots. She could see Rachid stealing glances in his rear-view mirror.

'Hey!' she snapped. 'Keep your eyes on the road.'

She put kohl on her eyes then folded the *jellaba* and placed it in the bag along with her make-up. She crossed her legs and gazed out of the window. She glanced at the rear-view mirror then crossed her legs a second time. As they drove round the roundabout at Avenue Moulay el Hassan Rachid slowed down. Then, at the last second, he pressed the accelerator to the floor.

'Stop!' cried Ayesha. 'You've missed the turning!'

The locks on the passenger doors clicked shut.

Karim drove through Place Bab Taghzout in a state of utter dejection. He hardly noticed the man who stepped out of the car at the entrance to his alleyway. Abderrezak! His face was drawn and he looked uncharacteristically scruffy in a hoodie and jeans.

'Karim . . . *labas* . . . I need to talk to you.'

Karim checked his watch. It was only nine-fifteen. He still had fifteen minutes before he was due to meet Ayesha. He got off his scooter and tried to adopt an attitude of disdain.

'I've been in Agadir. I heard reports that the wedding is not taking place. Tell me that those reports are mistaken.'

'Things have changed.'

'Nothing has changed. Khadija is ready, we are ready.'

Zak held out his palms in a gesture of supplication. 'Karim . . . I am not in love with Khadija.'

'That is no reason to call off the wedding. You have an obligation to my sister.'

'I love another woman.'

'Is she rich? Does she wear fancier clothes?' *This was ridiculous. There were more pressing matters to attend to!*

'Khadija is a good woman,' said Zak. 'She deserves a good husband. It's better this way.'

Karim was silent for a few seconds, then said simply, 'You're right.'

Abderrezak's eyes filled with tears of relief. He embraced Karim. 'Should I come with you to see her?'

'No, it would only give her false hope. Write a letter instead. I must go, I have to meet Ayesha.'

'Ayesha? I saw her walk past.'

Karim's jaw went slack. 'When?'

'Ten minutes ago.'

'Where did she go?'

'To the square.'

'Did she come back?'

'If she did, I didn't see her.'

Karim climbed on his *moto* and drove pell-mell back to the riad.

'Where are we going?' cried Ayesha.

The taxi swerved violently as Rachid whipped round. He seized her phone and tossed it out of the window. 'You like nightclubs, do you?' The taxi had left the city walls behind and was speeding past the Agdal Gardens.

Ayesha clutched her seat in terror. 'Where are you taking me?'

'You haven't answered my question. Do you like night-clubs? Or just that African cesspit? Do you like showing your tits to black men?'

Ayesha struggled with the lock on the car door, breaking her fingernail. 'Stop!' she sobbed. 'Please stop!'

Rachid's mobile buzzed on the seat next to him. He glanced at the screen: Karim. *What did he want?* Rachid let the phone ring. He turned off the main road onto the side road and then down the *piste* towards the Sherezade. A faint light shone in the hut. Rachid braked abruptly.

'You want to show off your body, do you? Come on then, bitch!'

Karim left the keys in the ignition and went straight to the courtyard. 'Ayesha?'

Lalla Fatima's face appeared at the upstairs railing. '*Salaam alikum!*'

'*Ou alikum salaam.*' Karim searched the salon. 'I just saw Abderrezak.'

'You saw Abderrezak?' His mother was dumbfounded.

Khadija appeared at the railing, her hair in disarray. 'What did he say?'

'I'll tell you in a second,' said Karim, dashing into the kitchen. 'Where's Ayesha?'

'What did Zak say?' Khadija cried.

Karim ran up the stairs to Ayesha's bedroom. Clothes lay scattered on the bed.

'What's going on?' asked Lalla Fatima, getting alarmed.

'I told Ayesha that I'd be back here at nine-thirty.'

'It's after nine-thirty. We heard the call for prayers.'

Karim checked his watch: it still read nine-fifteen. He got out his mobile. To his horror it read seven minutes past ten. He tore the fake Breitling from his wrist and hurled it against the wall.

'*Zbel hada!* Piece of shit!'

His mother took a step back, terrified. Khadija ran to Karim and clutched his jacket. 'Tell me what Zak said! Tell me, tell me!'

Karim looked past her at his mother. 'Did Ayesha say where she was going?'

'I didn't hear her go out. *Ash andek?* What's got into you?'

'Tell me what he said!' demanded Khadija, beating her fists against Karim's chest.

'He's going to write to you . . .' Karim punched Ayesha's number on his phone. It rang twice then went to voicemail. He pressed redial.

'Forget Ayesha!' Lalla Fatima shouted. 'Talk to your sister! What did Zak say?'

At that moment Karim heard a voice come on the line, a man's voice. '*Aloo?*'

'Who – who are you?' Karim asked, fending off Khadija with his free hand.

'Me? No one. I just picked up this phone. It was lying on the ground by the side of the road. I heard it ringing.'

'Where?' cried Karim. 'Where are you?'

'Me? I'm outside the supermarket, on the Route d'Ourika—'

Karim descended the stairs two at a time and tore out of the house, leaving Khadija sobbing in her mother's arms.

Fouad stood in the door of the hut as Rachid pulled Ayesha from the car.

'Help me!' Ayesha begged.

'Save your moans for later,' growled Rachid. He dragged Ayesha by the hair, stumbling, towards the hut. As he was trying to yank her up the steps Ayesha broke free and fled towards the undergrowth.

'Get her!' Rachid yelled to Fouad. 'Get her!'

The other man stared at him without moving.

'Imbecile!' Rachid marched angrily to the boot of the taxi. He took out a torch and started after Ayesha. She was groping her way towards the derelict building, thorns tearing at her skin, looking for a path or a way out, but the nearer she got to the building the denser the thickets became. Suddenly she stopped, teetering on the edge of darkness. Rachid came up behind and grabbed her arm.

'You stupid slut! You nearly fell in! You're as bad as that Talal bitch!'

'Please don't hurt me!'

Rachid shone his torch at the ladder on the side of the empty pool. 'Get in.'

'What – what do you mean?'

Rachid pushed her roughly towards the ladder. '*Ziddee*. Get into the pool – slowly!'

Whimpering, Ayesha climbed down the ladder. Rachid jumped down after her. He struck Ayesha across the face with the torch, sending her sprawling. Then he kneeled astride her, placing the torch on the ground so that the beam shone on her cheek. He ripped open her blouse. 'You even look like her . . .'

With his knees he forced Ayesha's legs apart. He grasped her wrists in one hand and fumbled with the fly of his trousers. 'She was a whore like you . . . a whore and a drunk who would spread her legs for any man, even the beggars in the street!'

The fear went from Ayesha's eyes. She spoke clearly, calmly. 'Amina Talal was not a whore.' She twisted her arm free and in one swift movement slid out from her boot the long wooden-handled knife she had used to cut up the sheep. Before Rachid could react she rammed the knife upwards through his ribs, grunting with the effort.

'She – was – my – sister!'

Rachid stared, transfixed, then slumped sideways, clutching his belly.

Ayesha wriggled from under him with disgust and leapt to her feet. She took his mobile phone from his pocket and pushed blindly at the buttons, finally managing to key in Karim's number.

'Rachid?' Karim's voice was suspicious.

'Oh, Karim! He tried to rape me . . .!' Ayesha's voice trailed off. A figure was silhouetted at the edge of the pool. She reached down to pick up the torch but when she shone it the figure was gone.

She looked behind her in alarm. Rachid was no longer lying on the ground. The next thing she knew there was a *whumph* and all the breath was knocked out of her. The torch skittered across the ground. She heard a wrenching sound and something struck her face. She tasted blood.

Ayesha was a fighter – hadn't Si Brahim said as much? She had wrestled all the boys in the alley. She could beat any of them, even Karim. She fought now, flailing and kicking, for a long time.

Then she fell.

Karim skidded to a halt behind the taxi. He ran towards the hut, throwing open the door. The room was empty. Grabbing the lamp he set off through the undergrowth, following the zigzag path he had used three months earlier. There was a new moon and the site was in almost total darkness. He searched the undergrowth on both sides but all he saw were shadows, ghostly apparitions.

'Ayesha!'

He veered off the path by the old cement mixer. A few steps further, where the darkness turned pitch black, he stopped and held up the lamp, gazing down at the shallow end of the swimming pool. A patch of dark liquid was soaking into the sand and dried eucalyptus leaves. Karim looked around. From the derelict building came a dull *clunk*. The iron pulley was swinging gently on its chain.

'Ayesha?' Karim bristled. 'Rachid?'

He took out his gun, cocked the trigger and crept around the pool. Beyond was an area where the undergrowth had been trampled and the leaves spattered with blood. He followed the trail, trying to see into the murky interior of the building. He stepped up to the ground level and pushed the pulley aside. It was much heavier than he had imagined. It made a *clunk*, followed by a lighter *clink* of the chain.

It was the first time Karim had set foot in the Sherezade. Pillars stretched away into the darkness. The floor was covered with glass and shattered breeze blocks. Every few feet, steel reinforcement rods sprouted in spiky clusters. There was blood on the concrete, smeared in places as if an object had been dragged bleeding into the depths.

Something moved, a fluttering.

'Rachid? *Redouane?*'

A bat flew past Karim's head, causing him to reel in shock. When he righted himself he saw the outline of a body propped up behind a pillar. He ran towards it, his feet crunching on clumps of cement. He held up the lamp, the shadow of the pillar moving away from him. Rachid was slouched with his hands on his abdomen and blood oozing through his fingers. He looked up in surprise.

'Karim! What on earth . . .? *Shouf* . . . Look what the bitch did to me . . .'

Karim gritted his teeth but said nothing. He could see another body – a female in a short skirt – lying behind the next pillar. It was Ayesha.

Her hair was wet, and her blouse was torn and covered in blood but she was alive, praise God the Merciful! He checked her for signs of injury. Her right eye was swollen and puffy and there was an injury to her head that, in the light of the lamp, looked serious, even life-threatening. He turned her gently on her side so her airway was clear, then took out his mobile and called for an ambulance. He went back to where Rachid lay.

'I am arresting you for the abduction, attempted rape and manslaughter of Amina Talal on 31 July—'

'I told you – my brother-in-law was working that night!'

'Your brother-in-law is a fantasy, like everything else in your miserable life, Redouane – Rachid – whatever you call yourself. Allah will judge you for this.'

'It was an accident!'

'You intended to rape her. You caused her death.'

'The whore was drunk,' Rachid said, his tone now one of sullen contempt. 'She was about to sell herself to a businessman.'

'I'm also arresting you for the abduction and attempted rape of Ayesha Talal—'

'She's a whore as well.'

'And for the abduction and rape of at least twelve other women.'

Rachid managed a sneer. 'You know, Karim – you were useless as a security guard.'

Karim saw Rachid's eyes flick to a movement behind his back and he whirled round. A dark figure was approaching with a cudgel – Fouad!

Karim grabbed some gravel and flung it in Fouad's face. He barrelled into the other man, ramming Fouad's hand against a pillar and slicing the skin from his knuckles. The cudgel clattered to the ground. Fouad cast around for another weapon. He went to the pulley and disengaged the chain at head height, bringing the great steel hook crashing down. He picked up the end of the chain and started wheeling the hook around like an Olympic hammer thrower, slowly at first, the heavy weight skimming the ground, then faster as it rose into the air. Mesmerised by this feat of strength, Karim backed away towards where Rachid was sitting. He didn't notice that Rachid had stretched out his leg to trip him up. With a cry, Karim toppled backwards, thrusting his hand out to break his fall but instead impaling it on one of the steel rods that protruded from the floor. The pain was blinding, instantly expanding to fill every corner of his being. When he could see again, Fouad was looming above him, the massive hook whirling around his head.

'Finish him off, Fouad, you cretin!' rasped Rachid. 'Do it!'

'Fouad!' Karim cried, tugging helplessly at his pinned palm. 'So far you're only an accessory to rape! If you kill me you'll go to prison for life!'

'*Allah inaal l-hmaar lee weldek,*' said Fouad. 'May God curse the donkey that gave you birth.' The chain arced through the air and Karim squeezed his eyes tight. *I take refuge in God. There is no strength or power except from God.* He heard a sickening crunch of metal on bone. Slowly he opened his eyes. Instead of bringing the hook down on Karim, Fouad had buried it in Rachid's skull.

Karim stared at Fouad. For several seconds he was speechless.

'It was you with the handcart at Sidi bel Abbès! You weren't cursing Amina Talal . . . you were cursing – *him*!'

He slid his palm off the steel rod, wincing with pain. He crawled over to Ayesha. He tried to lift her but his hand was useless. With Fouad's assistance he pulled her upright and draped her over his shoulder. Fouad led the way back to the hut, lighting the path with the lamp. Karim laid Ayesha's unconscious body on the ground, then ran to the standpipe and grabbed the old grey robe. He kneeled down and laid it over Ayesha to keep her warm. Fouad took off his overgarment. He folded it into a pillow and placed it under Ayesha's head.

Karim looked up. Fouad stood before him in a black *jellaba*. He watched as Fouad removed the scarf from his neck and wrapped it twice around his head, leaving a slit for his eyes. In Touareg dress he looked noble and impressive, very different from the cowed wretch of three months earlier.

'I'm going home to the desert. It's cleaner there.'

Karim nodded. He stood up and clasped the other man by the hand. 'May God protect you.'

Fouad's eyes creased slightly then he turned and walked through the tamarisk bushes until his silhouette merged with the darkness.

Karim sat beside Ayesha, stroking her hair. Her breathing was coming in fits and starts.

'You crazy girl. You poor, brave, crazy girl.'

Karim prayed for Amina, and for the other girls – blameless girls whose only offence had been to go out for the evening wearing a dress and make-up. He thought of Fouad, forced to keep watch while Rachid raped his victims, and decided to gloss over Fouad's role in the tragedy: the police were unlikely to follow him across three thousand miles of desert.

He checked Ayesha's pulse.

Hold on, my love.

He remembered an incident, a long time ago, when a boy from the alley shouted insults at Ayesha. *Where are your parents you dumb orphan?* She beat him black and blue, then, as he lay on the ground, she reached out her hand to help him up.

As the wind stirred the cypress trees Karim let the tears come. 'For as long as I live, I will never love another woman the way I love you.' Karim was still weeping and stroking Ayesha's hair when the ambulance drove down the track.

In Guéliz the November sun warmed the pavements. At the crossroads where Avenue Mohammed Cinq meets Boulevard Zerktouni the shoeshine men were sitting on the pavement, tapping the sides of their wooden kit-boxes and looking hopefully up at the passers-by.

Sébastien was at a table outside the Négociants, dressed in a linen suit. He reached for a cigarette then thought better of it and put the packet in his pocket. *There he was* – Laurent, making his way through the crowd towards him. Sébastien rose for an embrace but Laurent simply stood, unsmiling. They shook hands awkwardly.

'*Comment ça va?*' asked Sébastien.

'*Ça va.*'

Laurent ordered a *citron pressé* and looked around at the other customers. Sébastien gazed at the handsome youth in front of him. He had dreamed of this moment for years, yet now that his son was here he found himself at a loss for words.

Laurent met his father's gaze. 'So – you got out of prison?'

'*C'était un cauchemar.* Two months in a cell. They break your balls, the Moroccan authorities—' Sébastien checked himself. 'Never mind about that! How do you like working at the Serafina?'

'The pay is nothing special but I'm enjoying it.'

'What do you think of the building . . . the architecture?'

For the first time Laurent smiled. '*Pas mal.*'

They made small talk for a few minutes, then Sébastien asked, 'Are you planning to remain in Marrakech?'

'I'm moving out of the riad tomorrow.'

'*C'est vrai?*'

'I've got a place with a friend, opposite the *lycée.*'

Sébastien breathed a sigh of relief. There would be more occasions like this.

'Kay's gone to Beirut,' Laurent said, stirring his *citron pressé*.

'Beirut?' A cloud crossed Sébastien's face as he recalled his dreams of escape. Then again, if Laurent was staying in Marrakech perhaps it was no bad thing for him to stay as well. Autumn and spring were the best seasons in Marrakech, and Yves had mentioned a friend with an apartment to rent – cheaper than his place in Zerktouni, in a quieter neighbourhood. If father and son were both around at New Year perhaps he could take Laurent on that desert trip he'd planned.

A young Moroccan in a Lacoste top and jeans walked up to their table. Taking him for a street vendor, Sébastien contemplated the youth for a moment. He was good-looking, sixteen or seventeen years old, with well-toned arms, grey-green eyes and a tuft of hair under his lower lip. Laurent stood up and kissed the Moroccan affectionately on the cheek, then turned to Sébastien.

'Papa, this is Younes.'

Sébastien looked from his son to the other boy. He stared for a moment, his mouth open, then threw back his head and roared with laughter.

In Jemaa el Fna the sanitation lorries were whirring and flashing, clearing the debris from the three-day holiday. In Houmane Fatouaki street Bouchaïb was chatting to the furniture upholsterer as he stacked mattresses on the pavement.

On the first floor of the commissariat, Karim sat at his desk with an irritable expression. He had a bruise on his cheekbone and his right hand was bandaged. 'You're not going to re-open the case?'

Noureddine was standing by the door, one hand on the wall switch, staring up at the fan. 'What would be the point?'

'You imprisoned an innocent man! Omar Talal died in disgrace!'

Noureddine sighed. 'We arrested him on suspicion of killing his daughter. Such things, regrettably, are not unknown. We have sent condolences to his wife.' He flicked the switch and the fan started turning.

'Condolences?'

'What else can we do? We can't bring him back.'

Noureddine turned off the fan and went back to his desk. 'As for what happened at the Sherezade, I'm sorry that your sister was attacked by Redouane Jabri, but she did take a risk going after him like that. Has she thought about a job with the police, by the way? We need women like her in the Sûreté.'

'The point is that Badnaoui knew. You knew!'

'Knew what? That there was a rapist out there? None of us knew that. I had suspicions, but no more.'

'You had suspicions?'

'Why do you think I told you to apply for the job at the Sherezade?'

'You mean you sent me there *on purpose*?'

'We'd been receiving reports of goings-on. Nothing definite, no allegations, *fhemtee*, just motorists seeing women in distress on the road, that sort of thing. When you said you were short of money I thought it would be a good way to kill two birds with one stone. If there was something going on, I knew you would sniff it out. It took a while but you caught the perpetrator.'

Karim was so choked he could hardly speak. 'Evidence was destroyed! Evidence that would have exonerated Omar Talal!'

'I wouldn't be too critical of the evidence if I were you. After all, it was you who destroyed the most important evidence against Jabri.'

A muscle twitched on Karim's forehead. 'What do you mean?'

'The mattress in the hut.'

Noureddine came over and sat on the corner of Karim's desk. 'Listen, Karim, we all made mistakes. It was Ramadan. No one was at their best. True, Aziz should have impounded the cart. True, the autopsy should have been done sooner. But you spent four weeks with Jabri. You sat in his taxi, you patrolled the site where he took Amina Talal, yet you didn't suspect a thing.'

Before Karim could reply Abdou came into the room, bursting with excitement. 'Badnaoui wants to hold a press conference!'

'*Al-hamdulillah!*' Karim cried. 'Some good will come of it, after all!'

'What do you mean?'

'Women are raped in this city all the time but it's never talked about. A press conference will bring the subject into the open!'

'No, my brother, you've got it wrong,' Abdou said hastily. 'The press conference is about the operation in Agadir.'

'The operation in Agadir?' Karim's voice was hoarse. 'Who cares about that?'

Abdou held up both palms. 'I didn't mean any offence, brother.'

'Counterfeit drugs kill people,' Nour commented. 'You said so yourself. It's important that we make people aware.'

'What we should be making people aware of is that a taxi driver has been preying on women for years!'

'And scare away the tourists?' said Noureddine. 'It's bad enough that our taxi drivers don't turn on their meters.'

'But other victims might come forward. They might testify!'

Noureddine walked to the window. 'That they've been raped? I don't think so. This is an old-fashioned city, after all.'

Four miles north of Marrakech a lorry trundled into a refuse-strewn wasteland that marked the municipal rubbish dump. It was a hillside with smoking mounds, wheeling storks and, if the wind was blowing in the wrong direction, a stench that could be smelled all the way from Hicham Cherkaoui's old house on the Route de Safi. The dump was an eyesore, an embarrassment to the authorities. They had plans for a new transfer station, boasting modern recycling facilities and a 250-ton-a-day compactor. The old site would be landscaped into rolling fields.

But on this day the lorry driver did as usual: he

manoeuvred up a steep incline, stopped, pulled a lever and a ton of egg shells, bones, fish heads, banana skins, wrappers and cartons slid down the slope. A tin can rolled twice and came to a halt on a piece of cardboard on which were written the words 'My name is Amina Talal and I am a whore'. The driver raised the tipper to its full height and the rest of the rubbish cascaded down the slope, burying the sign completely.

Khadija lay in the *salon* with her head in Lalla Fatima's lap, watching television. Up on the roof Karim and Ayesha sat with their backs against the bedframe, looking up at the night sky.

'See that star?' Karim pointed. 'That one – *Yad al-Jauza*, the hand of Orion.'

Ayesha shifted position. Two of her ribs were broken and it hurt to sit for too long. A bandage covered the top of her head and the area between her mouth and her left ear was bruised, but she managed a grin. 'It looks red. Like my face.'

'That's because it's about to explode. The explosion will be so bright that people will be able to see it in daytime.'

'Will we be able to see it in Marrakech?'

'Perhaps. If we're still around.'

Karim could hear children's cries drifting up from the alley. The press conference had gone ahead as planned. Badnaoui came up to Karim afterwards to congratulate him on the operation in Agadir. He didn't mention Redouane Jabri or the Sherezade.

Several minutes passed. Then Ayesha said, 'I'm going to go

and live with Lalla Hanane. Abderrahim's in Kenitra and she has no one but me.'

Karim nodded. It changed everything – and yet it changed nothing. Ayesha would remain his sister in the eyes of God, from now until the end of time. He pulled a roll of banknotes from his pocket.

Ayesha stared. 'What's that?'

'The money we saved for Khadija's wedding. I managed to get it back from the *traiteur*. Here.'

'I don't want it.'

'Khadija wants you to have it. We all want you to have it.'

'What would I do with all that money?'

'Go to college. Get an education.'

Ayesha took the bankroll and put it in her caftan. 'I wonder what would have happened if my father had got an education.'

Karim considered for a few moments, then chuckled. 'We probably wouldn't be sitting here now.'

Just then there was a movement by the parapet. Ayesha sat up in alarm. Karim scrambled to his feet. He could make out a small head and shoulders above the line of the roof.

'It's one of the kids from the alley! He's climbed the wall! What does he think – no, wait – it's . . . *a monkey!*'

Momo scampered along the parapet and cocked his head at Karim and Ayesha.

'You're right – it *is* a monkey!' cried Ayesha, clapping with delight. Momo leapt onto Ayesha, his skinny arms clinging round her neck. 'Oh, Karim – can we keep him?'

Author's note

This book is set in 2011. Ramadan fell in August that year. On 28 April a bomb exploded in the Argana Café in Jemaa el Fna square, killing seventeen people, mainly foreigners. Around the same time some hoardings for a property development featuring the actress Eva Longoria were defaced on a road outside Marrakech. And a new nightclub called African Chic opened in Guéliz.

Acknowledgements

This book took a long time to write and several people were instrumental in it reaching publication. Eileen Horne, my first editor, was a constant source of encouragement and good advice. Mary Jones at literary agents Gregory and Company (now David Higham Associates) picked the manuscript out of the slush pile and helped patiently with rewrites. My Moroccan Arabic teacher, Peter Solomon, made valuable suggestions on culture and Arabic transliteration. Thanks to Khalid and Clare Minejem for hospitality, Arabic lessons and more; thanks also to André Attanasio for proofreading the French. Finally, I'm grateful to my wife Czarina for her unfailing reassurance and support.